T0064465

THE
HIMALAYAN
BOND

Reviews from distinguished readers:

In this colourful journey to the heart of a pastoral landscape, Dani returns home to India with his friend Roland. Dani leads Roland to his ancestral mountain landscape revealing the treasures, the simplicity and spirituality of Dani's heritage. This is a didactic wander through modern and traditional India providing a rare insight into age-old values somehow untarnished by modernity. Exploring the life and values of his native Himalayas near Shimla, Dani introduces Roland to the charm and magic of India and leads him through any confrontation he may have had. A good and informative read for anyone wanting to travel to the country. – **Devdan Sen (Co-author: Rough Guide to India)**

THE HIMALAYAN BOND is a real-life adventure laced with exploration, history and planetary survival. India and The Himalayas are the backdrop, with Dani the perfect guide, in this fascinating insight into a part of the world embracing ancient traditions and modern technology.– **Brian Perkins (Former Presenter: BBC Radio 4)**

"A must read to understand the impact of our fast paced lives on our natural system and the climate. Explains age-old sustainable facts, very simply described by eye witnessing stories."- **Dr Prashant Kumar (Reader: Dept. of Civil & Environmental Engineering, University of Surrey, UK)**

I enjoyed the story very much. It's actually a bit like Kim! (By Rudyard Kipling) really interesting! – **Neil Stourton (English Scholar: Newark Academy, USA)**

The Himalayan Bond gives a fascinating insight into the way of life in India, especially of course in the descriptions of life in the village where Puran was born. I think it would be an invaluable "**Vade Mecum**" (a handbook or guide that is kept constantly at hand for consultation) for those travelling in the area. I especially see it as appealing to the young adult market, especially those exploring India. Puran is very fair in his criticisms of India as well as his praise. His warnings about scams would be very useful for anyone travelling. –**Maggie Pringle (Former Publisher: Sunday Express, London)**

Puran Bhardwaj is an accomplished guide as well as weaver of tales in the Kipling tradition, as readers of *The Kukri* (Journal of the Brigade of Gurkhas) know. He richly deserves a wider readership. "Child of the Raj"-**Roger Massie (Former Secretary: Council of Europe)**

The area Puran Bhardwaj describes in his book *The Himalayan Bond* is quite familiar to me. It is because of the fact that I came to the area in 1958 as a young medical officer of the town Suni. The village, Thali, was just on the other side of Suni on the north bank of the mighty river Satluj, a small Jhula (steel ropeway) over the river connecting Suni and Thali.

However, about 56 years later, while reading his book in its manuscript form, I initially thought it as the nostalgic reminiscences of a young man for his childhood days. But after serious reflection, I realised that notwithstanding his laments for the disappearing old ways, there is indeed a universal message in his writings.

It goes without saying that extolling the virtues of the old ways is not the underlying message of Puran's writings though he describes them in some detail. However, by doing so, he vividly illustrates the sharp contrast of the old ways and the modern ways which are virtually wiping out those old ways. Therefore, he has tried to express his intense concern, and has tried to send the unmistakable message that in spite of the tremendous advances in every sphere of life, we the inhabitants of this planet can no longer behave like the biblical Prodigal Son. A time has come for tightening our belts in order to curb the wastefulness, and to learn to live within the resources available in our planet preserving the eco as far as practicable. For that message alone the book will be invaluable reading for those who care for our planet. And as such, I can recommend his book *The Himalayan Bond* without any reservation whatsoever.
–Dr S Ghosh (Former Doctor: NHS, UK)

THE HIMALAYAN BOND

BETWEEN MAN AND THE ENVIRONMENT

PURAN BHARDWAJ

PARTRIDGE

To order additional copies of this book, contact
Partridge India
000 800 10062 62
orders.india@partridgepublishing.com

www.partridgepublishing.com/india

Contents

The Himalayan Bond

Between man and the environment.

"Gifted to all those wonderful faces that I have met in my life."

I DEDICATE THIS BOOK TO MY
LATE MOTHER AND FATHER
&
My appeal - Save water
Aqua vitae – Jalam jivanam

ACKNOWLEDGEMENTS AND CREDITS

This book has been a dream and a challenge for me in equal parts. The experiences and tales gathered from my childhood and recorded in my small dairy since the age of nine, juxtaposed with the huge changes taking place in the Himalayas in recent years, created a pressure in my head which demanded sharing and release.

Gradually the book started taking shape. First, in bursts in the middle of the night, then continuously throughout the day and finally on to paper in my customary broken English. So please bear with me and after twenty pages or so you will understand my appeal.

The finished product was possible only by virtue of the help of various people whose input was unquantifiable.

Special thanks go to:

Maggie Pringle – former London publisher, who lit the flame after reading my initial draft and inspired me with her confirmation that it was indeed worth publishing.

To Tonya Gabrielle Steward, for early corrections and advice.

To my editor Richard Sheehan, who worked hard to help me give it a good shape and focus. He took great care to keep my style and story safe.

To Lynne Choo-Choy for her support and advice with the text in reading and re-reading for errors and general advice on text. Her corrections and tips were invaluable from start to finish.

Additional heartfelt thanks go to the following for their advice and support:

Brian Perkins – BBC Radio 4, Neil Stourton – Newark Academy, Devdan Sen – Rough Guide, Dr S. Ghosh, Mrs Elizabeth Passingham, Roger Massie, Cristina Aldaz, Hellen Faus, Isabel Lahoz, Prem Adriano Merola, Yuko, Raaja Bhasin for his words and inspiration and Kanishka Gupta of Delhi for his critique report.

Also to Aki Schilz – The Literary Consultancy – London, Irene Black, Tim Dowling, Media Molecule – Guildford, Hari Ram, Basant Lal Thakur, Vikas Gupta, Ved Prakash, Mahender Verma, Dushyant Sharma, Yugal Kishore Sharma, Jagdeep Syan, Gajender Sason, Prem Raina, Jane Fairbank, the late Peter Allsop, Murray and Ann Campbell, Swami Divyanand Tirth, Mohan Bhandari, Parmarth Niketan and Shivananda Ashram in Rishikesh, Cundall Manor School in UK, Senior School Suni in H.P. India, Mark Robberds, Yogasarita Ginny Morris, Daragh Anglim, Jackie and Walter, Lalit Sharma, Major General Kishan Singh and Dr Yajvender Pal Verma for their support.

I am grateful, too, to my publisher Partridge India for their encouragement and support and to Roland Bourne for his contribution and to his agreement for the use of his name and part of his trip as the basis for this book.

Photo credits and gratitude go to Alison Fairbank, Bredan James, Bailey Galvin-Scott, Alexandra and Mark Berthon, Alexandra Mahoney, Eleanor Marriott, Prabhoo Janabalan, Prem Rain, Satish Kumar, Kirk Newton and Ingrid Timmerman. Their photos bring the story alive and capture the unspoken.

Finally, I would like to express everlasting thanks to my late parents, brothers, sisters, family and friends in India, and in particular to my dear wife and children, without whose support and tolerance none of this would be possible.

If just one single idea from this book touches a single reader or makes a small change, that is reward enough for me.

The Himalayan Bond – Book Map

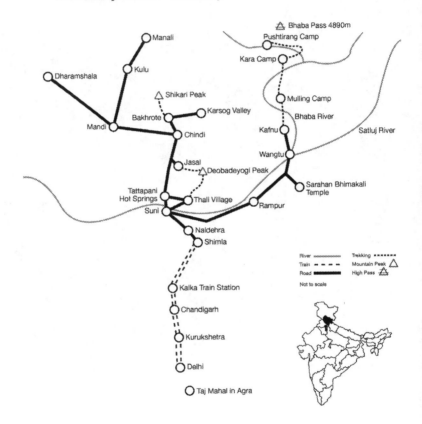

PREFACE

The Himalayan Bond – Prologue

A good English summer is one of the best things one can experience in England. The parks, streets and countryside are charming, and overall, people are in a happy mood. In this kind of weather, people can be seen walking their dogs, running or cycling, having picnics and playing games in parks bursting with flowers, greenery and trees. The surrounding scenes are full of life, and everyone is making the most of every moment in the sunshine. There are also people jogging and running to be fit or preparing themselves for running marathons to raise money for their favourite charities.

Within such a group was a young man called Roland Bourne. Roland was nearly twenty-six years old and full of life. His weekends were normally spent learning to fly a helicopter or running or pursuing other physical activities. He was well read and well educated. He occasionally used glasses with a thick frame which gave him the look of a scholar, and in the past he had his hair longer, but since qualifying as a chartered accountant, his long hair had had to be sacrificed. Roland's belief was that children and today's youth needed to get out more often in this iPhone and computer age, and they needed to do more outdoor and sporting activities. He was concerned about global issues such as food wastage and negative changes to the environment. He had travelled Europe extensively, but now he was drawn to visiting a very different country – India and the high Himalayas – which he had admired from documentaries, movies and the many exciting stories of his friends. He was fascinated by what he had heard of the British Raj and from such sources as *The Jungle Book*, Rudyard Kipling and Charles Dickens. The country where a snake can look you in the eyes and hypnotise you and where people have to check their shoes in the morning for scorpions before putting them on, and where numerous gods, holy rivers and the highest mountains on earth co-exist. India has the world's second largest population (1.2 billion) and yet the world's lowest meat consumption per person. It is the world's largest democracy and the third largest economy on earth.

Roland felt the urge to make a trip to experience all of this before it changed. He came from a family where education, exploration and knowledge was highly regarded. His grandfather, Arthur Bourne, was a motorcycling journalist who wrote a column under the name Torrens. He later became vice-chairman of the RAC (Royal Automobile Club). He also helped design a Royal Enfield bike known as the "Flying Flee". There is a trophy to his memory called the Torrens Trophy. So curiosity and interest was the back-bone of the family and later came the association of Royal Enfield with India. This was enough fuel for Roland to build his fascination and to encourage him to take the challenge of exploring India and the high Himalayas. The time was ripe. Working life had become all-consuming recently and the efforts of modern living were taking its toll.

Roland had heard from some friends about a Himalayan guide from North India who was currently living in Southern England. After some research on the internet,

Roland found his name. The phone number started with the same area code as his parents (01483), and in fact he was living in a town that Roland knew quite well, Guildford. Having moved away to Newcastle in recent years, Roland was confident that the familiar connection was an omen.

And that is how Roland got to speak to a man called Dani on the phone, who spoke with a pleasant Indian accent, and a connection was established. After a conversation about a possible itinerary, a meeting was arranged for when Roland would next be visiting the south.

Dani's background was a very different one. Born and brought up in the foothills of the Himalayas, he grew up in a small farming village called Thali, close to the hot springs at Tattapani on the banks of 'the' Satluj River in the western Himalayas. He had memories of happy days at school followed by daily chores on the small farm his parents owned, such as picking fruit and vegetables, tending goats, ploughing with oxen and planting rice, herding cattle, weeding onion and garlic fields day after day before and after school and during the weekends. It was a simple upbringing, but he treasured his memories of the times sharing, learning and working with his family members and his community. The air was clean, the landscape inspiring and the friendships strong. Now Dani was in his early thirties, with the face of a highlander and the lungs and fitness of a mountain-bred person. He liked scientific reasoning and logic and was put off by ignorance or superstition.

His interest in further education coupled with his desire to learn about different cultures and people led him to further studies away from his village, to the capital town of Himachal Pradesh in Northern India, and Shimla, the old summer capital of the British Raj. While studying at evening college, he gave tuition in maths and English to children, as well as working as a waiter during the day, and later with tourists, teaching them Hindi. It gave him the opportunity to improve his English in return, because he had gone to a Hindi village school and hadn't started learning English until the age of nine or ten. Though his fascination with the English language had continued to grow, school did not offer the opportunity to learn it to a very high standard. Now he could satisfy that desire while answering the questions any Western tourist might ask about the mysteries of India and its culture.

This gave him the impetus to investigate and question rituals and practices performed in day-to-day life in India as he led various tourist groups to the villages of the high Himalayas in India and Nepal. The Indian culture is complex, old and long, and the more Dani observed and learned, the more it deepened his interest.

Some of his treks went on for two to three weeks at a time, climbing on foot to unfold the mysteries of the Himalayan wilderness and its villages and the diverse communities living by the melted glacier waters on the banks of the holy rivers. Eventually he started to travel to various travel exhibitions in Europe. He spent three or four years on and off between India and the West, and this gave him the opportunity to compare his simple village life to the fast-moving, sophisticated Western life that was going on the other side of the world. He had discovered that many of the age-old skills and sustainable ways were being overtaken by modern methods of living, and many of the simple and practical eco-friendly ways of the past were being destroyed by the new generation. The gap between the old and the new, the rich and the poor was getting wider and wider in many ways.

As much as he was seduced by the comfortable life in the early days, he became frustrated with the modern fast pace of living, which left precious little time to enjoy some of the simple things in life and the values that went hand-in-hand with them.

Recession was about to hit, and talk of climate change and uncertainty about financial stability was on the rise globally. Global warming and sustainable living was catching the interest of ordinary people. This was the catalyst that was to bring Roland and Dani together at this time.

A few weeks later, and typically, Dani was enjoying a wonderful soak in a hot bath. Lost in his thoughts and enjoying the comfort of this luxurious experience, he reminded himself how important it felt for him to have a moment of complete silence and calm in his day.

His eyes were fixed on a round lampshade above him. It formed an umbrella shape, hanging upside down from the white-painted ceiling and cast a circular beam of light on the ceiling above. There were four dry leaves attached to the shade, arranged in a square shape around the rim. Looking at these leaves took him back to the small Himalayan valley – 8,000 or so miles away – where he had spent his childhood. There he had lived a life close to nature with his parents, brothers, sisters and friends. He remembered how he would often collect various types of leaves there. Some of them were then used to propagate new growth, while others – because of the hot, dry climate – quickly dried, and after a few weeks looked very much like the leaves on the lampshade above his head. He would store them between the pages of his books.

Dani was soon lost in his childhood memories, thinking of all the things he used to do back in those days. Then suddenly, with a start, it occurred to him what he must do. He must remember all the traditions and values that were so dear to him and the community around him – the natural, simple ways of living and growing up charting the life of his parents' village back in India – and write them down in his diary somewhere so they would not be lost to time. Most of the games that he played with his friends, for example, were re-enactments of the jobs that he witnessed adults doing in the valley: important tasks like building houses and making things – everything from wooden ploughs and other farming equipment to flour mills and kitchen and cooking utensils.

Building a simple flour mill model, for instance, was a real skill; with the help of older children, they would create a perfect model of a water-operated turbine, made out of a mango seed, by cutting it into a robust circular shape and making "wings" from thorns from a local blackberry bush and water pipes from a small piece of bamboo, which they also used for making home-made pens. Other games would be played when the children would go along with the adults of the community to herd cows and goats in the jungle. These excursions gave the children the opportunity to explore different terrain to find the perfect places to play hide and seek, marbles, and old traditional games like *Gulli-Danda* – known as tip-cat in English, played with two sticks one small, about six inches, sharpened and pointed at both ends. You flick the small stick with the longer stick and hit it while it's in the air. There was also Punch Gate (played with five little stones of marble sizes. It's a sitting game and can be played with a few players and has a sequence count of up to five and so on), *Khatru* (known as Mancala in Africa and the West), *Dhekli* (where one team has to build a tower from circular slates or round flat stones and the other team then has to throw a ball to break the tower. Once the tower is broken and the ball is taken by the first team, then they have the ball, and then you knock out or hit the players one by one, whenever they try to erect the tower again. If the first team have knocked or hit all the players of the other team before they can erect the tower, then the first team wins; if the other team has built the tower then they win. It can be played between many players), and Chippy (a hopscotch game, hopping on one leg while attempting to hit a piece of circular slate to move or retrieve through different boxes on the ground, without losing balance, and only one box allows rest; you cannot let the circular stone rest on the lines or you will be out).

Dani remembered wonderful days spent living in the wild: exploring birds' nests, having close encounters with snakes, tigers, snow leopards, wolves and foxes; trying their hand at riding buffalos and rams and organising bullfights in the jungle. There was such a sense of freedom and exploration. Running to the local shops, or with goats to the jungle or into the open fields; all these and more were very much a part of their active, physical lifestyle – so different, thought Dani, from life today.

As he pondered these things, he missed his home and felt a need to go back and re-experience the basic traditions and customs again and understand the practical importance of them. He had spent a good few years in the West, and it was now time to reconnect with the community of his childhood, to help them to have the right balance and improve their lives – who were living their lives in much the same way as past generations – and record the process. He felt a sense of sadness that their old traditions were not available to modern life and had a sense that modern readers would glean a lot from these ancient, simple, sustainable ways to live with less.

As Dani was digesting this idea in the days that followed, he soon found out that his new friend from England, Roland Bourne, wanted to confirm the plans to visit the country. Not only did Roland have a lifelong interest in India and its culture, but he also wanted to meet Dani's family and experience life in the village near Shimla, the Himalayan village that Dani had mentioned.

Things were starting to fall into place. Dani had good experience in tailor-making and leading expeditions, so after a short time, they had put together an itinerary, booked their flights and arranged all the necessary accommodation and transport for their trip, which was to take place over a period of two weeks at the end of the year. The countdown to their adventure had begun.

CHAPTER ONE

The adventure begins

Three months later found Dani and Roland at London Heathrow airport for their eight-hour flight – Roland had to fly first from Newcastle to Heathrow and then catch the flight to New Delhi – a smooth journey punctuated by a few films and naps before arriving at Indira Gandhi Airport.

Dani noticed a dramatic change as soon as he disembarked. The airport seemed much better, cleaner and more colourful than before. It had clearly undergone a recent refurbishment. They rushed to the immigration queue, and after a little while they got through.

The first thing they noticed were huge three-dimensional copper hand-sign models on the wall. Dani explained that these were different *mudras* (hand shapes which had their roots in yoga). There were also elephant heads and colourful exotic paintings that made them feel that they had arrived in the land of wonders. As soon as they made their way into the arrivals hall and the waiting throng, they saw a sign welcoming them to "Incredible India".

Dani greeted the man holding the sign, a driver from their hotel, who introduced himself as Harminder Singh. Dani introduced him to Roland as Sardar Harminder Singh the great. Mr Singh had a warm personality and a wonderful smile, a nicely set grey beard and a turban covering his hair as is the tradition for Sikhs.

Harminder Singh took the trolley and offered them small bottles of mineral water. Dani asked whether they could stop at a historical monument en route to the hotel and off they went to the exit.

There were lots of people waiting in long queues, but, to Dani, everything was much better signposted and well organised than before. Dani was impressed with the new orderly parking and prepaid taxi systems that had been introduced. He was really surprised to see that all the empty parking places were indicated by red flashing lights and all the occupied places were indicated by green flashing lights, so that spaces could be noticed from a distance for the convenience of the drivers. There was no need to drive around trying to find a place.

As they drove through the city, Dani continued to notice massive changes. There was a lot of construction in progress together with newly planted trees, flowers and plants on the side of the roads and big flyovers and road-widening schemes. The driver pointed out the new metro in the distance. They were comfortable in the car and Roland was very excited by his first impressions of India and couldn't believe that he was in New Delhi already. This was soon apparent by the scenes outside: the roads were full of rickshaws, and the cars and buses were full of people.

Harminder Singh was very proud of Delhi and told them that by next year Delhi was going to be much better as they had replaced most of the diesel vehicles with gas for the Commonwealth Games, and the city was going to be in perfect order to host the games for people from around the world. They discovered that Harminder Singh was from the Pahar Ganj area of New Delhi. He lived with his daughter's family and drove his taxi around Delhi. He was satisfied with the work he got from hotels around the area and seemed happy with his life.

As they drove through the streets they marvelled at the people dressed in their bright colours and the buzz in the streets. Roland was not disappointed.

"This is incredible India," announced Dani.

***

As they drove and entered the smaller roads, they noticed many green trees by the roads and through them, Dani pointed at a tall tower called Qutab Minar, which was the tallest tower in India.

The driver parked the car and they jumped out to visit their first historical monument and a UNESCO world heritage site. Harminder Singh took them to the ticket office and waited for them over a cup of tea while they went to see the tower. A local guide from the office was hired to escort them, who then hurried them up to get to the site.

As they wandered through the crowds of visitors, the guide explained that the tower was 72.5 metres high and had been built in the twelfth century by Qutab-din-Aibak and that's why it was called the Qutab Tower. It had around 379 steps, and had been completed by different rulers down the years. It was really quite spectacular, and they had to look up to appreciate its full size. The rulers and Sultans of Persia had conquered Delhi and destroyed some of the old monuments and temples in the process of establishing their power. Around the central tower was a collection of other gates and towers together with much older carved pillars and stones and a mosque dating from the thirteenth century. The site was much more than just a piece of history: it was a great introduction to the heritage of India: it showed how powerful armies from abroad had conquered the land and about the struggle for the native people to adjust to these conquerors.

The most impressive landmark the guide pointed at was a wonderfully made iron pillar in the middle of the courtyard. The guide explained that "the tower is a masterpiece of art and history and was built in a way that means it is still preserved well today, although some rulers tried to melt it down in the past. This is no ordinary iron pillar. It is called the Ashoka Iron Pillar and it goes back to the third century BC, and had been built by forge welding and it contains only pure iron. The inscriptions on it are in one of the oldest languages of the world and go back to the dynasties of Chandragupta Maurya. It was he who had driven the armies of Greece and Alexander the Great out of India. Ashoka was the grandson of Chandragupta Maurya and was a great warrior, but after the Kalinga War of 261 BC, Ashoka erected lots of towers around the Indian subcontinent. As he came to terms with the massacre of so many people in the war, he tried to convey the message that peaceful existence was the only way to live, and this tower symbolises that message. Sanskrit and Brahmi scripts on it indicate that it was erected to honour Vishnu, the god of protection, by Chandragupta Maurya.

"Another inscription is from the twelfth century, when there may have been an attempt to remove and melt it, so it really is a pillar of victory and the old ruins around it are a fascinating glimpse of past architecture, workmanship and art."

Roland could not believe that all this had been happening in India when Romans were marching in Rome all those centuries ago. It was a lot to take in but it was fascinating, and soon they were ready to head on to the hotel after buying a few postcards and saying goodbye to the guide.

Dani explained in the car that during the Mahabharata time, the land where Delhi was built was called Khandavaprastha, but the Pandavas turned it into a very prosperous city and called it Indraprastha, and it became the centre of the raja and maharajas dynasties for many centuries. Its history went back to more than 1,000 BC, while the civilisation of North India went back much further to the time of the Indus Valley, Harappan and Mohenjo-daro civilisations.

They drove through the main centre of Delhi and soon entered a busy junction near the New Delhi Railway Station, and it was quite a shock to Roland. The sounds, smells, colours and the general disorder of the traffic began making him nervous. There were cows by the side of the road as well as horse and bull carts. Many people crossing the road cut through little gaps in the passing traffic. There were beggars knocking at the car windows as well as many people, young and old, selling water bottles, snacks and sweets and flower garlands for those in expensive cars. Dani reassured him that this was all perfectly normal in the big cities.

Dani was excited and telling his story with great passion and interest. He said, "Roland, you won't believe what happened the second time I came to Delhi. I came by a luxury night bus with a friend and arrived very early in the morning, five o'clock, much earlier than the scheduled arrival time. We got an auto rickshaw, or tuk-tuk, and asked him to drop us at our hotel. We agreed on a price of thirty rupees and he got going, but after a few minutes, once he'd got us out of the range of the other rickshaws and the busy street, he stopped and said, 'Sir, sir, sorry, oh no! I forgot to mention, we can't go to the main centre because there is a bomb blast and you can't go to that hotel.' I said, 'What? What? Come on, let's just go!' But he said, 'Sir, sorry, really, I promise I can't go there, you can take any other driver.' He pointed at the auto rickshaw coming towards us, 'Ask him.' He stopped and asked him, and I did too, 'It is no joke? Is it true?' The other driver replied, 'Oh ya, so and so market is closed until morning as there are police everywhere. They are asking everyone. You must not go there. Go when it is daytime.' Thus in this way we were convinced, and decided against trying. I just couldn't believe it, but we were very tired. I said, 'Ok, you show us any another hotel nearby,' and I was keen to see what he did next. He took us to a hotel and quickly went in before I could, as it took us time to get out of the rickshaw. I went in and asked the receptionist to make a phone call to the hotel I had booked. I gave him the number and he dialled it and put me through. 'Hotel Moon Palace?' 'Yes sir?' I explained about my booking and asked him about the bomb blast. He replied, 'Yes sir, you can't come until two o'clock as there is a curfew.'

"I still could not believe it, but couldn't be sure if they were right. So to test them further I asked how much their rooms were. They said that as it was now very busy and there was big demand, due to the bomb blast, so they only had a limited number of rooms – one was three thousand, and the other was five thousands rupees. We had a look at the room and could not believe that they were genuine. I soon understood that the number they had dialled was to their own rooms and one of their friends was tricking me, pretending to be the manager of the Hotel Moon Palace. I was getting really exasperated as the rickshaw driver and hotel manager were trying to cash in on this story. I felt I was being completely manipulated and it made me very angry. I really wanted to bash his rickshaw's windscreen, but as there were a few of them and we did not want to get into a fight, we just walked off without doing anything. The rickshaw driver now demanded ten times the price for his services – around three hundred rupees. I threw thirty rupees at the floor and we walked off with our luggage.

"By now it was around six o'clock in the morning and the sunrise was taking the darkness away and a few locals and commuters had started to appear on the road. I stopped an elderly man on a scooter and asked if there was any bomb blast or curfew. He said, 'Oh, my son, don't believe these stupid cheaters. They always make these stories up.' So we stopped another rickshaw and didn't even ask him how much he was going to charge. I was swearing about all of these cheating drivers so he didn't dare ask me a thing. He had realised that we were very angry and he tried to calm us down by saying that all the nightshift drivers were hoaxers. I handed over thirty rupees and he didn't say a word, just dropped us at our destination. So you have to really be aware in these streets. Now, after seven years, they can't use that story with me." Roland couldn't believe that it happened to an Indian and laughed in disbelief.

Some of the areas they drove through were busy and chaotic, with people selling things everywhere and all kinds of transport moving in every direction. But everyone looked purposeful and calm and there was no panic of any kind, so it made Roland feel that it must all be normal. He was surprised that transport continued to move despite the surrounding chaos. Harminder Singh was a determined driver, and as he moved forward he explained that a new pedestrian bridge was about to be built by the busy junction outside New Delhi Station to the main bazaar which would make life easier for all the drivers.

***

After the train station, and zigzagging through more traffic, the car turned in to Arakasha Road. The driver stopped the car outside some big glass doors and a *chokidar* (door guard) with a handlebar moustache, well dressed in a long *sherwani*, or *Achkan* (traditional Indian royal dress), opened the doors of the car and welcomed them to the Grand Godwin Hotel. While he was saying, "Welcome sir, welcome sir," some boys helped to take the luggage from the car.

Once they were inside, they left behind the sounds of all the traffic, motorcycles, people, horns, dust and smells. All was calm. They were welcomed with a small bottle of water as it was hot and they felt tired and thirsty. The staff took all their luggage and wouldn't let them carry a thing.

Harminder Singh came in and Dani handed him a tip and said goodbye.

After a slow check-in process, they were shown the rooms where they could rest after their long journey from England. It was much needed, and luckily it was cool and comfortable. Roland had a shower followed by a very long nap.

After a few hours, they met on the rooftop for dinner in the early evening. From there they could see the street below and everything going on in it. A few kites were flying in the sky from the rooftops of high residential buildings, and they could see telephone or mobile towers with umbrella-shaped satellite dishes keeping communication alive for the millions of people in this bustling city through a complex and entangled network of wires running through all the streets and houses. There was an orange and red reflection of the sun in the sky and a few birds flying in the distance.

It was a pleasant evening and they enjoyed their authentic Indian meal with a Kingfisher beer. Roland was relieved to find that the beer helped neutralise some of the more robust spices. Dani told him that it was not advisable at this stage to have anything that could make him dehydrated, as it was not good for the body; it needed time to adjust and adapt to jetlag, the changes of time zone, weather and food, as well as tiredness. Dani continued drinking mineral water. They met the very helpful manager, Peter Raymond, who was local to Delhi and he introduced them to a waiter called Tara Singh. The manager wanted to make sure that the guests were looked after well. Dani wondered where he was from, and Tara Singh told them that he was from Almora, a little place in the beautiful hills of Uttarakhand in the Himalayas, and had come to Delhi to work for a few years. Dani in turn told him that he was from Shimla, and that he thought that Tara could have been from Himachal or some other mountain region, as his face was like that of a highlander.

***

After an early morning wake-up call from the reception desk, they got up and met again in the rooftop restaurant for breakfast, where there was a buffet with various choices of continental and Indian food. It was an enticing scene with the chef and staff dressed in white aprons and hats, frying and steaming food in the kitchen, from where the smell of spices reminded them of the freshness of the fayre.

Dani availed himself of the Indian spicy paranthas, which he ate with hot pickle and yoghurt. Roland found that too spicy for the early morning. He preferred a light continental breakfast. They had to finish their breakfast quickly as the taxi had arrived to take them to the train.

They were booked on the early Shatabdi Express train from New Delhi Station to Kalka, a small British-built station in the Himalayan foothills, and then by narrow gauge railway to Shimla, famously known as the Toy Train. It would take them one more day of travelling.

New Delhi Station, with its rush of people and traffic, was almost impossible to imagine. People were carrying all sorts of bags, baskets, rucksacks, suitcases and bundles on or about their person. Outside the station you could be hassled by beggars, despite police being on the continuous look-out. There was a mad rush of people running to catch trains and long queues at every desk and gate. There were huge staircases to climb, which was very difficult for families with children and heavy bags to carry.

Dani explained that porters take advantage of those passengers who have too much luggage and know that they can't manage it themselves so are forced to pay for help. The porters were not regulated so could double or triple their prices, but luckily Dani and Roland didn't need one. Roland wondered if there were any authorities supervising their rates or behaviour. Even so, the porters did try to pull their bags from them, but Dani had experienced this before and knew how to cope with the situation. It was quite hard for them as they had to go up and down many steep staircases and make their way through huge crowds.

Another incident, before they even got into the station, was when someone approached and asked to check the validity of their tickets. But again Dani didn't fall for this trick and said he knew his game and his story to boot and told him to vanish.

"Very often these people, *dalals* (brokers), can trick you by saying this is not the right ticket or you need to approve it in an office opposite the station, especially when it is an online ticket. In these 'offices' someone may sign it and make you pay extra or may prolong the discussion which results in you missing the train. They may then attempt to sell you their services or even change your entire travel plans, such as offering to take you by car to your destination or book you a completely different itinerary. This, of course, makes them more money. So you may have the correct ticket and be on time at the right station, but you can still be taken for a ride. You must only check with railway officials in proper uniforms behind the desk or with the police."

Dani was more than familiar with these kinds of encounters and knew these fraudsters shied away when they spotted travellers who knew their game, but they were always on the look-out for innocent new travellers from villages or abroad.

"I remember a time when I was coming from Pune via Mumbai to Goa in South India," said Dani. I had to buy another ticket in Mumbai. The train was to leave in three minutes and the queue was so long that it would have taken half an hour. Suddenly, a beggar, no older than fifteen and barely able to walk, approached me and asked if I was going to Goa, as he knew that the queue I was standing in was for Goa tickets.

"I said yes and he said that the train was leaving in three minutes and that I would never be able to make it, and that the next train was in three hours. So, what to do? The beggar showed me a ticket and asked me to follow him. I had no choice but to trust him and was led like a dog on a lead, asking myself if I was being a fool or just stupid. But there was no other option, so I followed him, feeling sorry for the beggar who was rushing up and down the stairs with his stick and unsupported leg to the train. We both rushed, and he took me to the first-class carriage and showed me the seat number and gave me the ticket.

"The beggar asked for a hundred rupees extra. I paid him two hundred extra and was so relieved I thanked him very much and I couldn't believe how lucky I was! The beggar rushed off the train, disappearing into the crowd, and I, having checked with fellow passengers that the train was going to Goa, was relieved and grateful for my brief encounter with the beggar.

"It could have been such a different outcome had the man been dishonest," Dani said. "So it is a very difficult position to be in. One person's actions may benefit you while someone else's could lead to confusion, loss of money, hassle and frustration in this crowded and hectic environment."

Dani and Roland had no problems in Delhi. They got to the right platform on time and the train was there. Their names were clearly displayed together with their age and gender by the coach doors and they got in. They had the option of English or Hindi newspapers as well as tea and breakfast, all included in the cost of the ticket, which was just a few pounds. It was a clean and well-organised train and, surprisingly, on time.

Roland had heard a story about one tourist who had got on a train and found someone sitting in his seat. The tourist showed his ticket to the passenger and said, "Excuse me sir, there must be some mistake, you are sitting in my seat." The passenger looked at the ticket carefully and humbly replied, "I am sorry sir, your ticket is absolutely correct, but this train is yesterday's train!"

So Roland was beginning to realise that in India anything could happen. Nevertheless, the people resting and waiting on the platform around the train with their faces and colours was something to behold and reminded him of scenes from old documentaries. It was quite extraordinary.

The eventual departure of the train from the station was a relief and Roland was looking forward to seeing the countryside. In the air-conditioned coach, they couldn't open the windows, but they could draw the curtain to look out.

The early part of the journey was quite dull, and the smells and scenes outside the first stations were not very interesting. They reminded Roland of scenes from the film, *Slumdog Millionaire*. Some of the activities you just can't fathom while others make you want to either laugh or cry. The train passed many old buildings and bungalows, small residential areas with shabby looking apartments, people outside doing their jobs and children playing in the dirt.

It was disconcerting to see so much rubbish by the side of the railway tracks. Roland just could not believe that people could live in such conditions, including the very small huts and shacks covered with multicoloured plastic or metal sheets. This seemed to go on for miles. Roland asked Dani about these people and how it was possible to live like that. Through the haze of pollution, they could dimly make out people urinating in the open, and furthermore they seemed to enjoy directing their flow towards the trains. In the early morning, such as now, this was quite a shock to the foreign novice, but for the people outside it was a daily occurrence and they didn't give a damn for passing trains.

Gradually the scene changed, with some small houses a slight distance from the track, but there were still piles of rubbish alongside swampy fields. Nearby there were shacks from which men periodically trod carefully through the scrub having completed their ablutions, dressed in a shirt or just a *lungi* or *dhoti* (a sheet around the waist but no lower than the knees, or even shorter for some men). A few ladies were in saris and their faded colours displayed their poverty. They were all carrying pitchers, or other plastic jugs or bottles full of water, to find a relatively clean and secluded spot to squat. If they could find a spot behind a bush or cover that was a bonus.

It seemed that some of them were close enough to have a conversation, to catch up with the morning news or any stomach issues – good or bad! Some people were already engaged in their morning routine, while others were rushing back with an empty pitcher. From the train the two could see people brushing their teeth, washing their faces, urinating and much more. It reminded Roland of Roman bath houses, with their separate squatting places for ladies and gents. These places were more than just functional – they were meeting points for catching up on the latest morning news: a bit like the pubs in Britain for the evening news and gossip.

For Roland and Dani the train was the best place for conversation, and the topics for discussion spanned a vast range: history, architecture, theology, politics, the education system, shopping opportunities and local sightseeing, or topics arising from the scenes before them. Religion, spirituality and many other discussions added spice to their journey.

It was completely natural for Roland to have hundreds of questions regarding the scenes outside. He wanted to understand the mysteries behind what he had witnessed, and to express his anger about the levels of rubbish and the sheer poverty he had seen.

"Why are rich people not doing anything about it?" he asked. "Some of the richest men in the world," he said, "are from India, and many of the world's millionaires are Indians. The country has world-class hotels, royal palaces and forts, IT parks, Bollywood and trains like palaces on wheels with every comfort in them. India has a very old civilisation and an outstanding way of life in the world. Why doesn't Bollywood feature some of these causes and problems in their movies instead of just love stories filmed in London, Paris or New York?"

The waiters came in and offered them a flask of hot water and a tray with biscuits and packs of tea, coffee and sugar on it. This pack was labelled, "Meals on Wheels" – very interesting, thought Dani! The waiters were all very smartly dressed, with colourful red turbans with yellow and white dots on and long sherwani or achkan coats, similar to the British tailcoat. Dani explained that the cloth belt on their waist was known as a *kamarbandh* (like the British "cummerbund") and it was adopted by the British to go with their black tie dinner jackets as a flattering way to present their paunches. They looked very impressive while working very hard, carrying piles of trays and fulfilling the demands of their fellow passengers.

Roland was thirsty and wanted to stand up and retrieve his water bottle from his bag, but realised that there was a bottle behind each seat on a bottle rack. He was very suspicious after seeing all the poverty and hearing, the stories about hygiene. He asked Dani if it was alright to drink the water and tea. Dani told him not to be too sceptical, "This is much better than many London restaurants, because in the train everything has to be fresh, and all the vegetables and grain comes from fields in the Punjab – as rich and fresh as you have ever had. In the West we buy lots of food from these areas which then has to travel to us." Dani pointed out the fields and yellow-looking crops beyond the windows. "Those are rice fields."

All the houses were gone now and all Roland could see was mile upon mile of beautiful farms and trees, and some tractors, oxen and buffalo carts. "It's like we're passing through the equivalent of Yorkshire," Roland laughed.

Another interesting thing was the number of people waiting at the railway crossings. Some cars had smartly dressed people in them, perhaps going to an office. There were also rickshaws full of uniformed children, and farmers with tractors, buffalo carts and bulls. Some curious faces and some cross, as if the train was causing them to be late.

Later, a guard dressed in army gear with a machine gun on his shoulder came by and asked to see their bags. He put a sticker on them which said "Security Check". Dani said if their bags were not approved they would be removed unceremoniously from the train. Roland felt secure and liked the idea of being assured that passenger safety was taken seriously, as millions travel on the trains in India.

Looking outside at the farmland, Roland said excitedly, "Oh, so they do have lots of open land to grow food!" He was discovering something new about India all the time, and he realised that he didn't know much about its resources and ways of life.

They finished their tea and their trays and Thermoses were removed. Roland wanted to return to the scenes he had witnessed just after leaving Delhi. They were still troubling him.

"Dani, why are all those people living like that and so close to all of that rubbish?" he asked. "It seems that those people are living on rubbish tips."

Dani said that he felt sorry for those people and was concerned about their situation. "The thing is that the train station is full of people who have come to Delhi in search of food, work and a better life. Seventy per cent of India's population live in the villages and many people think life in the city is much more glamorous and wonderful, without knowing the difficulties and dangers. Others are victims of poverty, as they have no parents or have run away from home. The police and social systems are now improving, as India's young generation are being educated, but there's still a long way to go.

"In the past there were no non-profit organisations or charities to help people, as everyone was so concerned with their own survival, and the people who live in big palaces, they don't even know it happens in their neighbourhood. Those are people who will know more about London and Paris streets and prefer to buy all imported products. India has millions of pounds in Swiss banks, hidden away from the authorities for tax purposes and suchlike. In a way they are the cause of India losing its craftsmen and its way of producing small domestic products of every kind in the villages. Because these poor people can't sell their products they are losing interest and becoming jobless. Also, because they see no future or jobs in these local trades, people are relying more and more on machine-made products and no one is ready to learn these skills in the villages.

"Most of them want to learn computers and be IT or medical experts in science and technology, so these old experiences and skills are on the edge of extinction. All the money locals earn is sent to big manufacturers in the city or abroad. A local snack maker is going out of business because people are buying the well-presented chips or snacks made and packed many months ago by huge multimillion-pound companies. A local tailor or shoemaker is going out on the streets because people send money to huge brands abroad by buying ready-made jeans and shoes. As the media, famous actors and sports people or other public role models advertise them so much, a labourer may not be able buy food for his family, but will buy an expensive mobile and keep sending money to a big phone company every month or a pay as you go almost every day. Some rich man is making good money out of it all and those on the bottom are getting deeper into poverty without realising it.

"In the end they become victims of cheap labour, and again these rich people use them for their own well-being."

Dani explained to Roland that if he had been landed in a town and had missed the train, he could take another train to Shimla, because he was well educated. But he may have to wait for another train. "Then, if your belongings are stolen and all your money is taken, as you are a tourist and look different, you will get help from the police and other people, or you will be able to ring your family to arrange everything on the spot.

"But someone from a small village will try to ask for help from the police, shopkeepers and from other people. If they don't believe him or because they have hundreds coming every day with the same story, what can they do?"

Roland was getting worried already, even though he was in a very comfortable train. All he could think of was to sell his shoes or clothes. The last option would be to ask or beg for help.

"But then, maybe people will think you have stolen them and you are trying to sell them," said Dani. "You may be in trouble, but they will take them from you too. Not so much when you are different, but when you look like them – and I am sure after a few hours of heat and hunger and thirst you will look very much like other beggars. By then you will only worry about water and food, because you are hungry and thirsty in the heat and worried in a crowded town. If the train comes, you may not be allowed on the train and you may end up with all those other people that have chosen begging, because it's easy money, or because they have no other option.

"I am sure they all detested the idea of being a beggar in the beginning, but soon people get used to it, and once they do, they can no longer face their family and friends."

Dani told Roland about the "professional beggars" whose aim was to trap you and offer you food and shelter and then show you the techniques of begging and making more money. "Many beggars in the big cities make more money than a basic wage and do it on a freelance basis. Of course an educated person will not be taken in by it, but those who are not educated and look poor or look like other street people can end up in this situation. Then they try to make friends so that they end up sleeping near the richer or more peaceful places," he said, "but because rich people don't want you near their house, because they suspect that you may steal or rob from their house, then this becomes impossible and they are moved on.

"It is still a big worry," said Dani, "because you see children begging and they don't even have a single piece of bread or drop of water to drink, because people don't allow them to come near a tap or houses. If they want to sleep or take a rest in the heat somewhere, the owner will kick them out." Dani explained how it was happening to the people near the stations. "They are there out of desperation and see travellers, who are often innocent to their tricks, as easy money and easier to beg and trick. Sometimes," he said, "I get worried when I see young female beggars with babies or toddlers. Sometimes they bring their mothers or sisters' children to beg with them so they get more money. Sometimes they are being snatched at a very young age by their guardian beggars and pulled into a situation of every kind of abuse, by assuring them of food and shelter. There's even the possibility of being pushed into prostitution. Beggars can earn more if they have young children or babies to display and so are given the burden of motherhood when they have not yet learned to stand on their own feet or haven't established themselves as mature people. They may end up in this cycle for life."

He said that in these cases, it was hard to see any way of escape for that child. "It will all be repeated again and again and will be rooted deeper and deeper – and it will lead to more crime and more beggars in society," said Dani, with a sigh. "If action is not taken, that is! If action is not taken in time."

Dani could not believe that big world banks were giving millions of pounds to their top executives as bonuses on top of their salaries, when even their salaries were in hundreds of thousands of pounds. He could not understand how the work they were doing in those eight hours a day or forty hours a week could be worth that much money. On the other hand, a common person might only be getting around two hundred pounds a week. This worker may be really tired and ready to drop after eight hours of hardship. Dani really could not understand this huge gap in salaries. He believed that there should be a cap or limit on how much one could be paid for eight hours of work so the gap could be bridged.

"If a corporation makes huge profits, they should contribute part of it to the development of those at a ground level. If this is not done, most of the world population will live in worse conditions than this, which is really very sad."

Dani could not stop saying that when he came to Delhi for the first time he was shocked as he couldn't believe that people could actually live in those conditions, with hundreds surviving on the trains alone by begging, cleaning and stealing, because these are the only options they have for sleeping. "They survive on leftover food or food given by kind railway staff. That's why sometimes it is good to give them a little attention, talk to them and try to give them a little care," said Dani, "so they don't feel useless and unwanted." Dani said that he felt it was always good to give them something to eat, as it would make them feel good. He said that he used to always do that on his travels, and after giving to one beggar, he would end up with a huge group of them gathered around him.

He spoke of the first time he had experienced this chaos, on the way to Rajasthan and Goa. All he had known before this was a mountain boy's experience, which was a pretty self-sufficient one. And he explained how some of these beggars would move away from home and fall into the bad habits of drinks and drugs, because of their own nature or habits. "Or because they have done something wrong, they want to be hidden away in these lonely and punishing places. To shelter themselves from the rain or the heat, they would, little by little, acquire colourful blue, black, white and yellow plastic sheets, or a little kholi, or hut.

"Yes, there are many people living below the poverty line like this," said Dani. "And it is a big issue for all those Indians who would like to solve this problem, bridge the gap, uplift these people and be proud of India. There are now some organisations which are helping them," he said. "But there's no easy solution, as some of the beggars are addicted and they don't want to leave this easy money-making profession. Some of them work hard and do become coolies, rickshaw pullers or drivers and learn some other skills to make a good and honest income.

"I wish that there was a place or school or institute for all these homeless people and beggars, where they could perhaps be trained in local crafts and handwork, like in bamboo and woodwork or music, knitting and stitching, so they could be self-sufficient and their brand could sell with a special mark. And begging should be like a way of protest to show that someone really needs help. Authorities and society should be aware of it and there should be a record of each person's history and background and a registered number for each beggar," he said. "Then I think we will not see so many 'fake' beggars pretending they are blind, have broken legs or arms, or coloured wounds to get attention, care and charity from the public."

Dani explained that he knew a boy in Shimla, the town where he came from, who was Nepali and used to beg on the streets. "We got to know each other," said Dani, "and I used to see him almost every time I was in the town. I used to buy him food or a bun whenever he asked for it and I could afford it. Later he started calling me *bhaiya* (brother) and would ask for money, or food or whatever he wanted, or tell me his stories. I always advised him against buying any cigarettes or alcohol, and asked him to save and do good things. Very soon after that," said Dani, "he had made many friends and I saw him selling balloons on the main mall. And Roland, you would not believe it, but a few years later he approached me as a six-foot young man smartly dressed with a mobile in his hand: 'Bhaiya, do you remember me?' I was shocked and so pleased to see him looking so well, healthy and normal.

"He told me that he was a salesman in a store now. I had never felt so good. But he was a charming little boy and many shops and stores got to know him and helped him, but that can only happen in a little town."

"That must be so wonderful, Dani, to know that he is doing so well," said Roland.

Dani explained how he wished he could have done more. But it had made him think that individuals can make a change in this world – at least to touch just one life – it is worth it.

By now the train was pushing on and passengers were busy reading newspapers or were busy in conversation. Some of them were office commuters and many were tourists from other cities in India or from the West, escaping for breaks to the hills, pointing at interesting things along the way to each other.

Observing a rubbish pile near some houses, Roland asked Dani why they had rubbish piles everywhere, even along the railway tracks, courtyards and close to houses?

Dani said, "There are a few reasons, including ignorance and a lack of knowledge. Before plastic bags or packaging were introduced, they used to use natural materials like bamboo, leaves or tree bark to make bags and baskets. They were used again and again until they came to the end of their life. When they were finished they used to put them in a corner with the other daily rubbish of the house where nobody would see them. They then used to decompose and convert it into soil or useful compost after six months or so, which was utilised in the gardens and fields.

"But as they have no knowledge about plastic and other machine and hi-tech produced plastic material, they do not know that these do not disintegrate, so due to a lack of knowledge, they don't know what to do. They are not to blame, but it's those who produced it and thought that they were intelligent and allowed this plastic all around the world who are to blame.

"I think the best way would be to put a few lines about it in the school curriculums, so that all children and teachers are educated about it and information could be sent to all villages, before a new harmful product is launched," said Dani. "They would have to introduce a strict law for it, before introducing it around the world. But the manufacturers see the colourful plastic material and bags everywhere purely as money and profit. This is a big problem in the modern world."

Dani explained, "Traditionally, when a family in the Himalayan villages needed any containers, baskets or bags, or any other crafts for farming and domestic use, they were made from natural materials like bamboo, plants and the bark of trees. Every village had skilled craftsmen and local ladies who used to keep up with craft making from all-natural materials. Every season villagers would harvest different crops and then use the hay, bark or leaves to make baskets, mats and other useful things for their daily use at home and in the fields. Very often you would see ladies sitting and working on some knitting or making mats, baskets, jumpers, shawls or scarves from all-natural local materials like wheat straw, banana tree bark or leaves, date palm leaves, corn skin, cotton and wool. What they or their fellow villagers needed was made on demand.

"For special bamboo crafts they had to invite an expert or a skilled craftsman," continued Dani. "The story is quite interesting how it all used to happen. They would wait for the right season and then a member of the family would walk in the early morning to Bansbunane Wala's (a craftsman who makes things out of bamboo) house so that he could catch him at home before he left his house. Very often you could just catch a craftsman in the early morning, around six o'clock or so, just before sunrise and deals would be done then. It showed the dedication of the visitor to the craftsman, as well as the fact that he genuinely needed some work done. So the day and date would be fixed, including how many baskets they needed to make, or any other things, such as bags or backpacks etc. The craftsman would also advise where to buy the bamboo and how many bamboo pipes they needed and who had the best type in the village. Once all this was discussed, the delivery day would be confirmed and then, finally, the craftsman would come to the family's house. By then they will have arranged bamboo to be there, or they may take him to select the bamboo pipes himself as he knew more about it and he would know which older shoots to choose, as they are much stronger than young shoots. They would drag the bamboo to the house, and very often the work was done in the courtyard. The craftsman would measure them and split them into very thin sticks. Sometimes he dipped them in water so they didn't dry, as the sun is quite strong, and very often he made them in February or March, depending on the rainfall and the wheat crop, as they had to have lots of baskets to take dung to feed all the young wheat shoots every spring.

"The process of making these baskets and containers is very interesting. Step by step they converted these bamboo pipes into very thin sticks, which could be easily bent. It could take around two days to produce three *kiltas* or backpack baskets. It might take around five to seven days to produce enough types of containers to fulfil the family's demand. The craftsman could be paid by day wage or by the numbers he produced. They varied in shape and size as well as being used for different uses, like carrying things on the back, or carrying baskets on the head, *shup*, *dal*, *chchaj*, *tokari*, *kilta* etc. Many containers, after drying, were covered in a layer of a mix of cow dung and some other small leaves of certain plants to make them windproof and leak free. They could then store grains and other seeds in these containers, as they preserve seeds very well.

"Farmers always used to use their own seeds every season. These containers normally lasted thirty to forty years but it depended on how much one used them and how they cared for them. After a good amount of use they started wearing and tearing and a few spikes might start falling off. Finally, when it developed many holes and could not contain much of the dung or grain anymore, even after the visits of the craftsman to repair them, then he would let them know that this was the last time and that next time they had better throw them away and make some new ones. Finally, at the end of the life of the containers they may be burnt in the kitchen fire to cook food or they may rot in a pile of dung or rubbish in a corner of a field.

"As the seasons changed and they started ploughing again, all that would have decomposed into compost or into the soil. If any thicker stick remained that would be added to the pile of wood to burn for cooking food. From earth to earth or from nothingness to nothingness. Once, again, the same cycle would be repeated, and this natural process has been going on for centuries in these hill villages. A respected and well-off farmer's family would do this to be self-sufficient, and they would have good relationships with the local craftsman. They may also give him his wages in grains, such as rice, wheat, onion or any other crop he may need, and he was always looked after well with food and tea, etc., while he worked. During his stay he might discuss all the stories and catch up with all the village gossip too. There may be a few more village members who would come along to catch up with the day's news, and children often watched, and sometimes visitors might help with passing this stick or that. Sometimes other villagers brought their bamboo to the same place or they might invite him to their house. But very often they would bring their bamboo to him to fulfil their needs.

"Different families would take shifts to provide a packed lunch and meals for him. You could see people bringing big *thalis* (plates) and jugs of food covered with leaves or cloths from their houses. In the evening he might visit different families for dinner. It became a social event too and this sustainable life went on without leaving any effect on nature as more bamboo would be planted to carry on the cycle. Luckily, that is good for rain and greenery too. Local life was simple.

"Then, after a lot of use in the villagers' daily life, people would burn or bury it or simply throw it towards the back of their house or to unseen corners. Most of the houses don't face towards the railway tracks, because tracks used to be very smelly, so they don't really like these train tracks by their front door so they just throw unwanted stuff to the rear of the houses, which for us train passengers is front facing. It is a real shame that plastic, which was a great discovery, is a complete disaster due to the lack of disposal options, which causes lots of problems and all these innocent people in developing countries are victims of it.

"It was all to benefit humanity, but these were all short-term experiments to make money. Developed nations have found different ways of dealing with this because of their wealth, but here these poor farmers are suffering and many old skills are being lost. And now, everywhere even on the highest mountains of the world, the landscape is colourful with these plastic bags."

Roland sighed. What a shame. He told Dani that this wasn't just a problem in India, but a very serious issue for the whole global community. "It is not even managed very well in developed countries in Europe. Only a few countries are doing it better than others, and overall they are all struggling. They have provided various big dustbins and are managing to hide it away from the community, but creating landfills in dumping areas is not the solution either. Landfill has no capacity to expand anymore. As the global population is growing and the amount of waste produced by each household is increasing so much, the whole system is simply exploding with waste of every kind. It would be best to block it at source and stop manufacturing plastic bags or containers at all, and they should allow manufacturing only from natural materials which are decomposable.

"How does this work in India, Dani – the whole waste management? There must be some old ways, where people had jobs to clean and clear all the dirt or waste from around the houses or the community?" Roland asked.

"Yes Roland, there were some simple ways. First it started with cleaners who used to come and clean your house and toilets. Also there were some people who were trapped in poverty, or were on the lower level of society, who used to come around the village once a week, or month, to ask for empty glass bottles or any containers, broken metal things of iron, copper and brass. They used to sell it to other dump collectors in the town and it used to go back to the factories to be recycled again. That was in the villages, and the rest of the food waste went to the cattle or was put on the compost heap with the cow dung. That is a crucial part of saving the world, a very natural way of converting waste into something very useful by using simple natural recycling methods without any expensive machines.

"All this bombarding of plastic, in many shapes and sizes, has confused everyone now. People mix all kinds of waste and food together and stick it in containers, and when it starts smelling they just want to dump it further away. That dumping has developed into landfill and waste mountains. There are many reasons for this, especially in India, as there are lots of people who hate dirt so much yet they have never cleaned any of it themselves. They hate dirty places and toilets, which smell so much. They just prefer to close their nose, do their business, and run away. Many of them haven't understood that if you simply clean it with some special cleaning liquid, that will be clean and then you don't have to close your nose or hate it so much that you simply want to run away. They don't understand that if they clean it well every time they use it, when they come next time, it will be clean for them too. If everyone understands this basic habit, their public toilets will be transformed.

"Sadly the problem is that this cleaning and rubbish clearing job has always been left to the poor and those people who were helpless and had to do it, as they had no other option for living. The gap between the rich and poor is so huge no one can believe it. Caste and class is also a big factor to blame for this problem too. Some people feel so superior that they are too smart to flush their toilets, let alone to sort out the waste of the house so they leave it for the rubbish collectors to pick and sort out. But society expects these poor rubbish collectors to go through the smell and the mixed muck for them. The rich always look down at them and think that it's their job. They do not even consider that they are human beings like them, and without their help their rubbish would not be cleared and their life would be hell.

"Millions of people in the world are now working on these waste or rubbish collection projects, and they are not just waste pickers or waste collectors. They are much more than that, because they are helping everyone to clear up

Mother Earth, so all that rubbish does not develop into diseases, viruses or nasty, dangerous, harmful chemicals or gases that damage the environment, otherwise our surroundings would be full of smells and waste and you would not be able to breathe or survive.

"They are helping the whole planet and here we are not giving them any credit at all. We call them rubbish pickers and they are at the lowest level of society. We need to upgrade them and give them better positions in our society. We have to value them and give them a better name, not just waste collectors or rubbish pickers. They should be called environment inspectors or sustainable managers or grading inspectors, who help in separating all kinds of rubbish and putting it in order. Households need to interact with them more and make them feel that they are an important part of society by having a conversation with them to understand what needs to be done in advance so they don't have to go through all the rubbish to separate everything. Families could separate plastic bags, bottles, glass, paper and cardboard and food, which would save lots of time and help them find dignity in their jobs. We all need to clean and sort out our own rubbish. Everyone is equal as human beings, and we can't expect others to do everything for us if we want to survive in this fast-moving modern world.

"Many people don't even think about these things and they just dump their muck in plastic bags. I have seen people throwing these packages out of their windows or from the tops of roofs, and these collectors have to take risks to go to these places to sort out any recyclable products, or they would still be piling up."

Roland asked, "Has the government done anything towards this at all or is this just the job of the needy or the very poor? Are the public free to dump their rubbish anywhere? At least the government or local organisations could provide them with basic equipment or tools which could make their life easier. That would be a good start."

Dani went on, "Well nowadays the government have put bins in different big towns and they have started different ways to convert rubbish into useful products. But villages have no access to anything like this and they are still wondering what to do with it. In Shimla, they have started a project to convert waste into gas, and they have put lots of money into the project, which is really good for the Himalayan states. I'm not sure if it's possible to do these kinds of projects throughout India, but sometimes they use money on big machinery and recruit well-educated and trained people for these jobs but ignore those who have been doing these kinds of jobs for many years, which is a big shame too. I hope they recruit and train those people who have been doing this for their living for many years.

"One more thing ... it is quite difficult in areas where there are wild animals like monkeys or other cattle, because monkeys take everything from the bins and spread it everywhere. If you don't have experienced waste pickers, new people and machines find it difficult to collect this kind of rubbish and it is left behind, so a lot has to be done, and educating everyone about it is the first step, so the public can actually understand about it. Special awards should be given to waste managers for doing this most important work for society."

Roland added, "It would be much better if people controlled their waste in the first place and tried to reduce their rubbish as much as possible and find natural ways to convert it into something useful. If they could manage it in the past they could do it now too. Have a community cow or cattle and use their dung for compost in the gardens and milk for the community. Simply improving things at home, like cooking just enough food, using biodegradable bags and baskets for shopping and not buying any plastic bags can save lots of effort and money too."

Dani was impressed and agreed heartily with Roland, saying, "If that happened, we would not see miles and miles of rubbish along the railway tracks like we have just seen."

Dani pointed out the piles of cow dung, *uple* (round dung cakes), made from cow dung, like a small chocolate cake drying out in the sun. "These *uples* are cooking fuel for many families, because they can save on wood if they burn cow dung. This is the economical and forest-friendly way to protect trees and wildlife." They could see piles and piles of it all along the railway track.

They were now in the area of Haryana and Punjab, famous for its farming and crops all over the world. Roland felt that in one way India was developing in line with Western standards, but on other hand, the old ways seemed very advanced, sustainable and well thought out. They could see piles of hay and farmers ploughing in the fields with oxen and tractors. It was something Roland had never seen before.

Soon the train passed through a big station called Ambala, which was famous for the army base that had been there since the British Raj.

By now they had had their morning breakfast with toast and stuffed *parantha* as well as a samosa and cutlets. The waiter was clearing the trays and Roland was ready to know more.

Dani said, "Now we are in Punjab and soon we will be passing the famous city called Chandigarh designed by the French architect Le Corbusier. It is a very new and organised town in quite a modern style, but famous for its rock garden. It used to be a huge farming area. During the construction of the town they found remains of old Harappan civilisations here too, which can be seen in the Chandigarh museum.

"Tell me about the rock garden?" asked Roland.

"It is a huge garden, or park, full of different art objects built out of unwanted or broken waste from households, like tiles or electronic parts. It was built by a great man called Mr Nek Chand, who was a simple worker involved in removing lots of waste out of the farming sites. So much clutter and waste was produced – piles and piles of waste were produced – that he could not just let it sit. For that generation, wasting anything was painful. They knew how long it took to make or produce a little pin or simply a handmade broom. To see wonderfully machine-made things broken must be so hard. Just a simple thought, how long a craftsman must have taken to create this, and here we just burn or throw the thing away, like, 'Oh, you can pick another one up in Ikea for next to nothing'. He had experienced the horror of partition and settled here in the end, but he presented sculptures in an extraordinary way without using anything but unwanted materials from the people in this town. It is all displayed in a wonderful setting that now has waterfalls, ponds, swings and other activities inside. It is a popular site. Chandigarh also has a very popular rose garden with hundreds of different roses, as well as famous museums and shopping malls."

Roland pointed out the mountains that they could see in the distance. Dani said excitedly that those were the foothills of the Himalayas and that soon they would be there.

By now everyone was getting ready to take their bags out, and some people were already rushing to the doors.

"Here we are in Kalka," Dani announced. Soon the train stopped after three big honks of the horn and all the coolies rushed towards the train, dressed in red shirts and white trousers with a cloth over their shoulder and a brass number plate on their arm. They were asking passengers if they could take their bags, but Dani and Roland collected their own luggage and took them out onto the platform.

***

It was a very interesting train station: an old colonial-style building with not many train tracks – two or three towards Delhi. The pace was much slower and not that crowded, a welcome relief from New Delhi Station.

They had another railway track towards the hills for the famous train to Shimla, called the *Himalayan Queen*, the famous "toy train", which was waiting for the passengers coming from Delhi. It had small coaches and quite tiny seats, so they all had a seat but not enough space. It was built in 1903 on a narrow track, and before that the only source of travel were palanquins, horses or horse carts, or bull carts, or going on foot.

Soon the train started and they hardly had time to use the bathrooms. They got some biscuits and juice from a nearby stall at the platform. After a slow start, the train picked up some speed and it went through various tunnels and curves; they could see the whole train on curves in a "u" shape, and it was zigzagging at a slow pace all the way uphill.

Dani explained that the train goes through 103 tunnels and travels from the plains of India to 2,180 metres above sea level up in Shimla. "This was a great gift to the hill station of Shimla from the British, although they had built it for their own interests. But one has to admire British management as well as Indian workmanship for creating something so useful and incredible, which is still in perfect working order and used by a lot of travellers and hill people."

From the train they could feel themselves moving higher and, leaving the level ground behind, they could see the terraced fields and small scattered villages and houses all over the hills. Further up, they noticed that many houses had yellow corn drying on their roofs. Dani later explained that villagers had just harvested the corn crop and they would dry it out on the roof before grinding it for flour. There were small streams in the distance and the train kept passing through tunnels and thick jungle and they could see monkeys sitting on tree branches and jumping from tree to tree.

Dani told Roland that when he had travelled previously with one of his family friends from London, he found out that his father, Major David Atkins, had served in India during the British Raj and was very fond of writing.

"Later, after retirement and his return to the UK, the major had written and published a few books like *"The Cuckoo in June"*, but one he had written during a train journey to Shimla for a vacation at the residence of the Governor General of British India had never been published and this friend had brought the script with him. It was really touching for him as the major had passed away a few years earlier, and it was very interesting for me to read all about the scenes outside the train before World War Two. He described the drying of yellow crops on the rooftops of little mountain houses, the monkeys outside, tunnels, vegetation, and all the things they had just seen and he emphasised the importance of the changing weather and the cool breeze, which reminded him of going home. It was interesting to know that not that much had changed, although now there is a quicker way of going by road which takes two hours less."

The train stopped at many different places along the way. A few people would jump on and off and a ring would be let out at every stop by the driver, in the old style, before leaving the station. Then the train stopped for a snack break and they had tea and sandwiches. The station where they stopped sold all sorts of local and continental snacks – all freshly made – and soon afterwards the train started again and left the small station behind.

Dani explained that Barog was around 1,560 metres above sea level, and he had a sad story about a Colonel Barog, who was the man in charge of digging the tunnel near the railway station.

"Sadly, the tunnel's mouth, dug from both sides of the mountain, did not meet and he was fined one rupee by the British government, which was not much, but the humiliation was so huge that he committed suicide. It was really sad to know what these young British officers had to go through, thousands of miles away from home, giving their lives for the British commanders who were well-looked after back home in England. All that dedication … Leaving behind their parents and loved ones, they were pushed out to fight or build in distant parts of the world at great personal cost, so the ruling class could harvest the world."

"It's hard to understand, just madness, digging tunnels in the Himalayas," said Roland.

Dani continued the story. "Finally, another tunnel was dug under the command of a different officer called HS Harrington, and he took the help and advice of a local sage, or wise man, called Balku, and he succeeded in making this the longest tunnel of all 103 tunnels on the railway, around three years after the first attempt."

Now all the trees and vegetation were changing. There were alpine and silver pine trees as well as beautiful rhododendron trees with some red flowers. They could see deep valleys and high peaks around them and towns and villages in the distance. It also started to feel cooler. It was making sense to Roland as to why British people wanted to leave the hot plains of India behind and come and live in the hills in Shimla.

"The main town is called Shimla, the present capital of the state of Himachal Pradesh and an old capital of the British Raj in India. The British could not enter Shimla before 1816 as the Gurkhas had a stronghold in the foothills and surrounding areas. They had to have a special treaty with them after losing several battles to these mountain fighters, who were experts in guerrilla warfare. Finally, they were allowed to enter the foothills and soon the British felt at home with the weather and the breathtaking scenery. Soon Shimla became a famous retreat for British lords and ladies. They built the first house in 1822 in Shimla, and soon romantic colonial couples started to rush to Shimla. It became a hub for those delicate British roses who were pushed into arranged marriages and were made to leave their comfortable lifestyle behind in England to find a suitable match and keep up with the British hierarchy in the unknown and mystical wilderness of India.

"The British carefully chose their spots on the hills of Shimla to build residences, and they understood why locals had built houses on certain slopes or sides of the hills while leaving other parts to grow as alpine forests due to the rain, wind and sunshine, as winters could be extremely windy and freezing cold. Soon it became a sport of the Indian royals and lords to leave their palaces behind for summer and have residences in the hills to hunt wild beasts or game.

It became the fashionable place to be in 1888 when the huge Viceroy Lodge was built, and wonderful malls were created to wander in so the British didn't miss home. Lots of treks for walks and horse riding were found. The trails led them to secluded and private hidden spots where you could hunt for British roses in the romantic hills. Landmarks like the Chadwick Falls, the Glen and Annandale ground and many other hill areas are famous for these outings. This summer capital witnessed a transformation from palanquins, hand-pulled rickshaws and horses and carts to the railway, motor cars and then to airplanes."

Roland found it interesting as Dani explained that this was the only escape for lots of British ladies and families from the heat of the plains.

From far away they could see beautiful mountains and green hills spotted with red-roofed houses. They couldn't stop taking pictures and Dani kept pointing at important monuments and buildings, as Dani had spent his youth and studied in Shimla for a period of around seven years, and it had been a turning point and a huge learning curve for him, and the most important place in his life.

He knew Shimla very well and pointed out the centre of the town, and soon the train was slowing down and Dani was excited to be back in Shimla, looking out for anyone he knew.

The train stopped and they collected their bags and made their way to the door. However the coolies were quite pushy and they wanted to help with the luggage and lead the tourists to different hotels in Shimla, but Dani and Roland had their own hosts this time.

The station was small and beautiful, nestled in the hills.

Roland said they'd had quite a journey from Delhi, "It was a bit long, around nine hours."

"If we'd taken a flight we would have been here in fifty minutes, but we would have missed all the joy and fun of the experience," joked Dani.

Roland was secretly pleased with their decision, as the whole train journey from Delhi to Shimla had been full of farming land, small villages and terraced fields. The trip from Kalka to Shimla had especially given him a real feel for the countryside and he could relate to it more.

They got out of the ticket checkpoint and were welcomed by Dani's relations. After a brief introduction they were then driven through the town. The traffic wasn't that great, even though it was just after five o'clock – rush hour in Shimla! Finally they arrived at a grand-looking hotel called Woodville Palace. Dani explained that it was a royal palace and was more than two hundred years old. "Himachal had a great history of royals as it dates back to around AD 1000 – a time when invaders from the plains and other countries had discovered the Himalayas and India and were attacking and looting it, as well as destroying its temples and monuments and stealing its wealth.

"Many Indian royals followed the rivers from the plains and took over small mountain kingdoms in the Himalayan valleys, although they could not stay in these hills, but the damage was done to the famous and powerful Kangra Fort in the Kangra hills in Himachal. There are some old native families and tribes as well as some very old temples from the first and second century. It could be that in the beginning people followed these routes to these temples as pilgrims, and then settled here later. Many royals had connections with West Bengal and Bihar state in the eastern plains of India, though. This royal family is part of an old dynasty and still partly lives in the palace."

Roland liked his room very much as it had lots of old pieces of furniture and paintings and was very comfortable with all the facilities that he required.

They had quick baths and showers and were then ready to hit the town. Dani suggested they walk into town and experience the main mall of Shimla – famous from British times for shopping. It was also said to be the longest pedestrian shopping street in the world where spitting, smoking and all vehicles were prohibited, except ambulances or emergency vehicles that used a certain route.

There were many famous hotels and restaurants in Shimla, but Dani wanted to take Roland to his favourite spot first. Dani had spent lots of his leisure time there with his friends during his college years and it was a place from where they could enjoy Shimla more. And it really was a wonderful place. Called the Ashiana Restaurant, it was perched on top of a hill called Ridge Maidan, (open ground), right in the heart of Shimla, next to the Gaiety Theatre and a church to the north. Dani explained that it used to be a bandstand, as the British had loved their music. The Ridge was also an open ground for army parades, making it a suitable spot for the bandstand. It had seen some changes over the years, including being a crèche for children and finally it had been converted into an enjoyable restaurant called Ashiana, with a bar downstairs called Goofa (cave). Downstairs was a bar and upstairs a very enjoyable restaurant. It was a spot in the heart of Shimla from which to enjoy watching the roaming crowds on the Ridge either from the terrace or through the big glass windows. They had a table booked and were spoiled by the hospitality. They even produced Himachal wine, and juice made for them out of Himachal produce; for sure a step to an eco-sustainable life, instead of importing expensive wine from around the world.

"We will lose the charm of travelling if the whole world becomes the same," Roland remarked to Dani.

They had delicious food with very different flavours, and the restaurant was very busy. After dinner they went for a walk on the mall.

Dani explained that in the daytime they would have an excellent view of the snow-capped Himalayas from the Ridge. They walked along the mall road and enjoyed the British look of the town: town halls, timber houses and slate roofs, all built by the British in the early 1900s. To Roland this town looked much like a street in England. Some of the buildings would have been at home in the UK and the weather was also very much like at home. Dani wanted to introduce Roland to the Indian coffee house. There they still wore full dress, with hats for waiters, and they had a fixed menu written on a board from which you had to order, pay at the counter and then wait for service on a designated table. There was old-style furniture as well.

After the coffee they went back to the hotel. They'd had a long day and were tired too, but it had been a great day to experience what the first British people might have felt when they arrived and settled there.

***

The first thing that Roland found as he opened the door to his room the next morning was newspaper in English slipped underneath it. It was still a bit cold; the sun was slowing rising higher in the sky and the shadows were disappearing from the trees outside.

Feeling a bit cold himself, Roland shut the door and began studying the newspaper and its top stories. He noticed that there were lots of stories about how to live a sustainable life. The main news was about the International Conference on Climate Change which was taking place in Copenhagen at this time, (see Appendix) and how mankind could change its way of life so that temperatures and weather conditions could stay reasonably stable. There were comments from world leaders, and in one corner of the page there was a small picture of Mahatma Gandhi with his spinning wheel and the words: "Simplicity is the key to a sustainable life." There were comments and arguments from various scholars and reformers about modern life and about the whole world following the same way of living; how modern chemical fertilisers were changing and damaging the farming in India and around the world; there were terrifying pictures of the drought and hungry children in Africa, and African leaders appealing for action and blaming the West for its booming development and lifestyle and demanding quick action and requesting emissions to be cut down to bring the temperature rise to 1.5°C. There was also a special appeal from the leaders of the Maldives requesting quick action to save their country and islands. Roland thought if a whole island like the Maldives is on the brink of disappearing, it means all small islands around the world, as well as our own British island, could disappear too, with global weather changes, unpredicted floods and rising sea water levels could destroy our world.

There were other articles about how everyone was ignoring farming and hard work, as everyone wanted to live an easy life and leave the hardship to machinery. In another article, the invention of the motor was described as a curse for nature, as humans were harvesting most of the resources from inland, from the earth and from the sea. How long will these resources last and what effect will that have on daily life, the article asked? Roland thought that there was no easy solution to the problem, as we are replacing all the natural gases, coals, oils and other minerals with smoke or toxic gases. He felt a bit down about the whole thing – the well-being of the world mattered to him – and he switched off the light to save resources. After finishing the newspaper, he was relieved that at least he was in among the beauty of the Himalayas and thought he'd better have a shower and see if Dani was already in the restaurant.

All packed and ready, he joined Dani and his friend from Shimla for breakfast. As part of their mission here in Shimla was to explore the sustainable life of the villages and the traditions which had been going on in the Himalayas from around 6000 BC, their discussions over breakfast veered towards the same topic. Dani was very serious about this and newspapers aplenty were on the coffee table as well. He commented, "The culture and way of life has travelled, moved and shifted over 10,000 years from Afghanistan and Persia, and from old settlements like Mohenjo-daro, Harappan and the Indus civilisation high up into the Himalayas. The way of life and culture has been passed on through day-to-day working practices, oral rituals and ceremonies throughout the generations, and is still being practised in the way of life in the villages of India."

After their breakfast they came to the conclusion that they may have to leave all this luxury one day and live a basic life and share and adapt their bodies to face the hardship of nature and to live with it.

Dani suggested that perhaps one day they may have to live the way Mahatma Gandhi lived and said that being in touch with Mother Earth to create a self-sufficient life with simple ways of living was a positive step.

"Gandhi really had a great vision and had foreseen the effects of modern living. He encouraged simple living and high thinking. He set an example to all of us for generations to come with regards to how we can face the difficult task with a smile and non-violence, just to prepare ourselves mentally and physically.

"First, to train our body to be strong from within and outside so that we can cope with a very basic lifestyle, because it is a fact that not all people who live a luxurious life or are living in a palace are happy or satisfied with life. Small and local is beautiful and essential needs are important, and unchecked desires can lead us to want more and more, which is a sure way to destruction."

Roland agreed, "It is madness the way much of the world is going, but we can't fix it all at once. I hope that people will soon realise and try to balance their life in a more moderate way."

It was time for them to get ready for their day ahead. They finished their breakfast after a little look around the old Maharaja palace.

They were soon ready to leave and, after paying their bill and checking out (the bags had already been put in the car by the efficient hotel staff), the local driver was ready to set off for a day of sightseeing.

They drove along the cart road to the famous Viceroy Lodge, once a formal residence of the British viceroys. The entrance to this building took them right back to Scotland or England. It was built between 1884 and 1888 and was a cocktail of Eastern and Western architecture: carved stones and stone pillars – an impressive castle on top of the hill, it could have been in the Scottish Highlands. It was awe-inspiring to contemplate how they would have built it without transport and modern machinery. Most of the stones had been carried from far away by local labourers and the craftsmanship was very impressive.

This was also the first building in Shimla to have electricity and it even had provision for a lift as well. Not only did the British rule from that seat in Shimla as a summer capital for the viceroy, but it became an important monument for decision-making after it was fully established, as the Independence movement was at its peak around twenty years after its completion. So the British couldn't really spread their wings around the hill state that much, and before fully settling, the struggle for independence had already started. Lord Curzon, Lord Wellesley and Lord Mountbatten couldn't help it even with all their force and policies.

Great leaders like Mahatma Gandhi, Jawaharlal Nehru and Vallabhbhai Patel, Maulana Azad and Muhammad Ali Jinnah had taken the partition decision along with Lord Mountbatten here, as well as the important Shimla conference being held here in 1945, which could not stop the flood of millions of people during the migration from India to Pakistan and from there to India. All the religious groups, who had previously managed to live together for centuries, were bloodthirsty for each other. A scar was left on the land forever.

So decisions were taken at the highest levels in these hills inside this comfortable, luxurious palace, away from the reality on the ground, and they ended up dividing societies, families and friends here.

After Independence, it changed hands and became the presidential residence or "Rashtrapati Niwas", and soon after became the Indian Institute of Advanced Study for higher level students who were pursuing PhDs or further academic research into fields like humanities and social and natural sciences. Due to its collection of books and the huge library, it could provide the right environment for the scholars.

After a guided tour inside the building by the excellent guide, Rajesh Verma, they finished with a photography exhibition and enjoyed witnessing some of the scenes taken from local history. It gave a useful insight into the work that British officers in India had done for the British government back in England, obeying their commands from all those thousands of miles away. Thousands of British men and women suffered, served and adapted to the customs and dangers in India so that the British monarchy could benefit from their tasks in these hills.

These included tasks such as expanding territories and constantly defending them from local fighters as well as harvesting raw materials and making use of them, and at the same time keeping the balance right socially and culturally so a relationship with the locals could be maintained and they could support projects like railways as well as creating a market for machine-made products to sell.

"It's a shocking thought, leaving all your loved ones behind," Roland exclaimed. "It's hard to imagine this when there were no aeroplanes or telephones. Travel by sea or orders from home depended on a postal system that could sometimes take months to arrive."

The two bought a few postcards and some books on Shimla written by a famous local historian called Raaja Bhasin. Soon after this they walked past other houses to the gate and got into the car and drove through the busy roads of Shimla again to go to Jakha Hill.

Dani explained about the hill, "The name of the hill was derived from a local word, *jakha,* which means the butter of the first produce from the milk of a cow or buffalo. When locals are proud and happy with the milk produced, they offer that first-produced butter to this shrine, which is now dedicated to Lord Hanuman. So the hill is called Jakha Hill, where they take their *jakha*, and they hope that their cow or buffalo continues producing milk and calves for years to come. The legend has it that Hanuman, an ape that holds incredible powers and strength, took a rest on this hill when he had entered the Himalayas in search of some herbs called *Sanjivini* to rescue the younger brother of Ram, the Royal Prince of Ayodhya in *The Ramayana*. It's an old Indian history, which is not included in the history books, but the kingdoms existed then and the names and towns still exist in India today.

"Lakshman was injured in a battle against a king called Ravan, who had kidnapped Sita, the wife of his elder brother, Ram. Ram organised an ape, monkey and bear army in the jungle to fight against Ravan to rescue Sita, as they were exiled for fourteen years to the jungle when this all happened. Hanuman apparently took a rest on this hill while taking the herbs back. Now there is a famous temple dedicated to him. The forest around this temple is filled with monkeys, and some of them are so clever that they can take your cap or glasses, so that you feed them in return, and then they will throw your possessions back. It is a game played out daily.

"Inside the temple is safe, and there are some old photographs which are worth seeing and it is a really interesting place. You have to take your shoes off and leave them on shoe stalls to get in, but the monkeys can take your shoes too, so you do have to be careful. There have been cases where they have even searched pockets, not for money, but for anything edible, and this can really cause problems. They are depending so much on people that they're losing their natural way of finding food in the woods and are making life difficult for local people. Now they have put some strict rules in place to stop tourists from feeding them, and special efforts have been made so that they don't lose their natural skills of finding their own food in the wild, because before this they were always independent in the woods. It's a really serious issue because if you are scratched or bitten by a monkey you have to have a rabies injection. Many tourist families have sticks to guard their children from the monkeys, but all this doesn't stop anyone climbing the hill. People trek up the hill for half an hour to admire this spot, visit the temple, and also enjoy the view of the Himalayas. There is also a beautiful garden in front of the temple, which must have taken huge efforts to keep it going with the monkeys around.

"The Bollywood actor Amitabh Bachchan and his family have visited this place for many years and it means a lot to them, and they believe that any wishes made on this spot are fulfilled with the Grace of Lord Hanuman. They have donated a 108-foot statue of Hanuman to this hilltop, which can be seen from down below as an orange crowned head with strong shoulders shining through the alpine forests. I'm not sure if the statue is the best thing one could donate to this hill. I think I would prefer something educational, maybe a museum or a craft or cultural centre to revive some of the old skills, or even a children's centre for creativity. That would give something valuable to visitors and the community. But if they had made this promise to build a statue, maybe they had to fulfil their promise, which they did. Nevertheless, it is still admired, and it marks this place as the highest spot on earth to have a statue of that height.

"Another alarming statement is about an old devotional song, dedicated to the monkey god Hanuman to praise the great warrior. It is called 'Hanuman Chalisa'. One of the lines in this song says: '*Yug sahastra yojan per Bhanu-leelyo taahi madhur phal janu!*' and means he leaped towards the sun by imagining it as a *madhur phal* (sweet fruit), but the fascinating thing is that it defines the distance from the Earth to the Sun with a formula, almost like in algebra. YUG SAHASTRA YOJAN per Bhanu. Bhanu means Sun and 1 YUG = 12,000 years, 1 SAHASTRA = 1,000, 1 YOJAN = 8 miles. So YSY = 96,000,000 miles and 1 mile =1.6 kilometres. So, 96,000,000 miles x 1.6 kilometres = 153,600,000 kilometres to the Sun. Today's science and NASA have now confirmed the distance between the Earth and the Sun; surprisingly, it is about the same: 92,935,700 miles."

Dani explained that this could be the main reason for the famous actor to donate the statue to the queen of the hills in the Himalayas, so it is not forgotten. "The amazing thing is how accurate and meaningful these ancient details are, and how did they know about it? How did they discover it all those centuries ago? The old astrologers and astronomers had studied about the planets, the Sun and the Moon, and they had calculated the distances between the Sun, Moon and Earth long before modern science did.

Thousands of people visit the temple every day to offer prayers as well as to trek up the hill, or simply for the sake of the view all around, and then to trek through the woods to Dhingu Hill.

"In our college days," said Dani, "we used to walk down from this hill to Sanjauli and then hire bicycles from there to ride back to the ridge, and it was great fun as we could leave the bikes at the end. It was a wonderful outing and good exercise, and we used to love it."

Roland could see the happy expression on his face. They enjoyed the view and after a cup of tea at a local stall, they headed down to the car for their final getaway from the town.

It took them forty minutes to drive through Mashobra (where the famous Sipi fair used to take place during the British Raj) and the alpine forests to a beautiful place called Naldehra, which was famous for a golf course built by Lord Curzon in 1905 (he is well remembered for building this golf course, as well as for the enforcement of the policy of "divide and rule" in India), where there were a few horses waiting for tourists to hire them to have rides in the hills, as well as a few stalls and restaurants offering snacks and tea.

Dani recommended a stroll along a footpath up towards the woods, where the golf club was, and an open picnic area with some small stalls and a chaiwala selling chai (tea). They went to the top of the hill for the view of Shali Peak and some of the other Himalayan peaks and then returned to the chaiwala for a samosa and a cup of tea, freshly made in the beautiful setting of the woods. The golf course was nice and they mused that it must be tricky to keep the ball from running down the hills. It was a very peaceful place and many families were enjoying picnics there with their children, and Dani said many of them were tourists from different places in India.

After a rest they headed down the footpath, encountering a few struggling horses coming up the hill carrying those who preferred not to walk but wanted to experience horse riding in the hills. Dani met a few people he knew from the golf club, including one member who had visited London. After a brief introduction they invited them to have a drink and Dani suggested that a short visit to the club would be a good idea as they were in a hurry.

After thanking them and saying goodbye, they headed down to the car and drove past a small government hotel

Golf Glade which looked like a nice place to stay in the hills outside Shimla. Dani said they had also got cottages which were good to stay in.

Soon after that, on the way down, Dani pointed out the Chalets Naldehra – a much more luxurious place – with a swimming pool and a spa with beautiful wooden cottages. "There's a small house further down called Naldehra House, through an apple orchard just after orphanage started by Mahatma Gandhi," said Dani, "where hikers normally stay a night when they want to hike down to the hot springs and the Satluj Valley. It takes around four hours through the alpine forests and mountain ridges, and from there the view is very clear to the Himalayas and to the river valley, and you can see the river winding its way down from the Himalayas. If you have a picnic lunch on the way, it becomes a great day out as well as good exercise."

They carried on along the narrow winding roads. It felt like they were really getting inside the mountains. Soon they left the alpine forests behind and the vegetation changed, becoming rocky, and Dani said that they were now at around 1,000 metres above sea level, and he pointed out big telephone towers and a temple lower down which was called Devidhar (*Devi* means female deity and *Dhar* means mountain range). It was at the edge of the mountain, and the road curved right to the other side of the mountain and they carried on.

Dani pointed out the beautiful view and the Satluj River down in the valley below. They could see several small bridges over the river in the distance from the top of the hill, covering the whole mountain all the way to the last village, Basantpur, and after a U-turn they drove downhill again to the base of the mountain, back to the other side and to the river bank, after passing through a market town called Suni, built on level ground.

After driving past a large market, they drove by the school where Dani had studied up to higher secondary level. They could see the old school buildings built very much in the old colonial style, together with a big playground.

Roland liked the look of the school and thought that it would have been a nice place to study. Dani remarked that it had been quite basic when he had studied there, but had vastly improved since. He pointed out some new buildings.

"To grow trees and have wood is very difficult for these people. So they don't tend to use any wood at all except for furniture," said Dani.

"So they're not cutting the trees in the forest down then," Roland exclaimed. "That's good for the forests and the land."

Dani felt a sense of pride. As they drove through the small villages and woods by the riverside, they remarked that that was perhaps why the landscape was still quite green.

"Before cement houses in the village, people depended so much on wood that many areas were cleared as locals used to cut trees at night, so the forest guards didn't notice.

"Not only that, people used to clear the woods and fields so that wild animals couldn't come close to the villages. Gas cylinders have saved trees as well. Villagers used to trim the trees every season for firewood. This has now changed and the modern generation can't do the same work anyway. They'd rather spend money to use gas and electricity than to walk to the jungle and to carry firewood home. Now there's a better chance for the trees, jungles and wild animals to survive. However, the number of wild animals has increased and villager's crops are being damaged. The fields have to be guarded at night, which is a serious issue as they are not allowed to hurt the wildlife!"

After driving for a few minutes by the riverside, they came across another big cement bridge, and once they were on the bridge, Dani pointed out another beautiful old bridge which had been built in 1957 from wood and iron, but was no longer in use as it had been damaged by fire and wasn't functional. There were some run-down shops and guesthouses which had been left because the whole market had moved higher up the valley now that there was the new cement bridge, and the lower riverside had been abandoned. Another reason was that the market had been damaged in a huge river flood in August 2000, when the water level had risen by around 40 feet and had ruined most of the houses and guesthouses close to the river. The main reason they didn't bother to fix the bridge or rebuild the shops on the lower part of the area was because the river was soon going to be flooded for a hydroelectric dam, so the higher bridge and a new market had been created.

"It's really interesting to look back and see how and why people preferred to live by the riversides," said Dani. "Traditionally, their ancestors had advised them not to go too close to the big river, let alone to build houses anywhere near the river, or places that might flood in summer, and also not to build houses on the hills or mountains which were in the way of strong wind currents or storms from the river valley. I remember many stories of lives lost in floods or in the rivers, or of roofs been taken off by storms when people went against old advice or principles.

"Well before there were bridges, there were fishermen who were expert swimmers and helped people cross the river on animal skin rafts, mainly buffalo or cow, and they also caught fish and exchanged them with other villagers for crops or grains. On the other hand, there were those poor or powerless craftsmen who depended on the rich and powerful households for their livelihood. They were pushed towards the lower-lying land which was of little use and could be dangerous and might not grow many crops either. Most of the accessible riverbanks were places of cremation and considered sacred and lonely places. The most fertile land was always taken by those who were close to the royals or the authorities. The lower classes were always struggling to survive in day-to-day life and depended for jobs on the ruling classes. As there were no bridges, fishermen became famous for their river crossing and swimming skills.

"Another group who moved to these valleys were those who were led by the demands of tourists who wanted to come and visit the white sandy beach and the beautiful Satluj River in this stunning and peaceful valley, way below the Shimla hills. Not only was it Western tourists, but this was an auspicious place for locals too, and people came from far and wide to have a holy dip in the natural hot springs. Tourists wanted to stay in Tattapani in winter due to its unique springs, and so the villagers built places for them to stay to provide some shelter, or offered homes for those who had walked a long way and couldn't return in the same day. During festivals, old temples used to offer shelter as well as food as a service."

"I remember a meeting with one of the first guesthouse owners, Prem Raina, who was a family friend, and he used to put soft drink bottles into the river to cool them down, so tourists could have cold drinks during the hot summer, and this was a good after-school business for him. When there were no real guesthouses, Western tourists used to go back to Shimla after their day out here. During his holidays from college and his masters at university in Shimla, Prem used to sell cold drinks by the riverside, and he realised that tourists were quite plentiful in the daytime and he could make a good income. Many Western tourists used to struggle to find any beds in the village and they advised him that any small guesthouse would be very popular and suitable for travellers. Soon his family created a small café for cold drinks and tea, and then a place for tourists to stay, and it became what is now the Spring View Guesthouse.

"After that, a race began and many hotels sprang up, ignoring ancestral advice of not building too close to the river banks, but the power of nature is always unpredictable. A number of these guest houses were ruined after the flood of 2000, and many have not bothered to repair them anymore, which is a terrible blow for families who depended on these small businesses.

"The high Himalayas are still places of thunder, lightening and cloudburst. If rain pours down on these mountains, due to a lack of trees on the Himalayan soil, rocks and landslides start rolling down the riversides, and these can destroy everything in their path. There have been cases where people have lost their lives, houses, fields, and animals too. The force it can come downhill with can be fierce, and landslides can change the whole geography of the river valleys.

"Now they could be underwater again as the government is planning to flood the river and there will be a dam or a lake here soon. A major hydro project is being built lower down in the valley to produce electricity and to make use of this river, so when we come here next time, there will be a huge lake."

Dani pointed out a large building under construction and said that it was probably going to be a three or four-star hotel with a hot spring by the next time they came to Tattapani. The dam company had given financial compensation to some local people who would soon lose their houses or land or businesses, and the amounts may have pushed the price of land up very high for ordinary people too.

The sensible ones are doing really well and are using the money to build hotels or buy more land higher up the valley to build new houses, and this brings lots of business and employment to the community as well."

Now they were very close to the Satluj River bank and Dani asked the driver to stop the car so that they could explore the sights. They all got out and went to the Spring View Guesthouse. They were warmly welcomed by the owner – most of the locals knew Dani and they were all excited to see him back – and were soon made to feel at home and served chai and delicious *paneer pakora*. Dani kept saying, "No, we just want to see the hot springs." The fact that there were hot springs was quite a surprise for Roland, as he thought that they may have been washed away. As the weather was a bit cold, Dani had planned it well and they were ready to jump into the small pools, which were, unsurprisingly, very hot. So hot, in fact, that they actually had to mix some cold water into it. It was a wonderful surprise for Roland and a welcome relief for his muscles after all the walking and travelling in Delhi and Shimla.

They jumped in and enjoyed the rejuvenating warmth of the naturally hot water.

Dani pointed out the way some of the local men saved their underwear from getting wet there. "Look, they use a string around their waist and tuck a little piece of material in the front and back to make a sling to cover up their dignity for a bath. To bath naked is not seen as respectful, and the villagers are always very private, they have to have something to cover themselves. There is an old saying, Roland, '*nanga kya nhayega or kya nichodega?*' which means that 'what will a nude bathe and what will he rinse?' especially if you are not used to it and you cannot relax fully. After finishing the bath, they just wash and rinse that piece of cloth and put it on the line to dry for the next day."

After a good hour lazing and washing in the hot tub and looking at the nearby river, they wanted to explore the main source of the water and also fancied a walk on the sand. They jumped over the fence and had a quick walk on the shiny grey sand and went to inspect the main spring. There they saw people bathing by the river in small ponds by the shore so they could mix cold water from the river to reduce the heat of the spring water.

Dani explained that the source of the Satluj River is a small river called Pareechu, which comes from the Parang La glacier at a height of 5,380 metres above sea level in India and goes to China, and then comes back after a U-turn all the way from Tibet over a 4,200 metre pass called Shipki La back to India, and it is all glacier water.

"It brings lots of goodness and life to the whole valley as it collects water from many streams on the way and provides water and fertile soil to many states in India, as well as to Pakistan, and it goes all the way to the Arabian Sea. It is one of the longest rivers in India," he said. "Once they flood the river, all those hot water puddles in the sand will disappear and all the sand will be underwater. That sand is free and a main source for building houses in the area with cement. A lot of rubble and stone will disappear, which will become a big problem and an expense for all the local villagers whenever they need sand in the future.

"In January they host a bathing festival here called Lohri, and it is almost a festival of the New Year. People walk from many parts of India to bathe in these hot pools, as it has been a holy shrine for many centuries. People walk to this village on the twelfth night in January, and they have lots of bonfires en route in many villages for the pilgrims to keep warm, as it is winter, and people also offer free *khichuri* (a black lentil pilao of rice with *ghee*). It is a very old tradition and people sing, dance, pray and worship, as they cover a long distance on foot, and above all have a holy dip in the natural hot water to wash away all their past sins and negativity and start a new life. Some people do charity and donate money, grains or precious things to gain a peaceful future for themselves or in an attempt to cleanse and improve their *karma*. Special astrologers and priests come to perform the *Daan* ceremony (charity or offering in the name of planets, nature and fish) and rituals on the day. It has been taken over by some commercial aspects, but there's a village fair with stalls selling all sorts of farming tools and entertaining things for children, which is good fun, and it makes an excellent outing for families, and if one can get time to think and sit by the banks of the river or in the temples and contemplate, one can benefit spiritually and obtain peace.

"If the lake takes over all the hot springs, this village could lose its visitors and pilgrims, which would be a big shame. Locals have been told that by 2014/15 the river will be flooded and the lake will be created.

"Having a huge lake here may also invite all sorts of different birds and animals, which may affect the farming and crops, or a lot of the vegetation in the valley. It is fine for those who have got money, but life will change in many ways after losing this river to a lake. This spot really is a wonderful place, and the lake may bring some tourism to the region, and I hope that the locals are given an opportunity for employment first instead of rich Shimla businessmen or corrupt officials taking away opportunities from the locals. That will be in the hands of the authorities, so let's hope they give some training to the local youth first, and that locals understand the prospects for water sports and boating."

***

Afterwards, they had another dip and then they dressed and Dani had a conversation with the owner, Umesh, who was extremely helpful, and soon after, they said goodbye.

They carried on their journey to a little village called Thali, Dani's family's village, and on the way Dani kept pointing out more places. The most intriguing one for Roland was a very old wooden temple at Tattapani which had been there for centuries, named after a great sage, or maharishi, called Jamadagni Rishi, who had stayed at the hot springs in around AD 1292, and it had become a place of worship and a shrine.

"Since then," said Dani, "this place had become known to outsiders as a *Narsingh* or *Narayan* temple. It is said that *Narayan* refers to the god Vishnu, the god of protection or preservation. He is the only god who can manifest or descend as an avatar to earth. He is responsible for looking after a new plant, leaf, flower or a being as well as the earth itself, after the God of creation has created it. *Narsingh* – 'nar' means human and 'singh' means lion, so half-human and half-lion – refers to the fourth *avatar* or incarnation of Vishnu. The first refers to *Matsya* – half-fish and half-human; second, *Kachcham or Kurma* – half-tortoise and half-human; third to *Brah or Varaha* – half-boar and half-human; the fourth to *Narsingh*; the fifth to *Vaman* – a dwarf-like man; the sixth to *Parshuram* – A caveman-like human with a long beard, much more developed than a human. Out of ten, nine have appeared on Earth to save the planet, and the tenth is expected in the future. Avatar means 'a manifestation' or 'an appearance in a different form'. It is almost like the secret millionaire, hiding to help the poor community, without letting them know, and he quietly completes his mission of rescue without showing off his real form. Throughout South India and in Central India there have been various temples and carved stone statues found which indicate these avatars' appearances. The most interesting occurrence is that scientists found a rare fish called a coelacanth, which evolved four hundred million years ago and is closely related to mammals. The coelacanth was thought to be extinct seventy million years ago, but they are still living today in the Indian Ocean."

Roland said, "Oh, lobe-finned fish, the living sarcopterygians."

Dani continued. "They may very well have been the first fish to move from the sea onto land as they can walk or crawl using their fins. Old stories emphasise the importance of each creature in saving life on Earth and the Earth itself. These go back thousands of years and are passed on to us through stories and songs as well as many tales. There are plenty of temples in India where you can see various statues carved in rocks from as early as the second century BC. If one gets chance while near Shimla or Tattapani one can visit some old seventh century riverside temples in Mandi and an eighth century Baijnath temple in Kangra Valley in Himachal Pradesh. There are various statues describing these different incarnations and there are stories that go back thousands of years. It is very interesting because it refers to the same evolutionary theory as Charles Darwin. Creation in water, and then the fish slowly developing into a land creature like a tortoise, then a wild boar, *Narsingh*, and eventually the human form of today.

"I like the story of *Narsingh* especially," said Dani, "because it refers to a cruel king, who is so taken by ego, pride and power that he wants everyone to worship him as a god, and he has protected himself with a wish that he cannot be killed, day or night, not with *astra* nor with *shastra*, meaning weapons, not on the ground nor in the air, not by human nor by animal, not outside nor inside. His own son's debate about absolute god and his divine presence in everything made the king go mad, and after losing his debate that he was the most powerful on earth and should be worshipped, the king was about to kill his own son, unless his son, Prahlad, could prove the almighty's presence there and then. To the king's surprise, Narsingh appeared as a half-lion and half-human and a fierce battle took place. Narsingh broke through the kings spell by killing the king at dusk time, with his claws, on his knee, in the middle of the front door step. The story suggests that nature has a solution for everything.

"The temple of Narsingh was built here, and now it will have to be removed because of the flood from the dam."

Soon they followed the road by the Satluj River and left Tattapani behind. Dani was very excited to be back in his village and pointed out his primary school by a little stream further down from some shops on the left-hand side of the road.

He said that the road was just a year old, and during his time, there was only a footpath through the fields and under the trees where they used to walk. They never imagined that there would be a bus coming along there one day.

Many people in the street or by the shops greeted Dani, and he waved back at them. After a few more bends in the road, they turned left into a small lane and the car pulled in front of an old slate-roofed house further down. This was Dani's family's house. It really was in the middle of nowhere. All they could see were a few fields and some trees, bushes and high mountains all around.

"What an amazing place!" exclaimed Roland.

As soon as they got out of the car, they were surrounded by the excited family members and children. Dani touched the feet of his elders and hugged everyone, while Roland shook hands and greeted them with "Namaste", while putting his palms together. Everyone seemed really happy and excited to see them. They were welcomed with garlands made out of marigolds and given a *tika*, or red colour dot on their foreheads, as they stepped through the big wooden door to the house. Roland was touched. He was introduced to all the relations, brothers and sisters, nephews and nieces and the respected mother, the head of the family called *Amma ji*. She made sure that everyone helped with the luggage and both boys were made comfortable. Roland was also introduced to a barking black dog, a Tibetan Shepherd called Tigger, who looked a bit like a bear cub.

Dani said that the dog had been a gift from a small student group and a teacher, Andrew Shepherd from Cundall Manor School in Yorkshire in England. "They were on a school expedition to the Himalayas and they did some trekking and helped in a nearby school in the village to support children through the support of a local charity, Asra. The charity helps education in the mountain schools by providing support to schools as well to those children who are good in studies but cannot support their further education after qualifying for professional training and courses.

"They had stayed a few days in the farmhouse and wanted to give something to the family as well. It was really kind of them as Tigger is a very good guard dog, and his voice echoes throughout the whole mountain valley when he barks.

"So Roland, you better get used to his barking," Dani said, "sometimes it can be quite annoying especially first thing in the morning!"

The two were shown to their rooms in the farmhouse, where they were scheduled to stay for a few days, and Roland put his things in his bedroom, while Dani caught up with everyone outside in the courtyard. It was the end of the autumn. The weather was very pleasant and the excitement of being there was in the air, with the mountains fading away in the dark after the sunset.

CHAPTER TWO

A power cut in the mountains

The farmhouse was quite basic, but was comfortable enough and all the essentials were there. Roland left his bags in his room and, keen to have a look outside and around the house, took his torch and went out of the door to the north from the main courtyard, a very secluded courtyard walled on three sides; the other side of it was the old house, which he had a closer look at afterwards.

Roland stepped out of the courtyard, through the entrance doors and up a few steps to a raised circular walled platform just below the roof terrace.

Soon after, Dani joined him and explained that this circular raised platform was called a *Khaliyaan* and that it was a harvesting and threshing courtyard for crops, like paddy rice, corn, wheat and lentils. It was in a circular shape because they used to walk cattle or oxen round and round on the crops to thresh the grains. In much higher parts of the Himalayas they use donkeys, yaks or horses too. "The circle is a symbol of life and movement, of carrying on the journey of the ancient traditions of India for more than 5,000 years. The wheel of life fits in with this round courtyard, because it produces the food and does the grading between what is good, i.e. healthy to eat and what is not, although all the hay and straw go to the family cattle."

Dani explained that as most of the harvesting depended on good weather and wind for grading and harvesting crops and grains, they needed wind, and that's why it was raised several feet above the ground.

"People here depend on the wind a lot," said Roland, "but nowadays people use table fans for a cool breeze."

"My father was the first in the village to buy a table fan from a famous Indian company called Usha, from Shimla, during one of his trips to Shimla town to sell farm produce," Dani told him. "He also had electricity first in the village too. My father was fascinated by all the modern inventions and by engineers who were able to produce that kind of technology. He had great respect for them."

"Is the fan still working?" asked Roland.

"Yes. It's had a few bashes and dents, but the motor is still the same and it is in good condition. But if there's no electricity, it is of no use. Sometimes, if there is no wind, people use big cotton sheets or shawls to produce a breeze, which is a very clever technique and not everyone can do that. You need two people to do it and locals call it *Pharkaval*," said Dani, as he walked off to catch up with his family.

This circular platform was a high enough spot for Roland to have a good look at the house and explore the area to have a feel for where he was. It was completely dark all around in the valley. A few tiny lights, like twinkling stars, were dotted around the mountains, which surrounded the village on all sides. There were little lights everywhere. At first Roland thought they were stars, but then the dark line of the shape of the mountains revealed that they were actually houses. Leaves moving in the far distance were making them twinkle or hiding them for a few seconds. He couldn't believe that it was so very silent and peaceful.

The silence was so tender that he could even hear his breath and the conversation from the distant kitchen, which were just exotic words to him – he couldn't understand anything. He sat down on the small wall built around the courtyard and just wanted to observe the mysterious beauty of this place. There were no traffic sounds. It was the first time in many years that he had experienced such a degree of peace and silence. He was so touched and surprised with it all, with the twinkling stars high up creating a sparkling umbrella up above him in the sky. The magical wonder and the darkness and silence made him feel that he was experiencing a real night. It took Roland back to his childhood days, when he was five or six years old, and they'd had a big storm in the south of England which had uprooted many trees, and hundreds of people had no power for days. He remembered how his dad had to cut lots of trees to clear the pathways. The interesting thing was that they had to go back to lamps and candles for light. Daylight had become much more precious and it had been important to finish the daily tasks before the dark nights drew in.

That's how these people live and have lived all their life, he thought. He pondered how Dani or any other villager from the mountains could live in the modern cities in the Western world, in our chaotic strange culture where thousands of cars pass through every day. Dani had told him once that he had done some part-time work in different stores and companies in England. One of his best jobs was at Fortnum and Mason, where shoppers seemed to be under pressure to buy the best in a very limited time, and another was in a restaurant or food store called Subway. It was quite a contrast. At Subway he worked on some night shifts at weekends and could not understand or believe how well-educated young people could behave like that after midnight – where they struggled to stand while queueing for food, and they tried to help each other but fell again and again, or fought to keep their place in the queue in fear of closing time.

He'd said he often witnessed drunken arguments and fights into the early hours of the morning between the customers and the exhausted and tired staff (mainly migrant students or workers) in these long queues as they struggled to get a sandwich just as these stores were trying to shut the doors after a long day's work.

The bumping music and the incessant sound of cars and motorways in big cities and towns just doesn't stop, thought Roland. Day and night makes no difference in our lives. Many of these party people go to bed around five in the morning or after sunrise. He wasn't sure how this had become a part of the Western culture. And this way of living was now taking over many towns in the developing world.

Dani had explained that they were having big issues with drinking and drugs outside pubs and bars in big towns in India too, as that was the fashion inspired by modern international culture and films. Taxis, buses and underground or overground trains ran day and night in the cities. Many people, especially young people, were attracted by these things and wanted to live in the city, whereas in the country they had open space, the peaceful life, fresh air and water. But no, many young people were inspired to go to the towns and rent a little flat, where they had everything within one room.

Dani had been joking that many young couples wanted to live a neat and sanitised life – no cows, cattle or any pets – far away from their parents. They criticised their mother-in-law or parents who work very hard with cattle and farming in the villages and many consider them backward. A lot of the modern generation in India was looking for a boxy kind of life in the city, which was planted in their mind by Bollywood and Hollywood, and they think that is the lifestyle to have. They forget that in the villages they had different rooms for different activities, big courtyards and fields to run around and plenty of exercise from harvesting fresh vegetables and other crops, or jobs around the house.

Sadly, later on, they had lots of health issues as they have hardly any real exercise or fresh air from their style of living. They have lots of bills as well as twenty-four hour television services with more then two hundred or so channels.

Soon after, they start the rounds of hospitals and depend on cheap medicines which they can buy over the counter, even without doctor's prescriptions.

Roland kept thinking about what was happening and how old and new were merging together and a new transformation was happening right here in this village. The most important thing was silence and to feel and respect the day and the night, he thought.

Looking at the dim lights on the mountainside made him think that in the so-called developed Western world we have lights which are almost on all through the day and night. Some people in the world hardly have a lightbulb in their house, and at home in the so-called "developed" Western world, we have five or six lights in one room: bedside lights, table lamps, chandelier lights. So many bulbs, why are we so mad for them and what are the things which have driven us to do that, he thought? He didn't think we needed more than one simple light in a room. He wanted to count the miles of roads in England and count how many lights they had just for the roadside – it must be millions! Do we really need all those, when cars have lights too?

Roland wondered about the discovery of electric light and the light bulb, and Sir Thomas Edison, who had worked so hard to remove darkness from the world in the sense that people could do things in better way. Would he be happy to see all this, instead of it being used just for necessity? We are removing the whole sense of night. Within a hundred and thirty years of the invention of electric light we have changed so much. We have gone mad and want to make the night like the day, he thought. Millions of bulbs and cars, as well as planes, operate at night. Why do we need so much and what do we want to achieve? Was it not enough just to work in the daytime and sleep at night? Before we had cars we had to walk even to send a message; it used to take a few days on horse or by passenger or passer-by. But now we have fast cars and mobile phones. We are still rushing and cannot seem to stop, thought Roland. One thing is clear, we have lost darkness and silence. We are lighting the outer material world so much that the inner world is getting darker and shrinking. Many people suffer from lots of illnesses and cannot sleep, even with sleeping pills, though they work very hard and feel very tired. Our bodies have lost the rhythm of the natural patterns of the day and night. Our minds and bodies are getting confused. If we really think about it, it does make sense that there are two types of creatures, and some live in the daylight and some live at night in the dark. If we humans keep producing more and more light at night and take over the space and make lots of noise at night, night creatures like owls, bats, rats and other wild animals and insects who completely depend on nights to hunt and survive may no longer be able to survive for long, and that may ruin the natural circle of life. That will affect not only humans, in the long term, but will also affect the plants and nature around us, which may have catastrophic consequences for the world and life on it.

All these thoughts were going through his mind, and suddenly he realised that he was in complete darkness. Everything was pitch-black. He heard Dani's voice asking if he was alright and whether he had his torch, as there had been a power cut. Roland felt his torch on his forehead but had not thought to use it, and replied "Oh, I actually prefer it dark. Do you think this power cut will last for long?"

Dani laughed and said that he had no idea how long it would last, but that a candle-lit dinner might make him feel at home!

Roland could see nothing now but the stars in the sky. All the dim lights on the mountains were gone and he could see the shape of the mountains marking the sky and the sparkling stars in the sky.

He looked around and realised that the power cut was affecting the whole valley. No one had any electricity. This reminded Roland again of a childhood storm in England when they'd had no electricity for weeks. But since then he had never experienced a situation where electricity was cut off and all modern electronics would be of no use. Here he was in the middle of this Himalayan valley, and they had all sorts of wild animals around too, but living side by side with humans. Dani had explained on the way that they have many types of wild animals in the village, and over the centuries they have learned to live side by side. Animals shied away from villagers in the daytime and villagers had to protect their cattle and animals in sheds at night, because wild animals roam around freely at night. Dani had said that to keep dogs alive in this village was a difficult task as leopards dislike them and often took them, but they never harm any humans.

Roland could see the dim flames of firelight from the kitchen and Dani suggested that he come to the kitchen as it was bit chilly outside and the food was about to be served.

Roland could not explain his surprise and pleasure at being in this wonderful place. He was amazed that Dani had been brought up here. Now he could understand the natural calm nature of his, because he really had lived a very peaceful life and had experienced the really natural rhythms of day and night as well as the different seasons in this Himalayan valley. There were no clubs or bars in the whole valley. His mind was full of questions and curiosity.

Inside the kitchen a few dim candles were being used for light. Roland felt he was living in the past and the complete darkness and silence in the valley was like a scene from a science-fiction movie. But here he was living this experience, and many people in cities don't have any idea that people still experience life this way in the world. Roland felt a strange thrill from knowing this.

CHAPTER THREE

A sensible use of water

As Roland came in he followed the light, and here it was, the light of burning firewood in the traditional oven built from local clay and mud. He was offered a wooden seat, which was like a rectangular-shaped stool, called, in the local language, *patda,* and *Tarpai* is a little hexagonal table to keep your plate on. The *patda* was quite low, six inches high from the ground or so, so that Roland was almost sitting cross-legged on it. He couldn't bend his knees like the rest of them, because everyone sat on chairs and ate at the table back home in England, and sitting on the floor or squatting no longer fitted it with modern lifestyles.

Dani explained that in Indian cities and towns, or even villages, things were changing and people were offered chairs and then traditional mats made from leaves or bark. But the stool was fine and Roland settled very well on it.

There was a beautiful carpet under the stool, and they were sitting around the cooking fire, which was very cosy and warm.

Roland noticed that there was a big pot on the back oven and a round metal sheet on the front oven. Dani's *Amma,* or mother, was making Indian bread, or chapattis, while everyone was sitting around and chatting, as well as getting things ready to serve for the meal. It was interesting and Roland realised that it was quite a simple process to make Indian bread. It was just water and wheat flour. Dani's sister-in-law was helping to finish them on the coals, as soon as they came off of the *tawa*, or metal sheet.

"Wheat chapattis are easier to make," said Dani, "and it is more difficult to make yellow corn bread or *makki ki roti*. *Roti* is a word mainly used for corn bread, which is yellow and bigger in size, often served with *lassi*, made from yoghurt and green vegetables (*sarso ka saag*), mustard leaves usually. All the boys and girls have to learn it from childhood as they are all given responsibility for cooking whenever there is lots of work on the farm. During harvesting or weeding time it is quite hard work. Our *Dadi ji* (Grandmother) and her mother, our paternal great grandmother, was a very good cook, and nanny, who had travelled to Africa and America during and after the British Raj with an army family. She had a lot of influence on my granny and indirectly on all the future generations, and now parents have to make sure everyone learns to cook."

Another younger brother, Roop, arrived, and Dani introduced him and said that he was a professionally trained mountaineer and had done rock climbing and ice climbing up in the high Himalayas. He was also a trained rafting instructor and was now doing a degree course in hospitality and management. Roop was quite skinny and tall, with wide shoulders, and he seemed quite shy to Roland. Dani and his sisters told Roland about how they had to produce lunches on this fire for the whole family during the hot summer, which used to be like having a sauna. Now life in the village had changed a lot. In older times, children would have been sent to collect firewood and bundles of grass and leaves for cows as well as to collect figs from trees in bamboo baskets. The difficulty was that they used to put more figs in their mouths than into the basket. It was really hard work to climb trees and collect enough so that you could bring some home, and they all laughed, as they must have all experienced it but never admitted it. They used to have lunch picnics on busy days on the farm with *Baturu* (a thick swollen bread) with fresh onions, tomatoes, small black *bhegre* (figs) and *chutany* from a local green and red berry which they just called *berr* (berries) and from *imili* (tamarind), *pudina* (mint) and from passion fruit or pomegranate or from mango. Sometimes they added ground sesame seeds and other seeds like *halo* (flax) with it, or created a churn or powder mixed with salt.

Dani's mother exclaimed, "But who does those things now? Many youngsters aren't even aware that those things used to happen, nor do they know those recipes and ways! Youngsters are very busy with mobiles and other electronics and hardly have time for day-to-day village activities. They all want to eat, wear and do what their movie stars do and advertise on television, and many are embarrassed at their own food and lifestyle as they think it is backward in the villages, but they can't understand that this is the most healthy lifestyle."

Suddenly a few voices were raised saying, "We all have enjoyed it and are proud of this, *Amma ji,* and we have worked on the farm most of our lives too."

"Oh no, not you lot. Luckily you had to help, which was really good, but generally speaking things are changing very fast!"

Working in the kitchen and on the farm had taught them how to get on and adapt to the changing ways in life.

Dani explained about the fireplace, or clay oven. "It has to be the way it is so they don't burn too much wood, and a good amount of heat can be generated with just a few pieces of wood. This wood is mainly leftover thicker branches, which can't be eaten by cattle after they've eaten all the leaves."

Roland noticed that they were burning very thin sticks and twigs, not solid wood at all and that there was plenty of heat, and he thought that the way that they kept it going with only a few sticks must have been a skill inherited through centuries of constant experimenting to find better ways of doing things.

Dani explained that they always had the copper pot filled with water on the back oven so the family have hot water whenever they need it. Roland recalled that in Britain they used to have open fires in the middle of the room and a big copper pot to heat the hot water as well (and this may still happen in some rural parts of Europe).

The fireplace was quite cleverly designed. Dani told Roland that it was always either fixed onto a wall at the back or in a corner. "Traditionally fires always face north, so that when you sit around the fire you are facing south.

"If you go to any traditional house you will find that fireplaces or these clay ovens are built the same way, and most of them are built onto the south wall. These are ancient ways and special attention is applied when building these ovens. This is a strong practice, almost like when someone passes away, their head is always turned around towards the north. The belief is that it helps the person to depart the body quicker and more smoothly, maybe because of magnetic fields," said Dani.

Roland found it fascinating and also noticed a very small chimney, which was really just a hole in the roof to let the smoke out. It was bit smoky and Roland wasn't sure if all the smoke could go out that easily. But the heat felt really good.

Dani pointed out to Roland that he must be finding it hard with the smoke, and he explained to him that in the old days people knew exactly what kind of wood should be cut at which time of the year and how long to dry it in piles and where and when to burn it.

"Well-dried thin sticks hardly used to make any smoke. But these days the new generation is struggling to keep up and has lost some of the knowledge about doing these things. In the old days they used to have huge piles of sticks stored, and every six months or so, they used to change to a new dry pile."

It made sense to Roland as it was quite a logical way of doing it, and it also made sure that they always had a water pot going at the back, as they didn't have any other reliable way of heating water for the family. They did have an electric water heater in the guests' bathroom, but the family didn't use it at all as they couldn't rely on the electricity as power cuts often occurred in the hills.

It must be quite a struggle to keep the hot water ready for everyone in such a large family, thought Roland. As they started to move away from the fire to eat, Roland realised there were around nine of them in that little kitchen.

By now Dani's mother had finished making chapattis and she had cleared all the waste flour from around the big copper bowl where she had made them. A bamboo basket on the shelf was full of chapattis, covered with some sort of cloth or tea towel to keep the heat in. Now the big flour bowl, or *parat* as they called it, was removed, and they had much more space for everyone to sit. The little round fireplace could fit seven or eight people around it; the more the people the bigger the circle so as to fit everyone in. It was very cosy and was a good way to get to know each other in the family.

Dani removed the big copper pot (*tambia*) from the back oven to the front and the *tawa*, the round iron metal plate in which she was cooking the chapattis, was also removed. Dani explained that the *tawa* was quite an important item of life which produced food for all. "Also, in the old days, whenever children were frightened, and shaking with fear or shock, ladies used to make bubbles by sprinkling water on it. It was called *Pani Jhadna* and used to create steam and bubbles, which used to take the fright away from a child. It may have been a very old trick or a remedy to heal children, or maybe a superstition to remove bad energy or black magic, but it made children take their mind off the pain or shock!

"*Tamba* means 'copper', so *tambia* is simply a 'copper pot which contains water'. In ancient Indian culture, copper purifies the water, so you find it all over India, and copper pots are used in the temples to store water, and many people have copper pots by their bedside to keep water overnight."

The back of the oven was blocked by a divider which was simply a thick piece of metal in a round shape. This meant that the heat would stay in front of the oven.

Dani then told Roland that he was going to show him some basic ways of saving water and how to really enjoy washing his feet. He brought out a shiny brass bowl and took jugs of hot water from the *tambia* on the oven and put it in the bowl. He then mixed it with some cold water to cool it. Then he asked Roland to wash his hands and face and to dip both his feet into the *dubra*, the large brass bowl.

Dani asked him to wash them well and not to wash his face again with the same water (as was the custom), because his feet were now in the water. "This is something that the family traditionally do – wash their face and hands before they dip their feet into the footbath and then not to use the water afterwards."

Dani poured fresh water for Roland from another brass bowl to wash his hands. The best thing was when Dani made Roland dip his feet into the water in this bowl. It felt very good and rejuvenating. "Science has found that human feet and hands have lots of nerve endings, and this is one of the best ways to heal and relax our whole body and mind," Dani explained. "This is the oldest method of relaxation in the Himalayas after a long day's work. It is also a very well-rooted belief that the feet, hands and ears have effective pressure points and they help to release pressure from different muscles. In the old days ear pinching was a punishment for little children, because it is believed that pressure points on the ears have a great effect on the mind and a child will pay much more attention after that, and it's still in practice in many Indian households and schools.

"But Roland, luckily for you, we only offer hand and feet washing. Ears are only if you are naughty!" said Dani.

"I will make sure no one needs to pinch my ears, and I will try to be on my best behaviour," Roland laughed.

"Traditionally, if someone is a close relative, a lady from the family will wash your feet too. But that is getting less and less common these days," said Dani. He told Roland that they use the Sanskrit phrase *Atithi Devo Bhava* to explain the concept that "the guest is god", and he or she has to be treated well. "To please a guest is pleasing God, and that is the way it is up here in the mountains."

Dani handed him a towel to dry his hands, and one by one everyone was washing their feet after him. They all followed the same rules and the pot was rinsed every time.

After this process of washing hands and face first and then feet afterwards, what really made Roland think was that back in England it was normal to wash everything in the bath in one go – it had never occurred to him before: feet, face and body in the same water after a long day's work. Roland and Dani looked at each other in amusement, indicating that they shouldn't talk about loo paper! He was sure that there was a big difference between a dry wipe and washing or rinsing with water.

"I found the Western custom of bathing very strange at first," Dani said, "and I used to have a shower after the bath to wash again. I thought that's what everyone did, until my wife, who had noticed it a few times, asked why I needed to wash again after having had a lovely bath infused with essential oils. For me the bathwater was just not clean enough to wash my face after washing everything else in the bath."

Roland said, "We hardly wash our feet in the West. We just have a good shower or a big bath. We are used to washing everything in bubbly water and we don't even think about it."

Because baths were very new to Dani and washing feet is an age-old practice, he said that he didn't see the point of a bath if you don't scrub your feet or bend your knees to give a little stretch to your leg muscles. "If young children start doing these things in a routine, whenever they have a bath, they could keep doing the natural bending movements of their knee joints, then they don't have to suffer in old age and they can still enjoy the luxury of a bath.

a—A man having a bucket bath. The old sustainable way of bathing the body, applying soap, washing and rinsing. Exercise gained while squatting and standing a few times.

Roland felt that washing feet was a beautiful thing to do instead of wasting lots of water. "We hardly used three jugs of water, so it's maybe two litres of water! What a wonderful way to save water. The thing is that they have to heat it on the fire here and then we just have it twenty-four hours 'on tap'."

Dani did enjoy the lifestyle in the West as everything was very well organised and made easy with modern technology. "Now the whole world is aiming for those kinds of luxuries and many old ways of surviving in the past are being forgotten. Using modern chemicals does not make water safe to use, for plants either, and it can ruin the soil too. In the old days they hardly used anything, maybe natural herbs or flower petals for essence, and the water could be used to nourish plants, and it helped the soil instead of spoiling it. Now the use of modern chemicals is increasing and the soil may not grow much in future and may even be left barren, which could be a huge threat to lives in the world itself."

Roland said that he'd been reading some details on the use of water in a book from UNICEF, a UN charity organisation, and he could not believe that some developing countries use less than ten litres in a whole day, and some developed countries used more than a hundred and fifty litres a day, and it was quite depressing. "The wasting of water is way too much. We use around three buckets of water to flush the loo on three visits and that's more than thirty litres of water. A full bath can waste around eighty litres of water, and our power shower can use up to thirty-five litres within five minutes. These are all modern ways, and it's because we have very easy access to water."

"That's absolutely true," Dani replied, and he explained how they had to carry water from nearby water sources, fountains or springs in the morning, before and after school, and they had between two and five shifts on Sundays to stock water. Duties and shifts were divided between all Dani's brothers and sisters, as Dani had five brothers and four sisters. By the time Dani started working, some of his older brothers and sisters had left or were married, so the younger group of four or five were quite close and busy and lived with their parents in the same house. Each had a round brass pot with a very small top, so it didn't splash, and it was the first duty of the day to bring fresh water. It used to be a morning walk in the freezing-cold weather in winter to bring water, and then again after school in the evenings. "We hated it, especially in the winter mornings, as sometimes cold water used to splash while we were walking and run down our back, wetting our clothes. It was not pleasant at all. Sometimes our fingers used to get really red and freeze. As soon as we got home we used to dip them in hot water, which was painful too, but it took the freezing away.

"The women and girls used to carry the pot on their heads and the men and boys carried it on their shoulders. But for the past fifteen years we have had a water connection, so carrying the water pot is very much a thing of the past. Traditionalists still get a pot, because natural spring water is cold in the hot summer and warmer in the freezing winter. Locals even used to have a bath at the springs in the early morning so they didn't have to carry water to their homes to have a wash. The cattle and goats, or sheep, used to be taken to nearby streams to drink water every afternoon or in the evening. The lifestyle was very different before taps arrived."

Roland said, "That's the thing, you face this right from childhood, that water is important and you have a very limited number of water sources in the mountains. If there's no water in the tap it makes you think more about the importance of water. We never had to think about it. Of course, now bills are really high and people have started to think about it, but here you experience it every day. If there is a lot of rain you have a good crop, or if not, no crop."

"Yes," Dani said, "that's true, we have very limited natural springs and people work so hard to connect them to their fields."

"Although we think there is plenty of water on the earth, most of it is not drinkable, and it's worrying to realise that drinkable water is very limited on the earth, and if there's no rain, that can disappear too," Roland said.

"The modern generation need to understand the value of water," Dani replied. "In the old days, when there were no taps, women used to take all their washing to the nearby streams or springs to wash. It was a social time for them too, and you could hear them catching up on news. It's a big shame that all this has changed in the last ten to fifteen years,"

"But we still see that sometimes," his brother Roop said. "Whenever the water channel is broken or blocked in the mountains, many families still have to walk a few miles to bring water home in pots to drink."

"Another interesting thing," said Dani, "is that whoever did that water carrying never had back pain or any physical aches and pains. My mother once told me, 'You were all fit and never had to go to the doctors.' The young generation is always complaining about aches and back pains. Their working habits are changing, and they don't do anything physical and prefer to work with machines, which is making them lethargic because they have lost a lot of natural exercise, which the older generation did naturally in their day-to-day jobs.

"New studies have suggested that those tribes in the world who carry water or heavy weights and walk a long way have very fit spines and hips. Walking for long hours forces the body to rebalance and centralise the whole spinal system as well as hip joints and knees. If you carry a little weight on your head, you will be much fitter and more balanced. The body finds a way to relax during the journey itself. One should always walk freely with the knees bending and arms swinging for the exercise of the spine as well. Now the only thing in use is the bucket bath," said Dani.

Roland had no idea what the bucket bath was. He understood the concept of a bucket, of course, but he wasn't clear about how to use it as a bath.

"Let's have some food," his mother said. "You must be tired and hungry."

They placed wooden stools in front of them and were presented with beautiful brass plates and bowls containing rice, lentils and vegetables and some wheat chapattis. They were told to just eat, and whenever anything was needed it arrived on their plates; they were served with more and more food each time they finished what they were eating.

Roland realised that "No thank you" or "No more" did not stop them serving him more food. They kept giving him more until he really couldn't take anymore and he had to cover his plate saying, "Bus, bus", meaning "Enough, enough".

The home-cooked food here was very different to what Roland had experienced in British Indian restaurants. Traditionally, the mother or elderly person in the family serves the food to the younger generation first or, if there are guests, the guests will eat first.

"Sometimes the children will eat afterwards if there's a delay in preparing the food," said Dani. "Sometimes if you are hungry and you haven't had food and a guest brings some sweets and offers you some, the children have to say 'No thank you, we just had some,' so it would show good manners. Sometimes, if they were hungry, children used to be offered sweets secretly by their parents to calm them down, so they don't complain in front of guests that the food is late, especially during the harvesting times, when parents had to work in the fields for long hours.

"But don't worry. Today children would not behave in the same way, and they have eaten already anyway," he said, pointing at his nephews and nieces.

Roland did think it was a most beautiful way of life, having all the family together and the mother making sure everyone has eaten well.

"Traditionally we talk much less while we're eating so we can just concentrate on the food," said Dani.

"But the food is so good that we've had no time to talk anyway!" Roland replied.

Suddenly the electricity was back and they all cheered, though Roland thought it had been much more atmospheric without it. The fire had now dimmed and they had moved the vegetable pot to heat on the back oven, and the copper pot was now on the front oven. Dani said that the copper pot didn't come down at all, unless they had to use both ovens for cooking. It did look more permanent as it had layers of black charcoal marks under it.

The group finished their dinner and Dani and Roland washed their hands in a special washing bowl again – a strange antique bowl, which had a circular plate on top so the water didn't run away and it drained through some holes in the centre plate to the bowl. It was passed around to them with a towel afterwards to dry their hands. Then everyone moved closer to the fire and started to dry their hands and feet in the warmth.

Dani's mother and sister-in-law then served food for themselves. While they were all chatting away, Dani put a pan for tea on the fire and stirred it a bit while adding a few more sticks to the fire by breaking them first so they caught on more quickly. Soon the orange flames created a good heat and they had to move back a little again.

Roland said that the way of making tea in the West was to switch on an electric kettle and get the cups and tea bags ready, and even that sometimes felt difficult to do. What an adventure it was here to make a cup of tea – first, collecting the firewood and making the fire, then boiling the water, adding some tea leaves, sugar, ginger, cloves or cardamom, and, when it's boiled, some milk. After boiling again, the tea (*chai*) would be poured into the cup and served.

Roland thought it was quite thick and sweet.

Dani explained, "Traditionally tea was just a hot drink with some herbs like *Adrack* (ginger), *Loung* (cloves), *Elayechi* (cardamom), *Nimboo* (lemon), *Tulsi* (basil), *Pudina* (mint) and other spices or roots. Sometimes the leaves of different plants were used: *Darchini* (Cinnamon), *Moolathi* (liquorice) which means 'mouth stick' and it was also used in hot summers to produce liquid in the mouth, and *Kherkath* (Kotechu) from a local tree to give goodness and colour. The drink was made frequently in winter as a protection from the cold. Different herbs have different medicinal properties and they are used accordingly to have the desired effect. Also, salt was used, not sugar, in the tea. Salt is better for the cold than sugar. That's why in the high Himalayas they still use salty tea in winter. Some people know that as 'butter tea'. I've tried it a few times. You get used to it if you have no other option.

"In the village in summer they use *sharbat*, a drink made with sugar, aniseed, cinnamon, cardamom and a few flavours from orange, lemon and mango. But this *chai* was a modified version of a winter hot herbal drink called *caru* or *Kaddoo,* and now people add everything to the *chai*. But a *Kaddoo* is the origin of all the tea in the world, because before tea was created, it was just a hot drink where the goodness and the essence of certain herbs and plants and roots were harvested by boiling them and then drinking it. It was simpler and fresher than today's herbal tinctures. We make *Kaddoo* in the family if someone has a cold."

"So tea isn't English?" asked Roland. "We tend to think tea is a very English thing to offer. We even have 'tea times' in England."

Dani explained, "Tea is actually Chinese, but British men brought and planted tea plants in India, and it was a British man called Mr Campbell who smuggled a few plants from China and planted them in the Darjeeling area. Once their first plant worked they planted more and more.

"I visited a tea estate called Makaibari in Darjeeling with one of my student groups from Cundall Manor School, accompanied by teachers Andrew Shephard and Jake Kempton. Both of the teachers were fantastic in introducing every concept and element possible during this trip to students in either trekking or cultural and historical events. It was really good to visit the tea factory. I remember a meeting with Rajah Banerjee, the owner. He said that Makaibari in Kurseong was India's first tea factory and was established in 1859. He was so proud of his crop and the way they were producing tea naturally. He told us the history of the tea, and his tea was still regarded as a mystical wonder, and he was so passionate about it. Rajah has written a book on it and has even produced a short documentary. I still have his signed copy and it was quite nice to read the note afterwards on the coach, as he had written, 'You are a veritable wonder. Find the jewel within you. God Bless' on it for me, which made me feel really good. He really was a very interesting character.

"Anyway, it was a 'cash crop' for the British and they were the ones who regarded it highly and made it fashionable to drink, and they could make money out of it. The British had a style for everything and they gave great value to tea for sure. There are tea-tasting ceremonies in many tea estates in India, and it's still a very exclusive event and a private ritual. Tea used to be a very basic and rare drink. People hardly ask for a glass of water – tea is always first – but soon it seems that this may be taken over by Coca cola or fizzy drinks," exclaimed Dani.

"I hope not," Roland added.

The tea was ready, and it was sweet and delicious and, "Thank goodness – it's not salty!" Roland said, laughing.

Roland was also very impressed with the efforts they had put in to produce the food in those circumstances. It was delicious. Roland asked if they used to follow certain recipes and, if so, if he could borrow any of the recipes. Dani explained after asking his *Amma ji* that it was all passed down from mother to daughter and nothing was ever written down. It was all done on taste and they always followed simple recipes.

"They hardly ever write them down. Some family chefs who cook for big events like weddings and celebrations, they do have some written lists. A proper knowledge of herbs and spices is essential, because some herbs are very powerful and can cause problems with our bodies. Their different properties can affect your digestive system as well as change your emotions and feelings. Nowadays, many people almost get addicted to spices without having a real knowledge about them and many of them behave in very strange ways as a result. Their hormones are all over the place and sometimes they can be like zombies. I wonder if many people behave strangely like that on the streets of Delhi, when it's very hot and people eat more than a hundred grams of spices on one chicken alone. I'm sure that's why they hardly move.

"Do you remember some of the street restaurants in Delhi, where boys made nan and *roti* in tandoors, which are very very hot, and in hot weather they work there constantly from morning to late at night? There's very limited space and narrow corners where they can hardly move. They spend all day in certain positions, which is really amazing. I wonder if it's their physical capacity, or some other drugs or whisky or the effect of heavy spices. Or are they kept there due to something else, like financial pressure, being treated as slaves, or is it that they have no other option? I'm always amazed by the skills of these people who work so hard for such long hours in extreme conditions.

"So a deep knowledge of each herb and spice is very important, and which herb to use in hot or cold seasons is also very important. But traditionally you use a small amount to get just the essence of the herbs or spices so it gives the food a refreshing fragrance and it tastes good as well as it makes you feel good.

"Kitchens are almost holy shrines for many families, and you only enter them barefoot and you can't take any unwanted smell or shoes in there. Cooking is like a ceremony and a ritual in itself. Great devotion is needed. The service spoon has to be different to the food tasting spoon, and often you take it outside the kitchen to check the taste. Have you seen the modern chefs on television when they taste food from the service spoon and then put it back with some of their saliva into the cooking pot? That would be considered a sin in Indian kitchens. Purity and the separation of each spice in different types of food is essential, as we know that in Britain food contamination is a big issue now due to allergies. But here it is a big sin, so, whether your guests or other families are watching you or not, you always pay attention and maintain these kitchen rules to get a distinct taste and flavour from each dish you produce."

Everyone was slowly disappearing from the kitchen, and they were quite tired too, so Roland got up to wash his hands and his thoughts went straight away to Dani's explanation of the Indian custom of the left hand being less holy, which was always kept away from food, and the right hand being used for auspicious duties and to eat. Most important tasks, like handling money and for ceremonial uses, were always done with the right hand. This was due to the left hand's main chore of cleaning that important body part – the backside!

Roland felt it was terribly interesting to think about it a bit more and he sat down again to contemplate who started these things in the first place: baths, bubbles, candles and essential oils to create a luxurious and pampering environment in the bathroom. But he had not thought before of the extra things they were adding to the bathwater. And now he knew why Dani had felt this way, because if a clean and wonderful bath is already waiting for you with heavenly fragrances, petals and bubbles and candlelight, in theory one would need to be quite clean already so not to ruin the essence and beauty of the clean water. Smelly feet and a day's sweat, and unwashed or unrinsed buttocks, would spoil the purity of that luxurious bath.

Roland's mind went straight to a scene from the Hollywood film *Crocodile Dundee* and he asked Dani if he knew about the film. Dani said he had, and he had enjoyed it because it was almost a mirror image of his first visit to London and he'd loved it. Roland shared the story of Mick Dundee, a Bushman from Australia who goes to explore New York with his smart lady friend, who takes him to the top hotels in New York. He was wise, with many mysterious Bushman tricks and skills and was curious about the big city. When he went to stay in a smart hotel in New York, his friend gave him a quick tour of his apartment. When he saw two toilets in one bathroom, he was puzzled as to why they had put two dunnies in there (as he called them). He asked his friend why there were two. As she was rushing out, she said, "You will figure it out, I will see you at seven." As he was already taken in by the whole rush and the strangeness of New York City and the lifestyle, he did his best, turning on this button and that button, and he finally figured it all out. He whistled from his multi-storey hotel window and shouted out that he had figured it out – "It's for washing your backside, right?" She smiled back and he realised he was right. That film really defined a lot of the great differences between small tribal communities in the developing world and the high life in the city, and a message that material wealth may not make you happy and all humans have many similarities, wherever we live.

Dani added that he also remembered a conversation with some elderly people in the UK, when this topic of the left hand came up. "They said that they used to use water to clean their privates and it was a common practice in high society in the old days. There was always a second washbasin which was very low, almost the height of a loo and one used to sit on it to wash the buttocks, and people even used them to wash their feet in. It was called a bidet, which is French, and it actually comes from Spanish traditions. It is a type of sink to wash genitalia or the inner part of the buttocks. But then somehow a new generation in the West have grown to dislike it and they are happy with loo paper."

Roland smiled and whispered quietly to Dani that it was becoming popular again among young couples and had apparently proven to be very useful. Roland said, "Nowadays you see bidets in bathroom stores again, and I'm sure many rich and famous people are still using them in their five-star bathrooms."

"I'm sure that if they provide these facilities in top hotels in New York, many rich and famous people must have them in their houses," Dani said.

Roland wondered how many households in England had maintained this old custom.

Dani replied, "The great thing is that as this old system is still in use in India and other developing countries, people are still used to squatting, and they have an Indian-style toilet at floor level where they can squat and sit, just bending their knees and hip joints, and they can keep their shoes on too. For washing purposes they either take a jug of water or a bottle with them, or have an automatic spray to wash by just turning on a tap on the more modern toilets."

Dani added, with a laugh, "You have to be careful in Indian hotels and households as they often have a tap on the side which sprays straight-on, and I've had shocks sometimes, especially in cold winters, when you turn it on by mistake."

Roland said, with a laugh, that he had actually had a similar experience, and he couldn't believe what on earth had hit him! "Why don't we come up with a new idea, maybe a better one, where we can still sit on a seat, but bend our knees and hip joints a little bit more. Not too low or too high. At the moment it's more or less a ninety-degree angle. Why can't we reduce it to something like thirty degrees or more? So at least the new generation can start with some exercise every morning, and their joints may be better than our current elderly who hardly bend their knees more than ninety degrees. After all, our knee joints are formed naturally and built for big bends like hinges. Somehow the inventor ignored that and made it up to chair level."

Dani was quite serious, and said, "Of course, with toilets the whole world has changed. Courtyards and hidden corners, bushes and fields are now clean and those bushes don't get any extra compost, but it's so nice with toilets, so we have to be grateful, but we shouldn't stop with one or two designs. How can one idea fit all? We need a balanced design, which cares for our joints and covers from ground level to chair level height."

Roland said, "Did you know that in some parts of Europe, especially in Italy and France, they still use squat toilets, and they also call them privies, or *alaturka*. They come with ridged footpads like the Indian toilets, perhaps better equipped, and they're always really very well cleaned and dried, but it's quite a shock for skiers to use them after having tired legs as it really stretches their muscles and ligaments, and they find them very difficult.

"Japan is mad on cleanliness and they have developed very high-tech toilets where they offer automatic buttons to keep you washed, cleaned, brushed and dried, or even perfumed! Some of the toilets even have sensors! Oh dear, that would be nerve-racking if you pressed the wrong button! So, finally, when they have a bath they can enjoy the real essence of that bath, not the polluted one with other kinds of essence!"

They all laughed!

Now it really was late and Roland thanked them for the very interesting evening and told them how touched he was by the whole atmosphere and by their whole way of life. They said goodnight and went to bed.

Roland had a peaceful sleep and hardly heard anything, apart from once in a while he heard a wild Himalayan wolf or a dog barking in the valley. Dani did say that he might hear wild wolves, tigers, snow leopards, deer or wild boar in the village.

***

Roland woke up with the chirping of the birds in the early morning. As soon as he heard them he couldn't sleep, and the sound got louder and louder as well as the morning light getting brighter outside. Soon he heard the main doors open and the cows mooing for their first feed. In the early morning, the lady of the house wakes up to give the cattle their first feed so they can be ready for milking by 6.00 a.m. Roland was quite tired, with the jetlag and the time difference, and his tiredness won over and he went back to sleep.

He kept sleeping until the bright sunshine and the heat started to warm up the room. He looked at his watch and it was 8.30 a.m., but it felt like it was already midday. He looked outside from his window but all he could see were hills in the distance and beautiful green birds on the trees near the house. They must be parrots, he thought. After a while there was a knock on his door and Dani came in, enquiring if he had slept well.

It was almost 9.30 a.m! Roland got up and went outside in the courtyard for his morning tea. They sat facing the garden, and the whole family were busy already doing their daily jobs. After tea, Roland wanted to get ready and to have a shower and Dani reminded him about having his first bucket bath. Roland was interested to experience that way of washing, so Dani got the hot water from the kitchen in a half-full bucket, which he assured Roland would be enough for his bath after he'd added some cold water in it as it was too hot.

Dani explained the whole process to Roland. "First, you must sit on a small stool and then, with two or three jugs, you should wash your whole body with water and then apply soap and shampoo and finally wash with the clean leftover water from the bucket. It will be quite an effort to complete the whole process, but if you need more water I will give you one more bucket, as it might be difficult for you the first time round, as you are used to having a full 'power shower' as it's called in the West nowadays."

Dani left one more half-bucket for Roland in case he needed it. Roland shut the door and decided to follow the rules and do it as Dani had told him. He was pleased to see that he didn't need to use the second bucket though. He had a perfect wash for his hair and body with just the half-bucket, because it was very hot water and he had added quite a bit of cold to it. So now he was confused about bathing and washing. He thought that to wash and clean the body and hair was one thing and to have a shower or bath was another thing. He thought that maybe we have mixed it up in the West; we no longer think a bath is to wash or clean ourselves. A bath is like a relaxing luxury and sometimes, he thought, he would even have a shower for a long time and just enjoy being under the running water. However today he could understand that eight litres of water was plenty to wash the whole body, unless you are very big. He couldn't believe the difference between eighty litres of water used for a full bath and around thirty-five litres used for a full shower. Here he could have a good wash with just eight litres of water. It really was something to think about. It means less energy to heat the water and also less in water bills. Not only that, but the way you sit, stand, wash and stretch your muscles, bend your joints and body is an exercise in itself. It is a whole cleaning ritual.

Later, Dani said, "Sadly, everyone wants a big bath in their house. In the mountains it would be a foolish thing to do as there is a water shortage in many towns already."

"It doesn't make any sense to me either," Roland agreed, "that five-star hotels and resorts are providing swimming pools and other water-consuming facilities to tourists, or for the rich, in places where people or villagers are losing their crops and plants, and trees which are used to provide shade to protect from the heat of the sun, and people are losing their lives because they don't have water to drink or to save their livestock. Although tourists are providing funds to help the economy grow, and it may be benefiting a few people at the top, a huge disaster could be being created for the common people. How can it be fair that someone is having a swim in a huge pool and splashing water around, and on the other hand, someone is craving a drop of water? We need a fair system so we can all survive and not ruin ourselves with extraordinary habits and lifestyles. Our children need to be able to survive in all kinds of environments – who knows what the future will bring?"

Dani said, "I wish that famous and powerful people like Bill Gates, royals of the world, other leaders or Bollywood and Hollywood actors, private organisations, or even the UN organisation would look to develop this old bucket bath idea into a life-saving eco-fit idea and make it the fashion for every luxurious bathroom to have an eco-fit bath. Then poor people could buy the bath too, and it would be a trend that could save lives, and the burden of having to have huge baths would be taken away from the poor. They could have a well-designed and good-looking bowl with a tray where one can sit and have a little cup attached with a beautiful chain to take the water out. That would give a good clean wash as well as a little exercise, and it would save water. As 'cleanliness is godliness and health is wealth', this bath would fulfil both purposes. It would be so popular among the population of developing nations, which is huge in number compared with the developed world. People in Asia and Africa alone would love to have a fashionable bath if it was advertised by Mr James Bond of Hollywood, or Mr and Mrs Bollywood. So people could save water and have some exercise to stimulate knees and hip joints as well, otherwise in old age they will seize up. More so for our generations as we hardly move from computers."

Another interesting example for Roland was when they were having tea outside. Dani's brother was shaving. It was interesting to see him shaving by the basin in the courtyard by the mirror, because it was new to Roland.

"In Britain we don't shave outside as it's either too cold or it's too warm or because we have become too private. You do everything outside here. The children are running outside and there's always many things happening around you."

The interesting thing was that although there was a tap on the basin, he had a bowl of hot water inside the sink and he shaved within that bowl of water, and it contained maybe only a quarter of a litre of water. After his shave he washed the bowl and his brush under the tap and that was it.

"Sometimes," Roland said, "I'm not even aware of my tap running for a few minutes or so, even when I'm brushing my teeth! We do it because we are used to this and that's how we've always done it."

It was truly eye-opening for Roland. The people he was with didn't even know about a sustainable life or the green movement. They may not have had any idea that there was something called global warming or an eco-friendly life. This was just natural to them, and that's how they learned it from their ancestors. They were living in the wilderness of the Himalayas and every drop of water had to be carried from nearby water sources and from rivers. To waste water, or even a grain of wheat, was considered a sin or bad luck in day-to-day life.

"Some people still have to carry water from at least thirty minutes or more away on the higher mountains," said Dani.

"If we somehow lost the water that we have," said Roland, "we may have to learn these ways too, as many water resources are drying up and every day we face a water shortage. We are importing water in plastic bottles from all around the world, but how long will that go on for? If the ice caps are melting and rivers are drying up, how will we survive? In Africa we have seen the drought and the pain and suffering of looking for water without having rivers or streams nearby. Wells are going deeper and deeper everywhere in the world. Australia is facing the same situation.

"I remember a programme on television that showed that when everything dries up in the heat in Australia, the aborigine people search everywhere for water and they walk miles in search of it. They don't build permanent houses as they have to move according to where food and water supplies are. When there is no water, they look for damp places under trees, to dig deep, so they can find frogs. They learned from their ancestors and they know that frogs carry a pouch of water with them to survive till the next rainy season. So they take a sip of water from that and bury the frog back deep again, so he can survive. But those techniques and that knowledge is rare and disappearing day by day. We must remember how important every drop of water is to survive."

Roland was impressed with this water-saving attitude in the Himalayas. Dani also explained that in India water sources and rivers are highly respected and worshipped.

"That's why they have the holy river Ganges where millions of people come every year to dip in it and worship it. It is against the natural principle to throw anything bad or dirty into the river or to go to the toilet in a stream or river. Nowadays, science and the modern way of life is pushing so much that the young hardly believe in it, they think that to worship water or the sun is superstitious and it's the business of old people. They believe that the modern bottle of mineral water is stylish and fashionable.

"In the old days there used to be places where locals would put clay pots in a shady place with a little cup tied with string to each pot, so passers-by could have a drink whenever they needed. No one carried a bottle around anywhere. The clay pot kept the water cool in summer, and it was considered a divine service to provide water to a thirsty passer-by. Now again, people are realising that their ancient traditions and the old ways are the best. We have to live in harmony with nature as we are a crucial part of it. We are taking millions of creatures and fish from the sea and replacing them with useless rubbish. We're chemically destroying and polluting water and dumping tons of clutter from machinery and electronic waste. Some countries are even using tanks to store dangerous and useless gases in the sea."

Dani explained that many villages are affected by modern living and lots of new houses were being built by rivers or beside streams. Sometime people have drains flushing directly into these streams, and Dani said that it was even happening to small village streams.

"Local authorities and villagers have no idea that soon, after a few years, these beautiful rivers can become stinking sewage and dumping grounds. The government and local people need to pay attention now, before it is too late, and they need to have separate drain and sewage systems in the villages. People have no idea how modern toilets, washing machines, showers, baths and all the liquids and chemicals they use will affect the whole water system. Their trust and faith in nature and simple living is being disrupted by profit-oriented firms and they're forgetting the advice taught to them by their ancestors. Salute water and rivers as you wake up, and salute the Sun and the Earth for a greater and longer life. Without water and Sun there is no life. These are the most important life-saving resources."

1 Arriving at Indira Gandhi airport, New Delhi,
copper hand gestures welcoming visitors.

2 View from the hotel window of the hustle
and bustle of Pahard Ganj, New Delhi.

3 Ancient Iron Column and Kutub Minar, New Delhi.

4 Heaps of rubbish by the side of the railway.

5 The Ridge with Church and Library, in the
Colonial Summer capital of the British Raj, Shimla,
in the foothills of the Himalayas at 2180m.

6 A porter climbing the high stairs in Shimla with a
heavy load common scene in the streets of Shimla.

7 View of Suni town and Thali Village on the banks of the Satluj river, showing the farm land and mountains, which are wanted for a cement factory.

8 Tattapani and the Satluj valley due to be immersed by the dam lake.

9 Tattapani now after the dam – August 2015.

10 Gateway entrance to the farmhouse at Thali with
a welcoming brass pot and flowers (inset).

"The sun is responsible for converting carbon dioxide into oxygen and keeping nature alive," Roland said. "Producing that much energy could cost more than fifty trillion US dollars to the world economy."

Dani wondered about why people started using tools like knives and forks to eat. "Maybe they used to work so hard in the fields, or maybe they didn't clean their hands very often and they used these tools due to the demands of time and necessity. I wondered if it has affected our teeth or mouths in any way? How natural it feels now to eat without them. Sometimes I have seen people burning their mouth with hot food because they can't sense the heat of the food with these utensils. Fingers can sense and feel the temperature of the food on the plate before it goes into the mouth. Here we are eating with our fingers, a single plate and fingers. One thing for sure is that you can feel the temperature of the food before you put it into your mouth and eat it.

"Did you know, Roland," said Dani, "that Arjuna, a prince from *the Mahabharata* story, who was a famous archer around five thousand or more years ago in India, went to the kitchen late at night during a summer night to fetch some water but found that his older brother Bhim, who used to eat a lot and was much larger in size and stronger too, was eating leftover food in the dark. Arjuna wasn't shocked at him stealing food at night, but the main thing that struck him was how his hand could find his mouth in the dark. Arjuna asked Bhim, 'Oh my brother, how can you do this and how can this happen?' Bhim was wise and replied, '*Abhyas, abhyas, abhyas* (practise). If you practise you can have eyes in your hands too, practise makes perfect.' So that advice made Arjuna practise day and night and finally he was known for his archery, and his ears had eyes as his shots never failed and he could shoot behind his back too. How interesting, and here we don't even notice it. So, from childhood if one practises, it becomes natural, but the effects of using your fingers as opposed to cutlery must be different."

***

By now they had finished their breakfast in the courtyard and the heat of the sun was making Roland relax in the chair. It was a perfect day and he would have liked a nap in the sun, but Dani wanted to take him for a walk and show him local people working in the fields. First, he called him to show how his mother was washing the dishes.

"She is using ash from the fire and some hair from a coconut shell. Hot ash is much more effective at cleaning grease. Sometimes they use any tree bark like banana tree bark, hard dry grass or any other hard material for scrubbing. If something is really hard then they use sand and soil with some little pebbles in it. There are no chemicals of any kind at all."

Roland also noticed that it was really hard work to clean the dishes, but every rinsed dish was really shining.

"You must have noticed that to clean these dishes you need good muscles, and this is hard work. One has to really apply lots of strength and effort and that's why they are so fit and strong," Dani said.

Roland replied, "I've never seen anyone applying so much strength to washing dishes before. When using gas and electric ovens at home, dishes don't really get dirty. We just clean them with washing liquid and rinse them, and I've seen some friends who don't even rinse them. They just leave them to dry with the washing liquid on them. No one really applies any strength as we have various types of brushes and washing-up cloths specially designed to help us, but I must say our big cooking pans don't shine like the ones here.

Sometimes we just run our dishes through the dishwasher, and we still feel tired. But these women are really fit.

"Here you don't have to pay to buy any of these things and there are no chemicals in the food chain. Dishwashers and chemicals have changed human habits. Due to machines and chemicals we don't hesitate in producing lots of dishes for very little use and we don't worry about washing up. Various types of appliances are produced, and we are made to think that we can't live without them. If we check our kitchen drawers we'll find many things which we have only used a few times or not at all. These things just fill up the sink until we shove them all in the dishwasher.

"If all goes well, it's fine, but if a fault happens or the machine is not cleaned regularly, you can sometimes find cups and plates with layers of washing chemicals and dirt all dried onto the cups or plates, and if you're not careful, you can end up eating all those chemicals," said Roland.

Dani couldn't believe that Roland had noticed that, as he himself often inspected every cup and plate before using them and had developed the habit of rinsing them with water beforehand. Dani's family used to go mad in England about this habit as the cups and plates used to be washed by the dishwasher, but he said that he simply couldn't trust the machines.

He wondered how many people did that in the developed world. "Meat contamination or bacteria, or God knows what, can go unnoticed with very little attention. It is crucial in the case of young children, what with their complicated milk bottles, as parents in a hurry can just serve milk in them and be unaware of leaving chemicals in the drink, which is supposed to be a nourishing and healthy feed."

Roland said, "With machines one has to be extremely careful. If we use any machine directly with food, all the tools, cutlery, plates, pots and pans should have very strict rules to follow so that we make sure we do it right and we don't kill ourselves with chemicals. It doesn't matter if you dress in 'black tie' every day for dinner or you eat in top restaurants or in a little roadside shack or stall. If the food is prepared with well-washed implements and rinsed with clear water and has no unwanted chemicals, you will be fine, otherwise you are not only contributing to killing yourself but spreading a message of laziness and we will be responsible for killing our coming generations too."

Roland was shocked by all these thoughts, because the modern generation are not even thinking twice before they buy washing-up liquid. "That's the only option they have. They are used to this and they will say, 'Oh my mum used to do that too, she was okay', but they have no idea that having a pure diet, with natural food, will not be seen again, because now we do things, not for quality, but to keep the balance sheet up and generate huge profits through mass production, injecting chemicals into cows for milk and modifying plants to produce more and more. That's what our diet is. We don't eat it all in the developed world anyway. We throw half of it in bins. Here, anything not eaten goes to the cows and special care is taken as everything grown is precious."

These were the thoughts going on in Roland's mind when he was sitting and enjoying his book, and he thought that he had better note some of the points down in his diary. He also remembered that around sixty pounds worth food was wasted by a family in the UK per week and millions of pounds were spent on shifting tons and tons of it by trucks around the globe.

Note:

1. Eco-fit bath: If the West encounters a water problem in future, there exists a solution already, which has survived the centuries and is still in practice in millions of homes. The bucket bath teaches us how to bend and stretch our legs by squatting, and it means that washing and cleanliness is not just about lazing around. It will save water as well as keeping you fit. You will use ten litres of water instead of eighty litres. That will save water, money, health and lives, and require less drainage.

2. Hand washing means the exercising of fingers and muscles: Hand washing provides very good exercise for fingers, carpal muscles and arm muscles. It may also help with reflexes and pressure points too.

3. Natural washing liquid using ash and lemon can save you money and you don't have to give your earnings to big companies by paying big water and electric bills. If this ash goes back into the fields, it becomes a fertiliser for plants and enriches the ground, whereas chemicals will poison the land. You will also produce less washing and it will save you water. A washing machine can waste around one hundred and thirty-five litres of water in one go.

CHAPTER FOUR

The seeds of life

After spending around two hours in the sunshine in the courtyard and garden, Roland felt it was time to move on and explore life in Thali. He was very interested in the sustainable lifestyle of the village. He packed a small bag and took some of his things with him for the day: his camera, sun cream and his metal water bottle with a purifying tablet in it (it could be ready to drink in one hour). It was warm enough for him not to wear his shoes. Dani wore sandals and Roland realised he could use his sandals too.

They went along a small footpath which led through the fields towards the farms. He followed Dani, who kept pointing to some of his family's fields as well as important trees and plants on the way and mountain peaks around the valley. He also pointed out where there was a temple of their local deity, suggesting that it would be a good four hours' walk to the top. They decided to do a trek later on, but for now they were happy to explore around the village.

Soon Dani started to talk with someone that Roland couldn't see, and he realised that it was someone up a nearby tree trimming the branches. Dani explained that this lady was collecting the leaves for her cattle and that it was very normal in the village to cut the leaves and trim the trees every six months.

"The tree is called *beaul* in the local language," said Dani. It is local to the area and grows at an altitude of around 600 metres above sea level. It can grow on rocky land and can survive both extreme heat and cold. It has wide, thick, juicy leaves, quite similar to the shahtoot tree, which is used to feed silk worms. *Beaul* leaves are delicious, and animals like goats, sheep, cows and horses or buffalos eat them. Once all the leaves have been eaten, the leftover sticks and thin branches are then trimmed and kept in bundles to dry. After a few months, once they're fully dried, they're dipped in streams for a few weeks. Once the bark has become soft, then the whole family takes them out and they hit or smash a few sticks against stones and rocks to get rid off the darker layer of the bark, each time giving them a good wash by dipping them in clean water. It used to be a great day out for children, especially in hot weather, and they used to love paddling, splashing and having a dip in the streams, as well as looking for live animals in the water like tadpoles, fish, crabs and water spiders and making sure that they don't encounter a snake hunting for his food.

"Once the sticks are fully washed, they dry them in the sun and carry the bundles home. Once fully dried they separate the white bark from the sticks and roll it and keep it for making ropes to tie cows, or even to make bags and baskets. Once the white bark is separated from the sticks, it's dried again and kept in small bundles and then used throughout the year as kindling as well as to make torches for dark nights."

Dani started to collect the branches into a big pile and Roland joined Dani to help. By then it was quite a big bundle, maybe around thirty to forty kilos, and the lady was under the tree trying to get her rope ready as well as getting some other branches together. Dani pointed out that the rope was made from the same bark, and it looked very strong and well made. Roland looked up at the branches of the tree and could see that it was all trimmed beautifully; all he could see was thick branches without any small young shoots or leaves, except one thin branch full of leaves at the top of the tree. He pointed at the branch full of leaves and said, "Look, you have missed that one."

They laughed, and Dani said this was to show respect to the tree as well as being a very old tradition to let the tree grow a little every year. "It is seen as a sin if you don't leave that branch. This is the only chance for the tree to survive and grow to its own height. Everyone in the village will leave that last branch as long as they know about the tradition. It is called a *Kalgi,* or 'new blossom'. Everything has a right to live and establish itself as well as it can.

"Which part of the tree and where it should grow are all part of the old skills, and the elderly know much more about it than today's computer generation. Sometimes due to a lack of knowledge people cut down very useful trees and many species are lost or disappearing fast."

Roland was impressed with the idea of not taking everything from the tree, giving it a chance to grow, so it could live longer. It made sense to him. He asked Dani if they did this to every kind of tree.

"Almost all, except if the tree is too high or it's of no use, then sometimes they cut the thick branches down to burn, but that was only done for bigger celebrations, to cook food, or for funeral pyres.

"There is a big tradition of worshipping trees in the culture, and in some farming villages, people still have 'divine' bonding with certain trees. In Bihar state in the eastern part of India, a man called Vishnudev Singh has started a tradition where girls tie a string around a tree in their childhood to make trees their godbrother or guardians and then they look after them all throughout their life like their siblings."

By now the lady had her bundle ready and Dani helped her put the bundle onto her head and then she walked off. Roland couldn't believe it. In England it would have been illegal to do that due to health and safety. It seems that we have gone a bit too far and have got some of our priorities wrong, he thought. These people must be very strong, and they must know what they're doing. What a life.

Now they could see the open terraced fields. Some of the fields had people weeding, and there were also people with oxen. There were many people ploughing and working in different fields all around the valley.

Dani explained that most of the fields were for growing cabbages and cauliflowers and the season was for winter crops like wheat, garlic, onion and mustard, and most of the people were ploughing to sow wheat.

Roland realised that there were no tractors, or any other machine or motor sounds. Everything was being done by hand and with simple tools. He was amazed to see their tools and equipment as they got closer. Some of the farmers had two oxen and a wooden plough tied to the centre of a wooden collar which in turn was tied to both oxen, and that's how they were ploughing the soil. In some of the fields they had a wooden log with two bamboo sticks to flatten the soil, as well as some of the villagers breaking the lumps of hard soil with wooden hammers that looked like they were made from bamboo. Dani explained that after the paddy rice, the summer crop soil gets very hard as it's clay, and it's also very hard to plough for oxen. The tools they were using were very simple and all handmade from wood and bamboo.

Dani told him, "They are eco-friendly and have no carbon effect on nature. If they go wrong they can fix them there and then, whereas tractors or other plastic or metal tools are manufactured in big factories, and most of them have motors because they all run on oil or electricity and pollute with smoke or by using energy. If they go wrong they have to be repaired or their parts have to be replaced, which are again made in big factories with the help of complex machines, and all have a cost on the carbon footprint. If there is no factory to produce that little part, the machine cannot work and will be useless and work will be postponed or stopped or a new product will have to be bought."

Roland could not stop thinking that this way of life was small, simple, and when problems arise they can be easily and locally solved. What a beautiful life.

"This village used to be cut off from rest of the world, as the river could only be crossed by raft to the other side and the bridge was only built in the early 1960s. Before that they had their own local rajas (kings) and village life was very self-sufficient," Dani explained.

"People must have followed the river from the flatland many centuries ago when they were just nomads with their cattle and animals, and then later they must have found the village sufficient to settle in, as there was flat and fertile land as well as good water sources. They found this land perfect in both winter and summer. They started living here on a permanent basis and soon built houses and shelters for their herds. They had to be self-sufficient, so they must have collected all kind of plants and started to grow them here. All they used to get from local traders was salt, because it used to come from a mine around 200 kilometres away, a place called Mandi. The rest of the medicinal herbs and spices were grown locally, but originally must have been imported from many different places, because it is not possible that it was all growing naturally in this place. At the same time they had to rely on all kinds of fruit, vegetables and crops or animals to have a balanced diet."

Roland felt very grateful that in a modern society everyone had access to all kinds of food. "We can buy anything we like and whenever we like. There are huge supplies and we are very choosy and can easily throw away any over ripe or under ripe food."

Dani replied, "In the old days, people had to look after their grain and use everything accordingly. They had natural ways to store crops and they used to share in the hard times too. They had to create their own seeds and then store them for the next year without any chemical sprays or machine-made containers. Everything was natural. To store grain they had big bamboo baskets, sometimes five feet high, shaped like barrels. They used to dry various types of vegetables, like *ghiya* (bottle gourd or calabash gourd), to produce containers, utensils or pipes. It was harvested young for eating, or dried to have a hard skin to produce containers of various sizes – long, round, big and small – and the lid would be the core of corn or wood to make it airtight, and sometimes they would just use a piece of material at home to block it fully.

"So life was self-sufficient but hard. They knew the old simple ways and they were able to survive among the hardships, and amazingly they lived a good life. But there are also stories in the village that if they had a loss of crops in one season or a natural disaster of too much rain or a drought, it could bring famine, and people even used to grind certain tree bark to make flour and bread. Or some people would have mutton to survive till the next crop. Our grandparents knew much more about it and how important every grain was for them, and it simply meant life or no life. That's why they had such devotion, dedication and respect towards tools, farming and food. They said it is not just a grain, it is a divine seed and it can save communities or lives. But for the supermarket generation it is hard to understand how they felt and why they felt the need to collect all kinds of herbs or plants from this valuable fertile land.

"There is a story of a villager whose house was two hours away up on the hill, and he came early one morning with his oxen and a plough and collar for his oxen on his shoulder as well as a bag of already-sprouted paddy seeds. You have to dip paddy seeds into water for at least twenty-four hours at home before sowing or planting. If you haven't known the hardship of ploughing with oxen in a field full of water, you may not understand. The farmer only wears shorts of some sort and it is a real marathon which goes on for a few hours. First you have to plough and then you have to level it with a special thin wooden log tied to the oxen collar like the plough.

"It can be hot, forty degrees or more, and maintaining good work and controlling oxen at the same time is a difficult and very skilled task. Sometimes other members of the family help to mend the edges so the water doesn't leak and the field is fully filled with water. So the farmer ploughed all morning and finally got the field ready to sow the sprouted paddy seeds. After finishing his ploughing, the farmer had to wash his oxen as they got very muddy and, of course, thirsty. That's done from the same water channels that feed the fields. After washing himself as well, he started his journey back home with his oxen, the plough and wooden collar on his shoulders, hungry and tired in the summer heat. Thank goodness it was lighter on the way back as he did not have the seeds to carry. After two hours walking up the hill, he got home and tied the oxen and put the plough down. He took his hat off and found that a sprouted seed was stuck to the top of his hat. He felt so sorry for not planting that seed that he took the seed and walked back to the fields to plant it, so it could live. He even forgot that the wooden collar was still on his shoulders. A seed is one life, and such devotion was there for that grain that it was considered a sin not to let that single seed live where all the other seeds were already planted in the field, and he had given life to all of them.

"This story shows how simple people were, and what kind of trust and devotion they had in the natural laws. He was pleased that he saved one seed and that seed could grow and multiply into millions of seeds in years to come. It did not bother him to walk up the hill again, hungry and tired. That is a true story and my grandmother told me it as she had seen that man, but it is around a hundred years old," Dani said.

"Fields were precious and looked after and ploughed so the land would not be barren, not because they had worked out a business plan to calculate the profit or gains, but simply because they couldn't bear the land not to be used or cultivated, food was precious and it had to be done. Today, there is an opposite way of thinking, more like, 'Oh no, what will you get out of all that hard work?' They ask their hard-working parents, 'A bucket full of grain! For all that hard work, all through the season and severe weather? I work one day and can buy more than that within a few hours.' That's how the modern mind has started to think. If all these little fields are left to wilderness, who will work hard to grow anything? And one cannot always rely on resources from outside! Sooner or later they will stop supplying too, because they think the same and will just do office jobs. That's the cry of the modern generation. Soon their generation will think that beans or grains are made by machines like sweets or chocolate, which can easily be found in the supermarket.

"We need to develop those old ways into affordable innovations for sustainable agriculture and for clean energy. We need to point out and control those things which are a threat to our existence, like too much sugar, alcohol and smoking. We need to avoid or ban those fashionable lifestyles which may put a stop to life on Earth through diseases like cancer."

Roland was really touched by that kind of trust in and dedication to the natural laws and to nature. "In the West we use lots of combine harvesters and God knows all sorts of farming machinery to harvest, and a lot of grain just drops out during the process and is not even noticed at all."

"When I was young," Dani said, "we used to get the job of collecting leftover grains from the fields after the wheat harvesting, and we used to collect around three to six kilogrammes of grain, and we were allowed to sell that and keep the money. It was a reward for us, and at the same time it taught us not to waste the crops and how valuable every seed was. We also used to eat a very varied diet. People could have two crops a year and sometimes three or four crops side by side. They had their local herbalist and for any problems they used to go to him. But now the problem is that lots of food can come from outside, and people are losing interest in many useful crops. They are more concerned with cash crops.

"Now, with modern medicines, young people do not recognise many herbal plants anymore," he said. "They want to study modern subjects like IT, and local knowledge is being forgotten. At the same time, in the race for more produce and more money, people are exploring more chemical methods, which are ruining the whole ecosystem of village farming. Lots of sprays to kill weeds or insects are being fed to the plants and it is not just affecting the things targeted, but may be affecting other useful herbs and plants, which we are consuming. This is disastrous for nature and the whole ecology of plants in many parts of the world.

"The pressure is on young children to study English, maths, computer studies or engineering, but not how to make a wooden plough or oxen collar, or any other handmade farming tools. I wish they would start teaching this type of subject, or have private workshops for local people, so they remember these sustainable techniques. It seems that we are doing our best to destroy the best and most eco-friendly way of life and building a way which is a poison for us and nature."

Roland agreed and wondered about the benefits of machines and the West's influence all around the world. He was very proud of their discoveries and inventions, but now seeing this part of the world and its use of sustainable science had given him doubts.

After that they went through the fields and saw garlic and cauliflower growing and people weeding and working hard in the fields. Some ladies had metal sickles to cut the grass and a very spikey sharp tool with a small handle for weeding. Dani helped Roland handle and examine the spikey tool, which had just one spike to poke with.

"Oh it's quite sharp. It must take them a long time to cover the whole field?" said Roland.

"Yes, it does," Dani replied, "but the idea behind it is also so that they don't kill any earthworms. Very often, people use forks or spikes so that they don't chop up many earthworms. It is considered a sin. Also, scientists have proven that earthworms shift and turn huge amounts of soil around the globe and are a very important part of the environment. So the choices of tools – a spade or a fork – are also quite practical, considering the preservation of other lifecycles as well."

Roland wanted to know who made the metal tools, and Dani explained that there were professional blacksmiths who made mainly farming tools, and in exchange they received rice, corn or wheat from farmers. "This helps them too, but nowadays many of them sell them in the market for money as well."

Roland pointed out some huts built from wood and metal sheets around the fields, and some of them were covered by plastic sheets. Most of them were high up off of the ground – around five or six feet.

"What are they for?" he asked.

Dani replied, "Villagers are having a very tough time with wild animals, like wild boar and sambar deer as they're growing in numbers, and their herds attack at night and ruin fields of crops in the area. It's a very difficult task to stop them as the Indian government has a law to protect wildlife, and the population is asked to live side by side with it, and villagers don't know what to do. They have few options but to guard their fields at night. Very often they lose part of their crops to these animals. They can't kill them or do any harm to them as it is not allowed. Due to a lack of the clearance of jungles or forests in summer for firewood, they have very thick cover to hide in and reproduce to multiply their population, which is a big worry for farmers in this area. They have multiplied hugely in the last ten years or so.

"There is a big change in many ways as older and more modern lifestyles are merging together. We may need some new rules and changes in the law, either permission to get rid of, or the forest department could control the numbers of these animals as well as increase their revenue by creating a wildlife park here in the nearby forest area, which contains more then fifteen hundred hectares. Or they could arrange special high fencing for farmers to protect their crops, otherwise their knowledge, skills and habits will change and we will find this beautiful community ruined and lost for ever."

Roland couldn't believe what was happening to this farming community and the kind of changes it was going through. He said he hoped that a proper balance would be created and the authorities would understand the ordeal they were going through.

After roaming around the fields, they followed a water channel up to a beautiful well-built white slate house above the farming land. They greeted a man, saying "*Namaste*", and he greeted them with "Hello" and then walked with them. He spoke quite good English and his name was Ramesh. Dani chatted in his local dialect and it seemed to Roland like Dani had planned it in advance. He opened the door to a small room away from the house and Roland could hear grinding sounds. As they entered the room, Dani explained and pointed to the grinding stones: it was a flour mill that was run by using water. Ramesh explained that it was a very old flour mill started by his great-grandfather, and it had served for whole communities way back before motor cars had even been in use in Europe.

They had a good look and also explored the small wooden turbines and their blades from outside. One was for the main wheel, or grinder, and the second very small one was to keep the flour level lower than the wheel. Inside were big bamboo baskets full of white wheat and yellow corn, as well as big drums of wheat and corn grains. The owner explained that it ran day and night and that they produced more than one hundred kilogrammes of flour every day.

He had lit the oil lamp to check the grain level, and Roland asked what kind of oil he used. Dani explained that it was mustard oil, and it was from mustard produced in their own fields. Roland found it interesting to see the whole process of growing things in the fields and then using natural processes and tools to turn it into flour by using a watermill, and this whole ecosystem was still alive and had been going on for centuries.

They said goodbye to the owner of the flour mill and walked down towards the stream. Everything Roland was experiencing showed him a very eco-friendly way of life, and he was excited to explore more.

He was just thinking about it when Dani shouted, "Oh look! They've dipped some sticks here in this puddle."

All Roland could see were some bundles of sticks dipped in the water under some heavy stones.

Dani reminded him about the lady cutting the branches in the tree. Dani explained, "Those leaves will be fed to the cattle at home, and once all the leaves have been eaten by the cows, the leftover sticks are then trimmed and tied in small bundles. Once they are well dried, they are brought here and dipped into these little puddles by the streams. After a few months, the villagers will take them out and take all the dark skin off by smashing or hitting them on these big stones, and then they will rinse and wash them in the stream to get rid of the dark skin, as well as to clean the bark. When only the white bark and sticks are left, they then put the washed sticks with the loose bark out in the sun to dry. As soon as it has dried in the sun, mainly within a few hours, they will carry it home and separate the bark from the sticks and store it to make various types of ropes for household use, such as ropes for farming jobs, to tie cattle and even to make charpois, or string beds, as well as any other nets and mats. Finally, the bare leftover white sticks are than dried and kept for kindling to light a fire in an emergency and to make fire torches to create light at night. It is very important for farmers and it is all produced in a very sustainable way, with zero use of machines and electricity. Also, it provides good exercise and activity for people. They may see this as hard work, but it's better than those working in big factories with huge machines to produce ropes with an environmental cost!

"That's why," said Dani, "I was telling you that the *beaul* tree is a very important tree for us here. It is never cut down until it dries or falls by itself."

Roland was fascinated with the morning's walk. It had been an excellent insight into these age-old natural and simple ways of living, into how self-sufficient these communities were, and Roland was amazed at their seasonal arrangments tied in with nature.

They walked by the stream down towards the market, and Dani pointed at some newly built houses, which were very close to the stream.

"I hope that they aren't diverting their bathroom or dirty water drains towards the clean stream otherwise all the soap, washing liquids and chemicals will enter the water and spread around the area, as well as end up further down in the Satluj River, and soon, as the number of houses increases, the stream will look like sewage. Local government and the authorities need to have some special building laws, and they should also mark all the river levels, so a space or distance is maintained for natural calamities like floods. Separate drains away from these streams should also be built so that the dirty water doesn't go to their kitchen gardens or the fields near these rivers.

"It will save the villagers from many future problems as this little river called *Thali Nala* can also flood in a monsoon and the water level can rise. We heard that once two boys were killed by a flood in this little stream as the flood was really high and it brought many boulders with it, as it comes from very high mountains and the forces are very powerful. In this modern world we overlook many incidents of the past and make a big mistake by trying to control nature by taking over rivers or more and more of the land. We forget that we have to learn to live with nature, not to control it."

Within a few minutes they got to the main road by the old school and the bridge and found the local village square containing a few shops and small tea stalls. Dani asked for two cups of tea and a local snack called vegetable *pakora*. Dani said that *pakora* was their local delicacy and that they were much better than other foods in value as well as being very fresh and healthy.

"I don't think we could buy even a small packet of crisps for what we paid for our little tea party," said Roland. "It's such a shame that many young people do not understand the value of local produce and how beautiful it is," he said.

They had a long conversation all the way home, though the family wasn't very happy as they were very late for lunch. Afterwards, Roland went out and put his chair in the courtyard and had a nap. He also read a few things in his guidebook about India, as he realised that he wanted to know more about the country and he was getting more interested in its culture and religion as well as its history.

Roland had every confidence in Dani as he had completed various trips to the Himalayas to do trekking as well as to explore the culture and village life there. Dani told him that he had led more than twenty-two groups in the eleven years since he'd been a college student in Shimla, and he showed him some pictures and explained about his adventures with different clients from Europe, as well as school expeditions for European and American students. He'd had to study and look deeper into the traditions and culture to give lectures and satisfy his clients over the years. The most interesting trip he'd had was over two passes from Kinnaur to Spiti, and then to Ladakh over the Bhaba Pass (4,890 metres above sea level) and Parang La Pass to Ladakh (which was over 5,580 metres above sea level). He said it was the trip of a lifetime and they did it in eighteen days on foot. He used to always quote one of his customers, Anton Muller, and his family from Germany, who were nearly sixty, and he had had great discussions with them about the Himalayas during the trip.

Anton had attempted to climb Mount Everest around forty years before and he had an excellent knowledge of the mountains. He had many wise people travelling with him from all around the world, and he himself was a great explorer and was interested in the mountains, old civilisations and in life itself.

Dani told Roland that on the day 9/11 happened he'd been having a wonderful, peaceful night on the Shikari Peak with his client Brian from England, and when they got down the next day villagers told them that thousands of people had died in America and that there had been huge plane crashes. That had been worrying for them, and they rushed down to finish the trek in a village called Bakhrote and found a Hindi paper to read the details. He was relieved that it was not England or Europe, but still found it unbelievable. They had parked their motor bikes there and were glad that they were away on a safe mountain.

"It is one of those thoughts one has on the high mountains – will something happen to the world when we are there and will we be the only survivors? Or will we be able to go back alive to see the world again? These are the sorts of terrible tensions the mind carries while trekking."

They were safe and they celebrated with local tea and pakora and felt sorry for those who'd been trapped in the buildings on that terrible day and they prayed for them.

So Roland had no doubts about him, but to understand the culture more he had to do some homework and guidebooks are always full of very useful information for a traveller like him. Another thing he realised while sitting there was that life was very much about living together with animals here. Young calves and goats ran around in the courtyard, although they were not allowed near the dog. Tigger used to bark at them mercilessly until they were sent outside the main courtyard of the house by one of the family.

Roland read in the guidebook about the holy river Ganges and also about the holy cows and how the whole of India admired and worshipped them. Dani's explanations were making sense, but he also wanted to know how they dealt with these things in their daily lives. He had noticed already that they used oxen for ploughing and for pulling carts, so it was not that they just worshipped them. Roland had even seen people being hard on the oxen yesterday while ploughing. They always had a bamboo stick to hit and poke the oxen to make them walk faster or turn and to make sure the job got done. So they can hit them, use them for work and at the same time worship them. He wanted to find out more about it, how it really all went together and how and why they honoured cows.

By then Dani had got back, as he had to go to see one of his cousin's brothers, Basant, near the bridge. He asked his family whether Roland had had tea, but Roland had been asleep when the family had tea earlier and they hadn't wanted to disturb him. Roland explained that he'd been reading about the cows and holy Ganges in India and wanted to find out more.

Dani said, "Oh well, this is the best chance to experience it, here in this family. You must see my mum milking the cow this evening, and see her making fresh butter in the morning. The whole process is done by hand and you will be able to taste the fresh butter. Every family in the village has at least one cow and they all make their own butter. It is very shameful if you don't have your own milk in the house, unless you have no one to look after them. Our family has four cows, two oxen and three young calves, as well as five young goats, but we gave twenty goats to a different family in the village as it was too much work for the family and *Amma ji*, as all the young children had left the village to study in the city and the young ones were in local school.

CHAPTER FIVE

An age-old sacred milk - making and natural recycling machine

His family were wonderful hosts and they produced cups of tea from time to time. Dani and Roland were not allowed to do anything, so all they could do was chat as the family wanted to make sure their son and his friend had a good rest.

While they were having some tea and biscuits, Roland decided that it was a good time to ask more about cows.

"Dani, my guidebook said that you worship cows in India, and I have also heard that Hindus are very protective towards cows," he said. "Is that true, and why and how does it all work?"

Dani sipped tea from his cup and agreed with what Roland was saying: that they do respect cows and worship them, and that they are also part of everyday life.

"But that doesn't mean that we don't treat them like cattle or that they are worshipped day and night like a deity in a temple. It is just that there is lots of care and protection for them, because farmers cannot live without them, especially in the villages or on farms," said Dani. "Modern science has discovered so much – huge planes which can fly with more than five hundred people in them and computers, mobiles and satellites and many more complex machines. On the other hand, they have produced ways to fertilise the fields with modern fertiliser. But to do that they have to create machinery and big factories and industries. And after a few years they find out that they had some wrong chemicals in it or it has some side effects on the crop. Many times it goes wrong, and sometimes they say that the greenhouse is the best way to produce things, but now there is another side to the argument – that greenhouses are dangerous for the environment. But the damage to nature has been done.

"Have you seen machines where you put dry hay, green leaves, grass or any twigs plus water in, and it will give you sweet milk and compost from the other side?"

Roland laughed. "No, I haven't seen anything like that so far."

"But that's the best way to describe what a cow is," said Dani. "If you ask anyone in the village about the cow they will just say, 'Oh, Gow Mata', which means 'mother cow'. It is very simple. This unbroken and huge respect and love for cows is unlimited. It does not mean that you don't use the cow or their services for daily life. They are treated very much like animals, and many times they are hit with sticks to control and tame them or if they don't do the job properly. But they have every right to live as long as they can and die a natural death. They cannot be killed because they are seen as a very important animal.

"They are natural machines to eat your dry hay and leaves and produce milk, calves, compost and anti-bacterial urine for you. Yes, cow urine is used to lay the floor in mud houses and is used to treat many illnesses too. If it has not been changed for more than 7,000 years, there must be a reason for it. People could very easily have a stone and marble floor, but they always choose to have their kitchen floors laid with cow dung mixed with mud. Dung is just broken down leaves and twigs. So the floor does not produce any dust either and lasts longer.

"As you know, babies can survive on mother's milk for more than six months. Mother's and cow's milk contains all that we need to survive to start life. The cow takes over after the mother to feed the baby, so it is a second mother, and the baby can live on milk for a year or more. Milk is not only very nutritious, but we can produce various products like sweets and other delicacies with it all around the world. In big Indian cities and towns in the late afternoon you can always find a very big wok full of milk. More than twenty litres of milk is boiled in many small restaurants, and every evening people have a glass of milk and they go out for a milk drink (*dudh pina*) instead of going to the pubs for a pint. Very often they will have *jalebi* (an Indian sweet dipped in sugar syrup) with the milk. People call it *Dudh Jalebi* and it is very popular, sweet and nutritious. Even here in Shimla there is a shop called *Nathulal Halwai* in the lower market right below the evening college after the mall road. So go for a glass of *Dudh Jalebi*, rather than for a beer or alcoholic drink, as people traditionally do.

"You still see that in the towns. So the different effects of milk and alcohol you can calculate for yourself. Again, you need machinery to produce alcohol, whereas milk you just need to boil it in a saucepan. The effect on health is very clear: as you sow so shall you reap. From the goodness of milk you can produce curd, cream, butter, *ghee* (purified butter which lasts longer) and *burphi* (a sweet and a delicious treat). Countless other delicious products are produced from milk.

"In the West, milk is used to make lots of cheese, and they create various kinds of cheeses with or without mould and you can keep it for years. It's the same here. We make *ghee* from butter and can keep it a minimum of three years in this hot weather. So we can keep milk or its products in extremely hot or cold weather to feed us for life," said Dani.

"These animals can also survive in extreme weather, in the heat and the cold. Here they are known as cows and in the highest mountains of the world they are known as *Churu,* or yak. They can live in the wilderness of the Himalayas up to around 6,000 metres above sea level in summer."

Roland interrupted and asked Dani if he knew about a cow called Audhumla, from the ancient tales of Norse mythology. Dani was interested and wanted Roland to explain more.

"Once I saw an old painting from NA Abilgaard about a cow. The legend has it that this creature, or animal, was the first to emerge from the emptiness at the start of creation; from the primal ice at the dawn of time. It nourished the first frost giant, Ymir. The cow herself survived by licking ice, from which she freed the first man, Buri. While Ymir suckled her milk, Audhumla licked Buri free of the ice. And Buri's son Bor and his children were considered the first gods: Odin, Vili and Ve. So it seems that this tale tells us about some kind of sudden ice age and is the tale of how a cow freed a human by licking the ice, and these humans may have been the people to start humanity again on Earth."

"It is difficult to understand what these old tales want to explain to us, because sometimes we lose things in translation," said Dani. "Cows live in sub-zero conditions in the Scottish Highlands and are known as Highland cows. These cows are from the same family and they have a long-haired coat to keep them warm when they are high up. These Highland cows have one more secret, which is an understanding of the snow and glaciers and other natural dangers they may face. When I used to go trekking in the high Himalayas in Kinnaur, Spiti and Ladakh, we used to take yaks with us to carry all the trekking gear and equipment. We discovered from elderly yak owners that apparently yaks can smell the cracks hidden in the glaciers under the snow. They smell them and step on safe places, and local people often depend on them for this skill and knowledge.

"For cows in this village it is a very simple and beautiful life here in the foothills of the Himalayas," said Dani. "They go to graze in the nearby forest, and in the evening they come home and they are fed by the family. Their food is always dry hay, green leaves and leftover food from the family. We don't waste any food and everything goes into a bucket. They only eat natural food, nothing from packets or produced by any machines."

Then suddenly Dani laughed. "I am going to tell you a very funny fact about the modern world. Do you know that most of the dogs in the modern world have no idea what their real or natural diet is? In Europe, have you seen a single dog or a cat eating meat or any cooked meat or hunting live animals?"

"Not really," said Roland, "but dogs in the country do catch rabbits or birds once in a while, and we used to have fox hunting, where foxes are chased by hunters on horses and hounds eat the live foxes in groups, but that's now banned, so, no, I don't think I have seen much of it in day-to-day life."

"Well, what do you feed them then," said Dani.

Roland had to think. "Special dog biscuits, and tinned food for cats?"

"Yes!" Dani shouted with a big laugh. "They are trained and that's all they know. Food biscuits, and that's what they eat. They have not tasted real food. What they used to hunt in nature or the wild or what their ancestors ate – they have no idea. After a few generations the mice will be dancing and jumping with the cats and rabbits, and monkeys will be chasing dogs, because our cats and dogs will not know what their food is! They'll be searching for biscuits! It is the same in Indian families. Some families are vegetarian and they don't feed any meat to their pet dogs either, which is foolish. Even in our own family some of the family members don't want to feed meat to the dog, they want to convert him to veggie too, and they forget that they cannot live without meat. Luckily, once in a while Tigger gets some meat, and very often he has a bone hidden in the bushes around the house. But if these domesticated dogs or cats are left in the wild they will be searching for biscuits day and night," laughed Dani.

"Imagine," Roland pondered with amusement, "if cats and dogs smelt the only store in town selling them, they would be queueing up to get them and then they would have to look for humans to open up the tins or the packs of biscuits for them!" How ridiculous would that be!

"Already many kennels have dogs without owners and they are being looked after by the government at great expense, because otherwise they will suffer and die in the wild. It's the same with wild animals in the developed world. Because of money and wealth they transport dangerous and exotic animals, such as cobras, elephants, lions and tigers to zoos around the world, again at high expense. They then have to provide them with the heat and other conditions they require and are used to in their native habitats. It is great for people or children to see them, but if they get out or somehow we humans cease to be able to look after them, what would happen? In the case of an earthquake or other natural disaster they could well get out, and then people would be hunted by lions or other wild animals in Europe. What would they do in the end but kill them too? So why do we do these strange things in the beginning?" said Dani.

Roland mused, "I guess things have changed, and nowadays we can see them in films, on computers and on television and so it shouldn't be necessary anymore. At the same time wild animals transport plants or other germs, bacteria and illnesses with them to these new places, which creates new problems. And of course they will never be able to provide what these animals are used to in the wilderness or in their natural environment. If they want to, they have to transport these things to feed them too."

"And it's not only animals in modern society that have lost the real taste of food," said Dani, "but people are doing the same."

"Yes," agreed Roland, "many young people go to the supermarket and buy sandwiches, fish and chips or pizza and fizzy drinks. What do the younger generation cook? That's all they know. Life is too busy and that's all they can manage. If they see a store selling raw vegetables, spices, herbs, lentils or rice, they think it's for professional chefs to cook in the restaurants, or they think it's too complex and they can't handle it. They'll have a takeaway or a meal in a restaurant instead.

"The other thing nowadays, Roland, is that many young people living in big cities don't have access to real fire anymore. People have microwaves and electric heaters or cookers. They have no direct contact with fire unless it's a bonfire outside or they light a candle. All they cook is done in five minutes with a microwave or cooked on electric heaters, even in Indian towns or cities. Some families have access to cook on gas or kerosine oil stoves. It is very rare that people cook over a direct fire, as life is so busy. Similarly, sitting together, watching a real fire and chatting with the family, like the households do here, is now a very old-fashioned ritual. They hardly get together for big festivals or occasions. And, of course, in the modern lifestyle, there is central heating, so why sit together? It is no good.

"It's the same here now with mobiles. A married couple goes for a walk together and both will be talking to somebody else on their mobile. So the whole sense of family life is changing and I don't think it's for the better. Everyone wants television in their bedrooms and many people hardly go out. People are happy indoors with just a T-shirt, even in freezing weather, because they have central heating. In the old days we used to have a blanket specially made for each person according to their size, and no one would put it away until winter was over. Now we are becoming so dependent on machines that instead of getting up to get a jumper or blanket, we prefer to switch on a heater that blows hot air at us. It is making us weaker and weaker at withstanding the heat or the cold or a natural way of living with nature. We are losing our ability to adapt. We have to always live in a maintained or controlled environment. The big question is, can these external factors sustain the human capability to adapt and survive?

"But this animal we have been talking about – the cow – has the ability to survive in any temperature around the world. In Africa, because of climate change, the weather has turned extreme and they are experiencing heavy rains and floods which are ruining a lot of their crops and their fields are turning into swamps. On the other hand, the heat is rising to a dramatic level and they are facing drought and don't even have enough water to drink. But the cows are still functioning and providing milk because they can survive in that level of heat."

Roland added, "I have heard that in some parts of Africa, if tribes have nothing to eat and they are starving and their cattle can't give milk as animals starve too due to the drought. They don't kill their cattle for meat but actually drain the blood from live cattle from their main arteries to survive until the rain comes and they can recover again to feed the people. Of course, for survival, people have eaten other human bodies too. Like in Australia, when British explorers were exploring or discovering the land, they had to survive on their fellow explorers' flesh when they were lost on the huge continent. How could they survive otherwise?"

Dani continued. "Even in Spiti and Ladakh in Himachal and Kashmir, they can only grow a single crop there in summer, and it used to be that the areas were cut off from rest of the world for around six months a year due to heavy snowfall, and they had no road or other connection with the outside. The area is a completely dry desert, and they can hardly grow any trees there, even in summer. Whenever they used to run out of food, they had to rely on dried meat, and when there was none left they had to eat their livestock. But I have heard stories that they used to feed their yaks really well in summer so that if they were in trouble in heavy winter, they could surrender the biggest yak to rescue the hungry community and pray for the summer to come. Even dead humans were fed to vultures so that they didn't kill or take their young goat kids. Cows in one form or another have stood by these people to help them survive for millennia, otherwise they could not live."

"But it must have changed a bit now, Dani?" asked Roland.

"Well yes, now they have got roads and air rescue services to deliver food in emergencies."

To make sense of all of this, Dani wanted to show Roland some cowsheds and how their cows lived in India. There were little stumps on the four corners of the square shed and also some stumps on the wall to tie up the cattle. The stumps were buried deep so the cows or oxen couldn't pull them up from the ground. Each cow was tied with a rope made out of the bark of a local *beaul* tree. Dani explained that when cows come back from the forest they all know their individual spot and will stand by their own spot or stump unless some food is around or they are up to some mischief. The ropes were handmade but quite strong. Dani explained that before the cows enter the shed they all go to the water trough and drink water. The shed was very clean and tidy, but not very flat, as there were usually a few holes in the soil together with some smooth inlaid stones. In some sheds they might even have some pictures of cows on the walls, and some bamboo sticks on the ceiling to hold bundles of grass for the cows to eat in winter.

Afterwards, inspecting the sheds they wandered down to the field behind and Dani pointed to a big heap of cow dung, which was collected in the lower field twice a day so it could be transported to another field every six months. All the collection and transportation was done by bamboo baskets carried on people's backs or even on their heads. Dani also showed him some *uple* (dung cakes) drying in the sun, which were used for making fires, as they were a good method of both for transporting fire and of keeping fire alive overnight. All the sticks were removed from the solid dung and then they were patted on the walls and stones so they could dry. They were made in one or two shapes – long and round like discs.

"The long ones last longer and are very good for transporting fire and are also used to produce smoke to get rid of insects and mosquitos in the summer, which helps cattle as well as humans and is a very old tradition. The round thin ones dry fast and are very efficient fuel for cooking fires. In the higher deserts of the Himalayas such as Spiti and Ladakh, they can't make *uples* because they don't have much dung or wood to utilise, so they just burn them in very small pieces, almost like sheep droppings."

Dani pointed at the fresh heap. "That heap is this year's compost for wheat and oats, which means we don't need any factories or machinery to produce fertiliser. So the cow is also a very important animal for our crops and fields. The very simple thing is that the cow eats the raw material from the field – what we cannot eat – and in turn produces food for us and for itself so we can work and plough and continue the cycle," Dani commented. "If every family had a cow in the West it would be the solution to many problems. There would be no food waste and no garden rubbish and no plastic milk bottles. They would keep it simple, tidy and healthy. They should forget the large-scale business of huge dairies and supermarkets or of mass production and modernising everything. Otherwise they will destroy everything small and make people useless and all the natural skills will be lost."

Roland agreed that mass production was affecting many parts of our lives, and he could see the importance of cows for humankind, but he had some more questions.

"What about worshipping cows? What happens to its body after its death?"

Dani explained. "There is a worshipping ritual once a year, and it is believed that cows are the only animals which can lead us from suffering to life. If we stand firmly with them (our ancestors talk about "holding their tail"), then we are led by them to a better life, not only in this life, but also in the next. It is a very old belief and many people also offer a cow with a calf as a charity to other families, which is a very highly regarded gift, because that action or ritual transforms lives for generations to come. That's why every year we have a cow festival, and a week before the festival, every mountain family sings songs of praise to these cows by the cowsheds, on each evening for a week. On the eighth day the cows are decorated with garlands and flowers and their bodies are marked with colours. That day is very special for them. The cows are taken to a common ground with music and lights made from burning sticks. Then there is a big bonfire and they are all let free and all the villagers sing and dance by the fire, but it happens very early, around 5.30 a.m. Drums and mountain pipes are played and the whole valley echoes with singing and drums. You see cattle jumping and running around in freedom. It seems that they know about it and it is a day of showing off and freedom for them. After a few hours they are brought home where there will be a big platform made of hay and grass and layered with green banana leaves topped with some cooked grains, such as oats, wheat and corn, as well as rice. As they arrive, all the cows eat from this platform together in the courtyard of every family. But before that a mother cow will be worshipped like you worship a deity – washing her feet and putting colour on her forehead and treating her with great respect. Once that has happened, all the other cattle will be allowed to eat at the platform. The family will sing and do rounds as if they are making the round of a holy and important shrine. At the same time, the family has lots of sweets and other special treats too to celebrate the festival.

"This is a great day of excitement. No one is allowed to work at all, even the farming tools. Oxen are freed too, but that also happens for every *Sakrat* on the first day of the month in the Hindu calendar, as well as for every festival and fair. Skrant is the name of the first day of the month, when the main lady of the house will clean the whole house and courtyard, wash the main doors, and then she worships the doorframes by offering *tika* or a coloured mark and flowers. They also worship the sun in the morning from the centre point of the courtyard, as marked by a red coloured stone or a tulsi (Himalayan basil) plant. None of the animals, such as horses, cows, oxen, donkeys or buffalos are allowed to work on these days, and even today many people still obey that law, so everyone gets to have a rest. It is considered uncivilised or sinful to make animals work during these rest days, but farmers and their animals will have no other holidays except these days plus weddings or other such celebrations. There is no Western habit of five days a week working and then lazing on the weekends. Work is considered worship and part of everyday life. The only pressure comes during the season from nature which requires harvesting or planting at the right time. The farmers start early, have a nap after lunch, and then simply carry on as the job dictates. So, the animals have their holidays alongside their humans, and I hope they enjoy them too!"

"What a life!" replied Roland. "What happens when the cows die?"

"It is extremely important in India that cows have to be respected. If someone kills a cow, that person can be killed by the public or put in prison or cast out from society. It is considered very serious, more serious than killing a human. It is acceptable if an ox is smacked or he kills a person with his horns. That ox will be punished or hit by sticks or sold, but no other punishment is permissible, because the ox has to live as long as it can naturally live. If the ox has some strange illness or goes mad, then in those cases, they are either starved to death or isolated and buried deep down with salt after their death. In the case where they die naturally, they are taken by an expert butcher from the village to a designated area. Such places already exist in every village, but are increasingly being taken over by modernisation and urban reconstruction. The butcher will skin them, by which time vultures will see and smell the body from the sky and attack in huge numbers, of maybe more than fifty or so and devour the body. As children, it used to be very exciting to watch this vultures gathering. The vultures would come very close to us, and they are really scary. Any leftover bones would then be taken by wild foxes, wolves and dogs.

"And so the body is disposed of. This process with the wild vultures is a very ancient tradition and vultures survive on that in the Himalayas and in India. Nowadays it is a problem for these birds, as many old animals are transported away from their homes far away to hidden slaughterhouses. Their carcass is sold abroad and the natural cycle is being destroyed. Vultures are forced to look for alternative food sources, which may not be sufficient. Going back to the cows, their skin is used for shoes and other leather products such as drums. So whenever we hear a mountain drum playing, it is that mother cow's skin. But they do not stop there. Cow's milk is running through our body as blood, and the next generation of their calves are pulling the plough and continuing to care for us. So they are truly mothers and we love them so much."

Roland was really very touched and noticed that Dani's eyes were filled with tears.

Dani went on. "Likewise, if we have a goat and we let her live, we can have lots of milk and more goats from her while she is alive. But if we kill her for her meat, how long can we eat off that goat? Of course, she will die one day and she can still provide her body then, but at least you will have a whole herd of maybe more then fifty goats by then.

"Due to climate change there are additional issues raised against killing millions of animals for their meat." Dani recalled a claim made on BBC News at Ten back in 2008,[1] when they announced that, "we can grow eight tonnes of grain for every ton of beef: it takes the same amount of water and land. It was shocking news when you bear in mind that eight million people in the world have no food every day. The BBC statement shows that meat eaters are effectively responsible for that, as people are not eating much grain and they consequently are growing less grain in Europe. Countless valuable fields are therefore left for a few meagre sheep to graze due to expensive farming techniques, which make them unaffordable to small arable farmers." Another article Dani recalled reading in 2009[2] in *The Standard* newspaper in the UK, "claimed that the vegetarian diet is less harmful to both nature and the climate than meat, and concluded that the UK should make a reduction in its meat livestock by thirty per cent. This is the movement for green policy. It means India is more advanced than the rest of the world as we have been operating this way for centuries. We don't even know who advised us and how our ancestors followed this principle but they did! This way of life is part of our culture and has been for many generations."

---

[1] 3 June 2008

[2] 27 Nov 2009

Now there are some block stamps with pictures of cows and oxen on them that were unearthed during the discovery of Mohan Jodorow, an old city and civilisation which is discovered to be between 3,000 and 12,000 years old.

"So it appears that this Indian way of life is even older than that," said Dani. "You will also find many statues of the cow and bull in temples all over India from 500 to 300 BC. But if we change this ancient way of life and start killing cows, maybe one day nature will turn against us, and instead of milk, cows may develop some nasty anti-human allergens which may be harmful to us."

"You mean like how lots of people nowadays are allergic to many types of food and even to animal feathers, hair or skin?" Roland replied.

"Well we will never know, Roland, but it's possible. So we do want to keep living in harmony with these cows as our friends and with nature as a whole," said Dani.

Dani continued: "Roland, to understand the depth of this bond with cows, we must look at the British history in India during the Raj. When Britain was at the height of its powers and had made a base in India, they had huge Indian armies and had won the hearts of the Indian people. Indians respected the British and the British officers were similarly taken with the lifestyles of the Indian maharajas. The officers were fascinated by the royal traditions and a friendship was slowly developing, but, in the end, these British officers were servants to their superiors back home and they had a job to do to keep law and order. Of course, there were some issues with tax and such like but gradually the British started taking over Indian kingdoms one by one. But India was not able to confront the British army or even ask them to leave. The British Empire was very powerful and widespread and they had a centralised system and power base which dictated how things were to be run."

"The sun never set on the British Empire!" added Roland.

"Yes, it is incredible that a little country like Britain was able to rule huge parts of the earth and have such an influence on the planet," Dani replied.

"But one thing the British did not pay attention to was the ancient Indian scriptures and traditions or its ancient history of warfare such as Ramayana and Mahabharata. They considered their traditions and lifestyle to be superior, and that the rest of the world was strange. They established clubs and churches in India and lived the way they lived in Europe. They introduced ballrooms and a hierarchy with the armies at the top and the missionaries at the bottom. They started shaping India for their benefit and comfort. Some British commanders were aware that Indian people worshipped cows and that Muslim people don't touch pork. But in order to destroy Indian faith and tradition they ignored this and pushed beef- and pork-fat gun cartridges on the Indian army. The big mistake was that men had to use their teeth and mouths on the cartridge before loading it. The day that was introduced, a fire started against the British and many Indians were ready to sacrifice their lives to fight against this huge empire. And all because of this belief in not killing cows. And to touch the meat of a deceased cow with the mouth is like the murder of their own mother, especially for a Hindu, and so because of this, one of the soldiers killed some British officers, and that was the first spark and the start of the 1857 mutiny against the British. Within ninety years of that spark, every single British person was out of India! So veneration for the holy cow was what made the Indian people realise that their British guests were not godlike at all, but were just hungry and greedy invaders. Once again, this rebellion happened not through war or violence, but through non-violence, by Mahatma Gandhi, something quite impossible and extraordinary in the context of the history of humankind."

By now, Dani's older sister, *Satya didi* (didi means sister), had produced tea and biscuits and *pakoras* she had bought from the local tea shop. While sipping his tea, Dani explained how Gandhi really did save the lives of thousands of British and Indian men through his policy of peaceful resistance and set an example for those who advocate peace in the world. "It is such a shame that some people have not found the wisdom and power of non-violence and that Gandhi's message has not gone through to those who are still trapped in terrible violence today," Roland added with a sigh.

"All those important decisions were being taken at a time when Europe was going through terrible massacres and suffering on a huge scale," said Dani. "Lives were being ruined, and young men were being forced to protect the desires of those who were merely thirsty for personal power and territorial power and who wanted to strip faraway countries of their resources, such as black pepper, chilli and spices from South India, coffee from Indonesia, tea from China and Darjeeling, and other treasures from distant terrains around the world."

Dani continued, "Consider World War One and World War Two. Every young man was forced to fight, and the retired were recalled for duty to lay down their lives for those in other European countries. New inventions, such as bombs, chemicals and bigger and better guns and flying machines were making them dance like a drunken monkey attempting to burn everything down. Millions of men lost their lives and acres of land mark the cemeteries and memorials of of those souls who lost their lives throughout Europe.

"Even women were forced to participate in the war effort and special home guards were formed to keep the nations' pride alive. Some of the boys who were flying and fighting on the frontline were as young as fifteen, and the lives of many horses and cattle were lost as many were caught up in the destruction. During these periods, Indian soldiers were fighting shoulder to shoulder with British forces, but with the approach of Mahatma Gandhi's non-cooperation movement, the British were falling short of them too. Those soldiers and spies from different battalions, like the Gurkhas, Rajputs and Sikhs, were masters in guerrilla warfare and experts in their own areas. They could easily turn around and go home, as British soldiers were nearly outnumbered anyway. British forces had experienced that shortage in the first mutiny of 1857, but they were lucky that they had a battalion on the way, which suppressed that first War of Independence. I believe that if Mahatma Gandhi had not embedded the idea of non-violence in the Indian soldiers' and leaders' minds after the First World War, there would have been awful bloodshed between the two forces within India.

"Mahatma Gandhi's movement and the idea of non-violent resistance avoided a huge loss for human kind, otherwise most British men serving in India would have suffered in the hands of an uprising of new India. The handful of British soldiers would not have been able to hold the forts for long. They were facing huge wars at home in Europe and thousands were being killed. I don't think that Churchill or anybody in authority fully understood what Gandhi had done to save the lives of British and Indian men.

He cannot be rewarded or honoured enough. I am sure many of these men who served in India, and their ancestors, are still grateful to Gandhi's non-violence, otherwise they would not be living. Of course, some hated the idea of going home, especially those who had adopted the way of the gentleman in India and were being looked after by native servants. Many of them moved to warmer parts of the continent after India. Nevertheless, the stories of death, and of men lost in the European wars, had created terror, and humankind was horrified, especially when the death toll of German and British solders kept rising. Not one single family was left undamaged by this war for hunger and power in many countries in Europe. These wars had also raised questions about Western civilisation and its governance or leadership, otherwise every well-off family in India was inspired to learn and behave like the 'Great' British.

"But those who were cheering the victories of wars, on cushioned seats with cigars and drinks, could only see Mahatma Gandhi as a little man with a walking stick. They could not see the greater meaning of non-violence or the values that Gandhi was advocating: self-sustainability and simple living for humankind. He was not just a spiritual or political leader, Gandhi was also a great thinker and environmentalist. His vision of sustainable development and simple living was one of the first to understand the impact of the global industrial race on the environment. To lead people to a sustainable lifestyle, he himself lived modestly in a self-sufficient traditional way. He warned against modern material prosperity and how this lifestyle would be a threat to the planet and its resources.

Dani explained that Mahatma Gandhi really had had a great vision; he had experienced the high life, the richness and comforts of Western life, but he recognised what was needed to lead the world towards peace and long life. He set an example by taking off all his machine-made suits and putting on a simple hand-spun cotton sheet. His ideology, of simple living and high thinking, and of sharing with truth and non-violence at its heart, was really a vision which could still help global issues today.

Mahatma Gandhi had quoted: "Earth provides enough to satisfy every man's need, but not every man's greed."

"Now maybe you can understand his way of life and why Gandhi lived a simple life in a small hut, with simple clothes spun by hand with a spinning wheel, and with wandering cows and goats for milk in a self-sufficient community," pointed out Dani.

Dani suggested, "The world will start changing when rich and famous world leaders like Obama or Prince Charles, or other famous European leaders, adopt Gandhi's ideology and stand shoulder to shoulder with the common man. Then climate change will be brought under control and the world can start moving forward in a different direction. How can a leader understand the problems of those who travel in a third-class train or in a local bus if he has never travelled on that himself? If we cannot leave home comforts or sophisticated suits and private jets to talk about climate change, it means we have not properly understood the problem, or Gandhi's legacy. He lived and showed us the path and we just need to follow his example. A meeting was taking place in Shimla before Independence, and Mahatma Gandhi was invited to stay at the Viceroy Lodge by the Governor General, but he refused to stay there, saying that his goat was accompanying him for fresh milk and he had arranged to stay at a alternative place. He did not use the *tanga* (rickshaw) either, as they used to be pulled by men, *tangawala* (rickshaw puller), and he preferred to walk, while other leaders could not stand that."

"So Gandhi really was an extraordinary man then?" Roland said.

Dani was in a different mood now and his mind was fully focused and every word was thought out, pronounced well and explained seriously. "Because the thing is that the desire for better clothing, cars or houses, holiday villas, private jets or yachts goes on, and in this rich circle, lifestyle changes to the higher and higher levels, and the struggle for discovering happiness in material things goes on till the man himself crumbles in this struggle, unless one has the contentment and resilience within for peace, and that can be achieved in a little hut too."

Roland could feel that every word he had said had a deep significance for him, and for Roland it was an awakening.

By now the sun had gone from the courtyard and it was only shining on the hills higher up. Dani said it was time to explore the other side of the village, where all the villagers took their cattle and goats to graze.

CHAPTER SIX

A traditional infrastructure

They went through the door of the courtyard towards the east and walked all the way along a newly built road through the village. A few houses were built from mud with slate roofs further up in the centre of the village. Dani pointed out that the old houses built from mud and wood were diminishing in numbers in the villages. Very simple houses made of mud, as well as many new cement houses, were being built instead.

"In the middle of this village," explained Dani, "there is a public area where people hang out – especially youngsters, or villagers passing by – and stop to catch up with news as well as have a rest. Here there are two trees and one of them is very old – several hundred years or more. Nobody really knows its age. They are called the pipal trees—"

"Or they could be called 'people' trees too," commented Roland.

"—as they provide a wonderful shelter from the sun, and their heart-shaped leaves provide great shadows and sounds, as the fluttering leaves blow in the summer heat."

"The older tree is an important tree and people are used to sitting in its shade on hot summer days," said Dani. "Many social gatherings and children's activities used to happen under these trees, and to sit under this tree is truly very pleasant and people don't want to leave its shelter or company, especially during the hot summer."

There were also a few yellow, brown and dry grey leaves around on the ground, a reminder that autumn was leaving and winter was on its way.

"There are two raised platforms built under each pipal tree, where people sit. They are built with local stone covered with cement and they give a good base and protection to the tree's stem and to its roots. These platforms also provide a good height of two to three feet, so that people can sit high off the ground, as the fear of snakes and scorpions is always there. Traditionally, all the village, *panchyat* (council) or other big meetings and gatherings used to happen under these trees, but sadly those have now shifted to government-funded small rooms, built with cement," Dani said.

"Alas! Leaving these wonderful open places behind," Roland exclaimed.

They sat under the smaller, younger tree, which was close to the road, and there was a small rectangular-shaped water trough built on the left side, which had a tapless water pipe, blocked with a wooden stick wrapped with a piece of cloth in a way so that it could still drip some water into the trough, which maintained the water level for passing cows, goats, sheep, horses and ponies, who could also drink from it around the clock. Under the big old tree, to its left side, villagers had dug a wide hole, and Dani found out from his friends who were sitting on the platform that they were building a water storage tank for irrigating the fields in and around the village.

They were looking at some little mud houses nearby, and Dani explained how simple and less expensive they were and still are to build.

"People used to get together from each family and all they needed were a few stones for the foundation and a good pile of mud or soil dug out from close to the spot in the local area to build the mud walls. It was a very quick and economic method. They didn't buy a single thing from outside the village or any machine-made equipment or materials. To build the mud walls was a real skill, and they had to have an expert carpenter from their village, or from a different village, who was able to build these mud houses. The timing was arranged well in advance to avoid harvesting or other busy times on the farms, like sowing or ploughing or weeding, so that at least one member of each family could come to help, and the days were divided into shifts – who is coming when – like a modern rota for jobs. It was very normal, and still is in some remote villages, to see these kinds of common events of building houses, walls, taking a tree down, wood splitting, and cleaning and clearing water irrigation channels (*kools*). But it was quite a hard job to carry mud in bamboo baskets as the walls grew higher and higher. So often other villagers and relatives used to get together to help. But these were also social occasions and people used to chat and catch up with each other as well.

"The walls were built in rectangular blocks. They would use two big wooden boards about six feet long and two feet wide fixed together with some bamboo sticks and batons, a parallel distance apart, as thick as you want the wall, one and half feet or a maximum of two feet high. Then you filled them with soil or mud and stamped or patted it with specially made long wooden logs. The patting job is quite easy but you need strength in your arms, and women are very good at this. This would continue until you completed one layer. Then, after resting for a bit, you would change the wooden boards and start a second layer, and so on and so forth until the whole wall is finished. Modifications and adjustments are needed to cut corners as you go higher, and men are good to lift and supply the bamboo baskets full of mud up the ladder.

"So the process required skill and would take a few days depending on how big the house was. The wonderful thing about these mud walls is that they have very natural insulation, and are warmer in winter and cooler in the summer's heat. People have lived happily for centuries this way and, of course, they design them differently for hot and cold climates so that air can circulate well in summer, or, in winter, less air can come in or escape due to the small windows."

Roland mentioned that insulation was a big thing now in England and everyone was talking about cutting energy bills by saving energy. Bills were rising and he could see that the way people had adjusted their lifestyle in this Himalayan valley was quite relevant to the adjustment necessary in Western lifestyles.

"Maybe the causes are different, but the aim is the same – a natural comfortable life without too much trouble."

It was really interesting for Roland to find out the parallels between the old ways, where they survived by making adjustments to their whole lifestyle, and how similar adjustments were made in the modern world to save energy today.

"Now," Dani said, "We'd better carry on exploring."

As they continued to walk, he explained that once the mud walls were ready, covering them up was the next important step and sometimes, due to rain, all the hard work could be spoiled immediately, as protecting the mud walls with slate or wooden boards was a difficult thing to do and even that process had to be planned very much in advance.

"Sometimes they will wait for particular trees to grow well, so that they have some trees ready in their fields to cut to produce good wood for window frames and door frames and for roofing or furniture.

"All the carpentry happens by hand, which is a very interesting process for outsiders to witness. They use axes and handsaws, which are used by two to four people at a time, to split big logs into boards and frames, then bamboo or thinner wooden battens to lay the slate or straw roof on top, or more commonly nowadays metal sheets and plastic sheets, which are very quick and good protection but not very attractive unless they are painted with suitable colours.

"Slates always come from nearby villages, but it can involve a two-hour car journey these days, which in the past would be one day by horse or mule. The thick short straw is plentiful in nearby hills, but they have to store it in advance and know what type of straw they need – thick, or just the thin straw from the hills. One is just a local grass called *jhinjara* and the second is called short. Short is very tall, the straws are like five or six feet high and quite thick, like pencils, and are hollow, which helps a lot with insulation, while *jhinjara* is very thin and hardly two feet high, but can be carried from as far away as two to three hours on foot. But to build thatched roofs, they really need someone who knows the techniques and has the skills to set and tie the grass with natural bark and bamboo so that it doesn't leak in monsoons.

"After that, they get some more clay-type soil from nearby local mines or fields. They mix it with the cow dung and some very thin-cut straw or grass called *munji*. Once the walls are dry and hard, they fill the holes and plaster the wall with that clay by hand. It's all done without the need to use protective gloves or any tools or equipment as it contains no chemicals or dangerous products. But every care is taken to filter and sieve the soil before turning it into the clay dows. Brushes are made from naturally grown *munji* from their own fields.

"Once that is dry in a few days' time, they will then make handmade brushes and the walls will again be painted with local mud with natural colours – red, brown, grey, black or white – using soil from the common land in the village. Different coloured mud will be available in different villages. So, from village to village the colours of houses can vary. But sometimes, if it is a main house and they want to make a big effort, they may do a day's journey on foot to a popular mine in a nearby village and carry a full sack of red or white soil home on their head or in a bamboo basket in order to make their house different.

"Black or *kala* colour was used only for borders. Often people used to have one- or two-feet borders at the bottom of each wall, as the lower part of the wall was prone to be damaged. But this fashion for borders is now almost dying out. Some of the remote villages still keep that art alive, especially in some of the traditional villages in the mountains, as well as in Rajasthan, where they even paint animal shapes or flower designs on the walls. Sometimes, during festivals, like the Diwali festival of light or during Shivaratri in the Himalayas, they do some special wall paintings for worshipping Laxmi, the goddess of wealth and prosperity, and of Lord Shiva. Those paintings vary from area to area, but more or less the style found in the oldest cave paintings."

Roland mused, "Nowadays, people don't have to do any of these basic chores or jobs at all."

"Yes, Roland," Dani explained, "they don't even know about it anymore. They just go to the hardware shop and buy any colour they want. There are no limits and the world has become a very colourful place. But it is all made in huge machines and produced on a mass scale. To build houses or just to paint them is a very expensive thing to do. Modern houses can't be built from village materials anymore and they have to buy everything from the outside world at huge expense – bricks, cement, iron, even sand, wood, modern handles, hinges and nails, while local blacksmiths and skilled men are no longer utilised. Modern people have lost some of that real knowledge and often these new buildings are dangerous in earthquakes.

"I can't stand the smell of paint, especially wood paint. Before, I was not used to it and they did not paint the wood in the villages, they just used to treat it in various ways, like burying wood in cow dung or in goats' sheds so that animal dung or urine would treat it naturally for six months or for a year. Alternatively, they used to dip it into mixed liquids such as cow or goat urine or dung heaps or apply some natural oil on the wood to help its long life, without spending any money on treatments. Now we cannot understand where the money goes.

"Although villagers have realised that cement houses are hot in summer and cold in winter, the fashion remains for cement houses, which are hard for living in, unless they have all the modern facilities like carpets, rugs, air conditioning or central heating. Some still prefer their old kitchens with a fire and soil-layered floor! The flooring in the traditional houses is always made with cow dung and soil, so it is very soft to step on barefoot. This is important as they don't allow shoes in their kitchens or in worship or prayer rooms all around India. No excuse of any kind is accepted."

Roland said, "This is understandable, as you don't want to take any unwanted mud or dirt inside and shoes might even damage the floor. So they feel much more comfortable on a soft mud floor, whereas in a modern cement house they cannot walk barefoot as they are freezing in winter and hot in summer."

"This is creating lots of health issues for villagers, and they complain that times have changed and that it was never like this, that they lived without fans or heaters in the old days. But many have forgotten that those old houses were built of mud," said Dani.

As they walked, Dani pointed out some older boys on the way because they had been his students when he lived here and he used to give them tuition in maths and English. Dani loved teaching and started part-time teaching when he was only twelve to make some money, and people were always approaching him and requesting him to teach or give some time to their children.

"In one way, it was not a good idea, because sometimes it used to be too much for me – seven or eight students and all from different classes learning maths or English. By the time I used to get home my mind was too tired to do my own studies. Some of the families have still not been able to pay me, as they are too poor. But I don't mind."

He said with a smile, "Some people were poor, so I did not even mention it, but some had money and very selfishly just used to think about themselves. They did not think about my time or my study; that was my problem. My parents were very innocent and just proud that their son was in demand and that other parents loved him, and I could learn more by teaching others. I did not consider that I should just do my own studies and achieve more for myself. My mother did warn me, but they never got worried about me. They thought I would always pass, so it was fine. They were more worried about my other brothers and sisters. Well, to give knowledge is a great gift and I have done that. The fee is just a token. But all of my students still pay respect to me today and that is quite rewarding.

"Well, we better keep moving, otherwise we will miss the sunset," Dani said.

They met a few boys and shook hands with them to say hello.

"It seems people love shaking hands in India. Something else left by the British," said Roland.

"In India they used to just say '*Namaste*' while joining both palms in a respectful way and bending the head in humble respect. The main part of the '*Namaste*' is not to smile, but to offer full awareness and respect to the other person, and by doing this one should obtain a stillness in breath and even in the mind, because if the breath is still, the mind is still. That's how it's supposed to benefit the person who is offering the greetings. If someone is worthy of even greater respect, such as an elderly relative, you have to touch their feet. This still happens everywhere in India," explained Dani.

Roland could see this practice within the family. Dani further explained that it is seen as a way to kill the ego, and a way to learn to respect the elderly.

"Also, of course, bending down a few times a day is healthy and will send blood to your heart and face. They always say that one changes his forehead lines or fortune by receiving many blessings while touching the feet of the elderly," said Dani.

Roland commented that even in England, the main way of greeting was to say "Good morning", "Good afternoon" and "Good evening". They pondered the question of whether hand shaking was even a healthy thing to do, as many germs and bacteria are transmitted or passed around through this touching of hands.

"Maybe in the old days, when there was the 'prevention is better than cure' attitude, it was good to avoid touching hands," said Roland, "but nowadays it has become the custom, and some people may shake hands with hundreds of people a day. It could be lethal in the case of deadly viruses such as Ebola." Roland was grateful that he was only shaking the right hand in India! At least he knew their right hand was a bit safer!

Dani had his own question to ask. He wondered why people in England say "cheers" when they drink. Roland suggested that it was for good health, or like "hurray!" But Dani had a twisted Indian answer to his question.

"To affect your sense of hearing!"

"What?" said Roland. "I don't understand? Can you explain what you mean?"

"Well, if you want to fully affect the mind you have to affect all the senses first, and then your mind will definitely be affected. So, first you see the drink coming and you start relaxing. Second, you will be touching the glass. Third, you will be smelling it, and then, finally, tasting it, but to hear it you have to say 'cheers!' So all senses are affected and thereby the mind is also affected. Well that's my theory! If you are alone and you pour it yourself, then you can hear it anyway, you don't have to say cheers."

Roland was amused and thought that it was a good drinking joke.

"Sorry, this is a made-up joke," Dani said, "but in a traditional way they say that senses are affected by material or matter, and to control senses one has to control or adjust the matter sense. Moderation in materials or matter could calm the senses."

"Yes, that's for sure, as environment and company definitely has an effect," Roland replied.

By now they had left the village long behind. They zigzagged through the hills and had to climb a little to the top of a hill to sit down to enjoy the sunset. The sky was getting red in the west and the sun was setting. The sun was still shining on the nearby hills and on them, but they could see the shadows covering the villages lower down in the valley. It was very beautiful and peaceful.

All this experience of a local family and their way of life in this beautiful Himalayan valley was fascinating to Roland. At first he couldn't imagine what kind of lifestyle was going on inside the small houses in the valley, but now it was all making sense to him, and he could almost imagine the first explorers walking up by the river and discovering the valley.

From where they were sitting they could see a village called Suni on the other side of the river. Dani said that there were big changes happening there. One was the hydroelectric dam project being built on the Satluj River and the second was a proposal for a cement factory.

"This river will be flooded by the dam and a big lake will be created near the village in Tattapani. There are big companies and firms involved in the development of these projects and they have paid a lot to those who have lost their land in the process. That money sounded very big, but in time they will not be able to buy the same amount of land with it. Money has affected the whole valley, and the cost of land has multiplied. People are building big cement buildings, buying fancy cars and living the life of their dreams as portrayed in television programmes while others are being displaced.

"Not only all that, but I'm worried that having a big lake nearby will encourage new birds to the area and our own native birds will be affected by it all. So not only people but birds, animals and other small creatures will be affected by these changes."

"But if the lake is beautiful, lots of tourists will be exploring the whole valley," said Roland. "So it depends how you look at it, Dani. In one way maybe it is a big change, but it will create some other sources of income in the valley. At some time change would have to happen to provide electricity to all these people around India, so that those who don't have a single light bulb, and study by candlelight, will have light."

Dani agreed, but questioned what was best in the long term for the planet.

"What is better for this little valley? I am sure it will give light to many, but because our desires are never-ending, soon these people will want many bulbs in one room, televisions, refrigerators, air conditioning, heating and much more, and they will also lose their own basic way of surviving and living," he said. "If a balance is not created or these technologies are not used in moderation, it will be a disaster for the human race.

"We somehow have got this idea that without modern facilities we cannot survive," said Dani. "But we have been living like this for thousands of years. We happily did what was needed of us and found ways to survive as well as enjoy life. All over the world we had a simple way of life, but if you now see London or any other big city in the world, you just see people rushing about, running here and there, travelling by underground or overground trains or by plane. Even the smartest, richest and most important man dressed in a suit and carrying an umbrella and suitcase in his hand is also behaving like a victim, as if he is being chased or hunted by a tiger, and he is about to lose his life. I really mean it. Just go to Waterloo Station in London and watch. I would have thought that if someone is that advanced, with the best cloths money can buy, that he should be walking with great pride and in a composed manner. But you see them all running and looking at the boards for trains and platforms, and at the same time looking around nervously at his neighbours. Or sometimes there is terrible news about knife crimes and bombs and loud announcements about suspicious lugguage and it makes one run faster and faster. It's like a hamster on a treadmill while at the same time trying to keep his eyes open for a bigger predator, that kind of rush and urgency."

Roland laughed. "That's what I used to feel whenever I visited London. Why are they running? Sometimes they even have a sandwich in one hand, or a drink, trying to run, eat and protect themselves from the crowd and not to miss the train. If you are two seconds late, the train's automatic door is shut, and you see their faces getting pale. But they just don't look happy, but sadly the truth is you soon get used to it, Dani."

"Modern men are made to think that's what the great life is – a big job and expensive clothes and having all the luxuries," said Dani. "That's why they are all rushing. Certain dreams and models are created by people and they are all trying to achieve and maintain those dreams at a huge cost."

Dani pointed at a very open and rocky area and said that the cement factory developers wanted to convert all the rocks into powder and also dig into the mountains because there are lots of valuable rocks inside.

"So if that happens they are going to destroy the hills and mountains around this region and also the creatures and animals living inside them. That hill, for example, is a big shelter for vultures," he said, pointing at a hill to the north with a very old wooden-built shrine on the top. "They will pay money to remove everything, even villages. Some villagers are looking forward to it because they would rather live in big cement houses and live a modern lifestyle like they see on the television. So local life and local ways will be forgotten. I believe that there is a fine eco balance and that's how these mountains are formed in the first place. This is home to thousands of creatures and animals as well as people who have a basic and healthy lifestyle and community here and all will be destroyed."

Roland agreed. "They don't realise that their own ancient system is a much more advanced system than many other eco-friendly communities of the world. This is truly a form of madness."

"So this will change too, this flat plateau and the jungle, and yes it may provide cement to many slums or poor people, but the thirst for this is generated from big companies," said Dani. "It is from big rich organisations who can see millions of dollars of profit in this whole project. They look at the figures and these factors do not occur to them, because they will be dining in Paris or London in famous hotels. They don't want to think about the consequences. They will be discussing their multimillion dollar deals over champagne and wine, and then the deal is done. That is the pity. Because if those people were living like Gandhi and saying, 'I am happy, this is all for my fellow people, or future generations', that would be good. They don't care about climate change or the poor dying, as long as they have the lifestyle they crave. They will fly from one country to another and they will buy a new palace in a safer place removed from the changes they have imposed, or even make further plans to migrate for good."

"But that may not be long, Dani," Roland said. "If we have lost the earth, that's it."

"Meanwhile these poor people in the villages will be robbed. They will have no fields, and they will all have to face the consequences of floods and the heat and cold. By then their generations will have forgotten how to make a wooden plough or how to grow any crops and the knowledge and skills necessary to know what to grow. Once the big organisations have used all the stones, they will leave the valley in a very different shape.

"Well, we better enjoy the sunset. When we come again this hill may not be here to sit on once the factory and dam project are here," said Dani.

The sky was all yellow and the sun was looking like a red moon, and suddenly all the colours were changing and the whole valley was in shadow, though they could still see the river.

They started to climb higher and could see the whole forest divided with a vast rocky area and with trees and bushes to the other side. "There are lots of wildlife in those bushes – wolves, deer, wild boar, tigers, and snakes like cobra and Burmese pythons, as well as peacocks and many other birds," said Dani. In the distance he pointed out a compound bordered with stone walls with lots of green trees in it. They could see it very clearly as other areas around it were very rocky and without many trees.

"That was an old settlement of shepherds living with their goats and cattle in stone and mud houses. More than a hundred years ago this jungle was full of big trees and wild animals. They used to have tigers, cheetahs and snow leopards and they used to lose lots of animals to them. Some wild animals still live in these jungles.

"So they finally moved from there to a village lower down called Dagao," said Dani, "which was safer. All those wild animals will find it difficult to survive without the jungle now.

"Once the new factory takes over that ruin and site will disappear as well, which will be a great shame.

"There are also *ajgar* (Burmese python) in this jungle. They are very rare. A few boys saw one attacking a goat, and they said his stomach was full, but he still killed the goat. At the moment they are deep inside the jungle and can't move much as they are heavy. But if they build this new lake, it could be a disaster as pythons can move very fast in water and they could really create problems for the lakeside villages in future."

"Like the anaconda, you mean?" Roland said, "Oh God, that wouldn't be good."

"At the moment the river water is icy cold as well as fast-flowing and they don't like it, but they may get used to the lake temperature."

Dani really hoped that it wouldn't happen, and Roland realised how challenging life was here, to live side by side with these dangerous animals.

"If the factory happens then it will definitely drive all the animals out to urban areas. But for now it's not certain that the factory will take place as some local villagers are against it."

Roland wondered why the whole area was full of rocks and boulders and why the landscape was so unusual.

Dani told him the story of *Dhar Giri* (*Dhur* means "hill", "range" or "mountain", and *Giri* means "fall" in local dialects). He pointed at all the rocky landscapes and huge boulders in the distance.

"There are boulders which are bigger than double decker buses and which are there as if dropped from the sky. They are spread over hundreds of acres. Near the villages they are taken for building houses and locals have also created fields. But much deeper in that area, there are plenty of rocks. The story is that there was a big palace of a local king, and he was asked by the local *deo*, or deity, to come up to the temple, which was on top of the hill. But he refused and said that his horse was not able to carry him up there. After that, whenever his daughter-in-law used to go outside the kitchen in the open after dinner to clean dishes, the myth is that she used to hear a sound, 'Can I fall, can I fall?' – '*Padu, padu*' in the local language. It was happening very frequently, so once she reported it to the king and he asked her to say yes when next asked the question. That evening, she said yes and there was a huge bang and the whole mountain fell. There were lots of efforts to dig them out and save them as people kept hearing the sounds of drums under the rubble indicating where to dig, but sadly they all died, except one of the king's chief secretaries, called Munshi, who had left the palace and was on top of the hill, so he was safe and later recounted the story. But in reality, nobody knows what really happened. Did a mountain collapse, or was there a cloudburst or a volcanic explosion? Something did happen in this valley, even stories say that this big river, Satluj, was lost for a few days, and it has changed its path too. During some spiritual rituals and shamanic ceremonies, they refer to a date around AD 1292. But looking at this landscape, it definitely looks like there had been a huge cloudburst or explosion at some point, because most of the heavy boulders are neat and clean, and left in various places, and the rest of the smaller stones and soil have been transported further down into different places. There are around five or six huge holes and five or six hills created, which seems like there were five or six huge gushes of water in different places at once. If this is true then it sounds like a really catastrophic event, which must have created floods as high as eighty feet in the river valley. Landscapes do tell their own stories, and it would be interesting if governments could do some research on these rocks and landscapes.

"There are mainly two types of stone here. One is blue, which is almost like flint and very heavy, and the other is quite light and not that strong or heavy. There is also a mixed one which looks like it comes from the sea or riverside. So it is really a very interesting story and event."

By now, as they watched the scenery from the top of the hill, shadows had taken over the whole landscape and the view was fading away in the distance. There was no more sun and the sky was still changing colour. Everything was calm and they could see that lots of goats and cows were coming towards the main path from the forest.

"Look," said Dani, "that's what all the young students do before and after school. They all come to garage their cattle and take them home in the evening."

All the goats were rushing to the main path in a queue, and some of them were still trying to nibble at the leaves of small bushes. Boys and girls were following them too. Some of the children were carrying bundles of sticks on their heads, which was, of course, firewood to cook food, collected by them while looking after their animals. It reminded Dani of his childhood and all the chores he used to do too.

Dani said the goats and cattle belonged to different families and they all knew their way home. "The children just have to make sure that they don't go to the fields and ruin the crops. It is really interesting, because they will all go straight to their homes and then to their own spot in the shed, where they will be tied to their stump with a rope. I used to do that in my childhood. Let's follow them."

So they walked down the hill and started to walk home as it was getting dark and cold too. On the way they could see many small herds of goats and cattle disappearing on small paths leading to different houses. It was the winter season now for them and the sun was setting early too.

Once again, they passed a group of young people on the same platform under the tree, sitting and chatting, as well as some older people wearing thick wool blankets or shawls covering them. Dani explained that people always have a thick blanket for winter as well as a woollen hat and a woollen jacket.

"Young people hardly use these as they think it is old-fashioned. They like to dress in an imported jacket of a more modern style, because that is cool for them or else they will just be in T-shirts. So if they do make some money they spend it all on imported products. The money goes to big companies in big cities, and poor villagers and craftsmen can hardly sell their products or live. So many of these skills are dying as young people have no interest, or there is a race to get machine-made products. Somehow the modern system of marketing serves only rich companies, and it is sad that no one has started a system which can support the skilled craftsmen in the villages. All the money is going out of these villages while they buy televisions, paint, packed snacks, cheap imported clothes, refrigerators, plastic ropes and machine-made farming tools, like metal ploughs and tractors – and much more is spent on these things. Many old ways and skills are now on the edge of extinction in the villages. Schools only teach modern education, and students can't learn how to make pottery, wooden or bamboo tools or handicrafts in these villages.

"A new fashion is mobile phones, which are useful, of course, but one family can have many mobiles and everyone wants to have a mobile, so big phone companies are making huge profits in India. They have businesses worth millions and they have made it solely on mobiles. A person would rather ring their brother upstairs from the kitchen than walk and talk to him. Even children don't interact with friends or parents anymore, when a call does the job. Youngsters are seen on phones all around the globe, so most of their earnings go on the latest technology, and there are a very small number of people who are reaping this wealth, widening the gap between the rich and the poor. How much of any profit is put into charitable community projects or development is debatable.

"Fifteen years ago they didn't know about these things. Computers and the internet were new inventions and since then they hardly move out of their houses. Farming is being left to the older people and soon young people will have no idea about how to survive. This modern race is no good for humanity. Farming is decreasing due to the lack of rain and changing climate, as well as because people are not that hard-working now as they depend more and more on machines and air-conditioned rooms. Those old skills are dying and young people have no training for old skills such as ploughing. They should include these topics in schools, and that could provide employment to old skilled people in the villages – how to make a wooden plough, how to make a clay pot or how to grow certain plants and crops in their villages."

Dani was questioning whether this could be called real development – losing all the old know-how and depending on machines. "It seems that there is no awareness about the old techniques in the villages," said Dani. "Locals are always embarrassed to show off their own traditions or old ways of doing things and teachers do the same. This is because rich people market imported products, which makes locals feel small. Therefore they can't be proud of their old ways as they are considered backward and to revive them or apply them to their technical studies in schools could be a brave step. But it's not considered modern, and the fashionable things to study are technology or other modern subjects. Schools should encourage handicrafts and technical village skills, so children can learn about them – instead of simply neglecting them without understanding or recognising their value. It is not even in their syllabus, let alone having visits to flour mills or farms, so how can that be revived? You can hardly find any carpenters to make a wooden plough or tools in the villages or people who know how to look after cows, goats, sheep or various crops in the villages. Of course, science provides tremendous advances in our lives, but it doesn't mean that they should completely forget the age-old ways which have helped the human race to survive for centuries in the Himalayas. They should not be mutually exclusive."

Dani said. "People prefer to go to the shops and buy everything these days. The modern generation of India wants to leave these villages and farms, and move to cities, to little flats, where they hardly need to move or walk, everything within a few steps – bathroom, kitchen and shops nearby. Very often they have most things in one room, their world becomes one room. Living in one flat, working hard, but due to a lack of space, exercise and fresh air, they may end up with all sorts of illnesses and end up living on medication for life, and in pain, especially those husbands and wives who have no jobs and have to stay at home. All they do is sit by the television. Again, they need more and more money to support that kind of lifestyle, which all depends on modern machines. This is often completely opposite to the lifestyle they had in villages as children."

All the animals were walking together, excited to get home. They had retraced their steps, past the same houses and the big pipal trees and had now arrived home.

Tigger, the family dog, was welcoming them with his barking, alerting the family on their arrival. Dani's niece, Radhika, opened the door and they went in. Now it was time for a cup of tea, and Roland and Dani joined everyone in the kitchen.

Dani's sister made some *chai* and they all had some roasted corn on the cob. Dani said that those were the last corn they had and that the rest would all be dried for flour.

There was a lovely fire again made with very thin sticks and one big piece of thicker wood. Roland pointed at the thick wood to Dani, as he was expecting thin sticks. Dani told him that the family had recently changed the roof on the cowsheds and they had some leftover old wood which they were going to use that winter to burn.

The heat was wonderful and all the children had started to wash their feet in the brass bowl, one by one, which they kept filling from the copper bowl on the oven.

In the end it was Roland's turn, so he washed his feet which he found really pleasurable in the warm water. Dani was commenting that feet are the most important part of the body.

Once they had all finished washing their feet, they warmed them around the fire after drying them with a towel, and then Dani invited Roland upstairs where all the children were gathered. All the ladies and older men were getting on with their jobs with the cattle, milking cows and closing doors, and one of the sisters-in-law was cooking in the kitchen, and another of the sisters was looking after the baby. It seemed like everyone had their own job and everything was organised very well.

All was quiet and the children were sitting on a mat as Roland entered the room upstairs. They offered him a seat on one of the cushions on the mat. He sat down with everyone but wasn't sure what was happening. There were drums and some other musical instruments nearby, so he thought there might be some singing and dancing.

And so there was! Dani played the drums and the others played the bells and various other instruments. They spent around thirty minutes singing, and before and during the singing Dani explained that this was their evening prayers and always took place before the children went to do their studying or homework. They were also chanting mantras in Sanskrit language, which sounded almost like poetry.

After the prayers they were all quiet for a moment, and then they had sweets and the children walked out after bowing their head to the main *oata*, where there were decorated deities on a shelf about two to three foot high. One of the statues was a few hundred years old. It was of the third incarnation of the Vishnu the Brah or Varaha avatar, half-boar and half-human, again from the line of ten Avatars of Vishnu. Dani said it was the best way to forget the day and clear the mind, so they could get on with their homework and all have a good evening.

"It is a very old tradition to get together like this after a day's work to convert our emotions from the whole day, good and bad, into devotion to the divine. Music is a good tool to clear or balance the mind as well as to reach something higher, which is beyond, absolute, unseen, unexplainable, to the creator or director of the earth and its movements as well as beyond the planets. The only example we have of that vital force is the Sun. We all know that the Sun is the main source of energy and that water is life. That's why we start our day with a salute to Mother Earth, Mother holy Ganges, or the water and the Sun," explained Dani. "These are very important for us, as well as some devotional singing and chanting. It is all to make us feel better, peaceful and happy. Food is good for the body, but devotional singing is the food of the soul. It is like after death in our culture, we believe that the soul lives around the house for ten days. To provide the food and water to that soul, there is a special ritual or ceremony. You hang a clay pot called *Baldu* full of water from where drops fall through a small string from a little hole onto the oat seeds planted in sand below. That goes on for ten days, together with other rituals, and the oats grow to three or four inches high before the soul departs from the earth. For those nine or ten days, that essence or aroma of the damp oats and water provide the food and drink for the soul. In that sense, devotional singing is food for the soul."

Roland asked, "What is the significance of the incense, flowers, bells and a flame?"

"All of these ceremonies and rituals involve the process of clearing the mind and bringing peace and blissfulness to our self. There are three ways to feel good. First is physical comfort, like washing your feet to remove tiredness, or sitting on a good seat to make our body comfortable. Once the body is accommodated then we can use the process to calm the mind through our senses. The information or messages the senses send can affect the mind. If you hear dancing music you feel the need to dance and if we see something fearful we get scared. Similarly, sitting in a quiet place creates calm for our minds. You see these incenses? They are to remove all the bad smells and to bring special and uplifting smells to our nose, because this sense is also very important. If we smell something strange, we cannot be peaceful. It will irritate us and trouble the mind. Once the mind is calm then we have this candle or *jyoti* created from cotton wool and *ghee*. This is to concentrate the mind as well as a reminder of the true light within us. According to the tradition, the light we see outside is not the real light – that is darkness, a bubble of desires, ever-changing illusion – and the real light is within us. That's why this is a reminder that real light, absolute energy, is within. Outside is full of illusion, both good and bad, and is impermanent. It is the whole drama of the cosmos which is ever-changing. But if the inner is stable, then you are the winner. Otherwise one may be sitting still, but his mind or inner self can be restless or disturbed, which can happen anywhere, in a hut or in a palace.

"If you go to any traditional temple, you will find that there are no windows at the *garbhagriha* (main shrine of the temple). That's so that there can be only you, your deity, and the flame in the middle. So the energy and force is being conceived directly by you as you face that candle and deity. Again it acts as a constant reminder that the life force is within you and it is nowhere else, and you receive it directly, so that energy can't escape, but connects you directly … to whom? To the real self within.

"As we sing, chant and play the bells, it transforms our emotions and clears our mind," said Dani. "As the flame moves and dances, our thoughts and mind flows, and unwanted and uninvited thoughts will fly away. By conceiving those sounds, the light and vibrations, you close your eyes and everything stops. Complete inner silence. That's the crucial moment that has to be experienced. When your mind is still, you are not crying, singing, dancing, sleeping, talking, eating, drinking or doing anything, but you are just still in every way, physically and metaphysically. That's the moment of being 'in the moment'. Once the mind, body and within is in balance, all is peaceful and blissful. No more desires or wishes arise but just a feeling of being happy in that moment. That's the whole idea behind all the spiritual rituals of the old traditions. He who obtains that peace becomes the happy one, and he is free from day-to-day dramas or suffering and he becomes generous hearted. We believe that the supreme God, or divine, is within us, and through our actions we can change most of the things in life, and our future will be according to our actions or karma. For us, God is not sitting on a cloud and making music or helping people. If he would be that giving, he would have created a very fair and equal society. But, take a child being born to a starving or dying mother in Africa on the one side, and on the other side a child is born in the lap of a rich queen, as a prince, who finds every comfort in the world for him. Through our belief in karma a beggar can become a king and a prince can become a beggar by his own actions – that is the theory of karma in India," said Dani.

Dani was lost in his conversation. "Roland, you may not believe it but I had an incredible experience in my childhood with regard to karma. It was a hot summer's day in June, and in the afternoon even the stones were boiling hot to step on with bare feet. This is the time of year when people are praying for the monsoons in the coming months. It is the time when children under eleven years old will go to school in the early morning at eight and come back home in the afternoon at two. On the way back home they pick some figs and walk in groups. I must have been around nine years old at the time, but we were already aware of snakes and other wild animals. If we used to see any such animals it used to be a big story to tell our parents or older brothers and sisters when we got home. When you go home for tea that's when parents or family are often having their afternoon nap. So they don't bother coming to the kitchen. We were two brothers in the same primary school, so we used to arrive at home together before our older brother and sister, who had to go to a senior school in Suni. *Amma ji* (mother) or *Dadi ji* (paternal granny) would shout from the balcony to help ourselves from the kitchen, and the best advice was that '*Beta dusre ke hisse main kabhi hissa nahi dharna chahiye*', which means, 'One should not desire any share from someone else's share', which means that all the food, bread and milk or curd should be divided in four and it should not be the first in that gets all, and the last one will have nothing.

"Anyway, it was about this time when I learned about the chanting. I don't remember how exactly, but maybe it was from the stories of the elders in the forest. They used to make many statues of Lord Shiva, the main Hindu god, known as the superconscious, or the principle of nature, or the transformer, who liberates and leads one from suffering to new life. He always has a snake around his neck, always, and lives without any possessions, like a *sadhu*, or ascetic, in the coldest and snowy kingdom. His consort is called Parvati, or Shakti (known as the vital energy or force of nature). They both balance the whole universe. Together they are complete.

"I must tell you that way before the Aryans arrived in the Himalayas there were certain old tribes like Dasyu and Nagas and a few others. They were Nag worshipers, and *Nag* means snake. There were also lots of stories of human serpent-like traits, Nagas marrying other races like Khash and Cole, who came later to the region from today's Iran or the Middle East. This was happening even way after the Mahabharata period, between 2,500 BC and 1,000 BC and up till now."

Roland interrupted, "So you are talking about 3,000 to 4,500 years before now?"

"Yes, Roland, these were the earliest tribes. Nagas were considered nature spirits and the protectors of jungles, springs, hills, rivers, temples and caves, and were regarded as the guardians of treasures. There are still many temples dedicated to Nagas in the mountains, like Mahunag in the Karsog Valley and Nag temple in Sangla Valley in Kinnaur. Also, there are very old temples dedicated to Shiva from the fifth century in Mandi, from the eighth century in Baijnath and from the twelfth century in Mamleshwar in Karsog, which are in very good condition and well built from carved wood and stone, and which are supposed to have been built during the time of the Mahabharata. These tribes called themselves Nagvanshi, meaning descendants of Nagas, and there are still many communities of Nagvanshi in the Himalayas.

"Anyway, what I meant to say is that there is lots of respect for snakes and it has descended over thousands of years from the ceremonies of the natives. So, as children we were told about the God Shiva and his special chanting mantra. I learned the chants and was able to gather a group of three to four friends to chant with them in the jungle on rocks while looking after goats or cows. The rest of the children used to make fun and laugh at us or make stories to have a good joke about us. Nevertheless, we were around eight to nine years old and we trusted in snakes and enjoyed our chanting and devotion time.

"We used to find soft soil from the termite's holes and mix it with water to create clay to make statues. We used to find a flat slate to give strength to it when it was wet and soft. To give support to its legs and arms we used to put sticks inside and cover them fully with the clay. It was hard work to carry water all the way from home to the forest. To build statues as well as look after our cattle and goats was not an easy task. We used to share the work between us and have these clay workshops. We had to discover little caves or areas to hide them so others couldn't find our statues and break them or steal them. We would build them in the morning at weekends, and when we returned in the afternoon they used to be dry and were ready for us to perform our rituals and *puja's* with chanting ceremonies. We used to make colours from flowers, as well as having some flowers and some sweets, maybe some *gurr* (brown lumps of sugarcane juice) and a few wild fruits and berries from the forests to offer to our self-made Shiva statues and his family and, of course, to deadly cobras. We even made others believe that cobras used to protect our Shiva caves, as someone had seen a snake near that cave and we were alerted about it. That could have been due to the sweets, or mice, or they could really have been protecting our statues! We sold that story really well, and after that other boys did not bother disturbing our treasures. These ceremonies were amazing and I still go to these places to sit and reclaim my memories. The only problem is these caves don't let me in anymore. As years have passed by, I have to really pray and squeeze to get inside. I can't believe how small they were and how small I must have been.

"Anyway, the chanting started from there and helped build a great confidence about nature, karma and a great trust in snakes, and we used to feel very powerful, spiritually strong, satisfied, happy and peaceful. I never thought about what others might be thinking. It made sense in my mind, and I believed in it without any doubt. To care about others and not to kill anything that is helpless, that was my motto. After all, we can only hurt or exert power over those who are weak or helpless due to their circumstances and nothing else.

"Anyway," Dani carried on, "on that hot summer day I came to school early in the morning and we used to have a break at eleven o'clock. We would play different games, hide and seek, jumping, chasing or running or watching the elders making toys like flour mills or balls or chasing butterflies or dragonflies. There must have been around sixty students in this little school, which was by a beautiful stream. The playground was always surrounded by thick shady willow trees after spring and was full of children's noise. Suddenly we heard warning calls in the air – kida … kida … nag … or even sarp … sarp … all these names meant snake, snake, snake! So everybody went quiet with fear, and wondered, where? Within minutes all the children had gathered under the big trees near a water spring and some of them had climbed on rocks and tree branches, excited to get a peek at the snake. There were a few adults and older men from the village talking in shock, 'Oh dear, huge snake', and 'Oh my God, how dangerous', and ladies were praying. Thankfully, they had spotted the snake in time, before any of the children had been bitten, as it was break time and children were playing all around.

"There was a lot of noise going on and the children were asked to be quiet and warned not to come too close to the scene because the snake might escape. There were a few men from the village to whom it was a challenge to kill a snake. Six or seven men were trying to hit the snake from every direction with huge long bamboo sticks. The poor snake was hiding under the bushes, but he had no chance. Being a little boy, I made my way through the crowd without being noticed until I was right near his head, hardly six or seven feet away, and then I was pulled back by someone. I could not believe how bloodthirsty these men were for this snake and I felt sorry for him. I was not enjoying the scene at all and my mind was wondering: Why was it alright that everybody was watching and waiting for him to be killed? Is there no one who can actually take his side? Well, a few elderly ladies came and said, 'Let him go, he will disappear in the jungle, what has he taken of your fathers that you have to kill him?' etc. But they were not heard by anybody. The men with sticks where hitting him and he was wounded in a few places. He was flat on the ground and the tip of his tail was coiling, like he was begging everyone to stop. His body was damaged and so was not able to pull himself forward. Tears dropped on my cheeks and my eyes burnt at the thought that not even one person was taking his side. Why? My attention was fixed on the snake's mouth and eyes, and I felt that I was talking to him. I said to him, 'Why did you get yourself among these cruel people? You are a king cobra, you have powers and you are mystical, why didn't you run away or save yourself? I am so sorry they are bringing an end to your life. I am so sorry! I am helpless and ashamed to be here and I cannot help you.' My body, mind and breath were still, and I was in shock, I could not believe that ordinary people could hit him like that, when he was supposed to be super powerful. I was very sad.

"Do you know what that cobra said to me in response, Roland? 'Do not feel sorry for me and do not be sad. Whatever happened, it happened because of the circumstances and karma. Remember this scene and watch my breath. I am really suffering. I am losing my breath. I am dying and leaving this body. But watch carefully and remember these faces and you may see these people in their last days too. You must remember this scene always. It is due to my action and they too will face their actions. I have played my role, but just remember this.' By now the snake was really opening his mouth and gasping for air, and this one person was just hitting his head over and over again. I was in shock and could not believe what was happening. I kept my words to myself and left the place in deep sorrow mixed in with some kind of relief.

"Soon lunch break was over and all the children were asked to go to the school playground for a briefing from the teachers about how careful we should be around the area as a huge cobra had been found nearby. Everybody in the school wanted to talk about the snake, but there was no chance as the teachers were strict and soon students were busy again with their studies. Some children carried on whispering about it, like how huge he was, and 'Did you see him running?' If the teacher heard, he would call the student by name and make a joke, 'If you carry on your stories, I will send you to him,' and everybody laughed.

"Anyway, time passed on and we completed our primary school and went to the senior school in Suni on the other side of the river, which was built during the British time and used to be the only higher secondary school in the whole valley. We had to cross the Satluj River over a wooden rope bridge built in 1961. I spent three to four years in that school and life was good, and I made many friends and lots of things were learned in those years.

"One day, one of my friends' brother had an accident during lunch break. It was an unfortunate accident and we were all in a big panic as we took him to the hospital. He was soon referred to the bigger Shimla Hospital as the injury was quite serious. My friend and the teachers were arranging their journey with their family and they left soon after. I was about to leave too, but I saw a few other people from the village at the small hospital and wondered if anyone from the village was unwell. I went in to find out and saw a few people gathered around a man on a bed. By now my older brother had come down to the hospital as well, so he came in. I joined them and noticed a familiar face from the village was on the bed and was seriously ill. I was shocked to see this person was suffering from a breathing problem, how he was trying really hard to say a few words but they wouldn't come out and he was really helpless. A doctor rushed in and put an oxygen mask on him, but I could very clearly see him still gasping for breath.

"It was so awful to witness this scene and how no one could do anything to help. I could not believe that even inside a hospital a patient had to suffer like that in front of a team of doctors. I wondered why no one could provide him with any relief. At that very moment, as my eyes were fixed on the scene, that same cobra face appeared gasping for breath instead, and I could not even see this man's face, all I could see was the same snake talking to me. A voice asked me, 'Do you remember my words?' I was stunned and shocked as he said to me, 'This is the karma. He was hitting me so hard and I was suffering and wanting to breathe. Do you remember? Do you remember? Today it is his turn and it is not because of me, it is because of his own doing. If he would have looked after his actions and life in a better way he would be healthy and happy. This is karma. That's what I want you to understand, so don't be sorry.' I could not tell anyone or cry or say a word. I had a feeling of relief in my heart, but I was equally shocked too. I found myself being pulled out by my older brother. He was reminding me that lunchtime was over and that we were late. But this conversation with the cobra was a great mystery and I could not understand it myself, let alone describe it to others. I took it as a great message from God, or from nature, and I kept praying to Shiva and the snake god to bless all of these victims of karma or their circumstances on this earth, so that misunderstandings could be clear and visible, so this earth could be a better place for every living being.

"Roland, I still can't get over that experience and I will remember his words forever. That scene, which fills my heart and eyes with sorrow on the one hand, and yet at the same time gives me great relief of sorts that while some things may seem unfair, somehow, somewhere, there is a balance and we shall reap the fruit of our own actions sooner or later. So, in a way you see, we are in control, and life can be altered. This thought gives me great confidence, and after this event I decided that my destiny was in my own hands. Before this I used to believe in astrology and fate, but after this event I was confident that my karma is my future.

"So action is important for us and we can only do that if the mind is clear and healthy."

Roland kept thinking that this world was very practical and that there were no stories like Santa coming down the chimney and bringing lots of presents for everyone, which can be disappointing once you understand or are able to use your own reasoning. He asked if they went to the temple every Sunday.

Dani said, "We don't have to go to the temple. We go maybe two or three times a year for *darshan* (presence and blessings), as people are busy working hard in their fields. 'Work is worship' is the way here, and it is said that you can remember God anywhere and anytime, as he is within us, and it makes temples more special and peaceful as well as a treat if you go once in a while. We have our own shrine at home and we just do our own practice to calm the mind and body and feel inner peace. Because temples are not really expecting people, temple priests are supposed to do their own practice for their own inner peace.

Dani's sister came to the door and asked them to come down to the kitchen as dinner was ready and their mysterious conversation had taken quite a long time.

"Sorry Roland, my stories go on a long time and you must be hungry."

But Roland was much more interested in the stories, and new layers of history and culture were unfolding as time went by.

They both descended to the kitchen and once again had a wonderful meal prepared from real home-grown mountain food. They also produced some ice cream for pudding; Dani's brother had bought it in Suni with some sweet *gulab jamun* brown balls made out of milk and dipped in syrup. It was delicious, though a bit too sweet for Roland.

After tea, Roland wanted to catch up with his diary, and he retreated to his room and played some music and wrote down his account of the day. It wasn't easy to remember everything, but he made his notes as best he could. At the same time he was thinking, maybe I can ask Dani to speak on a recorder, so I don't miss anything next time.

He found it much better to write at night, because it was peaceful and not a single sound disturbed him like in the daytime. Maybe the mind itself is less active at night, thought Roland. He finished his diary by 2.00 a.m. and made a note of some more questions he wanted to ask.

He ran his mind through the plan for the next day and thought about how many days were left on his trip. They had planned a small walk to visit a mountain village school where Dani had taught a few years ago, so he was looking forward to that very much and for now he was exhausted and asleep in no time, as not even a single sound could be heard this night in the Himalayas.

CHAPTER SEVEN

These precious lands

The bright sunshine streaming through the window let Roland know that it was another beautiful day outside. He was buoyed by the new and interesting insights he'd had into this culture which was hidden in this Himalayan valley. He also thought about his home, his parents, his brother and friends, and what they would be up to. He looked at his watch and realised it was a bit late, nine o'clock, which meant it was around four o'clock in the early morning at home. He also thought that they would be finishing work soon for their Christmas holidays as there were only a few weeks left.

The excitement of Christmas would have already started in England. Wonderful memories of Christmas celebrations and the excitement of opening presents reminded him that every street would now be decorated with lights, and shops would be driving people mad with their Christmas offers, decorations and non-stop music. It's Christmas time, it's Christmas time, he found himself humming, which reminded him more about people rushing around, panicking, confused, trying to find suitable presents. But he was looking forward to seeing family and friends and was especially missing that feeling of not doing much and being spoiled with delicious meals and treats such as different varieties of chocolates. Roland had mixed feelings and was glad to simply send some Christmas greetings for the year. I am glad that these people in the villages have no idea, Roland thought, except Dani, about where I come from, about busy London, and about that rush of last-minute present hunting and shopping. He felt better off away from the pressure and couldn't imagine what would happen if these people were transported on to the busy streets of London or other cities during rush hour – they would go mad with it all. The shops would be full of frustrated people trying to find the right presents at the last minute. He couldn't believe how the modern world had evolved and how life was such a huge pressure now with the day-to-day commute whether by train, car, bus or bike. Everyone aspires to a great lifestyle, but to keep it up they put themselves under huge stress and pressure. He was pleased that he was away from all that, but he wouldn't want to live without all of it.

There would be parties with friends in December and family get-togethers, and, of course, exciting presents and some holiday time to relax. He usually enjoyed the food, the drinks, the fun and the games that usually took place during this season. But I will enjoy my time off here, he thought, looking out from the window towards the peaceful guava trees and fields beyond.

Roland noticed a villager passing by in the lower field with a load of green grass bundled on her head. He thought he better start moving too and got up to have his shower.

What a peaceful and quiet spot, he thought, as he came out refreshed after his wash. He had not heard the dog at all that morning.

Dani was in the kitchen and Roland greeted his sister outside and for her he switched to Hindi greetings, "*Namaste! Namaste!*"

Dani joked, "Lucky you woke up now, otherwise it would soon have been afternoon."

Roland couldn't see the dog outside and was worried, "Where is Tigger today?"

Dani laughed and was surprised that Roland had noticed. "Well, my brother moved him away behind the house so you couldn't hear him barking, as he wakes us up early otherwise."

"How kind," Roland said. "No wonder I had a long sleep."

"No, no, you are fine, no panic, come on in and have something to eat, Roland," said Dani. "I am afraid it is now brunch time and then we must get ready for our walk to see the fields and visit the school further up the mountain."

Roland said he was looking forward to it. "I finished my diary at 2.00 a.m. this morning. I am still a bit behind, but not that bad now, but I may have to add a few things to keep it up-to-date."

"Well that's no problem, Roland. We'll catch up. We might include something funny or strange to share with your friends in England."

"I think they'll really appreciate that as they will all be fed up with the Christmas rush and shopping to buy presents and writing cards," said Roland. "We must have a day when we can send some emails to them."

"Nobody here in the village knows that it is Christmas in a few days and no one is reminding you," said Dani, "but I can still see the excitement in you. Are you feeling left behind Roland, that everyone will be having a big party at home, while we are in the land of 85 million, where people have not even heard about this festival?"

Roland could feel a little of the excitement, but not for the same reason he had as a child. "Those days are long gone. Now it means parties and get-togethers with friends and family. Of course, the excitement of receiving presents is always there. I was thinking in bed that nowadays Christmas is more about the shopping and is promoted more by markets which starts a few months in advance. It has become very commercial, and by the time people sit and enjoy Christmas Day, they are tired and stressed. As soon as they feel they have bought everything for everyone, it's over. But it is a festive season, and it would be better if the family simply had a get-together with nice food, without the panic or pressure of presents, greeting cards and then thank you letters soon after.

"What people buy and eat is a big thing and everything is decorated with special lights, from streets to gardens, trees and parks, and I hope that people stop and take time to enjoy that. But very often they are too busy buying Christmas trees, food and presents."

"We have to find a Christmas tree to decorate then," Dani said.

"Oh Dani, I wouldn't like to do anything like that here. I am really happy with the trees and mountains here."

"It could be fun, Roland, but the problem is that in this land we don't have enough trees. See how we burn the sticks and cook food."

"And you don't want to start that in India." said Roland.

Dani agreed, "Yes, you are right. Our population is more than one billion, and if everybody gets into it, after one Christmas that would be it. All our forests and trees would be cut down within a week, especially in the mountains because that's where those kinds of trees grow. Global warming would arrive very soon then. I really hope that our people don't get into that type of celebration," said Dani (he was a bit serious now), "because we don't waste any wood here, trees are very precious.

"Look at this ash from the firewood," he said. "We don't even waste that." Dani moved out of the way so Roland could see his sister washing the dishes, and he pointed at a little bowl full of ash. "That is our washing powder," he said, "which shines the dishes very well. Although television advertisements are bombarding and manipulating these villagers with all their modern products, and young people prefer to use fancy liquids and sprays like the Bollywood or Hollywood actors who advertise them on television, but the villagers forget that those same actors may not even wash a single dish after eating.

"This is the best product thing to use – it is free and natural. The family don't have to spend any money on it, although we have many companies in India trying to say otherwise through paper adverts and some pyramid businesses.

"There's a company from America, for instance, who make a very clever channel and have some clever Indian people involved in it, first taking some money from them and then driving them to make more money with sales. Once they get trapped in this pyramid business they have to go to every small village and try to sell them all sorts of washing liquids and so forth. When I was here last I met someone from the village who I thought was a very bright student in school and was from a well-educated and traditional family. He was trapped in that business and was introduced to me by a gentleman from my village who thought he would impress me with his marketing skills, their profit and huge turnover, as well as his English speaking and modern selling skills. There are special videos and recordings to brainwash and train them and then make them sign-up by showing them projections about big earnings, cars, houses and a prosperous future full of leisure time. But I am afraid they were very disappointed when I talked about this ash and how they were trapping and misleading innocent fellow villagers into this chain when they have all these natural products in the village," he said. "They were cheating the poor villagers while telling them, that various people had made thousands and thousands of rupees from selling these products or by recruiting new members into the chain. And so they perpetuate the business. This is simply madness.

"Not only that, but one of my own schoolteachers and a close friend was also involved, and they tried their best to push me, but they failed. One of my friends left some products with me and I tried them. Of course the products were effective, but villagers do not need them," he said. "They need to be self-sufficient. In the end, that friend even paid my entry fee too, so I could be a good influence to help grow his chain or pyramid. But I did not want to be part of a chain which was corrupting our natural system and asking people to use their machine-made products so they give up their own ways and start paying money to these international companies. This modernisation is destroying the natural ways, and all these big companies are looking into how to make money. They don't care what happens to the old ways as they are making large profits every year. If half of the world population is dying with hunger, it is none of their problem, they simply drive people to use their products, and if people don't have food to eat even two times a day, again it is not their problem: these companies are simply out to make money."

Roland added, "Now there is not just one company, but countless numbers of them trying to create new models to generate profit and they would even love to sell refrigerators to people in the arctic who have lived for centuries in ice houses!

Dani explained that in cities there are centralised drainage systems for bathroom and dirty water diluted by these chemicals. "But in the villages, a big problem is that there are no proper drainage systems, or even in many towns. All the bathwater and dirty water, with those chemicals, is flowing out to little streams, rivers and fields. Traditionally, all the water from dishwashing used to go to the fields, because it was only ash and water, which used to enrich the soil and worked like compost for plants. But these days, when people use these chemicals, that all goes into the fields and ruins the soil and the results are much more devastating and long-lasting, which local villagers do not understand yet, but the effect is being felt already as their crop productivity has suddenly dropped and their food tastes different. Then they wonder why something is not right, and now they are being pushed to use even more chemicals to increase their productivity so they can make more profit. It just does not end," said Dani in frustration. "How do you teach and educate everyone? Just say 'Stop, you have what you need already with the old ways so just stick with that and you will be better off. You don't have to spend all your hard-earned money on these new and expensive products'. Ash was very good for crops and our parents used to sprinkle it on plants to keep the insects off as well as use it for washing dishes. If there was too much of it they used to put it on the compost or dung heap. In summer they used to add it to paddy fields too with some other leaves to lubricate and fertilise the soil, that's why the fields used to have healthy crops."

Roland was amazed that Dani kept coming up with such extraordinary information. "Dani, you are absolutely right. We now understand that climate change is happening and we are still influencing these indigenous people to leave their natural ways behind and use Western machine-made products, instead of learning from them and creating something eco-friendly for ourselves. I am sure we had some old and beneficial ways in Britain too, but with the race towards machines and new technology we are now completely dependent on these inventions.

"Not only do we have one type of product, Dani, we now have at least more than ten different types of product to clean or to do the same job. For everything, they produce something different and people buy it, although nobody uses all of them. Why don't we have one simple product for cleaning? We hardly ever clean or wash dishes or clothes by hand. We have machines, and we need other chemicals to clean those machines too. Or are we using such complex modified parts that normal cleaning is no longer any good? For washing dishes or clothes, it's all done by machines."

Roland was thinking, are we really that busy or are we simply getting lazy? We hardly wash anything by hand! We use modified mops, washing-up cloths, tissues and many more complex brushes and objects. Here they produce food for more then ten people in the family and don't use a single machine, just by burning little dry sticks over an open fire. Roland was quite shocked at this realisation. Wow! To cook for myself with modern machines like microwaves, electric kettles, electric or gas stoves and ovens feels like hard work after a long day's work, yet here, to make a cup of tea they have to first collect wood and make a fire and then keep the fire going as well as do other chores at the same time, which seems like a long process and very time-consuming. I just have to switch on the kettle, and even that feels like a pain to make tea. Dani said that here they are always asking for tea. He said that another thing he found difficult in England with making tea was that no one really cleans their electric kettle and very often it has lots of particles in the bottom. I wonder if those little particles or substances which seem invisible are often drunk by people with their tea? Because when we make tea or chai here, the pan is always well cleaned and it is always freshly boiled.

"Well, Dani, we don't have to rush here, we'll just explore more and chill out. All we have to do is send a few emails in a few days time – that's plenty. I'm enjoying the peace," Roland said.

Dani agreed adding: "And email cards are the best anyway otherwise it would be very expensive as well as using lots of paper and postage."

Dani added that he would not be able to find any cards in the village anyway as it was a new thing and people didn't really send greeting cards or thank you letters here and it is now a new trend.

"If villagers started doing that they will not be able to work on their fields or look after their cattle. These things must be started by those who have less to do at home," Dani laughed. "But anyway, Roland, please tell me good things about Christmas."

Roland said, "Yes, it's good to look at the positive side, but to be honest, Dani, some families just go mad and spend money on things for their children which they just play with for one or two days and then throw in a corner forever and wasting all that hard-earned money. A huge number of people even take out loans or have big credit card bills during this time. That is the biggest negative, and, of course, the more you give them, the more they want, and they become very materialistic, and little pleases them in later life, because they search for contentment and happiness through expensive gifts. The real Christmas values of family get-togethers and sharing, love and games, is being forgotten."

"But this is the same everywhere now, Roland, even here for the Diwali festival. People go mad and spend a fortune in a panic. These festive activities are becoming very materialistic and people put themselves under huge mental and financial pressure just by seeing others do the same, and they are all victims of the same thing," Dani said.

"I'll miss my family get-together and the meals, the drinks and decorating the tree, and the whole charm of the day. The excitement of opening presents is something very special," Roland said. "Everyone will be having their turkey or roast for Christmas, and that's what I'll miss most."

They wondered how many turkeys and Christmas trees would be used this Christmas across the world. It was interesting to think about, and they could not believe the fact that, while more than two hundred world leaders had gathered in Copenhagen (See Appendix) to talk about climate change, millions of people back at home were getting ready to cut trees down to decorate their houses for Christmas.

Dani also wondered whether there were many people using young trees. He said it would be so brilliant if everyone who bought a new young tree for Christmas replanted it afterwards in their garden, or in a park or forest, if they had no garden, instead of cutting an established tree every year.

Roland agreed. "It would be a great thing to plant a tree for Christmas and New Year rather than to ruin the life of a tree by cutting it down. Well, our population is around sixty million in Britain alone and not everybody celebrates Christmas. If only twenty-five per cent of people did this, that's fifteen million people. If you take two people living together, although many people live alone in big houses in Europe, that would make seven and a half million trees planted per year. So we may be cutting down around ten million trees. I hope they think about that at the Copenhagen summit. We really must understand this and change this tree-cutting attitude, otherwise climate change will happen much earlier. If we think about the whole modern world it amounts to billions of trees. And many of them don't burn them for fire or cooking either. They all become bonfires with the rest of the garden waste or another machine has to dispose of them."

"There's a man in South India called Mr Jaggi Vasudev," said Dani, "who has planted the largest number of trees on earth. His name is now in *The Guinness Book of Records*. It was only because he was told by global environment agencies that their state, Tamil Nadu, was going to be a desert in the next twenty years, because they were suffering from a huge drought. When he was asked how he created that miracle and turned the environment around, he simply said that when he heard it he was shocked, So he researched how to change that prediction. He was advised that only forests could change it. On that day he decided to plant trees, and schools and hundreds of volunteers started helping him, and now his Isha Foundation is not just planting but fully supervising the whole establishment of those trees and forests. It has also made it very difficult to cut trees down in India now, and one has to seek permission to cut trees down, even private trees on your own land, which will boost wildlife and human life itself as we cannot live without forest cover and rainwater."

By now, Roland had finished his brunch and his plate was taken by Dani to wash with the ash.

"Let me try to wash it so I can have the experience of washing with ash," Roland said.

Dani offered him the metal plate, as they only used metal plates in the villages, either that or they use plates made from leaves like banana or *shal*, which can be seen in traditional weddings and celebrations in the villages. Roland realised that the sponge he was using was made from coconut husk, and Dani said that they also use other natural material like bark from the *beaul* tree.

Dani applied some hot ash from the fire with the coconut husk, and then rinsed it with hot water poured from a jug. It was all really clean and the job was done.

"That's wonderful," said Roland. "Magic, nothing from the shop or from machines and the dish is clean."

Dani explained that ash is also different and depends on the different woods it comes from. "Some trees produce very good ash for cleaning, while others don't. My family knows which ash to store for cleaning. The rest of the ash goes on the crops, like coriander, spinach, onion and garlic, to protect their leaves from the insects and caterpillars. It is good for the soil too, as well as having many other values."

Roland dried his hands as they were getting ready for a walk. They got their bags to start their journey, but before that Roland noticed some flowers and a small pot of water on the doorstep.

Dani explained that this was a way to welcome the sun in the morning. It was an old tradition to leave a profound and fulfilling impression on your mind before you leave for your daily work.

"We ask people to sometimes drop a penny into it before leaving the house, but you can get by without doing that!" Dani joked. "But the idea behind it is that you encourage people to do it more often."

From outside the door Dani pointed out a mountain peak to the north and said that was their goal for tomorrow. "It will take us about three hours. It's not difficult to conquer a goal when you can see it. The problem is only when you cannot see the goal. If one knows the goal, paths are created automatically with little effort," Dani said, and walked off.

Roland was a bit nervous and not sure how far and how long the trek was going to take. Oh well, he thought, I'm sure we'll have many interesting things to see on the way, and at least we don't have to run, that would be a real challenge. Anyway that's tomorrow. Let's enjoy today.

Roland got his rucksack, with his camera and water bottle, and followed Dani, and they were both looking forward to seeing the school. Feeling free of responsibilities, all they had to do was walk and talk and explore and enjoy. They passed through the farmland, and it was green with very young wheat plants, as well as some peas, cauliflowers and potato fields. Dani kept meeting people on the way and saying a few words to them in Hindi, then translating them for Roland. One farmer was complaining about sambars, or deer, that had spoiled his field of wheat. He was not happy at all. He was saying how he wanted to shoot "the bloody beasts" one by one.

Dani had said before that deer and wild boar were becoming a big problem for villagers, as they were not allowed to shoot them in India. There were some cases where some were shot in the night, and police teams searched and hunted for the culprits, but they didn't find anything, so the villagers were really in some difficulty about what to do with them, as many fields were ruined. There were no proper insurance or protection policies for farmers, which was not a very good way to encourage farming or to encourage youths to get into farming.

Dani also pointed out some common land around the villages which villagers were struggling to save from some greedy people. It was government land and was an open space where their children used to play.

"Some greedy people are constantly moving their boundaries forward a few metres every year, and gradually those open spaces are being taken over by encroachment. Nobody wants to argue about it and the authorities are nowhere to be seen, as some of these dominating people have links with corrupt ministers, and a simple call can quieten the revenue inspector, or *patwari*, or a bottle of whisky or cash under the table can stop him coming to inspect too. It's a big shame as all the common land is disappearing into private courtyards."

He pointed out many places during their walk through the villages and that when he was a child it had been common land and free for children to play and run around on, but now was being acquired illegally, so for the village community there were no open areas to build community centres or parks. He hoped that it might be improving a bit due to people recording incidents live on phones and many revenue officers being sacked.

They went through the fields again and saw a few farmers ploughing with oxen, and a few people were weeding or planting new vegetable plants for the winter season. There were also two or three big poly houses: huge white plastic covered structures, a little like greenhouses. Dani explained that they were partly funded by the government so that a farmer could grow rare crops and it was an easy way to protect them from winter frost. But not every farmer was happy with these as lots of diseases which used to be killed by winter weather and cold could now survive in these sheltered areas.

Roland asked Dani if he could have a go at ploughing with oxen and a wooden plough. Dani spoke to one of the farmers and he was very happy for them to have a go. The farmer instructed Dani a bit about which ox was obedient and which one was difficult. Roland discovered that there are some ox that hate edges or heights, and others that are very stubborn and clever and will try to just lay down or kick or run away and refuse to obey orders, particularly if they think that the farmer is not confident or inexperienced.

Dani had a go first, and he explained to Roland about firmly holding the plough handle and to stick to poking the ox to move or patting its sides to turn left or right, and then if you need to turn around, either stepping on the plough hard, so they feel the weight and then patting on the side you want to turn them from, or simply lifting the plough in the air and then gently hitting the ox on the side, which will push the ox to the other side. "Hut" meant "to move", "chalo" was "let's go", or a long "H" sound meant to stop, and "co co co" was to move on or carry on.

"Oh well, lets see if I can manage," Roland said, and he hesitantly moved forward to hold the plough. He tried and did a few rounds, but he found it quite hard to keep the plough in line, and it was not that easy to walk on the bit which was ploughed and had big lumps of earth. After a few turns, the oxen had realised that they were having fun and they started doing long turns so they could have a free run around the field. Roland handed the plough over to the farmer and the farmer laughed as Roland thanked him.

"He said that you did very well considering it was your first time," Dani said. "It's quite easy compared to ploughing paddy fields in the mud and swampy water."

"It wasn't that easy," Roland said, "but it was really amazing." Roland inspected the wooden plough and collar to tie both oxen and found that it was simply a stick.

They said goodbye to the farmer and walked by a big white mud house and the flour mill they had visited before. Then they walked by a little stream and past a fountain from where locals took their water.

They passed another two big pipal trees and both of them had beautifully built platforms under them. Roland was surprised that both of them were funded by a school from Yorkshire that Dani had mentioned before, called Cundall Manor, through the Asra charity. The school they were visiting was located next to the trees and very often they had classes underneath the trees. Roland couldn't believe that Mr Peter Phillips, the headmaster of the Yorkshire school, plus other teachers, had been to visit this local school, and one of the teachers, Andrew Shepherd, was the first to push this trip forward. The local school had benefited from the charity and was also now promoted as a middle school, whereas before it had just been a primary school.

Roland couldn't believe how hidden the school was. "What a place to study. This is amazing. There's no road, just high cliffs and hills all around."

"All the children come from nearby villages and they all have to walk fifteen minutes to half an hour maximum to get to the school."

As they entered, the whole school stood up in honour on the command of the monitor. Dani said that he used to teach there, so a few of the teachers and students knew him. One teacher spoke English and offered them chairs and water. They talked about the school and what kind of development and changes were happening. Dani also found out that all the students study English, Hindi and maths from the age of four.

"That will really change India," Dani said, "and in twenty years that generation will be much more open and able to understand what happens in the world as they have access to television as well as to computers and the internet."

They had computers in the school, which were again funded by charity. It was a state-run school so there was equal attention paid to both languages. Roland was shocked to find out that some of the private English schools in India fined children if they spoke Hindi in the classroom.

"That is madness," Roland said.

"There is a huge pressure from parents. They all want them to speak English so that they can compete at an international level. Those are the parents – they set goals and careers for their children even before they are born."

"Really?" Roland said. "That is very strange."

"Well, they all want to be doctors, engineers and so on. I doubt it if any of them want to be a craftsman, farmer, toolmaker, blacksmith, or a traditional drum or pipe player or a weaver. All the skills that can provide them with food or help the land are completely removed from the text books – they are only in stories now. This is the only weakness of the Indian education system," Dani said, and the teachers sitting with them agreed.

"That's why I couldn't understand those advertisements on the walls around Delhi and from the train. Now it makes sense. But it is not good for the country if they don't learn other skills, as India is a huge country and they need to produce and manufacture food and other things to live."

"For that India has China. Everything comes from China. All we are producing are call centres due to the speaking of English, which is not good enough yet, as many of these schools either speak very old English or in very different accents. So although India is moving forward, in certain fields it's losing and stepping backward."

The teachers said that their students were all from villages so had access to local jobs and activities and they all helped in the fields. But English was still considered important, and even the Prime Minister and President of India lectured in English, and more than half of the population of India doesn't understand them, but they have to speak English.

They all laughed, and Dani said, "That is India for you, Roland. But a leader should be able to reach out to everyone and he should have different speeches in different languages."

One of the teachers said that without the national language the nation is mute, and those were the words of Mahatma Gandhi. "Otherwise what's the point? He can't just represent those who understand certain languages."

Roland said, "You are so lucky to have this peaceful corner for the school."

They smiled and thanked him, but they may not have really understood why Roland liked it so much.

One of the teachers explained about the fence wall and how they wanted to protect the flowers and keep the cattle out as there was no boundary. They had built the wall on one side, and on the other side they needed more fencing. Dani knew some of the teachers very well, but all the teachers who had taught with Dani had left to go to different schools. They also had a new art teacher called Hament Verma, who Dani had given tuition to as he was from his own village, and he had a great interest in art and photography too. Hament showed them some rooms and the computers which were being used by students.

Finally, they said goodbye and shook hands and the children waved as they left.

"Dani, that was really good, did you enjoy your time there?"

"Very much, Roland, and it was really very interesting to teach and see how these institutions work. Education is one thing, but politics and social structure and interaction with different teachers, students and parents is different and has to be learned in a way where the teacher can treat every single child equally and fairly. That is the most important part. Because it is very easy for teachers to get to know certain parents due to family connections, class or caste, and then they may favour certain students, but for a good teacher that does not matter. All those presumptions have to be left outside the school gate if they want to really change lives.

"In Sanskrit, teacher is *guru* – '*gu*' means ignorance and '*ru*' mean remover. The teacher puts the light on darkness and, like the sun, shines on all the same way. A teacher has to shine on everyone equally. He is the real teacher and his karma will be considered best, and he will even find comfort himself as they will respect him likewise."

"That's absolutely true," Roland said. "Teachers have to direct students onto the right path and help them along the way, make their way clearer. I had some friends who felt that in some schools teachers were so pressurised that they had to make sure their league table was looking good overall and that the school had achieved on all levels and subjects. In that race, if someone liked maths and wanted to study maths, but was not great at it, the teacher would prefer him to study something different where he could achieve more marks for the league table. But in reality it didn't assist students in studying what they really wanted, and that can ruin someone's life forever. In some cases students have to be firm about what they really like, although teachers may suggest something different."

11 Thali farmhouse nestled in the foothills of the Himalayas with swing, courtyard and countryside around.

12 Huge trees with sitting platforms and water troughs for animals.

13 Building mud walls the traditional way.

14 Woman carrying bundle of heavy leaves for animals back home.

15 Village women worshiping a tree, binding with holy cloths, thread and offering water.

16 Typical evening kitchen scene, cooking on a fire and washing of feet in a brass bowl in a traditional way as well as dining afterwards in the old Indian style.

17 Village ladies carrying fresh water pots on their heads in the summer, from natural fountains.

18 Amma ji making butter by rocking the clay pot by the fire in the early morning.

19 A local woman making the cow patties or dung cakes and drying in the sun before collecting them in a bamboo basket to store them to burn as fuel or burn as a mosquito repellent.

20 Preparing for worship on Vishvakarma day with decorated farming equipment and tools, a holiday for all animals, people and even for tools.

"Teaching is a very responsible job, and with modern tick boxes and pressures it must be very difficult for them to keep the balance right. But there are still many good teachers," said Dani.

They walked down through a different village path leaving the stream and trees behind.

"Roland, you would be surprised to know what happened with my maths exam. I had two amazing maths teachers in my main school, and the best one I liked was Lalit Sharma. He was very supportive and always treated everyone equally. I always felt I could approach him without any hesitation. He taught me maths from class six to class nine, and then, for the last year, in class ten, they put me in different section with a different teacher, and I had to adjust to his new style, which took some time to get used to and was fine later on, but it was not really suitable for the last year in school to have a different teacher for the final exams, which counted significantly, like GCSEs in the UK. Anyway, I loved numbers and had no problems.

"But a very unfortunate thing happened to me in the exam. There was a different schoolteacher on duty as supervisor, whose relation was also sitting with us in the exam. He was much more worried about supporting this student than paying full attention to the others, to keep things in control, because the exam in maths was quite difficult and some students were trying to get help from each other. But I was happy with it and I took two to three extra answer sheets. I had left one of them on the floor to let the ink dry, as we were all sitting on mats, and I was busy working away. One of the boys behind me was copying from that sheet, and in the end he just grabbed the sheet and kept it with him. I could not stop it as that teacher was busy somewhere else, and I did not want to waste my time arguing or fighting. This boy was almost crying, and he was begging for help and said 'just one more and then I will return it'. So I let it be, and I kept asking him again and again, but in the end, when we finished, I had to get up to collect it and found that it had gone all the way to the last person in the row."

"Where was the teacher?" said Roland.

"Oh, he was busy sorting out things, I guess. I snatched it in anger and tied it with a thread to the other answer sheets, but did not really check as my time was up. I was confident that I had done everything properly and hoped for eighty-seven marks out of hundred. But when the result came, I was so mortified that they had given me only thirty-five marks. I could never understand why, maybe someone had replaced my sheet or snatched my other sheet while I was collecting it, or someone wrote on it, or they thought it was a copy. I have no idea! And I couldn't tell anyone. My favourite teacher asked me why I was not in the first division and my face went red when I explained I only got thirty-five marks in maths, and he obviously doubted that because he thought I was better than that. But when he asked why, I couldn't say anything. I just felt hopeless, and he said, 'Oh well, never mind'. But he was disappointed and so was I. But no one really advised me to sit the exam again."

"Oh Dani, that's really awful. So what did you do?" asked Roland.

"What could I do, Roland?" Dani said. "I thought I would cover it up and try to study higher maths at the next level. So I took the admission in maths, economics, history and English. But the first day I entered the maths class, the teacher gave a speech saying that if anyone had got less then fifty marks in maths, he or she better change to political science. It was really embarrassing, because I used to deliver milk to this teacher and he knew me. He asked me what my marks were, and I told him thirty-five and he went, 'Hmm … may be very difficult'. Everyone looked at me, possibly thinking, oh boy, you are supposed to be better than that!

"After that class, with huge frustration and hopelessness I went out and filled in the form to change my subject to political science, and I never went back to maths. But I loved politics so much that you would not believe. But it did not end there. In the next year I changed to public administration in the hope that that would be harder and would have more scope, but I was misguided by other teachers. They had suggested that, in the modern world, public administration would have more possibilities in future. But they never had a permanent teacher and the teacher kept changing. It was really a very bad decision of mine to change. This was also the year when my father had an accident and he lost his memory, and my responsibilities at home increased. So I did my A levels in economics, history, English, and public administration, with reasonably good results."

By now they had left the streams behind and arrived at a little village called Shavag, from where the view of the whole town, the fields and the river valley was clear and beautiful. Dani suggested they sit there for some time as there was a big pipal tree with a clear platform underneath. They enjoyed the view of the green fields and the whole flat plateau underneath from there.

But Dani's interest in maths hadn't ended there. After finishing school, Dani and his brother, plus a good school friend called, Ved Prakash, worked part-time after exams with builders and painters to earn some money and then went to Shimla to study and they also had the challenge of working there as well. They decided to study in the evening college so that they could work in the daytime. With the help of an older student called Kishore Sharma from his village, Dani managed to change his subject again to do a business and commerce degree, higher financial accounts and other business studies with economics. Although Dani had not studied commerce in school, due to his economics and his English he managed to pass the admission test.

"That must have been a relief for you, Dani," Roland said. "At least you could study numbers in finance, accounting and statistics."

"Yes it was, but it would have been different if I'd had commerce in school, which was not a subject available in our school. To cover two years basic study and then the first year in college had a huge impact on my studies and jobs. Nevertheless, I was quite proud to finish my degree in commerce, on top of all the part-time jobs of teaching, being a waiter or a Hindi teacher for tourists, or finally a tour leader."

"Wow!" Roland said, "That sounds a challenging life, and interesting too."

"Yes, Roland, it's funny how one step or decision can change your whole direction in life. It shows how alert, fair and responsible teachers have to be, otherwise they can ruin the lives of children. This is still a big black hole and burden I carry. What if that would not have happened? Where would I be?"

"Absolutely, Dani, that is really tragic, and we can never know where, but all these challenges have made you what you are today," Roland announced with a smile. He added, "Isn't this the best view of the valley from this spot, Dani?"

They tried to figure out where the family house was and also the royal palace in Suni town. It was nearly past lunchtime and they decided to move on as they still had around twenty minutes of walk to go. They walked back down the hill and through the fields again and collected some spinach and cabbage from Dani's family fields to take home. His family was already waiting for them and lunch was ready, but his mother saw the fresh spinach and said that she would cook that for lunch too. By the time they washed and got ready, lunch was served, and after that they had a very easy early afternoon, except they helped to unzip corn from its covers as Dani's *Amma* and his sister, *Satya*, had huge bundles of corn straw which needed separating. They managed to clear all the corn and then it was lifted in bamboo baskets onto the main circular harvesting platform to dry. They finished very late in the evening, when they could see no more because of the dark. After that they had a quiet evening and Roland also wanted to finish his book on Mahatma Gandhi.

***

They woke up the next day at around eight o'clock and had a shower or bucket bath and Indian paranthas (stuffed chapatti with potatoes) for breakfast with curd and green vegetables and pickle with massala chaye, so they could be ready for their trekking adventure to the peak. Soon after, they gathered their bags, water bottles, torches and cameras, and, of course, this time, proper trekking boots. Dani explained to his *Amma ji* and brother what the plan for the day was and asked them if they wanted to join them, but they couldn't and wished them well, saying that they must visit relations on the way and send them love from the family too.

They said goodbye and went through the fields down towards the main village, again crossing the little stream near the local primary school where Dani had studied. They passed a row of small shops and Dani bought two newspapers – Hindi and English – and put them in his bag so they could read them later. They also bought snacks and some fruit juice made of mangos. Dani loved this juice because the monsoon season was just over and most of the mango juice was the produce of the fresh mango season, which finishes in August and September. Dani also bought *gachak* (peanuts mixed with sugarcane liquid, which is quite hard once dried) which comes in big circular pieces like a chapatti. Dani offered Roland some; it was quite hard to chew, but very sweet.

They left the shops and greeted a few people, as Dani knew everyone in the village, and he pointed to the peak and told them that they were going to the shrine on the top called Deobadeyogi Tibba. "Deo" meaning "deity" and "badeyogi" meaning "The Great Yogi", who the shrine was dedicated to – a great master and teacher for royal princes during the period of Mahabharata – his name was Dronacharya. "Acharya" is a rank and means "teacher". "Dron" was a master in archery and expert in all warfare.

b–A Palanquin (palaki) of a local deity, Deo Bade Yogi, during its visit to the villages decorated with old gold and silver masks and a pile of rice, rose petals, to offer for devotees or pilgrims, as a blessing.

"He was the dearest teacher of Arjuna the Great Archer Prince, one of the best archers known in the history of archery in the older era," explained Dani. "There was a huge temple dedicated to him as well as a very precious gold and silver *rath* (chariot or palanquin), which has one of the oldest antique sculptures and masks made from gold, silver and a mixture of eight metals. It isn't on wheels or pulled by horses, but has two long wooden logs, which you can hardly see as they are covered with embedded silver coins and decorated with silver lion heads on both ends. It is so precious and beautiful that many people come from afar to admire it and to be blessed. But this *rath* only comes out twice a year and travels from village to village, where people organise village fairs to welcome it. So the teacher from Mahabharata is still highly regarded for his wisdom and knowledge.

"The story goes that his five student Pandava princes and their mother had spent some time in the Himalayas after their escape from a huge fire, when their cousin, Duryodhana, had planned to burn them alive in Varnavarat Palace, but the brothers escaped by digging a tunnel underground and ended up in the Himalayas. Not because they could not fight back, but because they did not want to live a life where anger, jealousy and greed could upset their inner peace. They preferred to leave the Hastinapur kingdom to his cousin and instead live the peaceful life of sanyasis in the Himalayas. There is a temple called the Hidimba Temple, in Manali, dedicated to Bhim's wife, whom he married after killing King Hidimb in the Kullu Valley and becoming a king, until his son, Ghatotkach, was born to be the next king. After that they left and there were a few temples built by them as well as dedicated to them and their teacher in the Karsog Valley, which is further north than Satluj Valley. The main one is *Mamleshwar* temple, which still has a replica of a big drum from that time, called Bhim Dhol. There is also a centuries-old seed preserved in the temple, which is huge in size compared to today's wheat seeds and is supposed to weigh ten grams."

Dani explained, "*Deo* is a common Sanskrit and Latin word and may be one of the oldest words that is still in use in Eastern and Western languages to refer to the divine. Maybe the word was even used before the human race separated during the migration from Africa to the east and west. There are a few words and games we have in our village which have connections with Africa and New Zealand. *Haka*, or *kui*, means 'call' in our village dialect and *haka* is singular and plural, and both are similar to the Maori people's war cry in New Zealand, as well as there are a few more words such as Vahini. Also, we have games that are similar to African village games like *Mancala*, and we use the same sling with two strings and a pouch to throw stones, like they do in the African bush. So this is really amazing that there are many common things in old villages.

"Anyway, *Deo Bade* means 'divine great' and *yogi* means 'master in yoga'."

This explanation was interesting to Roland, as he wasn't sure how tough a yogi he needed to be to get to the top of the hill. But the concept of the roots of language was quite intriguing; at least Roland could relate to the word *deo*. He asked Dani if he had heard the old hymn, *Gloria in Excelsis Deo*, meaning "Glory to God in the highest".

"Yes," replied Dani, "I like the old Latin words as they are quite similar to Sanskrit and sound like poetry."

Soon they were away from the villages, and Dani offered some more *gachak* to Roland.

"I find it very strange that people in England eat most things all year round and food seasons mean very little to them," Dani said, "whereas in India people use certain snacks or sweets and fruit in winter and different ones in summer. It's like in summer we will eat lots of mangos, bananas, oranges and sour things as well as different seasonal food – sour chutneys from green mangos, mint, pomegranate, *imili* (tamarind) and pickles are the special things for summer. And in winter we will eat sweet things and more warm things like roasted nuts, peanuts and popcorn. Everyone ignores bananas in winter, as it only grows mainly in summer and it helps us with the heat. Bananas have some cold properties to them and that's why they are really avoided in winter."

Roland said, "That's interesting as in supermarkets we see them all year round."

"That's right," Dani added, "I find it so difficult when I see little children eating bananas in winter and you see their noses stuffed due to a cold. They should not be having banana or yoghurt, or even ice cream, if they have got a cold. But you can't tell anyone. Bananas do not grow in cold countries, nor in winter, so this means that nature does not want us to eat them in winter. The plant flourishes in summer and we should eat it in summer, so it saves us from heat and cools the body down."

Dani went on. "More or less we should eat seasonal food that we grow during that season. Indians eat what they know from generation to generation and also it is taught to us what kind of *guna* (qualities or properties) certain fruit, vegetables and grains have, what is good to eat if you are feeling a cold or if you have indigestion or diarrhoea, and what not to eat to be safe during these illnesses. We are also influenced by herbal medicines – "prevention is better than cure" is the best rule or medicine here in the villages. I think the most important thing here is that we follow *Ayurveda*. The word *Ayu* means 'life' and *veda* means 'science' or 'knowledge'. This word again comes from Sanskrit. The body is seen very much as part of nature, and in Sanskrit it is called *prakriti*, which means 'nature'. So it is like a moving plant in nature. We see the body as a plant, and if it is cold, more cold water on a plant is not healthy for it, or in hot weather, more heat will kill the plant, whereas in winter it may give life to it. So the villagers go along with nature and provide what is available in nature during that season.

"For that, everyone has to know the seasonal crops and their qualities, which I found very difficult in England," said Dani. "Because you can buy anything from all over the world and many things are so strange because they cannot grow in England at all. They all grow far away in Africa, India, Peru, Australia or Japan. And people eat them all year round. Sour oranges and bananas are eaten in freezing winter, when they only grow in summer. But they transport them all the way round the world, and often they are picked raw and then frozen so that they can travel."

By now they were climbing a steep hill, leaving the road below behind, and they could look down into the valley. The river and green fields were on the left and a town, Suni, was on the right. Dani pointed out the new bridge that was being built – people wanted a Jeep-accessible bridge – and an old wooden footbridge that was too low for Jeeps, below the new bridge.

"This footbridge was built by the local raja, Vir Pal Singh, and there is an old temple to the left of the bridge. The new bridge will be Jeep-accessible and they will be building a road through that green field, ruining all those fields. So the next time you come here there will be a road through here and these local people will soon build houses and shops by the road, so all these fields will be full of shops and buildings soon. It is very sad and people just don't understand that they should not build houses or shops by the road, because lots of cars will produce dust and noise, and in summer there will be sand and dust in the air, which is very damaging for children and for everyone. The peace they have here in this valley will be gone in the next few years. Villagers would be better off creating a special market centre in the middle of the fields or a forest somewhere away from the roads."

Roland wondered if the whole idea of roads and motor cars was a good idea in the long term. "Different types of metal have been dug out of the earth and put on the roads. The amount of oil they use and the trouble caused by this oil and the smoke is huge."

Dani said, "In the old days, if there was an accident, such as someone falling from a tree or from a horse or a rooftop, these were small casualties. But now, not only in India but around the world, huge numbers of people die within minutes – plane crashes, car crashes, and especially in the mountains here, buses full of people just disappear in deep gorges, rivers or valleys. For example, a bus full of working people and students goes from one village and within minutes they all die and the village loses all those breadwinners of the family. So this is a curse for humanity in that sense, not a blessing at all. Another thing is that in the developed world they have all the emergency services and all the health and safety, but here they have nothing. All the income they have goes on buying the vehicle and they can't afford anything else. So in the end it becomes a tragedy."

"That is really very true, Dani. It's not only here. There are thousands of people dying on European roads every year. But, at the same time, different inventions can be useful if used carefully for the right purpose. It is impossible to imagine the world without motors now. Everyone is trying to have not only one but a few motor cars, and that is really crazy. If ninety people go from a village to work in a market, they take ninety cars, more or less, instead of ninety using a couple of buses or, in other words, use three to four engines instead of ninety. This use of private cars is creating trouble for parking and even traffic on the roads. We can't move that fast anymore, and until all the smaller roads get blocked, and people won't start walking or using public transport again. I'm not sure how this will change. Maybe if celebrities and famous people travelled by public transport it might? Let's see if we can figure out how much land is taken up by the roads all around the world and if that balances what good it has done for civilisation," said Roland.

"I read somewhere," said Dani, "that London alone uses around twenty per cent of the land for roads and the figure is around twelve per cent of land for roads all over England. Houses cover much less land than the roads in Britain. I'm sure that India is rushing in that direction too, but it will be difficult to make roads through the mountains. It is sad that we have less flat land in the mountains, but they are trying to build roads on that too.

"While travelling around Europe and India I found that men were building lots of new roads through the fields and villages. The people were very excited to have roads by their houses, because that's the lifestyle that television shows promote, and everyone wants to travel right up to their doorstep. They have no concept of the smoke, noise, pollution and crowds of people it will bring. The government and political leaders call it big development and it gets votes because it is seen as progress."

Dani went on explaining as they climbed higher and higher, and after a while they took a break so he could finish what he was saying.

"All around the world I have seen drivers getting upset while driving through village side roads because local people are coming with their cows, goats, sheep and children, carrying heavy loads of firewood or grass or leaves in baskets and bundles of grass on their heads or on their back for cattle or for themselves. It must be very difficult for these drivers to drive through herds of sheep, goats and cows. How strange that these local people can't see the cars and understand that the roads are built for cars! They just come and block the whole road. They don't even care that these drivers are in a hurry. These local people are not good and are disturbing the life of travellers – that's what the drivers and the passengers now think. Sometimes they hit and kill the animals or have fights with locals, because they tend to think that the road belongs to them.

"What a modern system these leaders and wise authorities have put in place which can't see just who is disturbing who. When there were no settlements in the countryside in this Himalayan valley, it was all wild and unknown. Brave explorers and local shepherds found these wild valleys one after another and travelled as nomads to these places and settled wherever they found water sources and a suitable climate and land."

Dani smiled. "Do you know, Roland, when I was young I used to think how clever God was that he had produced water near every village and wherever people had built houses. But later I realised that it was not God. These were clever people who settled wherever there were water resources and suitable spots."

"Good point," Roland laughed. "Well, you've sorted that out, Dani."

"But Roland, we don't even know how many difficulties they had to face and fight with to make these remote places their homes, as there were lots of wild animals and thick forests. Slowly they gathered animals and went out into the jungles from these bases. Shepherds found routes to go higher up in the summer to the snowy mountains and down by the rivers in winter with their cattle to escape from the snow and cold. This is still happening here in the Himalayas. But now their paths have been converted and taken over by big modern roads for cars and lorries, where they can't even walk anymore with their cattle. We have ruined their peaceful little footpaths. It takes them much longer to walk than they are used to because they have to stop for every car or truck. It is very difficult not only for villagers but also for nomads, as they walk for weeks and months with cattle and goats. Sometimes, in a panic, their cattle, sheep and goats run here and there and it takes a long time for the shepherd to gather them together again, while motorists just rush off without noticing the trouble they create for these poor shepherds.

"They had these footpaths discovered so that nobody could disturb them, and they could easily walk with heavy loads and animals and continue with their lives in the villages. So it means we are disturbing local people by allowing fast traffic on their private footpaths, without giving them an alternative pedestrian path or byroad where they and their cattle could be safe. We have destroyed their paths and now we blame them and get angry with them?

"These road builders should give villagers a new pedestrian path before they start to convert their old footpaths into big roads. Because of this, many villagers and shepherds are selling their animals and changing their ways of living towards the modern world, where there is only a blind race, without a common or considered goal."

"It is a big shame," Roland agreed. "It's the same in Europe. They build roads to every village and every house, and when we want to walk there are no footpaths because they are all taken up by roads. In many places even to take your dog for a walk is difficult as the traffic is too bad, and instead of enjoying the walk, walkers are always worried about traffic.

"Do you know about the old railway line near Godalming and Guildford to Brighton in England? It was no longer needed and was converted into a footpath and is a very good path to walk and cycle, it really is, free from any traffic, and it goes through the countryside to the seaside."

"Yes, I've heard about it, I'd like to visit it one day," Dani said.

Roland, as he stopped to catch his breath, pointed out the route of the footpath they were walking on. "They won't be able to make a road here. It's too steep. This is quite hard. You knew this, didn't you!"

Dani laughed. "Come on Roland, you're tough. This is nothing for you!"

Roland realised that they had done a lot of climbing, and they were now quite high up. They hadn't stopped that much and, with all the conversation, had been walking an hour already and were on a very high spot from where the wooden bridge, the river, Suni on the right and Thali on the left, were very clear to see, as well as beautiful green fields.

What a beautiful view – and they felt they were doing really well.

"On the other side of the river opposite us, behind that mountain, is Shimla," Dani pointed out.

As Roland looked along the river, he saw some smoke and could smell a gentle smell like roasting or the burning of meat. He mentioned it to Dani.

Dani joked, "You never know who's roasting turkey in the houses around here, Roland. They'll have some rice and chapatti with it or maybe it's mutton."

"Oh, that would be good," Roland replied.

"I hope you're not missing your home food too much!" joked Dani.

When he looked at the smoke coming from the right-hand side of the river, he realised that Roland had been right, it was indeed a cremation ceremony, and Dani wondered who it might be for.

"Someone must have died in that town, or further up in the other villages in the mountain. Because we don't have much flat land in the mountains, it is in our culture to cremate the body, and there is a belief in returning the five elements to their original sources through the fire ceremony," said Dani. "There are different sites marked for different areas by the riverside to burn bodies. One person comes from each family with a piece of wood and that's how they build a huge pile, and if they really need to they might cut down a tree. I've witnessed several cremation ceremonies since childhood, and they're very moving as you witness the human physical existence disappearing. There is also a lot of superstition and many rich and famous people are cremated with sandalwood or with some other expensive wood for a better essence. All your life you do bad karma and then in the end, through superior wood, you go to heaven. They conveniently forget the karma theory. Of course, you have to treat the departed body and soul very respectfully, but sometimes people can go mad with superstitions."

"Oh, yes – you cremate here and you don't bury the bodies," questioned Roland. "But how do you keep a record or remember the dead if you don't have cemeteries or memorial places here?"

"We also believe that the body is a part of the soil, or earth, and through a very complex system the soil is converted into food by nature, and then the body converts food into the body. And we believe that the spirit never dies and so that kind of thing is not important. But saying that, Roland, this body is very special, and after burning it, ash is taken to a holy riverside, mainly to holy Ganges in Haridwar. Every family has a family priest there and a record book or log where they enter all the names of newborns in the family, and the day you go with ash for the final departing ceremony for soul and body, that name is crossed to show that this soul has departed. And then you can remember them as long as they remain in the memory, and family life moves on."

"So all Indians who have died in India are not buried at all and they are all cremated?"

"Yes, that's what has been done for centuries, and this is the culture," said Dani. "Otherwise we would not have any land left for ploughing!" he laughed. "It is enough that roads have taken so much land, it would be a disaster if they started having cemeteries here too. All the terraced fields built by our ancestors would be filled with cemeteries within a day after all the dangerous bus accidents."

"If you go to France and Germany, even the First and Second World War memorial grounds and cemeteries are huge," said Roland, "and I think thousands of acres are lost to cemeteries and the expenses to maintain them are huge too."

"They do provide a memorial place for loved ones," Dani said.

"Dani, you may not know, but there is a big struggle in Europe for cemeteries to accommodate everyone, that's why they have started electric cremations."

"Well, it is a place to remember loved ones and it is good to remember them," Dani said, "but the most important thing is to give them a place in our hearts and memories."

"That's very true," Roland said, "but Dani, in India, if you can remember your ancestors without memorials then I am sure we can too. But many people leave their elderly relatives in care homes when they start complaining or become a problem to us with our modern freedoms and lifestyles. Sometimes those elderly people are not even visited by their children, and they are left alone with other old people. It's just because their children are too busy with work or life to care for them. Once they die, after suffering in the homes, they make a wonderful memorial stone for them. What's the point?"

Dani said, "In the old days in India we never used to leave our parents in a home, and it is an awful thought, because in a joint household it's very easy to look after them and they often die while seeing their children and grandchildren playing around them. They look after children and do house-sitting too. It keeps them stimulated and they have fun. I'm sure sometimes it is hard for the elderly to look after the grandchildren, but that's all part of the entertainment and the days pass quickly. Well, at least that's the way in the villages. Cities are following the modern style now as children are working overseas or faraway or have no time at all from their working life with the modern pressure to keep up with targets. And some of them don't want to have the responsibilities of elderly people, or they prefer an independent life where no one can ask questions if you come home at midnight, or not at all. If that carries on in India it will create huge suffering for the elderly as social care here is not that great in comparison with Europe. That would not be good."

"I'm sure these old homes have excellent care," said Roland, "but if family and loved ones aren't around or don't visit you, then what's the point? Many families do have private carers full-time at home in Britain, and that's much better if you find a good and reliable person or if you can afford it. But maybe life does teach us enough coping skills and to cope with this one may be the last straw for the elderly."

"Anyway, now we have done the hard part," Dani said, and he pointed at a house. "I think we are going to have a break soon."

Dani stopped near the house and greeted a lady collecting wood in a nearby field. Dani mentioned that she was the mother of the wife of one of his brothers – Gita's mother. She stopped working and welcomed them in.

"We'll have lunch and tea here," Dani said, "because otherwise they will mind that we came through and didn't stop to say hello."

They sat on chairs in a big room while looking out through a window. She brought some water so they could wash their hands and offered them some water to drink.

"In the mountains they always cook extra food in case any visitors come," Dani said, "and it's a normal thing to have a visitor, but I'd already informed her about our visit through my brother, and it's always fine, as they always make sure you have food or tea in the mountains. There are few houses and each house is quite a distance from the next, so people are pleased to have visitors and often welcome the opportunity to have a rest and a drink. Especially in summer, they stop for water for sure. Because locals don't carry water like tourists do, Roland."

Dani went to check out a different room and asked Roland to come and see, saying that her daughter-in-law was giving a bath to a baby, and would Roland like to see it?

Roland misheard and wondered if Dani was going bit mad. He felt in an uncomfortable situation and worried whether it was some sort of tradition to witness the birth of a baby.

"Sorry Dani, what did you say?"

"Roland, do you remember, I was telling you about a tub bath for a baby?" Dani said.

"Oh yes," said Roland, with a deep breath, and, feeling at ease again, he stepped forward, but was still a bit unsure.

Dani burst out laughing. "Roland, did you think I said that she was giving a birth to a baby?"

"Shush," Roland said.

"Ha ha. No wonder you were getting a bit worried." They both laughed, but quietened down to show some respect to the host.

To Roland's great relief the new mother was giving a bath to the baby in a brass bowl, like the bowl they had used to wash their feet at Dani's house. The baby was nearly three weeks old, they were told. As Dani had experience with children, he was quite happy to hold the baby, whereas Roland wasn't so sure. All Roland enjoyed doing was taking some photos. Dani pointed at the baby's tummy and at a little piece of cord attached to the belly button, and said that in England he had seen newborn babies tied with a big plastic clip to close the cord.

"Here they tie or close it with a very thick home-made woollen or cotton thread. Again, here the old-fashioned way is very simple, as that plastic clip has to be produced in a machine. I wonder which is the safest way to keep the germs out?"

Roland had no idea what Dani was really talking about, but Dani said he would show him some photos on the net to help him to understand the concept, how they block the umbilical cord by cutting it from the mother. But the baby was very tiny and Roland found it amazing how one day that little baby would be a man like them and they had been like that little baby just a few years ago. Roland asked if there was a hospital nearby, and they explained that it was in Suni, about thirty minutes away.

"In the old days," explained Dani, "they used to have a *dai,* midwife, who knew much more about these issues and had skills to turn the baby in the stomach and they were experts in massage and delivering babies.

"They used to look after the baby and the mother and knew what kind of food to have or to avoid as well."

Another interesting thing Dani pointed out was a cummerbund on the new mother.

"After having a baby, it is a very old important tradition to wear a cotton material around the waist. It is quite long and you roll it around you a few times to keep your abdominal muscles tied for at least four weeks or so, and they are not allowed to do anything except feeding and looking after the baby. They can't even cook for at least two weeks. It's so they can fully recover and be strong again to look after their baby. Their mothers look after them, or in these remote villages you can still find an expert *dai* who will pay a visit every day to the new mother and baby. But, if there are any complications or other medical issues, then it used to be really difficult to save one or other. In most cases the dais are excellent, but in other cases it is better to rely on science and hospitals. Nevertheless, that old knowledge should be added to the midwife profession too, so a balance is created."

They left the mother as she was dressing her baby and went off to wash their hands and have their lunch in a different room.

They were ready to eat as they'd had quite a steep climb and there was still around an hour more to get all the way up to the peak called Badeyog. They had rice, dal, chapattis and green spinach vegetables, as well as some yoghurt and *ghee*. It was really delicious and had a very different taste to other meals they'd had in India, washed down with tea.

Dani had a good conversation with the lady of the house, and she was asking how her grandchildren and family were, and how were Dani's nephews and nieces. After lunch, they shared their biscuits with the family, then they both thanked them and said farewell.

It was time to start again and Roland kept thinking back and realising that the house had been very basic, only what was needed to live a happy and healthy life. Far away from all the crowds and in a wonderful location, they had an amazing view and one could easily be touched by the peace there. Some people now feel superior to this way of life and others feel shame that they have lost the ancient traditions and the roots of simplicity. It was good to remind themselves that the life our ancestors or forefathers lived hundreds or thousands of years ago was much harder and more rudimentary. They collected wood, made fires, lived their lives in caves and made shelter from hay, straw, wood and slates. Nobody was dropped straight into big palaces, or cars, or with the modern comforts and luxury we enjoy today. Most of us these days want to live like kings and queens and have servants do everything for us. Roland felt that life had gone too far in the modern world. This simple life was more peaceful than he had ever seen or experienced before. They had no roads, and even for the postman there was a trek of two hours to deliver a letter.

"I wouldn't like to be a postman here, Dani, just imagine this trek to deliver a letter."

"Oh no," Dani said, "you just hand it to a person you see from the village and the job is done, unless it is registered, that's why sometimes things never reach their target!" laughed Dani.

But Roland did think that we all have our ups and downs and needs, whether we live in a big or a small house. Life is a responsibility and it may be bigger for those who associate themselves with bigger palaces, with enormous valuables and possessions. They have bigger issues to deal with, although there are many people looking after them. Often a man contented with inner peace can sleep happily in a simple hut, while a man without it may not sleep in a palace even after many sleeping pills.

As soon as they got to the top through the pine trees, they had the most beautiful view all around them. All the hills were lower than them, and they could see the river and the little town far away in the distance. Finally they trekked through a very steep and rocky path past silver pine trees to the top where they found a pond and a little village called Badeyog, with six or seven houses, and Dani explained that it was just a little farming village and quite remote from any modern comforts, but the great thing was that they now had electricity.

"Lots of things used to come up on horseback and the nearest shops might be three or four hours away."

They climbed some steps to the top of the peak where there was the little wooden temple to the local *deo,* or deity, Bade Yogi, and part of it was more than eight hundred years old. Some villagers said that there were plans to modify the temple now, because someone from the cement company had donated some money to the temple.

There was a small pond behind the peak, and near the pond there was a little stall, where a man was making tea and selling sweets.

They needed tea as both of them were feeling their leg muscles were weak because it had been such a climb. They spent just less than an hour there reading the newspaper and looking at the views, as well as having conversations with the locals. Roland also discovered that the main temple, where they kept the precious antique rath, was further down in a lower village. But they didn't want to go there now as they hadn't much time and they needed to get back. The sunshine was perfect and the most amazing thing was the view below to the Satluj Valley, and all around they could see the villages, the river and all the mountains with snow-covered peaks to the east in the northern Himalayas.

CHAPTER EIGHT

The erosion of ancient and new traditions

Dani pointed out all the villages and how far up the dam would be coming and how much land all around the valley would be taken by the cement factory. In addition the mountain could be destroyed as there was lots of stone which could be utilised for cement.

"Lots of forest and valuable plants will be cut down and lost, and how much of the wildlife is in danger?" said Dani. "It really is very sad to see, and after a few years the whole of the Satluj Valley will be unrecognisable. There could be a lake created by the flooded river and then there will be more bridges for the factory and convoys of trucks all around, and slowly village life and the old traditions and culture will disappear being replaced with industrial town traffic and pollution."

A further disappointment arose from reading the newspaper they had bought that morning including the coverage concerning the lack of any agreement, and confusion, at the climate change summit in Copenhagen (See Appendix), on carbon emissions. More than two hundred world leaders had failed to reach a deal on carbon emissions.

"It sounds like they're discussing some kind of commercial deal instead of giving one hundred per cent to save the planet," commented Roland. It was hard for them to imagine an industrial town by the beautiful river from the top of this peak, which would destroy the vegetation and convert a self-sufficient way of life to one that was very dependent on machines. Roland just could not believe that all these nations were still discussing it.

Dani had explained to Roland that it was almost the end of autumn and they hadn't had enough rain that season, and some of the fields in the village were not ploughed, because they can only be ploughed if it rains. Roland wondered to himself, if all the water sources are dry due to rising summer temperatures, a lack of rain and melting glaciers and less snow, how would everyone survive? And when it does rain, it would flood because there will be no vegetation to stop it. Climate change was having a very real impact, not just in the Satluj Valley but all over the world.

"In England, most of our food also comes from far-off countries on whom we rely heavily." Roland was wishing he could send this message to the climate summit in Copenhagen. Here, this village was on the edge of becoming a cause of climate change due to the hunger and greed of rich corporations who want to convert these villages into factory production zones, paying little regard to local landowners or giving them any hope of working with the firm; they all think they have found the treasure and they will be rich. But in fact they are being robbed.

Dani remembered a conversation with one of his English friends once about harvesting nature on an industrial scale. One particular topic which had left a mark on Dani's mind was about mining gold and other precious stones.

"Many lives are put at risk to find gold and other precious metals and minerals. Once, my friend had spent her holiday looking for a particular precious metal in Australia, but had no luck, but she had witnessed one of the world's top gold mines in the process, which extracted huge amounts of gold. Gigantic holes had been dug to harvest the precious yellow metal. The demand is so great that no one pauses to consider the consequences. I'm sure that if the mines were owned and operated by local residents alone they might have hesitated to mine so extensively to change the whole landscape. But once outsiders come in, take over and start running the mines, the attitude changes, as they have no personal attachment to the area or the traditions of that land. Only those who were born there and lived there all their lives care deeply for it.

"There has already been a big exodus of builders and other craftsmen from states like Bihar, West Bengal, Uttar Pradesh and Odisha into industrialised areas. As the demand for building rises, they are being employed by big companies to complete projects like bridges, shopping malls, hydro projects and other large-scale constructions.

"The other side of the coin is that skilled craftsmen are diminishing generally as school leavers are feeling disinclined to pursue manual labour or local skills. They spend their lives looking for medical, engineering and computer jobs, which are insufficient, and, consequently, unemployment is rising. Once that generation sees money as being the ultimate goal and loses interest in their land, they will soon sell it to big companies and that's what these big companies are trying to achieve.

"At first, big companies offer them financial inducements to sell, and the lure of jobs, which are of a very low level, due to villagers not having the proper expertise for the top jobs … those top jobs are always reserved for the outsiders. Villagers have no experience of dealing with such large amounts of money, and they soon spend it on cars and other short-lived luxuries, and they end up landless and penniless, as well as learning bad habits such as drinking and drugs. In developing nations, where you can buy medicines without prescriptions, a lot of people soon become addicted to drugs like sleeping pills, and if they have nothing, they end up committing crimes and finally becoming a problem for normal society, who sees them as a danger to their lifestyle and prefers them to be locked up in jail or dead.

"I've noticed that some people, depressed because of family issues or some other issues, soon become drunk or alcoholic, and then they depend on sleeping pills. Many chemists are very happy to offer them these pills without any prescriptions, and this is ruining their lives, as well as their families. Many drunks are now not only seen outside *theka* (local liquor shops) but also seen by the chemist too. They hand over the drugs when no one is looking. The police authorities may not even notice as these things are new in these villages and the chemist is happy to make money, rather than to inform the police or any welfare or social services to help the victim. This is a big shame.

"What my friend had noticed while visiting the gold and opal mines is very different," continued Dani. "Most of the outsiders had a very good lifestyle and had benefited from the gold rush. On the other hand, the locals who had been there for generations were living in extreme poverty and were labelled as drunks, drug addicts, depressives, or lazybones. They were considered a rotten part of the community and hardly had anything, even when living next door to a world-famous mine, where they produce more than 28,000 kilogrammes of gold every year. These huge companies are turning over billions of dollars, but have no funds to reinvest in these communities through education and support, which could be done at a relatively low cost.

"They are immune to the sight of these disenfranchised people, drunk and hopeless, while they carry on digging gold under their noses. If the world could adopt a fairer system, these companies would train the local community through a suitable educational process to work and benefit from the mines, so they don't suffer. This should be made the primary precondition of these mining companies before they grab the land.

"The desire for diamonds, gold, precious stones and oil around the world is age-old. But it should not be permitted for the wealth to be taken by a few while the many, or locals, are left to suffer with nothing. Stealing their treasure and only giving them small jobs and compensation to shut them up, while big rich companies loot and snatch their wealth is simply not ethical.

"If something like this was discovered in Europe, would they let these companies plunder it with no conditions? No, they would put all sorts of limits and leases in place such as tax, royalties etc. on the projects generated, so that they could get a fair benefit. But if it is being taken from the Bushmen of Africa or the tribes of the Amazon, or from the Aborigines in Australia or the communities of the Himalayas, the world simply watches and no one is there to stop them. So where are the world organisations and their justice?" questioned Dani.

"All the precious stones, metals and diamonds being dug, smuggled and sold on at high cost are part of the assets of these rich countries. No compensation is paid to the communities where these things originate. I believe that any country which consumes such a precious asset should pay a royalty to the country where it originated. With inventions, every user pays a fee to the inventor for a new invention.

And so it should be with natural resources. There should be accountability.

"In the modern world, people talk about harvesting elements of nature on a huge scale. Now they are digging deep into the ocean floor for oil, gas and more precious metals and minerals. Soon, in the future, they will start digging on the Moon and Mars," said Dani.

It reminded Roland of the film, *Avatar.* "What a great vision that writer had. In truth what really matters is the body, and we are making it weak by ruining the fresh air and the climate, or even life itself. We can't cope with the heat or cold. We need air conditioning and heating to survive. Even running a little to catch a bus or a train nearly kills us and makes us feel out of breath. If we face a permanent power cut or energy loss, half the population may not survive for long as the new generation hasn't lived without these comforts. Everything is on the shelves for them under one roof in supermarkets.

"People don't need to move, as online shopping can be done from their phones now. In the bush in Africa or Australia, in the Himalayas, or in any other remote part of the world, whether in heat or in cold, a tribal man's body needs no external comfort. He is naturally resilient and is not brought up with air conditioning or heating. He can live, fully fit, just by training his body according to the natural conditions."

"Are we losing something fundamentally and profoundly precious?" Dani asked. "We have an old saying, 'if you have no ears, what's the point of earrings?' That's what we are heading towards – digging to the core of the earth and the sea floor to fulfil desires which are spoiling the real human self. From one perspective, they want to dig these mountains for cement to make life comfortable, but in a real sense they are ruining the lives of all those farmers whose ancestors have lived here for the last thousand years. So it is a very difficult balance between the old and modern life. In fact, in developing nations, cement house building is of a poor standard and many lives have been lost due to the collapse of these buildings, for example in the Pakistan earthquake or the Mumbai buildings collapse, because they are not built properly with metal reinforcements. Very often villagers don't have enough money to do it properly. Houses are built room by room or joint by joint over a long period of time, without any structural engineer or a qualified builder overseeing them as well as these are modern techniques and they have no advance training."

"Why doesn't the whole village get together and protest against this cement plant?" asked Roland. "If the villagers don't allow the company into the village and demonstrate against it, nobody can plunder their resources. After all, this is their land and they have a right to protect it."

Dani said, "The problem all over India is that people have not fully understood the ways of the democratic system and they enable the ambitious people to exploit them. Democracy means the government of people for the people, they don't realise the power of their private vote, that through that they choose the candidate to work for them. Some selfish leaders utilise the democracy in their favour by tricking the innocent villagers through false attractive promises. From the local political authority, called the *panchayat,* to the *Sansad*, or parliament, it is all a game of voting and the party system. Today's democracy is a bit difficult in India. If there are nine good people and ten bad, the ten bad people will control the government. In the old days the Himalayan villages had their own democratic electoral system, which was thousands of years old and still functioning in a village called Malana in the Kullu Valley. It is known as the oldest democracy in the world, but it is different in that they have a deity, or *deo,* who is fully in charge of the community and people have unlimited devotion to him, and he oversees all the assemblies, and they daren't do anything wrong for fear of sin, bad karma, curse, or even punishment from the *deo*, as you can be cut from the community for any crime. But without having a father figure and a role model in charge it can be difficult. I wonder if Indian maharajas could be revived in a modified and constitutional way, so they could provide a moral and ethical figurehead of traditional India and its values. Otherwise, it will be a long time before India gets a proper, working system in place to deal with corruption and other abuses of power."

Dani said, "To tell you the truth, Roland, this political voting system and choosing of a candidate has divided every family, community, village and *panchayat* and district here in the Indian villages. The problem is that the wrong kind of people want to be in power. They see it merely as a way to make money for themselves as well as being able to rule over other poor and ignorant or innocent people. Within each village, one member will be pushed by congress, and another from the same village by the BJP party, and a few by other parties. Sometimes these can be from close families or second or third cousins. But when they show them the power and the money, or links to big political leaders, everyone starts dreaming of climbing up the ladder and they forget about unity and the community. They start to dream of being an important person with big cars, drivers and security.

"Party people will tell them that's how you will become president or maybe a minister of state. They know how to tempt these villagers. Finally, two people will stand for a small seat, and each will start to ask, and count from the families in the village, who is voting for whom. It is very hard for villages to handle this situation, because it causes problems and many people like to stay neutral.

"Soon they find out and it creates divisions and makes two different communities within the same village. This is awful. Sometimes families will not even communicate or be social with each other once this happens, almost in every village in India."

"This is very serious, like in Northern Ireland," Roland said. "Both are Christian but each wants to defeat the other just because of narrow mindedness, misunderstanding and ignorance. Many of them don't understand the meaning of democracy, or the voting system, or the meaning of spirituality. They think they are the best and that they deserve the power. In real terms they are both victims of the same enemy. If they leave behind the issue of God power or man power and use power for the benefit of every human, they will all live a better life."

Dani went on. "Because these aspiring politicians have forgotten that they are accountable and have brothers and sisters from the same village, their land will end up being exploited by outsiders who have already completed projects like this cement factory and have moved on to bigger and better projects and have far more experience in exploiting, and so you see why this project will happen, and local people who are involved in the process will be unknowingly facilitating it.

"The strange thing is that some rich people who can afford it have bought some land from poor villagers in these places, as soon as they discover the plans about the projects, so they can claim compensation on it. They are in favour of these factories because they will benefit most from it. So you see, Corporations do benefit from this division within the villages. A local villager will have sold his land on at very little cost, way before people will have known about the factory. After the news of the factory, values go sky high and new owners grab the compensation, while the original owners lose out. I even urge the government to introduce a new law to protect locals, and they should definitely receive part of the compensation for the land, which is sold after the commencement date of the project."

"So what will happen to them, Dani?" Roland asked.

"They will be landless, homeless and jobless, and will become, in the end, the stone grinders, the hard labourers and such for the rich and powerful. Their land, their culture and their way of life will be taken over by greed and power, and these big companies will make huge profits from it. Once all the stone has been taken and the mountains disappear, this valley will be left for dead. That's what I feel, Roland," Dani said. "And here we are sitting on this mountain, fortunate enough that we can discuss it and enjoy the best of the valley. Do you know, Roland, that the British also enforced this 'divide and rule' policy in India, because some of the local kings did not understand the policy and they were always fighting and killing each other. The British grasped that and kept their army for a big fee, and one by one, most of the rulers fell under them."

"So that's what is happening here again, and in the battle of two, the third party wins, until the two parties get together and fight the outsider united," said Roland.

Now it was time to move on and they could see Thali far away. They went to bow at the main shrine, which was a carved wooden temple right on top of the peak. The priest offered them flowers and sweets and they thanked him and gave a donation before starting their descent.

Leaving behind the top of the hill and walking down the steps from the temple, Roland's mind was full of thoughts about what other issues there may be to fight. He asked Dani if there were any other issues in the villages.

"There are many," said Dani. "You cannot escape anywhere, as we humans like to create issues, and it's all because someone wants power or to rule over others, or it might simply be the desire to be better than others or wanting more. We are all the same. In Europe they had the class system: royals, upper class, middle class and lower class. Here in India we have the caste system, which is very old and still remains in the villages. Thank goodness, though, now it is disappearing."

"If this was in their religion," Roland asked Dani, "how did it work?"

"Roland, if I explain it in short you will misunderstand it," Dani said. "To understand this system you have to know about its origins and the reason behind it and why, sadly, it is still carrying on."

"In that case I better put my recorder on," said Roland.

Dani smiled. "Then I really have to explain it accurately, otherwise whoever listens to it will blame me and misunderstand this old system."

Dani went on as they walked downhill. "All over the world, Roland, people live in different communities with their different traditions and rules to survive and to have a better life. They share many things and work together to progress. Before we understand the caste system in India and talk about it, I would like to explain the natural division among human beings and what the ever-changing societies and communities on earth are.

"To discover this we have to go back thousands or millions of years in human history. Science has now proved that the world was not divided into as many continents and islands as it is now. India used to be part of Africa, and as the Indian continent moved and pushed the land mass, it created the Himalayas, the highest mountains on earth, which are still growing.

"We may have all come from the same origins in Africa, but humans had to adapt and make changes in their lifestyles according to the weather, climate and wildlife around them, as well as the options for food and vegetation to live on.

"In the Arctic, they had to resort to ice houses and hunting bears, seals and fish or reindeer. They used the skin of animals to keep warm and to dress up. Carts pulled by reindeer or husky dogs were developed. In hot countries they caught and rode elephants, camels and horses, and didn't need to use warm or thick clothes or the skin of other animals. These different ways of surviving led us to create communities, and we had pride in our societies and traditions. They got used to those ways and it became their lifestyle. All those rules they developed in order to survive, or what to do, and what not to do, became the traditions that were handed down through the centuries.

So the first divisions that occurred in the world were due to living in different parts and in different climates. The second division was due to the sun, which caused the variations in skin colour from dark and brown through to white and red. Some other physical differences included differences in appearance such as being tall, short, round face, long face, long legs, short legs etc. Eyes wide open or slit eyes. Again, this was due to the various climates they lived in, such as windy or non-windy etc. It is like if you go to Ladakh in the state of Jammu and Kashmir or Spiti in Himachal Pradesh or to any other high, cold, windy mountains in the world, like Nepal, Tibet or China. You will find people here who cover their faces from the wind or the dust and they hardly open their eyes and in time the eyes adapt so you open your eyelids very little, even just looking through eyelashes. Their eyelids develop different muscles and their eyes look different from people who live in the lower parts of the mountains that don't have these conditions.

"I experienced that in the Himalayas. I wonder if my eyes and face would adapt too if I spent a long time in the Himalayas? People kept thinking that I was local and asked why I wasn't speaking the local dialect. In Nepal I had to show my passport during the Annapurana trekking to prove that I was from India."

"But these physical changes must have taken thousands of years," Roland commented.

"Of course, once your body has adapted, your physical attributes pass down to your children through the genes and they then adapt further and further, because human evolution includes a drive to survive and carry on life. As Charles Darwin is reported to have said, 'It is not the strongest or most intelligent beings who survive, but only those who are most adaptable' – so we can conclude that all those species that are alive today were the most adaptable.

"The second difference comes from the way people look. They could be dark or fair and have red hair or blonde hair etc. People sometimes use physical features to differentiate one person from another. These attitudes cause natural divisions in humans, and they are passed on from one generation to another. After this comes ways or habits regarding dress. Although we look alike we cover ourselves in different types of clothes. What is easy to wear and less expensive will be worn by normal, ordinary people, and what is thought to be stylish, more rare, or luxurious, will be worn by the important people of the community. This is so in every race and society.

"Once they had created a way of living according to their own possibilities and limits, the community started to live together and people were divided on the basis of intelligence, wisdom, strength, civility etc, and subdivided further as workers, labourers or slaves. The strong and clever people held power through the generosity of the rest of the community or because they benefited their community, or they knew how to gain respect and favour from the public, or simply because people regarded them highly.

"One family would become the prominent family and anyone else related or connected to them would also be considered more important. One thing to remember is that although these people are considered important and they have the power to rule, some intelligent or wise people cannot be dictated to by these people. They are not impressed by false positions. For them, kings or queens are not important either. Their own morals and way of life is more precious to them and they prefer truth and justice or fairness. But this process of division carried on regardless and people were finally divided into different classes. They always found their class better or more comfortable than others. This is still very much alive within every community throughout the world, though it can be flexible over generations. One upper-class family can become working class if their property or power is lost and they cannot maintain their previous position. Many people in the West love their upper-class ways. They do things within their class and society, and this can be seen even more in those countries where kings and queens still rule.

"Some people live and do well in the shadow of these people. They are linked to important people somehow or they find a connection and use it to impress others so they can be respected. In most developed societies one can see that a person with a big name, a big house or expensive cars is treated better, so they naturally attract their hangers-on."

"Sometimes people may take an expensive present or gift to a rich host and a cheap present to a poor host," said Roland, "when it should really be the other way round."

Dani continued. "The real difference, or division, is explained as *gunas* (qualities) in our ancient Indian science. This goes back thousands of years. Human beings always find differences. You will see a village where people will be from the same religion, the same class and with the same amount of wealth yet they will still find issues to argue or complain about and will often fight. They will soon create a new branch of religion, club or organisation. And the root of the problem is that human nature always wants more and more and is never satisfied.

"The difference between humans is not because one lives in the north or one lives in the south, or that one is dark or one is white. The differences lie in the real science of qualities, or *gunas*.

"From the oldest texts and Sanskrit descriptions," Dani explained, "We are told that there are three types of *guna* and they create a big difference in humans.

"The body is part of nature and seen as a plant, according to the *Sanatana Dharma* (*India's oldest system*). Nature consists of the three *gunas*: *sattva, rajas*, and *tamas*. *Sattva guna* manifests as purity and knowledge, *rajas guna* manifests as activity and motion, and *tamas guna* manifests as inertia and laziness. These three qualities of nature or the body always exist together. There cannot be pure *sattva* without *rajas* and *tamas gunas* nor pure *rajas* without *sattva* and *tamas*. The difference between one being and another lies in the balance between the *gunas*, which can be affected by the types of food we eat. As long as a person is attached to any of the *gunas*, he remains bound. Even the super-intelligent are under their influence. *Sattva* binds a person with attachment to *anand* (bliss). *Rajas* binds a person with attachment to activity, and *tamas* with attachment to delusion. They are present in varying degrees in all objects, including the mind, intellect and ego. The *gunas* can be seen as operating at the physical, mental, and emotional levels."

Roland was a bit lost about these three qualities and wondered if a simpler explanation could help him to understand them.

Dani gave an example, "Suppose there is a big rock in the middle of a footpath which can be removed with a little effort, and these three people influenced by these three different qualities are passing by, one by one. If a *tamas guna* person, who is careless, lazy and dull, passes by the rock, he will not even think about it and may even add some more stones or give it a good kick.

"If a *rajas guna* is passing by, he will see the stone and realise that it's in the way. Because of his active nature and ego, he would want to remove the stone but preferably when someone can see him doing it, so he can get a reward for it, or he might tell everyone that he has moved the rock and how strong or good he has been so he will be praised. Then he will feel good as it will feed his ego.

"The *sattva guna* is a very different person and not at all influenced by external factors. This person has a balanced mind and as he is walking he will notice the stone but may not even think about it. He will just move it out of the way and not give it further thought. For him it is just something that needs doing because someone may trip over it and hurt themself. This brings him a sense of justice and righteousness. It gives him pleasure and does not add anything to his ego. This type of nature binds us with happiness, and in this quality every action is enjoyed simply.

"Actions of mind and body are always taking place, so the best thing for a balanced mind is to enjoy the present action, to enjoy whatever they are doing at that moment. That is the only way to bind action to happiness there and then. *Sattva guna* helps with the mental balance and this person will act or speak when needed and will otherwise be peaceful. His actions will be powerful, fast, profound and skilled, because he is storing so much energy and life in balance. This is unlike the action of a *rajas guna*, who is fast but active at first and then his energy wears off later on.

"So these are three differences in humans. Anywhere we go in the world, to an upper-class black tie party or in a very rough pub in the town, you will always find some people of the wrong type, some people active and some people very sensible. It does not matter where they are or what they do and how they dress. They can be labourers or royal princes or beggars, criminals, rich or poor. But *gunas* will put them in different categories and that is the real difference in us according to Sanskrit scriptures," declared Dani.

"I have been to some parties where people were dressed in black tie or tail suits, and called Lady this or Lord that. Although they will all be titled, their *guna* differentiates them. One can recognise who is the *sattva*, *rajas* or *tamas* among them. So in every society, class, community, religion, race, colour and organisation or family, these three different qualities exist. For example, they may all talk to you or ask you for a drink, but their way and their behaviour will define their *guna* within those lines."

Roland was quite taken by this interesting explanation and the concepts of qualities and how they divide us in every level of life. By this time, they had completed around an hour walking to the little village of Jusal, where their car was supposed to be waiting. It was time to look for their driver as they had planned to drive halfway back so they weren't late for the evening. There was a small tea stall and they could see a man there making fresh samosas and pakoras.

"Oh delicious," said Dani. "We also need to remember to fill our water bottles, and they sat down on a wooden bench to view the scenery.

There were a few small terraced fields further down around the hills where they could also see cows and goats grazing. Dani explained that they grow lots of pomegranates and make delicious fresh chutneys here.

"We may not get real chutney like these people make anywhere else in the world," said Dani, and he asked the stall keeper if he had made some for the afternoon. He handed over a little saucer with Dani's favourite chutney. Dani also inquired how his business was going and whether people bought lots of snacks and tea from his stall.

"Not that great," he said. "Only old people buy tea and pakoras. Young people buy chips and Bombay mix and other packets, even though they are three times the cost and not freshly made at all."

Dani said, "But it is your fault."

"Why?" the man asked.

"Because you sell them these chips and encourage people to buy them, and these companies increase their sales, and once people like them they always want them. Who will buy your fresh and delicious pakoras, because Bollywood actors are not advertising or promoting pakoras or samosas made by local stores in the villages, they are promoting big brands and that's the fashion for all youths. If you start selling cold drinks, people will not buy tea either."

The man laughed and said, "You are right, sir."

Dani suggested, "Well try to sell what is local and made in the village, and tell the villagers that that's how they can save more money, and the money will go back to the village as profit from the sale of sweets, pakoras, samosas and tea. Because those villagers can also sell you their milk, flour, vegetables and all the ingredients you need to make these delicious snacks. Otherwise, cold drinks and machine-made packet-sale profits will go to the big companies in big cities and the villages will get poorer by the day."

Dani was also upset because he could see empty chip packets etc. littered all around the stall. Roland paid and it was only twelve rupees (15p) for two cups of tea and some pakoras and samosas with the chutney free. If they'd had chips or cold drinks their bill would have been almost seventy rupees or more.

By now the Jeep and the driver, Sanjay, a great friend of Dani's from near his family's village, had arrived. He saw them having tea and joined them for a cup too.

"Perfect timing, Sanju (his nickname from school)," said Dani.

"I would have been here long ago, but this road is new and I had to slow down," Sanju replied.

Soon they started their journey via Sanvidhar village to Tattapani and Thali village. They enjoyed their ride down the hill along the winding roads and were pleased that they had avoided the descent on foot. Dani was happy to have a break from speaking English and he carried on chatting in Hindi with Sanju, but on the way he stopped sometimes to point out a few things to Roland.

When they got back, Dani continued. "Another difficult thing on earth is God and religion, Roland. Not everyone can be kings and queens, or rich, so some people take shelter in God and religion, or conjure up mysteries to control the less educated and feed their ideas. Sometimes these religious people become very powerful and even many kings and queens or political leaders fall into this trap too, or go along with these religious people to increase their power and attract more people to their own cause or for popularity.

"We humans do need something higher to believe in when we can't find adequate answers to our suffering. There are many questions for which the answers are lacking. Such as why is one person born as a prince and one as a beggar? Or Is God sitting on a cloud and looking down at everyone, and directing the whole world like a play? Or are we ourselves the cause of our own sufferings? Has anybody met him and discussed all these issues with him?"

"Not I, Dani," replied Roland.

"Not a single person has been able to provide us with the answers or proof. But then some people don't want answers or proof. Some people are emotional and are driven or brainwashed by childish stories, tricks and explanations and they cannot live without them, whether they make sense or not. These leaders build their lives around these stories to find comfort and security. Because if they didn't, then all these religious people would cease to become powerful overnight and they would lose their income and the lifestyle they have. So they have to push these ideas onto everyone and they always look for some vulnerable moments, like when someone has died, or is suffering with illness, or has had some major disappointment or is happy expecting a baby or just had a baby etc. These are the moments for religious people to get hold of you and to influence you. Once you believe in it, they have you for life. And even though they have their own family and life problems, they say that God is testing their devotion and service."

"So people should tell them, 'Yes this pain or suffering is also from God and I don't need you'," Roland said.

"People from alternative belief systems have proven that people can live without God and religion. Like in the Western world, secular life is becoming much more popular. After all, we are all human and one family. The spiritual aspect of life is always there and is private to each living being. Nothing against the existence of a God or spirituality, but one has to question fully all impractical religious practices and dogma. In the ancient times, spirituality and worship was a sort of thanksgiving to nature and a celebration of its elements. It is only when religion or powerful leaders crept in and they tried to use it to their own advantage, so they could be in charge of heaven or hell for ordinary people, while they enjoyed the fruit of their receipts and tax-free donations. They don't tell their followers what joy freedom is in the shelter of God's power! Otherwise everyone will have freedom of choice – that cycling, singing, dancing, eating, meditation – anything can be their religion if they so choose.

They can follow any principles or rules to live with nature or in harmony with one another. It could be with the obeying of the local law or constitution, if it is fair. There are now people who love food so much that restaurants are their temples, and it makes them happy. One of my friends, Devdan Sen, who is a *Rough Guide* writer and is a very keen cyclist, took me once to a huge bicycle showroom saying that for some people that was a temple and cycling was a ritual and a religion to keep fit and healthy and balanced. There are cyclists who go to huge bicycle showrooms to admire new bicycles and that is a shrine for them. They worship the bicycle god, who produces beautiful cycles! A motorbike man may say that his way is faster or his God is more powerful, but that's it. But cycling for sure is safer and is more harmonious with nature."

"Religion is a very dangerous tool," Roland said, "and because of it millions of lives have been lost in the world, especially in Europe and the Middle East. As soon as new faiths and beliefs were adopted by the important people in society, the new religions meant the old pagan, Roman, Greek, Norse and Germanic stories of worshipping the water, Earth, sky, Sun or fire ceremonies or nature were eradicated. Soon they updated and slightly changed the way they used to celebrate the Roman or Greek festivals or ceremonies. The meanings contained in the old myths and stories were all forgotten, even though they may have had some useful messages and concepts for society.

"Now there is a growth in non-believers and atheist groups, due to the nonsense of God," continued Roland. "Although religious organisations and churches are well developed, God's word is difficult to digest as everyone fights for his own idea of God."

"Religion should be very private and should not be fought over or imposed on others," said Dani. "It depends on the individual – what we want to believe in and to worship. It should not create an attitude of only our God is best and the rest are damned and will go to hell. We should all learn about each others' beliefs and appreciate them. Otherwise it creates fear, ego, power, war and crime and suffering. Religion should be private to each person. Everybody should have a little shrine in the corner of his house and pray or meditate according to his own wishes. We should learn from each others' ideas of peace and praise others' ideas and respect them. All shrines should be respected.

"This issue is very difficult. In the name of religion, thousands or millions of lives have been lost over the past one hundred years. The people who are supposed to achieve peace are actually creating war and crime. This is happening all around the world. We should be recognising the extraordinary men who have made a positive difference in the human family instead.

"For example, intelligent people like Charles Darwin found a common denominator for all humans and tried to encourage us to live in harmony with nature, animals and ourselves. He saw all beings as one family. You have some of the wisest people in the world born in the UK," said Dani. "People who invented light and engines and some of the most complex inventions on the earth. Darwin gave a message to all to learn and be one family."

Dani pointed at the river. "Here we are, we're in Tattapani."

Now all they wanted was to jump into the hot pools as the sun was setting and the weather was perfect for a hot bathe in the natural sulphur springs.

Sanju drove down towards a restaurant on the bank of the river and stopped. He parked the car and they all went for a drink. The hotel staff welcomed them and offered them a table, and soon the hotel owner, Umesh Raina, came out to greet them and asked them what they wanted to drink. Dani tried to avoid ordering anything expensive as he knew they wouldn't charge due to being related, so they ordered chai.

They enjoyed their tea while having a chat about their day, and then went for a dip in the pools and watched the people passing by on the bank of the river. They really needed their hot bath after the long trek.

"Many villagers come to have a bath in the evening in these natural springs. They are so lucky to have them in their village," Dani said. "They don't have to pay any heating bills at all. It's like a communal bath, but with all the men in one pool and the women in another, more private one."

To their surprise they were offered beer and some vegetable pakoras as a snack and they had a long and relaxing bath as the sun was going down and the riverside was becoming quieter and quieter. They enjoyed their evening and went home after dinner.

***

It was the next day in the village, after a village celebration, that Roland got the chance to ask Dani about the caste system again. They sat down at the table and Roland had his notes with him as well as his recorder. Roland had already read a little about it in his guidebook, but wanted a better explanation from Dani, so that he could understand it better.

They talked about some different caste systems in Africa and also the class system in Europe and in other parts of the world.

"The great thing is that the slave trade has gone and all those people sit and live together now and share life and its values," began Dani. "That is a transformation and a great step forward in human history, that we are all the same and equal as one human family. This has all happened within a very short time.

"But some people are still lacking in that understanding in India. Indian traditions introduced four types of caste system into the world in such a way that you can't move out of castes, from one to another, unless you are born into it. It is a strict rule that you have to marry within your caste, though a daughter can be known as half-caste after marriage if she adopts the caste and surname of her husband, though this applies differently in different parts of India. It is a difficult struggle to move higher in caste. A king or a monk, or *sadhu,* or a person who has renounced all material or worldly comforts is above all castes traditionally.

"From ancient oral knowledge and the written scriptures we are told that there was a great king called Manu, who was spiritual, kind, wise, and just, as well as a great warrior and a protector of his people. He looked after his kingdom with great devotion and pleasure and everything was in peace and happiness. Life was going very well. With the help of his wise and spiritual teachers, or gurus, they discovered that a huge destruction was going to occur on earth.

"So with their great knowledge and vision, they had calculated from rain, clouds and from the behaviour of a big fish that heavy rain and terrible floods were going to take over the land. We are told that the king had coincidently picked up a fish with the handful of water to offer to the Sun during his morning visit to the sea and his kindness brought her home to protect her. He first got this indication from observing this fish, which was behaving wildly and abnormally, getting bigger and bigger, So the king had to provide bigger water sources like tanks, ponds, a river and finally the fish had to be taken back to the ocean when it had grown too large. This incident was brought into the assembly of his wise people, and was first seen as a blow to the king's ego as he had promised to the fish that she was very fortunate to end up in the king's hand, and he could provide her plenty of space so she could grow as much as she liked, as well as that the astrologer had already predicted that the ocean and water would take over the land. So that fish was seen as a divine messenger, or a saviour of the people, and was considered as the first incarnation of the Matsya avatar of the god Vishnu, or the absolute force that looks after or preserves the earth. An incarnation means a super-intelligent mind that comes in different forms to life on earth and stands equally with normal people, without showing his extraordinariness, unless it is necessary for the protection of the people.

"They called it the Matsya avatar, which simply means fish incarnation, and everyone knows about it now, and in many temples all around India you can still see eighteen-hundred-year-old statues of this half-fish and half-human being. Who knows, it could be the same rare fish scientists have found and is now called a coelacanth, which evolved four hundred million years ago and is closely related to mammals. The coelacanth was thought to be extinct seventy million years ago, but they are still living today in the Indian Ocean."

Roland agreed, "Oh, yes, I remember you told me that. I think it is that lobe-finned fish, the living sarcopterygians."

That's right, Roland, but artists have tried to explain that incident in many different ways. But it was simply an extraordinary fish who wanted to warn the human race, like during the tsunami in South India, many elephants started to run away from the shore to the higher jungles and their *mahouts* or keepers could not control them and had to follow them too. Another story comes from some tribes who sheltered in the higher lands of their forest dwellings in the Andaman Islands after an elderly member of the community had read the clouds and wind and had predicted the terrible storm and waves in the sea, which we now know as the 2004 tsunami. Sometimes I am really surprised at the knowledge of these tiny birds and animals, how they sense things in very extraordinary ways."

"I wonder if animals are much more in tune with natural happenings than us?" said Roland. "Not only that, if we go to Scotland for walking holidays in the Highlands towards the Angus mountains, you always find these beautiful white birds, geese and other small birds flying over your head in large numbers, sometimes they will be fifteen or twenty, sometimes more than two hundred and you wonder what they are doing."

Dani agreed: "I tried to count them once and watched them for hours to understand their pattern and their way of flying. They make an angle to fly, maybe around sixty degrees or more and then they swap positions after a few minutes to the front to lead. The tired one goes to the back and the back ones come to the front to lead to do the shift."

"I wonder if they have some way to rest while flying," said Roland, "as they fly for hundreds of miles from one place to another, and furthermore, how do they know the directions? We get lost with paper maps, satellite maps, compasses and even with our own recollections, but they don't have any of that, and we hardly think they even have much of a brain. How do they remember their unmarked paths?"

"I think that humans have definitely lost some of their ability to read nature and our inner sense, or navigation, has disappeared whereas those birds, elephants and so-called primitive tribes have kept that knowledge," said Dani, "but we are depending more and more on external machines and losing our innate knowledge bit by bit.

"Anyway, King Manu believed all the indications and advice of his scholars and got ready to save his people as much as possible. Soon the king had ordered a huge boat to be built, and on the astrologically calculated day they gathered and took as many people as they could take with them, as well as important seeds, plants and animals and precious scriptures. As predicted, there was a huge storm

– rain and floods – and after many days of struggle and after losing countless lives, the storm abated and finally they could see some land, and it was the high Himalayas which became visible to them first." Dani wondered if this had happened after the formation of the Himalayas a few million years ago.

"So finally they took refuge on the dry land after the storm and the floods had gone down, and King Manu set about starting a new way of life to survive in the wilderness for the people who had made it through the terrible sea storm."

Dani continued, "Roland, if we go further up into the western Himalayas and follow the Beas River through Mandi and Kullu to Manali, there is an ancient temple dedicated to King Manu that has been newly restored, but it is centuries old, and some of the original statues have recently been discovered by the shepherds' families when they started to build their houses in the mountains.

"If we get a chance to go to the old village in Manali, we will hear stories from elderly people about the discovery of Great King Manu's statues. The story they tell goes back a few hundred years. A *sadhu,* or wandering holy monk, came into the village and said that there was a very old shrine in the village of King Manu and that he had received that old knowledge from his former teachers. People did not believe him or his tales. Then he asked a lady if it was possible to have some milk. The lady apologised and said that her cow was expecting a calf and it was not possible to have milk. Then he said to the lady, 'Well you villagers don't believe in me. Why don't you try your cow and see if she gives milk for her special guest, as they have great respect for *sadhus.*' So she did what he said. She was shocked that the cow gave more milk than it had ever done before. Then the villagers thought he was not just any ordinary wandering monk and they should believe him and follow what he said. So they dug at the place he indicated and found some very old ruins and old statues of King Manu, and since then the temple has been in service and is now a newly built shrine and attraction for tourists. So it is possible that Manu may have landed in these mountains because the Himalayas were the only places high enough above the water. And this story was preserved by the old tradition of oral story telling, which is still alive today.

"Well, wherever or however they started their new life, I'm sure that it must have been a challenge and they had to adapt to new changes and had to struggle to survive and keep their community alive. They had to live together and help each other. It is obvious that jobs would be given according to their experience, ability and interest. So one person would tend the goats or cattle and others would do other jobs. Like the way families still live together and everybody has a responsibility and a job according to their ability and capacity. It does not mean that their children have to do the same. No money was exchanged for any kind of job, like it used be in a kibbutz in Israel. It was a happy community sharing jobs and community work. Then it started to grow bigger and bigger. Many people became careless and lazy about their jobs, and some people disliked their jobs. Maybe they found it hard or felt that others had easier jobs than them. But the friction must have started within the community. People would be changing jobs all the time from hard to easy, and everyone wanted to avoid the harder jobs.

"That must be the time when this became a big issue and finally the issue was presented in the assembly of King Manu. After long consideration, discussion and thinking, it must have been very difficult to decide how jobs or work should be divided between families so that every family would have to stick to the same job forever, as it was a better way to train and retain important skills."

"Maybe the options were laid out to everyone," said Roland. "Whatever they liked to do they had to make a choice and then stick to it. Of course, even today, everybody is doing a job based on whatever they can do. Although theoretically we would all like to be in the top jobs, when it comes to reality, we all have to settle with what we are good at."

Dani went on, "So, according to their interests and abilities they must have made their choices and started to do the jobs they were most suited to. So the formation of this social system was fully based on a man's intelligence, not due to his birth or skills.

"After that, a system called *Manusmriti* was produced, and four *varnas*, or castes, or trades, were introduced to the public in order that everyone be able to serve their community in the best possible way. These trades were given to the community as: the top caste: *Brahmin* – scholars; including the sub-divisions, which were priests, preachers of all scriptures, community cook, astrologer and *vastu* architects. *Vastu* is a word in Sanskrit, which simply means site, space or location. This is an art concerning the way people built their temples, homes, living spaces and work spaces. *Vastu* art also has a balance of karma and *dharma*, the way of bringing these concepts of unity and completion to a physical space in the world as well as creating balance in our physical and spiritual space. The second caste was *Kshatriya* – warrior, who has ability to protect the community. They are supposed to be very fair to all. The third caste was *Vaishya* – traders and artisans. And finally, *Shudras* – workers and labourers, which was later divided into many sub-categories because of their different jobs. Kings and *sanyasis* (i.e. monks who had renounced everything) had no class and they were above all. But they still depended on the community for their living, and they could preach greater or higher values for the well-being of humanity and nature.

"Now everybody started to do their work and tried to be harmonious. Each caste had to do its work and they all depended on each other.

"The farmer would grow food for everyone, traders would take it around, and warriors would protect it. The scholars would teach, preach and give new ideas on any spiritual matters. Only the *Brahmin* would study the scriptures and go door to door or family to family to explain about weather through their astrological studies and calculations. Lectures were organised for the public on different topics or problems, because they had studied everything inside out and had become masters and scholars of their topics. So the other three castes didn't have to worry about studying, and they were well informed, or they could consult the scholars anytime. This system is still in order, but some aspects have changed. When I was young the scholars used to accept whatever you offered them – grain, rice or any seasonal crops, but now that system has almost fully been replaced by fees and cash payments. The advantage of this system was that no one needed to change their jobs but just had to get on with whatever they were used to and pass it on to their children. They must have learned much more than they would today as they had seen their parents doing it from childhood. They must have had relationships within their class so both people would have a good knowledge and understanding of the same skills and they could pass it to their children to be further advanced and skilled. Anyway, it did not look like a bad idea," said Dani. "It was a positive and practical division of labour. In the long term, though, it developed some issues. The problem with human nature is that there is always a race to be better or superior than the next person. Or we get bored of doing the same old job day after day, generation after generation. The conflict must have started when one would no longer do the job properly. If a carpenter is making a door, maybe he would start doing the job better for some and less well for others. Maybe the scholars started to say that all the knowledge and books were their property. Maybe they did not pass on all the knowledge and wisdom they had found through their studying and practice of spirituality, food, ways of working, astrology and other knowledge including, for instance, of Ayurveda. Or it could be that one of the trades completely died out and they had no one to do the job, and they had to recruit new people from different trades. Or maybe scholars wanted to rule and they misled the others.

"All the three lower classes used to eat meat and other types of food, but the scholars, or *Brahmin*, were pure vegetarians, eating fruit, nuts and milk products. This tradition is still alive today all over India. *Brahmin* will come to read scriptures door to door and will reveal the general forecast for the year as well as astrological predictions to each household, and how to survive in that year. They will even tell you about rain, heat or any other natural calamities including earthquakes, cloudbursts, lightning and fire as well as give you dates and timings of major moon and solar eclipses. And families very often give them grain, as in rice, wheat or corn in exchange for this information. But now some city scholars prefer money or cash and some of them may not even be authentic. But at some point something must have happened to make the classes dislike and mistrust each other.

"Another cause might have been that people just became exhausted. For example one is cleaning the sewage and another is studying books. One would get very tired physically and the other mentally. Maybe it became too much to keep doing the same thing. Or perhaps the children started to tease each other, 'Oh, your father is a cleaner or butcher. Your parents are doing dirty jobs and we are more clean and superior.' Somehow the friction began and they started to dislike each other and wanted to stay in their own trade and did not want to mix with other castes.

"Of course it was not easy to leave their jobs and switch, so professions carried on from generation to generation, and a change must have been very difficult, because everybody was dependent on each other to live.

"But friction was definitely there. The higher castes did not want a person who was involved in the lower jobs like cleaning and slaughtering to join them at the table, and they did not go to each other's kitchens. The kitchen became very private and not everyone was allowed to enter it. Because the age-old knowledge of different spices and herbs took place in the kitchen, a special food with a mind-blowing aroma was produced to satisfy the senses and taste buds. They started to serve food separately for each community and avoided any other strange smells in the kitchen. This did not go down well with the community, but although people started disliking each other they still had to do their job to survive, which is still the case in many rural places in India.

"The caste system has not disappeared yet and many ignorant people are still very superstitious about it. The most important thing was that all the different trades had surnames and one could recognise from the name which caste he belonged to. If someone wanted to leave the area or go to a different place, he had to change his name, which he could do, but people could still discover the person's history by his work or if he had knowledge of higher trades. This was not easy to hide, unless someone had access to it or were highly intelligent.

"Don't forget," Dani said, "that what I am trying to explain within a few paragraphs and examples evolved over thousands of years and this was a very slow process. Within these communities *Brahmin* and *Vaishyas,* or traders, became quite close as *Brahmin* had to depend a lot on the traders, and the traders had significant powers as they controlled all the trade and food. After the second century, traders became rulers and the Gupta (famous traders still today) dynasty became a golden era of India. *Brahmins* were also quite close to the royals, because they used to advise them on every aspect of life. But as the mistrust gradually grew, people wanted to become independent, they started to do small-scale farming and kept a few animals for milk, and many jobs were done by everyone. Also, people started to pay for services and become independent and were in competition with each other. Some castes grew in wealth and comfort while others were left behind. And the population must have multiplied many times over thousands of years. The tradition of working for food for someone has disappeared and everyone wants to have their own house, farm and good life.

"So this struggle to be self-sufficient and free was happening in all the castes. Life carried on like this for a long time. There is some mention of it in the *Mahabharata* period, which was around five to twelve thousand years ago, where they only allowed royals or *Kshatriyas* (warriors) to study with the scholars in their ashrams. These were like boarding schools where students lived with the teacher's family away from society and family life, and the princes had to leave all their comforts to live with the scholars in the forests to develop resilience, strength and wisdom, which is where the idea of boarding schools sprung from.

"So the warriors or royals would live with the gurus. Gurus bring the real light of knowledge and wisdom to a student, until they are perfect in all aspects of life, but spiritual development was first, followed by military and fighting skills. Teachers were chosen on the basis of their knowledge, wisdom and oral skills through live debates and practical performance. They were always older as they were supposed to have more knowledge of the world and life which they could pass on.

"When students used to return to the palaces after ten to fifteen years of this education, they would have debates and competitions to prove to the king and their parents that they were perfect in all aspects of life. But many people were being suppressed due to not having had such an education, although they might have had better skills than the royals in warfare or in archery or in swordplay, and also in the knowledge of scriptures and morals. But they had no right to challenge the royals unless they were a prince or royal of some sort. The royals believed that it was all in their blood, and of course the training they received through the generations influenced the whole of their society.

"You could recognise them from their appearance and their walk and how they held their head high with pride. This went on for generations," Dani went on. "Now if you study more about India and its ancient philosophies, you will find out that there have been many great people that never accepted any difference between humans of whatever caste, and did not hurt anyone with their ego or pride.

They stood shoulder to shoulder with the people and gave everything to protect *dharma*, or righteousness, justice and peace among people.

"In the story of the Ramayana period, way before the Mahabharata period, Lord Ram spent fourteen years with apes and different tribes in the jungle during his exile from his kingdom, following his stepmother and father's wishes. He did not see any difference between low or high caste. The story goes that he ate berries offered by an old lady called Bhilani from the tribe of Bhil, who was so overwhelmed to meet him, all she could offer him was wild berries, but to make sure they were sweet and not bitter or sour, she kept tasting them herself before handing them over to Prince Ram. Ram kept eating them, and his younger brother, Lakshman, was getting upset with him and reminded him of his princehood and social status and also that she was biting every fruit before handing them over to him and her spit, germs or a disease might harm him. But Ram smiled and kept eating, and then told Lakshman that she was tasting every fruit to make sure that he was offered the best one. Then he asked his brother if he recognised the love, hospitality and generosity of the elderly lady, and told him that 'Oh my dear brother, when true love is there, all the differences disappear. There is no difference of any kind between two beings.'

"Another great person from the Mahabharata period is Lord Krishna, who was a prince too, and he lived all his childhood with cattle farmers. He showed people that every human is equal by demonstrating to the public that materialistic differences were not real. He was the one who satisfied the great warrior, Arjuna, with his wisdom, when Arjuna nearly collapsed in the battlefield after seeing his uncles and cousins on the other side, before a great war began and refused to fight and wondered what life was all about. The desire for a kingdom seemed just a game, and the conversation between them became the book of wisdom known as the *Bhagavad Gita*. Today, it is around five thousand years old and it discusses the body, mind and senses as well as duty and righteousness.

"So Ram and Krishna both lived wonderful lives, and later they both became great kings after removing those who just wanted to rule by terror, greed and injustice in order to serve their own purposes. Because the good have to protect and rule in order to save *dharma* and justice for its people, if the rule goes into the wrong hands then the whole population has to suffer under greedy and cruel dictators.

"We had another great warrior prince called Siddartha, who was born in 522 BC. He was brought up in a very privileged way and lived a life of luxury. A special palace and garden was even built for him before his birth. All the dry leaves and dead petals used to be removed from his garden before he went out for his morning walk in the garden, and he had a joyous and happy life. He did not experience pain or suffering or other negative things that happen in the world.

"Whatever he did was well-planned and he had a routine for everyday. He was given the best education and knowledge of ancient wisdom and yoga. He married young and enjoyed all the worldly pleasures. But one day, when he was bored of being taken along the same route by his charioteer every day, he asked him, 'Why do you always take me through this way?' His charioteer replied, 'Royal Highness, because that's the only path I have known all these years.' But Siddartha said, 'No, you are wrong. This is not the only path. You think this is the path, because you are told that this is the path. How can there be just a single path? You need to discover your own path, and there are many paths to the same reality.' And he left the charioteer and walked off through the streets, jungles and river banks.

"As he went through the streets and riversides, he saw beggars with leprosy, without limbs, all kinds of suffering and someone being taken to the riverside for cremation. He found out everything and he was guided by his staff, who answered all his questions. What he discovered gave him a shock, and he could not believe that real life was like this. It made him decide to leave his palace and his comforts behind and he went off to live in caves and jungles for years and years to study, explore and discover the real truth of life and the cause of all the suffering. After meditating and self-realising, he had a vision that desire was the cause of all suffering, and through the power of the mind one can overcome desire and live in peace and harmony with oneself. He taught that there were no differences between humans and asked them to live in harmony with every living being and even nature. In time he became very popular, so that today all around the world people know his name. They may not know his real name, Siddartha, or later Gautama Buddha, but they know him as Buddha, and his statues and posters are found in all corners of the world, including famous galleries in London and Paris and so on.

"Gradually, India began to learn that wars were not the way forward. After the Kalinga War in 261 BC, the great King Ashoka was attracted by the teachings of Buddhism and Jainism. Seeing all the killing in the Kalinga War, he renounced wars and spread a message of peace and harmony. It was also at this time that there was a surge in Indian architecture and art. Art could be seen carved into rocks in caves during this period and also victory towers were erected to spread the message of peace all over India. Some people had also found ways of finding inner peace and pleasure through renouncing worldly comforts and living a moral life. They were also seeking to explore the science of worldly pleasures, and the *Kama Sutra was written.* Gotsyan wrote this book to help people understand the science of lovemaking and harvesting the goodness of our bodies and hormones. That's when lots of stone temples were built, and caves were carved out in some parts of India and exceptional art was produced for the world."

"Oh, so this is all the fault of this guy called Gotsyan. He is the cause of all the madness happening in the world!" Roland joked.

"Yes, Roland, that's the guy. If you find him, you need to punish him!"

"No Dani, not to punish, but to find out more secrets!"

Dani laughed. "He spent his whole life on this research and now you can buy a copy in any bookstore. He did really well, it's still on sale after eighteen hundred years or so!"

"I'm sure that during this time genes were being passed on or mixing. Many lower-class people were working for the richer just for food, and some higher castes had grown very rich and very powerful. There must have been some illicit affairs, as some rich and spoiled men often desire beautiful ladies, and it doesn't matter to them if they are from any class or caste.

"I hope you are enjoying the story, Roland," said Dani.

"Oh yes, this is very interesting, Dani, carry on," replied Roland with a smile.

"Beautiful girls would be chosen from fairs and local celebrations and taken to royal courts, and they were happy to be mistresses, and the girls felt pride that they were the chosen ones. But maybe this happened much more after the second and third centuries as that was the time of art, stone carvings, and the *Kama Sutra*. That's why 'diamond cuts diamond', an old proverb meaning that 'iron cuts iron' happened, and soon there were lots of battles and uprisings among the public.

They were fully immersed in worldly pleasures and indulged themselves fully, while they treated the lower class or poor people as their property. There are lots of stories of the most beautiful girls being picked by these rulers, who would then be their mistresses, and these poor people thought that was the best thing that could happen to their families. Many lower-caste people had great devotion to their superiors and their duties and regarded them and the higher-class people as their destiny and the only way to survive. Low class people were also made to believe that, otherwise it was a sin.

"The value of the lower class was becoming less and less, and they were treated like slaves. Great teachings like the *gunas* and karma were being ignored because it meant hard work for the higher class. Those of lower caste were seen as objects to play with. In some parts of India, many higher-class people called them 'untouchable' and did not even let them touch their houses. The seventh and eighth centuries were the time when many scholars and thinkers, as well as wise people, were worried about what the system had become, and spirituality or higher morals were in danger.

"Then, a great sage of the Indian civilisation came to the notice of normal people at the end of the eighth century – Shri Adi Shankaracharya ji, who was born in South India. He is considered the highest and most intelligent scholar of Indian traditions, history and culture. He introduced the original system of *Sanatana Dharma* (*Sanatana* means everlasting natural law, which is the same for all, and *dharma* means righteousness or justice. This is the main tool and foundation of Hinduism and *dharma,* or action for justice, is the path that leads to inner peace. Also, *Vedanta* (*Ved* means 'knowledge' of 'higher enquiry' and *anta* refers to 'inner' as well as to 'end') was reintroduced to the people, for he understood that the caste system was a new and inferior system compared with the ancient system of *Vedanta*, which had existed way before King Manu. He was a great scholar and passed the knowledge orally, and even now they still pass it on to other Shankaracharyas in Sanskrit hymns and rhymes, or *shlokas*. There are four Shankaracharyas in India at any point in time for four parts of India. It is the highest seat in Sanatana, equivalent to the pope for the Catholics.

"Now what is the *Vedanta* secret, and what is the message he wanted to give to the public? It was to tell them that all the kings and queens and men and women and *Brahmin* and labourers were equal. They all belonged to one family. He defined the philosophy of one individual soul and one absolute supreme source of it. He called it *Omkar,* or 'absolute', or *Per Braham*, the supreme identity or Almighty God, who is beyond explanation, and that, absolute alone is real, the world is illusory and the individual self and absolute is one. We are all part of it and come from the same source and will go back to the same source. That true source of energy and life is pure and blissful."

Dani went on and explained the theory of action and karma. "Just do good to have a better life, for as you sow, so shall you reap. The right action and duty towards nature and humanity can lead us to absolute peace, and one can emerge in the absolute source, or inner self, as that absolute is within us and we are all part of it, because the real energy of life and creation is within us. So God is within all living beings. This revived philosophy made sense, and many attitudes started to change, and people were feeling more free to choose their work and so forth. But surnames did not leave them, and to get out of it was not that easy. But they had gained a great respect for each other again and people were getting on better with each other as a result of this new attitude. Respect and consideration were getting better and were being valued.

"But the caste system had lived in India for thousands of years and it was an old tradition and very firmly entrenched in the higher classes who did not want to see it abolished, and some new versions of texts were manipulated in favour of the higher classes as they were the only ones who could read or write or even touch these texts, especially in certain parts of India, where knowledge of the *Vedanta* had not reached. Because of this ignorance, the caste system is still alive in many villages in India.

"Around the ninth century, invaders had started to pillage India and to destroy its temples and traditions, from the Sultans of Persia to the Mughals. It continued until the British, Dutch and Portugese left India. As India was struggling with its own complex traditions and superstitions, many didn't even know what they should call themselves religion-wise, as such formal titles were not required in the past, they were simply living under different names and to a devotion to one absolute ruler. On top of that, outsiders were trying to push their own traditions and faiths onto India.

"The conversion of native Indians became a big thing in the Mughal's time and anyone who resisted was brutally tortured or killed, so others would not refuse. It was then in the fifteen century that a great scholar and teacher, Guru Nanak Dev, witnessed the suffering, torture and death of his own people. His wisdom and guidance helped people to stand up against the social and domestic divisions and become one as a spiritual army called the Sikh. Soon after,

Sikhism became the way forward, and many accepted Guru Nanak's vision of a casteless society. He brought Hindus and Muslims together by combining the architecture of temples and mosques, by having no statues or idols in the temples, and by always having free food in Sikh temples for anyone, because he recognised that a hungry stomach can't meditate.

"All are served from the same kitchen and all sit together. There was no difference. All are one in the eyes of the guru and absolute. Strict measures were taken to remove the castes from society and Singh was the main surname given to most, which means 'lion' or 'king'. Their generosity can be seen at the Golden Temple in Amritsar, where thousands of people eat free meals everyday, as well as in any other Sikh temple in any part of the world, London or elsewhere. They are considered to be brave and honest because they will never steal and you can rely on them anywhere for safety. They will give safety to children, women and the innocent, and they don't tolerate any discrimination against caste, which is amazing. Once again, the knowledge of *Vedanta* is purified and simplified in such a way that everyone can understand it and experience the essence of it.

"But there continued to be a struggle for profound knowledge in India, and from the sixteenth century to the twentieth century India was still trapped by various traders, missionaries and the British Raj, who wanted to establish their institutions, churches and the machinery they required to rule India. They mainly targeted the low-caste communities, who were fed up with the untouchability and had no knowledge of *Vedanta* or Sanskrit, so they were easy prey for outsiders, who were using them as a hidden weapon to destroy the ancient knowledge and traditions, and as soon as they introduced them to wine and alcohol, they had never felt better.

"But soon after that, Mahatma Gandhi emerged and understood the problem and recognised the difficulty and suffering of these people in the villages. He gave a lot of thought to the problem and took it very seriously and called all the lower-class people *harijan*, meaning 'God's own people' or 'blessed humans'. He provided land and homes and special rights for all the lower castes as well as other minorities after Independence.

"Credit also goes to Dr Bhim Rao Ambedkar. He was a scholar and had studied in America and London. His qualifications were in law, political science and economics, and he became famous for his work on behalf of the 'untouchables'. He had suffered the social discrimination of the caste system in his childhood and he wanted to remove it. He was a key influence in the Constitution of India in favour of full support and rights to untouchables now known as scheduled castes, tribes and backward classes. I have heard that he could not take water from a jug himself in school and he had to wait for a caretaker or a peon to serve him water so he didn't touch the main clay pot or bowl. One day the peon was on holiday and he spent a baking hot summer's day thirsty without water. So he had experienced the suffering first-hand, and his intelligence and hard work saved many lives from discrimination. He was a reformer and a key figure in the creation of the Indian Constitution to provide an equal platform and status for the lower class.

"After that, capitalism and modern culture such as Bollywood were moving India towards a more equal life for everyone. Nevertheless, if you visit a small rural village the caste system is still deeply rooted and many people are under pressure because of this. Not only the lower-class people, but higher-caste people dislike it as well. One of the issue and old job reservation in the villages is that they still prefer higher-caste *Brahmin* families who cook for weddings and festivals alongside most of the priests, because they still carry the old knowledge and recipes. If you have a lower-caste cook, you cannot invite your superstitious higher-caste guests to eat the food cooked by harijan or untouchables. It gives less opportunity to lower castes. Similarly, if a lower–caste person opens a restaurant, nobody will come from a higher caste to eat or drink there, mainly in the villages. Sometimes higher-caste people will not drink the water from a glass touched by the lower caste. It used to be worse in the old days, when the lower castes couldn't even touch the water sources directly and even wells were divided separately for them.

"This is a big shame for India and that's why many villages and communities don't develop. It is too engrained in their lives. But in high society, the corporate world and in the educated world, it is changing fast, and anyone can train as a cook or a chef, and no one has any objections, which is a major step forward for India's growth.

"On top of this is a statement from one of the greatest yoga teachers, called Baba Ramdev, who is watched by millions every morning teaching yoga on television and for his fight against corruption in India. He has appealed to everyone saying there is no such thing as lower caste and people should grow out of it. The caste system is mentioned nowhere in ancient yoga or in *Vedanta* scriptures, and society should eradicate it for a better, more healthy and corruption-free India. It has made people think and question. Other famous scholars like Shivananda and other yoga gurus have eradicated it from their yogic system too," said Dani.

"This is really very interesting, Dani," Roland said. "I had no idea this was going on in India."

Dani went on. "Although many reformers and leaders in government are doing a lot for untouchables, providing them special reservations on jobs etc., it is not removed from the villages. It is a big obstacle in love marriages as well as in arranged marriages because men cannot choose a girl in the higher caste, because nobody wants to be demoted. It is hard for both sides. If a higher-caste person is in love with a lower-caste woman it is not easy to marry her that simply, because he could be pushed down a caste by his own family and fellow caste people. So it is very difficult for both sides, and young people are fighting against it, but the older generation is holding firm and continuing to preach.

"For example, if there are five beautiful girls in a lower caste and a not-that-suitable girl in a higher caste who are looking for a match to marry, and on the other hand, a higher-caste boy is desperate to find a girl to marry, he will not be able to choose from one of the five. The only option he would have is that of the one unsuitable girl, and very often that's how they are making matches, by forcing arranged marriages through social pressure between two unsuitable people. That is absolutely wrong.

"This cannot create a healthy society. If there is a girl and boy who are both intelligent, good and well-suited, who could have a wonderful family together, but one is from a low caste, they may not be able to marry. They may have to accept other more limited options for marriage. This is the real downfall of the caste system. Although the government has introduced a inter-caste marriage reward to support these marriages and pays money to both parties to take this forward step, but there are not that many brave enough. They could live a secluded and unhappy life, but they are afraid of being kicked out of their castes to a lower caste. To climb the ladder is easier only for more influential families.

Three or four marriages happen in every generation, but the struggle for children is harder. Their parents' love marriage can bring them to a lower-caste level, but that is slowly changing now.

"Another issue with these classes is that it impedes the brighter, more intelligent people from getting better jobs. The old-boy network for jobs in some sections of society plays a big role. Recommendations and contacts promote their loved ones or same caste people forward. Sometimes there may be a much more suitable candidate somewhere else, but they are obliged to employ someone who has come through someone they know rather than a person who is slightly different to them in outlook. It is corruption for sure. And this has to stop," said Dani.

"Very often you will see in India a policeman's son will go into the police, or in similar government institutions or departments. It seems that whoever has a government job, their son gets those jobs first. Thank goodness that due to technology and the media it is getting harder for this to continue and the system is gradually getting more transparent. In some departments you will find the same surname all the way up and down, because they are all racist and they all employ each other's relations without disclosing proper information and using a fair recruitment system. How can real and fair development happen on this basis?"

Roland could not believe that this could still be happening in these little villages. "I'm sure they will soon realise the downside of it and they will soon mix more, otherwise even friends might not be able to eat together."

"Whenever I used to go to village weddings or communal events twenty-five years or so ago," Dani said, "I noticed, lower-caste children waiting desperately for their turn to eat with tears in their eyes, while even the higher-caste grown-ups ate first. I could not believe it. We were leaving and it was getting dark, but they were waiting for their turn. I felt so bad. And they say children are like gods, but here they ignored them, because they are used to this discrimination and arrogance. So it clearly shows that even some higher-caste people are ignorant, stuck to the old traditions or superstitions. They can't see the absolute or divine in every living being and they have no idea of *Vedanta*, or they simply don't understand it. They need to do more work to understand the essence of their ancient scriptures and *dharma, or justice.*

"We had many friends in the village who always ate together, but whenever there was a wedding or a big occasion they had to sit separately. But I have noticed a change that now everyone is served food at the same time, although they may be sitting separately, so at least little children of lower caste don't need to watch higher-caste people eating first or higher castle people don't want to feel guilty by hearing the moaning complaints from hungry lower-caste children. Most people are desperate to change this system, but they have not managed to do it even in the twenty-first century. I remember a man from the village called Liladutt Thakur, who was from a higher warrior caste and had married the love of his life from a lower caste. Thakur was a very brave man and always fought for the rights of the lower class and equality for the poor people in his village. Although his own brothers and family were ashamed or scared to be seen with him in public, he was not bothered. He lived a good life, even though he found himself in a struggle with his own people, and he became a great man in my opinion. He could stand against all odds, due to the love for his wife, and he stood firm with his decision until his last breath. But instead of learning from him about love and respect for all, his people shunned him and blamed him.

"So we need to remove the hate and disrespect between castes first, and once that is gone then people will be ashamed of acting superior and they will understand the message that we are all one family," said Dani. "There are millions of people in India who belong to these lower-caste categories, so this division is a huge division and very difficult to get rid of overnight. Poverty is another cause that people cannot move forward. But now India is going through some real changes due to the media, and people are much more open and absorbing the facts about equality for all through education. Differences between people will always exist, but discrimination has no place in any society. If a village wants to do well, it has to care for all its children, to educate them so they can improve the whole village. Scholars can be born in slums too.

"I remember an incident from one of my school expeditions once when I was trekking in Ladakh with a British school. I used to always pay attention to what all these well-educated teenage children discussed and what topics interested them most during their travel. On the way back from a high altitude trek in the Markha Valley, I heard one of the boys talking about posh people and how he hated them, the way they dress and how boring they were, '… I hate them and I just can't stand them,' he kept saying, but a few of them were trying to defend them. I commented as soon as they took shelter in the shade of a willow tree, (there are no trees in Ladakh and you only find willow trees once in a while) by telling him that you can't simply hate due to how someone looks or the way they dress. Sometimes the way someone dresses can be deceiving. Maybe there is a man dressed in very rough clothes and looking a bit strange. He may be a wonderful and kind person, if you talk to him. On the other hand, if a person is dressed smartly and looking posh, it does not mean he is arrogant. He may be more down to earth and a very kind gentleman. You can never say until you know them. So just by looking at them and saying you hate them is not fair. I also told them the story of the rock blocking the way and about the different qualities of people and how they will react to that according to their own inner nature, and not because they are dressed in a certain way. It was quite interesting how they all agreed, and their teacher, Mr Shepherd, who was a sensible man, and carefully paying attention to the conversation, indicated to me 'that was interesting'. It is really fascinating how these topics go on in every society and in every country," Dani said.

***

Roland had spent nearly a week in the village now and was discovering the hidden secrets of India through Dani. It had given him a much more in-depth understanding of Indian society, as well as its spirituality, religion, customs and history and how old and complex it was, and the changes taking place currently.

Roland finished his diary very late that night and he was thinking about the system they had in the West. Roland thought that although we don't like to talk about it we have a class structure too. A lot of what Dani had described about caste system, was likewise in existence in the West, including in our way of speaking and dressing. Whenever one British person meets and greets another, he will automatically make certain assumptions based on their dress. It could be a signet ring or a blazer. And sometime might look the part, but once he speaks he will betray his class. It could happen in a single greeting: 'How do you do?' Roland felt that as a young man with an open mind he didn't really notice these things, but if someone were to look down on him, he would feel uncomfortable. But it makes sense that it doesn't matter where we are born. We can still change our attitudes and ways and achieve a better life through our own actions and hard work. Some people get stuck in one mindset all their lives while others change and progress and see no difference between people and get on with everyone.

Roland thought hard about his own culture and wondered how Western society had changed too. One can easily move up and down a class, if you made changes to your way of dress and speech. But most people have moved on and now there are different groups. These groups can be formed based on lifestyle, habits or other common interests, such as age, gender, marital status, professions, hobbies, or even (or Harrods shoppers, have the same dogs or horses, go shooting, hunting, singles, youths, new mothers, cricket clubs, golfers, garden lovers, authors, doctors, bankers, engineers, corporates, skiers, cyclists, yoga groups, runners, builders or body builders, rugby or football players, travellers,) Facebookers or Twitter-users. So these are the new challenges of the modern age. There are many more dividing factors for modern society over and above religion or caste or class. But we will all enjoy life much more through practising equality. Live and let live.

Roland also understood Dani a lot more now, after seeing how deeply he thought about everything. Roland was pleased that he had decided to come to the village and to discover these mysteries and at the same time he thought how dangerous ignorance can be.

***

The next day they had nothing planned, so they decided to go to the riverside near the wooden bridge and read their books. At the same time Roland had decided that he wanted to study more about Darwin, as Dani had talked about him a lot. Dani had also mentioned that Darwin had studied different religions in great detail as well as science. He was first ear-marked to be a doctor and then a clergyman. Darwin had experienced many personal challenges too, as his ideas had gone against the grain of life in Western traditions and religion, so it must have been quite a battle for him to explain what he had felt and discovered to his family and to the world at large. We owe a huge debt to Darwin for his discoveries, thought Roland. What an extraordinary man, who is famous all over the world. Even people in villages in the Himalayas know him. Dani had pointed out that that was why the British government had put his face on the British ten-pound note: in recognition of his wisdom and contribution to science and humanity.

***

Roland had had a really interesting two days and could not believe the discoveries he'd made about the local schools, hidden culture and the ways of the village. His mind was full of the good and the bad things of society and in particularly of the sustainable model of living he had witnessed in this village. He thought about home, about how the West was going mad on trying to cut down on carbon emissions while using more machine-made products and encouraging people to consume more. Here, an ancient model existed and was still in good use but was unnoticed and close to extinction. Here, every waste product was used one hundred per cent and nothing was left unused. For example, a tree is planted and established. Its leaves are used for cows, they convert it into dung, then the dung into fertiliser for plants and crops, as well as being made into dung cake to use for fire and ash. Also, the leaves are converted by cows into milk. Leftover sticks are used for fire torches or firewood, and bark is used to make ropes. Ropes wear out and become soil again and sticks become ash. Purified ash is used for washing dishes and sprinkled over plants to save them from insects. Cows are highly regarded, respected and protected, and fully used as living machines until their death. Until then they produce enough calves, cows and oxen. Once they die, their leather has various uses and the flesh is left for vultures to survive on and to keep the food cycle going. Roland could not believe all this, and it was quite a thing, coming from soil and going back to the soil, nothingness to nothingness, "dust thou art to dust returnest." These thoughts kept going round in his mind as he was enjoying his music and resting, until he fell asleep.

CHAPTER NINE

On arranged or love marriages

Roland woke up as soon as the birds started chirping the next morning. They'd had a nice evening at the hot springs the night before and Sanju had dropped them back home by car after an early dinner, which had provided them with a long and restful night. Roland started to read his book *The Life of Mahatma Gandhi* by Louis Fischer, and was fascinated to learn about Gandhi and his early life, education and travel. He was equally impressed to find out about famous people like Sir Edwin Arnold who had already translated the *Gita* from Sanskrit to English in a publication entitled '*The Song Celestial*' as early as 1885 in an effort to build a bridge between East and West and to explain the origins of this ancient civilisation.

It must have been something very different for the British at that time too, thought Roland, when the British Empire ruled so much of the world and when many royal and wealthy students from these colonial parts of the world came in exchange to study in England. At that time with the spread of literary and education many people began questioning aspects of life, and debate groups and clubs were arising in different parts of Britain, especially around academic hotspots like Oxford, Glasgow and Cambridge, where young scholars wanted to question the creation, the creator and God, such as Charles Darwin.

Many overseas British must have adapted to the lifestyle of colonial life, and contemporary Indians like Mahatma Gandhi encouraged them to translate their ancient Indian deep-rooted texts, knowledge and scriptures from Sanskrit to English, so that a wider public could have access to this wealth of alternative thinking and to debate it in English while they studied in Europe, so the Europeans could understand their new guests better and the values they treasured. Gandhi studied the English language, then Latin and French as well as Hindi, and his own local language. It must have been quite something for Mahatma Gandhi to move from a little village in India to a distant Empire in the West, to survive and learn and then set an example to the world by getting every single British man and woman out of India using non-violent means, particularly in a period when today's media and internet did not exist. Roland found it extraordinary that the human race is still stuck in wars, one after another despite Gandhi's example with many people suffering and dying. Thousands of British and Indian army men saved from killing each other during the struggle to Indian freedom itself was a result of his non-violent efforts. But Gandhi's singular message of non-violence had not been taken seriously by other leaders, today. What a dreadful shame.

Roland stopped for a second and looked out of the window at the dew on the trees and the white frost on the young wheat plants. After a long sigh, he carried on with his book. After more than an hour's reading, Roland thought he would go and see what was going on in the kitchen, as he had missed the last few mornings' activities. He heard a few sounds coming from the kitchen and noticed that the main doors to the courtyard were open as he entered.

In the kitchen, Dani's mother *Amma ji* was getting her clay pot ready to make butter. Roland greeted her and she offered him a seat, saying "*Namaste*" and making signs to him that it was cold. She had made a little fire with sticks, a dried dung cake normally used to store or keep fire alive all through the night, as well as some very dry hay, so that she could light it quickly. The flames from the fire were warm and Dani's older sister *Satya* joined them.

They didn't speak any English, save for "Good morning", and Roland could only speak a few words of Hindi: Such as *namaste* meaning "good morning," *Acha* being "good", or *Acha Laga*, "liked it", *Pani* being "water", *chai* being the word for "tea" and *Dhanyabad* meaning "thank you". *Amma ji* put the pan on for tea and added some tea leaves to it, and Roland helped to break some wood sticks to add to the fire. Then *Amma ji* brought a big jug of milk, and when she started to pour it into a clay pot, Roland realised it was a mixture of milk cream and curd to make butter. After that she added some hot water from the copper pot and put the clay pot lid on. This was placed on a soft thick mat of around two foot by one foot in size. Then she started to move the pot backwards and forwards and the sound was like a wave gently hitting a rocky shore and returning again and again. Whenever they stopped talking, the sound echoed all around the kitchen. *Amma ji* had done this early morning routine for more than sixty years: opening the doors, making a fire, getting the milk ready and moving the pot backwards and forwards. Roland admired the simplicity of her routine, the patience and stability it nurtured in their lives and the sense of belonging at home, with the family, and keeping an eye on everything on the farm.

Satya didi, meanwhile had already swept the main courtyard first thing and done her early morning chores.

21 Local farmer ploughing with oxen while on his mobile phone.

22 Traditional flour mill in the village.

23 A monk exploring a digital gadget, comfortably
and in reach of digital technology.

24 Boy sitting comfortably with his family cow, living
side by side, tied with a natural bark rope.

25 Herding the goats and cows home after
grazing all day in the forest.

26 Old traditional mud house with beautiful carved woodwork.
Unfortunately due for demolition to make way for a new road, Thali.

27 Thali- Suni wood and rope swing bridge due to be taken down for the hydro dam as the water level will rise above it.

28 Hari Ram, a wise old local farmer, taking a bath in the natural Tattapani hot pools on the banks of the river Satluj.

29 A village cremation on the banks of the river Satluj,
supported by all male mourners, now all that flat
space is due to disappear under the dam lake.

30 A shepherd struggling to keep his herd of sheep
and goats together on his ancient path way now a busy
road, while a truck hassles him to clear off.

The tea was boiling and Roland added some milk from the cup. Once it had boiled, he lifted the tea pot and they offered him a sieve and some cups. He poured it into three cups and offered it to both of them. They smiled and said "Good" (meaning "Well done – you know how to make tea,"). At the same time, *Satya didi* moved the copper water pot from the back oven to the front where there were more flames and heat. During this time, *Amma* pointed out and showed Roland the butter, which collected on to the lid, and Roland was amazed that it was white, not yellow, like Roland had seen it at home. Roland had never seen fresh, natural butter like this straight from the clay pot before. She offered a lump of it to Roland to taste on a piece of chapatti, and he could not believe the taste. It was so fresh and delicious and melted in the mouth.

"Oh yes, this is really *acha*," he said, as he tried to finish his mouthful.

By now they had finished their tea and the water was hot in the copper pot and the family asked Roland if he wanted to have a wash or a bucket bath.

Roland fetched his bucket and filled it with a mixture of boiling and cold water and the copper pot was refilled to heat water for the next person. Roland was amused to observe that even the squatting was feeling less demanding by the day, so it was obviously benefiting his knees too!

After his bucket bath, Roland was ready for the day, and by now Dani was also up. "You are up early today," said Dani. "What time is it?" It was eight o'clock.

Roland told him that he had wanted to experience the early morning. He asked Dani if he was missing his wife and son.

"I am, but I know that I'll be home before long. We were chatting on the phone until late last night – that's why I'm a bit late up today," he said with a smile.

"Good excuse," Roland said, "Well, I'll see you later then," and he left the room.

Roland went up to the roof terrace with his second cup of tea and kept reading his book until Dani was ready, and he was called for breakfast in the kitchen. Roland feasted on fresh butter combined with vegetables and chapattis, which was a really delicious, salty breakfast.

Dani asked Roland if he was missing his English cereals and toast.

"Not at all," said Roland. "Mind you, our traditional cooked English breakfast is quite salty, but nowadays people are too lazy to cook it and they just have ready-made cereals, which are sugary and instant, nothing like a proper English cooked breakfast." But he was enjoying his traditional Indian breakfast, and it was washed down with fresh *lassi* a new drink (the liquid remaining in the yoghurt after taking the butter out; sometimes people add mango, banana, salt or sugar into it to make it more tasty, but now they had it plain).

After finishing their breakfast they decided to do some washing, and Roland got his dirty clothes out in a pile. Roland had been thinking of sending them to the dry cleaners in the nearest town, Suni, but then he decided to try and hand wash them like the others did. He gathered his washing outside in the courtyard and was fetching the washing powder, but by the time he re-emerged, they had already been taken by Roland's elder sister, and she would not allow him to wash them himself. "Well, that's the thing with being part of the family in India, Roland, they do look after you and don't let you do much," said Dani. But Roland still wanted to help, which he did.

The sun was shining now, so they washed the clothes at a tap in the field outside the main courtyard. Dani's sister did all the hard work and the boys just rinsed and wrung them to get all the water out and hang them on the washing line. *Satya didi* made it look like it was a very easy and simple process to wash the clothes, though it was clearly not. Roland thought how interesting and fun it was to do this all together and reminded himself that they did everything by hand, both clothes and dishes, but seemed to prefer it that way rather than to change the old overnight like in the modern world.

Dani said that he was quite keen to get a washing machine, but his *Amma ji* resisted and said what would they do if everything was done by machines. They would have to sit around and get fat and ill and she didn't want that. It was good for everyone to at least wash their clothes and have some exercise, if nothing else Dani said that *Amma* was generally anti-machinery and preferred to rely on her own hands and furthermore was reluctant to waste electricity.

Roland felt that in a way they were more in control by doing it themselves and they didn't need to depend on electricity, or to worry about what temperature or what type of material or what type of liquid or capsule they needed to use – only one type of washing powder, hot water from the kitchen or cold water from the tap. The job was done in thirty minutes and the clothes were hanging on the line, adding colour to the view. Little can go wrong this way. In contrast if anything goes wrong with a machine, the replacement part has to be made in a factory. You have to call the plumber or company to fix it, and it takes days to repair as well as lots of money, even if it's just a small part, they have to come with their big vans and all the tools they carry with them. So the bills reflect that. Likewise with a power cut, an expensive machine is rendered useless in seconds. And also there are no carbon emissions by hand washing the clothes, only the energy to manufacture the washing powder.

Roland thanked *Satya didi* for the washing and after that went to the garden and sat with his book on the swing to enjoy the sunshine. Dani had said that in winter all the students used to sit outside the schools, and you could see most of the classes taking place in the playgrounds, because it was much warmer and so they didn't need to waste energy heating rooms, although children sometimes did find it difficult to sit cross-legged all day.

Children were playing outside with their wooden toys, though they were really more interested in the farming tools and sticks. But the toys were all very simple – there wasn't even a single toy which needed a battery like he had seen at home in England. Dani was thankful that they didn't have as many toys as many children have in England.

"I never had anything like that," said Dani. Children were much more active and creative than children are today in making their own toys," he said. "But we did have two puzzles of a map of India and the world with its states and countries in pieces. That was a very rare and precious thing in those days."

"Nowadays, children love the television and computers so much that it's very difficult to get them to switch them off. They can sometimes even operate televisions, DVD players and computers from the ages of two and three," replied Roland.

Roland had experienced the same with his friends' children. So he was thinking these things while watching the children playing in the courtyard. In a very relaxed and lost manner, someone was trying to catch a dragonfly or someone was watering the plants or feeding a calf, while the elderly were weeding in the garden. They were using old tins or some wooden sticks as well as playing with the seeds and farming tools around them.

Their families didn't really have time to play with them, as they were all very busy with the cattle, crops and farm. The children were kept busy by being given little jobs around the courtyard, or with their mothers. It was very interesting to see one such mother, Gita, carrying a bundle of leaves on her head and a little three-year-old grandchild called Lucky carrying a small bundle on his head too and chatting away with his mummy and *Amma ji*. The bundles were full of green leaves and they walked with difficulty through the courtyard doors. His little bundle of green leaves was for the little calf they had in the family. Roland was very impressed to see this process of training and the transmission of knowledge to a younger generation.

Once they had deposited the leaves by the cowshed, they picked up some firewood or sticks from the dry pile of wood, which they collected every day throughout the year, to make a fire to cook the food. Lucky carried some sticks with him too so he could help to cook the lunch. The children often sat around the fire and the mother or grandmother gave them a little dough of flour to play with or to make a *chapatti* or *roti or* animal figures.

While observing this scene, Roland mused at how toys are marketed in a way that convinces us that we cannot possibly live without them, when in truth children may miss something far more interesting or valuable in their surroundings while fiddling with a useless toy. "Of course, there are some good educational toys, but some of them just end up in piles and they fill the house up."

"Most of the products are brought out to make money. They are marketed in a way that the whole world forgets that they have lived till now without this product," Dani continued with frustration. "But all the shops, the media and the world goes mad about it, until it's in every household, and then a little percentage may use it, or it will be lost among all the other clutter which is bought because we have been pushed to buy it by the children-friendly designs and marketing skills to simply get money out of us." He wondered if a lot was being done for money and how can every little idea be turned into a game or plastic toy? "Parents can't escape from the childcare either, just by handing over a plastic toy, how can it help in long term? Of course, most of the things in the world are entertaining and interesting, but one cannot start dreaming a small business from it. It is like if a person is busy on the train or bus and lost in reading, he may miss someone interesting sitting next to him or something interesting happening outside the train."

Roland also realised that not many families could cook from scratch nowadays, because most of our food is pre-prepared and ready for consumption in the supermarket. Here a girl of about four years old would help her grandmother pick out the stones from the lentils, or *Kali Dal*. That happens with every grain they grow and eat, including rice and pulses. It is a real and practical way of learning for life – a process of training to live and survive in life. These were the thoughts happening while Roland was resting in the garden on the hammock.

By now, *Satya* had arrived from the local market in Suni, where she went every morning to deliver the milk, and she would come back with shopping for the household as well.

Roland discovered that she took three litres or more of milk every day to the town, another three litres to schoolteachers in three different places, and half a litre to a tea and sweet stall. She carried a brass *balti* or a small billycan or bucket with a lid in her hand all the way to Suni every day, together with a half-litre measuring jug.

Dani explained. "She has done that since childhood. All the children used to do it before school, when we were young and big enough to carry the bucket. It provided a very basic income for the house and gave enough to pay the bills for a daily newspaper, sugar, salt, and other staples."

At the same time, she brought over some fruit and a newspaper for them.

Satya didi seemed very caring, and it looked to Roland like she kept a general eye on everything at home: the children, checking the cattle and dog had been fed, as well as looking after all the members of the family. Dani explained that she was also very good at telling the time without a watch.

"If you ask her the time at any time of the day, she will just look around for a few seconds and tell you the exact time without a watch. She simply figures it out from the location of the sun and shadows.

"*Satya*'s almost forty years old and not married and lives with my mother and brother's family. She has some physical issues with her eyes because her skull has a dent towards the inside from the back, which pushes the eye sockets to the front, and so her eyes cannot sit fully in their sockets. Also, her hearing is not that good, but her mind is sharp, and she is very caring and hard-working. She always makes sure that the house is in good order and all the domestic duties are done on time and the cattle are looked after. She's very straightforward and direct in how she deals with everyone and her responsibilities.

She handed over the newspaper to them and asked them if they wanted some tea, but Dani explained to her that they were going for a short walk and to visit the family land and flour mill down by the river, "Otherwise you will spoil us and we will become very lazy," Dani joked.

She smiled. "Don't be late for lunch."

Roland took his small rucksack and put his sandals on. They went through the main gate towards the east and then followed the road for ten minutes, passing a pipal tree on the left side, taking a short cut by an old mud house with a slate roof, and then went through green wheat fields and some cabbage and cauliflower fields further on. Dani pointed out the flour mills, houses and temples on the way. He also showed Roland a fountain called *Sua* (meaning 'birth' or 'source') where they used to come to have a bath in the hot summer. His family mill was just opposite and they could see eucalyptus trees on the right-hand side planted by his father a long time ago. Dani began talking about his father, who died a few years ago, saying that he was very strict but had wonderful principles and values in his life.

"He began his working life as a skilled workman during the British Raj and had witnessed the slaughter in Shimla during the partition in 1947. That's why he was forced to leave the town, and he left behind a house and belongings in Shimla after the partition. At that time there were no cars or roads to Shimla. They used to walk around 40 kilometres to Shimla as well as carrying up to 60 kilos on their back. Once he left Shimla, he looked after the farm as well as worked as a mechanic in the village first for a short time and was also involved when the new road and transport came. He was the go-to technical man for anything mechanical.

Sometimes he had to walk for two or three hours in the morning to get to work and then the same to come home in the late evenings. After dinner at home, he would sort out a few things in the house and the farm and then be ready to walk to work again the following day. He was an exceptional man. Finally he left that job and started his own farm as well as doing some private mechanical work as he used to have the most up-to-date tools in the whole valley."

Dani took him down to the fountain to feel the water from the natural spring where people used to come to drink water, wash clothes and bathe in summer.

"My father was very popular and he helped so many people, and the house used to be always busy. He employed other people for ploughing or farming jobs, but he enjoyed the technical jobs himself. He would help with anything from cutting a ring from a swollen finger to repairing guns, or welding brass and copper pots and pans for villagers. He was also very good at taking out teeth. But the funniest thing my *Dadi* (paternal grandmother) told me was that once he took out my granny's back tooth, which was really hurting and painful for her. He kept asking, 'Is it this one? This one?' She kept humming, 'Yes ... hmm ... hmm ...' He was very firm, and with his pliers and tools, he got it out with some difficulty.

"She stood up and, after gathering her breath, as there were no painkillers or anything, as she rolled her tongue over it, she screamed, 'Hey Bhagwan (Holy Supreme), you rascal,' and chased him around the courtyard as he had taken the wrong tooth out. No wonder it was really hard to take out. He apologised in shock, "On no! I am really very sorry. Are you sure?' Finally she calmed down and instructed him that he had to take the bad one out too. She said he was careless because it was only his mother

303

and with others he was always very careful, but it became a joke for my *Dadi* later on. Unbelievable," Dani said. "Older generations were much more resilient, and could tolerate pain, although sometimes they used opium as a painkiller. These days life is much easier as dentistry has developed. I hope that this does not happen anymore."

Roland laughed out. "These days the dentist would be fired, and possibly sued as well! Lucky it was only his own poor mother."

They were now standing on a small hill called Riddu, by a pipal tree close to the river, where a little stream met the big river, and from here they could see the beautiful river valley and some palm trees on one side of the bank.

Dani pointed out the bridge on the river, which was a simple design of a wooden structure suspended by metal ropes. "My father was one of the main mechanics and engineers for this bridge when it was built in 1961."

Due to the potential rising water from the new dam, a new Jeep-passable bridge was being constructed, which was much higher up, above the old bridge.

"My father had a vision of a free and self-sufficient life, and his best advice was to work for yourself, and if possible do farming. Business was second, and working for someone else was the last option. He liked to grow various types of fruit and vegetables so he always had a cash crop as well as providing the family with food for themselves. That's why he also planted lots of different trees for wood like shisham, tunni, eucalyptus and bamboo, as well as banana, mango and other fruit trees, and he also built a flour mill to convert his home-grown grains into flour. Sadly that mill will be flooded by the new dam and the river will rise within a few years," explained Dani with some frustration. "Again, that is so called change or modern development, I guess."

Then he pointed to a nearby gorge created by a little stream on the right-hand side.

"There were five or six flour mills in that gorge just by the river, but they were flooded in the terrible flood of August 2000. Normally, after monsoon or occasional floods, people used to rebuild them every year. Now, because of the dam project, people are not bothering to rebuild the mills as they will be submerged again sadly, so all those flour mills are lost forever, and people are depending more on flour mills further up the stream, which are now depleting in number. Mills are now working on oil-run or electric motors and machines, and everything is bought from outside, so local skills are being forgotten. Nowadays there may not even be any skilled carpenters who could build a wooden flour mill from scratch anyway."

On the opposite side of the river people were digging the sand from the river bed and loading it on to ponies to transport it up to the town, or forming it into piles to transport by lorry later.

"It's a wonderful source of sand and stone to build houses with, but soon these banks are going to be under the floods once the dam is built, and all these locals will lose their livelihood as well as these materials. This will drive the cost of local housing up as people will be forced to look elsewhere for material," Dani said.

Roland was enjoying the sunshine and observing the steady flow of people walking over the bridge and asked Dani if everybody goes to the town to sell their fruit, vegetables and milk from the village.

"Yes," replied Dani, "if the villagers have anything to sell, they take it to the town. But if they have it in large quantities, then they take it to Shimla on the roof of the bus. Most villagers have only small quantities to sell and they can't afford to pay the travel to go to Shimla, so they prefer to sell them much cheaper here in the village. Not everyone has much land, and so survival can be a bit of a struggle for them. But they depend on each other and it generally works well. I do think that there's some hidden unemployment in the village as well."

Roland asked Dani if he knew how much milk the village produced every day.

"Well it's difficult to say, but I think that the whole area must sell more than two to three hundred litres every day, and the rest is kept at home to make curd, butter and *lassi*. *Lassi* is also used a lot for cooking or is fried on its own to eat with corn *roti* (bread), or is made into a yellow soup with spices called *Kheru*. The butter is boiled or purified to make ghee which can last for years even in hot weather without a fridge, which most people don't have."

Roland was thinking about Dani's hard-working older sister *Satya*, who did that walk early every morning to deliver the milk to the town as well as bringing the shopping home. Roland wanted to know more about *Satya*. For example, how long would she live with Dani's mother and family, and who would look after her when she was older, and would she ever get married?

Dani sat back comfortably and took a deep breath. My father tried many times to arrange her marriage, and she had many men interested in her, but she is completely against marriage. Of course, the men were not perfect either. In some cases, their wife had died or they already had children, or they could not have children, and it seemed to be those kinds of men who were interested in her. But she hates to even discuss it and now she is over forty. She is much happier with her mother and family," said Dani. "My father left some land and part of the house for her and gave instructions in his will for all the brothers to look after her. He had also arranged a disabled pension, though you can't call it that now, the new term for this in India is 'differently able'."

"Oh that's a perfect term," replied Roland.

"He had opened an account for her at the bank as well. She is very happy and loves what she does at home. She is in full charge of the household, and she has a very good relationship not only with her family but all the other relations and friends, and they all care for her as well. She visits and stays with them once in a while, and the interesting thing is that certain people always ask how she is and what her news is, but may not ask about the rest of us! Due to her warm and giving nature, she always makes sure that she takes vegetables, or other presents whenever she visits them, so she is always popular!

"That's why I think that arranged marriages are sometimes useful, because not everyone gets the opportunity to fall in love, or is able to find a partner in life. Many people are shy or reserved and are not able to attract partners as much as others. So arranged marriages provide everyone with the opportunity for marriage and family.

"Arranged marriages could be the best option for them. After all, the arranged marriage system has been an ancient and well-trusted system for thousands of years."

"How did the arranged marriage system start and how does it work?" asked Roland.

"Arranged marriage is a system of matchmaking, a way to let two single people meet, like and hopefully love each other, as well as a marriage of two similar families. Power, wealth and certain family values merge together. These couples are fully committed to the marriage for life. If it works, it is wonderful, but if not, it can be very harsh for one or both sides, because divorce is not considered an easy option.

"But this doesn't only happen here in India, even among the British upper classes there has sometimes been pressure or influence for their children to marry someone from the same background to protect the family's power and money. In the past, many estates and country houses exchanged hands and were preserved this way or were united through these methods.

"Roland, India has the second largest population in the world, with twenty per cent of the world's population.

"What is the cause of the increase in population in India and China?" Dani wondered. "Is it the simple and basic way of life, or are they following ancient ways of healing and lifestyles, or is it the diet or food they eat which makes them procreate?"

They both laughed.

"Or do they have a thirst to carry on the race and so everyone has a chance to marry and have children due to arranged marriages?" Roland replied. "Or is this good weather the reason that they can't stop making children. Indian people today have an identity of their own from their food, which is famous all over the world, as well as things like yoga, lifestyle, and a knowledge of the *Kama Sutra* too?"

"The other by-product of arranged marriages is that the two households are then joined and the children can have care for their elderly members while sharing all the jobs, so the parents have less pressure looking after the children. So the young and the old all live together and share the responsibility, and the food is always prepared in the one and only kitchen in the house. They will know each other intimately and everything will be discussed openly. Not just among your own family, but also with other relatives and friends, as they all live in very close communities, not unlike many parts of Europe.

"Here, the matriarchs of the families in particular will have a big role in knowing about the various girls and boys in the different families and their characters, as they love talking and exchanging information, both good or bad; the process of observing starts from a very young age. So that by the time the girl is eighteen and the boy is twenty-one (the legal age limit for marriage) they have a good idea of the possibilities within their community and connections. Often they have in mind, 'Oh, that girl or boy will be a good match for their child', though that opinion may change if they hear some other stories, otherwise the hunt is on and parents keep asking if they like that girl or boy.

The process starts through uncles and aunts as well as through relatives and friends. Traditionally, the boy's family will approach the girl's family. But if the girl's family want to approach the boy's family first, they can only do so through a relative or a third party who knows the girl's family very well and will say, 'Oh, we know a very nice girl', and likewise from the boy's side. If they don't know the family directly but they see a girl or boy at a wedding or a get-together, for example, they will try to find someone who knows the other family and then approach them that way. But you have to find a mutual connection to enable trust and confidence. The middlemen/women will then visit the other family and have a chat to discover more about the intended spouse.

"Once the intended has been vetted and approved they agree to bring the boy for the next visit, so the two can see each other and have a chance to talk, which is the modern way now. In previous generations this was not necessarily done and the groom did not get the chance to see the bride until the wedding day in some families. It could be a surprise for some brides or grooms with a blind trust on their parents.

"If the girl's family is happy and would like to agree, they will invite them again. But before that they will do all their research about the boy from other relatives and friends, or for more they consult local shopkeepers or the people from that village. So a lot of reliance is placed on the middleman and the community to get it right."

Roland commented, "Social media has probably made it much simpler now."

"Absolutely," Dani agreed, "now there are other ways to gather information. The boy's parents will explain about the girl and family – their way of life. But mostly people look for a similar family or a better-off one. They will also consider what type of work and lifestyle their daughter will have after marriage into that family. For example: is the family traditional or modern? If a farming family has lots of work on the land, they don't want a girl who only likes to read books or use a computer and has no idea how to stitch a button or milk a cow. She will be of no use to their lifestyle.

"Likewise, caste is a very big factor in arranged marriages. Even now, people feel more comfortable marrying into the same caste. Sometimes there are also divisions of wealth and standards within castes. It is not often that arranged marriages happen out of caste. Sometimes if two people find and like each other very much and if their parents are open-minded people, they can encourage their parents to accept it if the families are on the same level, then it happens, but this is considered more of a love marriage than an arranged marriage. Also, nowadays, people want a better lifestyle and environment for their children, so wealth is becoming an increasingly bigger factor rather than the stamp of caste or, above all, a good and peaceful life.

"Sometimes, of course, the process grinds to a halt if the couple decides they don't like each other, which will be communicated through their middleman, and if so, the same process of hunting for another person will start, unless they have a few alternative options already.

"Otherwise, the parents will take the birth horoscope of their children to an astrologer and find out if the couple would suit each other according to their birth stars. If so, then they will choose the right auspicious time according to their planets and stars for the couple to meet or even to marry. If the horoscope does not match, then the process will stop there. If the match is not one hundred per cent, most traditional families will drop it there and then, but modern families may still go ahead with it by performing some astrological ritual if they are determined for the wedding to happen. But this will depend on the boy and girl being willing.

"Traditionally, the couple will now wait for the wedding day before they have any further contact as this union is now considered sacred and special. Love, respect and wholeness depends on it. During this time parents may visit each other and ignore any further or negative information, unless it is considered to be so damaging as to be breaking news for the relationship."

Roland asked about what might amount to breaking news?

"Well, Roland, those can be things like if he was married before and was violent towards his wife, or abandoned his children, or he is an alcoholic or has ruined many girls lives or is involved in crime. Then it will be goodbye. And in her case it could be the same or she is pregnant already by someone else etc. Otherwise, the marriage goes ahead. It is very rare that such marriages go wrong. When they do, the main causes are usually things like bad habits, such as drinking, or mental or physical issues. Adjustments in arranged marriages are necessary in the first few years but finally they surrender and accept it, and the children and wider family help too.

"Another big factor is that in arranged marriages the children can quickly blame their parents if the marriage is unsuccessful and the parents have to stand by their son or daughter, because they have arranged it, so the parents and wider family all try their best to support it and make it successful. So there's a lot of responsibility on those who have arranged it to get it right!

"Nowadays in India things have changed, and young people are happy to try and find their partners themselves, but sometimes, after disappointment, they revert to their old traditions and opt for an arranged marriage. And of course some people don't want to get married at all, like my sister *Satya*."

"You said that she refused to have an arranged marriage?" asked Roland.

"Yes, many do," Dani replied.

It was getting cold now, so they decided to move to the sunshine further down. They had some bananas, and then Dani carried on, which Roland found interesting as he tried to understand the similarities between East and West and the differences between love marriages and arranged marriage.

"The funny thing, I think," said Roland, "is that we supporters of the modern lifestyle are always criticising these ancient ways. Many are mad for the modern lifestyle and what they see in movies. They make fun of arranged marriages and don't value them at all and forget that millions are single in big modern cities and now they are all relying on dating agencies or social sites."

"They all talk about love marriages and falling in love," said Dani. "It would be interesting if those from modern cultures were to step back for a minute and to look at their inherited modern system. Most of the 'love marriages' seem to be arranged marriages in disguise. The couples concerned are arranging their own marriages, instead of their parents doing the arranging directly. But indirectly it starts from a very young age, when a mother has just had a baby. They will join new mothers' groups and will carry on friendships with the type of people they like and want to be with or have things in common with. So from a toddler's age you will be divided from the rest, and you will meet, play and study with the children you are introduced to.

"Even schools are selected for them to mix with the kind of people parents want their sons or daughters to mix with. In some cases games will be selected for the sake of meeting like-minded people, like tennis, football or rugby, horse riding or rowing or cricket. Sometimes, after finishing school, children will be sent for work experience or on holidays with certain friends to certain places, or with specific organisations to do charity projects or expeditions, where it will be scheduled in advance through connections in like-minded environments. These links work and in some cases help them to get a job in certain companies. Sometime even lunches or dinners, theatre evenings, concerts or parties are specially planned to introduce certain friends and children they think may have potential to get together. That can be done by friends, family, parents or by grandparents or simply by well-wishers."

Roland interrupted, "Well that is part of life. These are the old ways to get to know new people and everyone aspires to a better life."

"Although these things are sometimes planned according to social structures and class, when these young people meet and 'get to know each other', a sort of informal interview process takes place using disguised questioning. This leads to learning key points about a person – their level in society, wealth and background – which can be figured out from the way they dress or speak, and also where they meet: at venues or places where certain types will live, walk, go, study, work and party or be entertained. Where are you from? Where do you live? Where did you study? Which in turn leads to: what job do you do? And a judgement of how much money you earn. Then an examination takes place: what type of person are they? Do they live in a flat or a house, in a town or the country? Overall, do they have most of the things they are looking for, and for some people it could be are they smart, cool or well-suited enough?

"Once an overall conclusion has taken place and the couple have got to know each other, they will be introduced to various friends to get the once-over. Perhaps they meet the parents. If the parents have done their job their child should be able to make a good choice, but sometimes it's a disappointment. Of course, parents will still have a huge influence. They have to be impressed, like in an arranged marriage, otherwise this may create a conflict between the child and the parents.

"If all the boxes are ticked and parents approve the match, they won't want the golden opportunity to slip away. Age is a big factor, and if they are older, then they just hope that they'll get on with it.

"After this, when the person is one hundred per cent sure about this, a conclusion is reached: 'I want to marry him', or 'her' or 'Oh no, it can't work'. Why? Nobody knows. Maybe it was because it was not a love connection after all and one pulled out because it discovered some new holes outside the box, and they could not compromise.

"Some people get to middle age and they haven't married yet, either because the right person didn't come along, or they were too shy to express feelings or because they have chosen not to. But how is it possible that they couldn't fall in love in all that time? I'm sure that every one of us can fall in love not just once, but many times. Sometimes one can't express it, and sometimes it is lost because too many doubts come in," said Dani.

"But if a human can't find a partner, it means that they have misunderstood love or someone else could not understand their love. Maybe they are hiding it away or may be they have found something else. It could be anything – work, a passion, activity, or even freedom – which they love more than companionship and they don't need a second person to share it with. But Roland, I feel that, in truth, it is not love that they could not find in these situations; it is some boundary affecting them. If there were no boundaries of any kind, would they not have jumped at the chance to have someone to say, 'I love you and I want to marry you'?"

"Yes they would have," Roland replied.

"But once trapped in a world of expectation and other such obstacles or boundaries, it is simply not that they could not find love, they could not arrange their marriage and they lacked advice and support from their own surroundings and on top they could not let go or surrender," Dani said. "I have observed an excellent thing among little children. If you put them together they are quick to interact with each other in seconds. Even two three-year-olds. They have play, even conversations, and they become friends and they want to see each other again. To these singles who are holding back due to caste or class or other boundaries, I really wish I could just say to them that 'Hey, imagine that you are going to die in a few days or years'. They should just forget some of these obstacles and enjoy life and have a partner they really love and want to be with.

"One of the significant, expectations these days is that everybody wants to be affluent and they can only find a good match if they have a good job, car, house and clothes. Especially in arranged marriages, if they don't have an income or employment, finding a good match to marry is very difficult, especially in India. They have to wait for a long time. And there are also certain religions or cultures that say no kissy-kissy or more before marriage. So now they can't find a good job or employment, they have no income, and they are waiting for a good income, because then they can get a better match. So they can have neither a good partner nor can they have kissy-kissy and they cannot marry. So what should they do? And their religious advisers tell them, 'Oh, no kissy-kissy before marriage'. Many people still believe it is a sin, that lovemaking is a sin. Truly these religious leaders are making these poor innocent people suffer.

"If you put two people on an island and they are trapped and have to survive on that island without any options, they would get on with life, even if they hated each other. They will grow out of any hate, dislikes and misery and look after each other and fall in love so madly that if one loses the sight of the other the life would go out of him or her. So, love can happen. When it comes to true love, it should be forever. Love is love. One can't simply stop loving. If they can't express their feelings, they may be in love with someone else. Love should have no conditions. It is the most wonderful thing if true lovers can be together without any conditions or social pressures. But in love marriages that should be the case, always. Love is like Indian gods, Roland, it comes in many forms and colours and one has to celebrate it in any form.

"Sorry Roland, I hope it make sense to you."

Dani's face was now lit with brightness as well as clarity in his voice, and a poetic impression in his tone. Why not, after all it is about love, which we all need.

"How simply we say love – I love you – but if we think about it … love … just the word … The trust, feelings and passion we need to gather are countless before we can even say the word, love," added Roland.

"That's amazing," said Dani. "I am not sure anyone can really describe it or if everyone feels that love, when they say the word.

"I really believe that if people are truly in love and they are united, their love should touch other lives too – who they see, greet and meet in day-to-day life – because they are full of love, and love affects every living thing."

Roland started to sing the song "Love changes everything".

"So Roland, what would you like to do: fall in love, or should I arrange you a wedding while you are here in India?" Dani enquired.

Roland laughed and said, "Well, I would definitely like to fall in love and choose the person I really like. But if that fails, I'd be happy to find a match in India!"

"Well, you better keep your eyes open, then," Dani laughed. "Who knows where that person is waiting for you? Wouldn't it be great if we could all know in advance? All this waiting and worry. What a pain!"

"Let's wait and see the miracle happen," Roland replied.

"Well it doesn't need to be perfect, because nothing is perfect in nature, it depends how one sees it. One person may look dreadful and scary for one person, and the same person looks loving, caring and wonderful for another, but the person is the same. With a few choices and adjustments one should be able to find the right person. I really wish you the best of luck for this adventure, Roland," Dani said.

CHAPTER TEN

The Himalayan trekking adventure, hidden cultures and the village fair

They were lost in their own thoughts and enjoying the sunshine, when suddenly they were alerted by men on the other side of the river who were shouting and gathering their horses and ponies. They must have been working since early morning, carrying sandbags, and now the horses were playing up, so they were shouting in frustration to control them for one more load.

It was nearly lunchtime and time to go home for Roland and Dani.

"Those people must think we're lazy and not doing much," Roland said.

"They are probably thinking, 'Oh, look at them, what a life they have'. But don't we think the same, 'Oh look what a natural life they have, keeping fit and working by this beautiful river bank, fresh air and water and a very peaceful valley'.

Dani decided that they would go and visit the nearby temple and then go to the local shops and home. They walked down from the hill to the river and on to the white sandbanks of the river. They drew some hearts and birds and names in the sand and washed their hands in the freezing-cold water. Roland could not believe how cold the water was. They heard the sound of people rafting and paddling down the river towards them. There were some tourists with some local boys in the rafts. An instructor on one of the rafts saw the two of them and decided to move nearby. They wanted to have their snacks and drinks there, because the locals knew Dani, and it was a good sandy beach to land on. The tourists were clearly having great fun with the activity. They said that the water was freezing and they were looking forward to reaching the hot springs. Roland found out that one couple was from Dublin, Ireland, and there was an Australian girl and another couple from England plus an Indian couple from Mumbai. The rest of the group were three local members of a rafting company. The main guide was called Rishi, from Sikkim, and there were two other boys from Suni: a friendly Sikh called Kulvant Singh and another boy called Jiya lal from Dani's village, who was a part-time farmer and an excellent rafter and swimmer.

The couple from Dublin were very friendly and offered them drinks, so they sat by the riverside to chat. The tourists were staying at the hot springs at Spring View Guesthouse, Tattapani. They were enjoying being off the tourist track and staying in the hidden Satluj Valley.

After their drinks, Dani and Roland walked all the way up the hill through the bushes along a little footpath, and after a few minute's climb, they were by the temple. They took off their shoes and washed their feet and hands by a tap and then walked up the newly built marble steps to the main gate of the temple. There were a few other people there and it was a breathtaking and peaceful spot right on the bank of the river, and they could see and hear the fast-flowing river below. They rang a bell and bowed down, then the priest applied a red dot on their forehead, and they were offered some raw rice, fresh coconut pieces and sweets as well as some flower petals with the rice. There was a smell of burning incense sticks and a lamp in the centre, and above them a goddess statue well-decorated with flowers and jewellery. The priest had very long dreadlocked hair and was dressed in traditional simple *kurta* and *pazama*. He had built the temple from nothing with the help and donations of local people and now gave free counselling and spiritual support to many villagers using traditional practices and rituals.

Dani also explained that the temple was very unique as it was a temple for the goddess mother *"Bhima Kali"*. "She is known as the female or maternal part of the original universal force, that energy which can direct one's life force in the right direction. Often people come for the *darshan* or for a face to face consultation with the goddess during their evening walk or in their leisure time, and it is believed that if you pray with sincere feelings, your wishes will be fulfilled here."

Dani had a personal connection with this place as he had taken part in its construction and had collected donations in distant villages for it. He recognised how the communities had benefited from its existence.

"Hundreds of people come every week to see the priest, because his spiritual and religious beliefs and rituals have helped so many people. This was also a temple where caste or class was not a barrier. In the mountains you will find many ancient temples devoted to the mother goddess."

Dani explained about the way the temple was built. "It has to be square because that represents stability, whereas a circle means life. Every object and corner has a meaning. The whole purpose of building a temple or other shrines is to provide clearance, balance and peace to the visitor and make the visitor feel peaceful. A visit to the temple should provide you with a profound but full feeling, like after a good yoga class, and then compassion, love and generosity flow from there. Temples are always supposed to be built in peaceful places like riversides, lakesides or on top of mountains or in caves. Natural caves directly represent the house of God. The main shrine area in the temple is called the *garbhagriha*. It is always square, which represents stability, and built with thick walls and no windows, only having the light from the doorway and from the lamp lit in front of the deity or idol. Everything is planned according to old science or astrology and *Vastushastras,* possibly the oldest texts based on oral traditions which are found in ancient *Vedic Vastu Vidya* scriptures (1500 to 1000 BC). These temples were not built for architectural benefit, but in accordance with strict *Vedic* (meaning the knowledge which reduces or erases pain or suffering, as *vedna* means pain or suffering) traditions and principles, so the benefit can be gained from just one single visit to these temples. The temple floor is raised so that the temple is higher than the outside ground, and one has to climb the steps to reach the main shrine. Raising it higher emphasises the separation of worldly matters from the divine. The porch is the transition from inside to outside and applies to both the physical and metaphysical, letting go of the external and connecting to the internal. There is also a bell. The idea being that one rings it to enter the inner spiritual kingdom for the individual self."

Dani pointed at the older temple called "Kalighaat" on the other side of river. "That was built in the eighteenth century by the royal family, ancestors of the present Kanwer Shyam Chandra Pal Singh of Bhaaji and was built properly with all those important aspects in mind, and one can still see all those aspects in that old temple.

"The main door and deity statue will normally face towards the sunrise or riverside. So the deity may catch the rays of the rising sun and the devotee faces the sunlight too as he descends down to the bridge towards earthly matters again. The main temple always has a big tomb, but the tomb in this old temple was built in the shape of an upside-down lotus flower – one can see the carved petals clearly – so sounds have a very special echo effect. The temple provides the most beneficial environment for visitors anytime and the whole community can benefit. Also, this was a way for the community or the local rajas or maharajas to display their wealth and power, by creating these well-carved stone temples with big elephant or bull statues. These were not really places for preaching, but for private worship, social gatherings and celebrations. Here one could leave all life's obstacles and problems behind and enjoy the presence of the main deity or god. Ganesha (with the elephant head), is the auspicious god of all beginnings, and so is present in each temple, as well as Bhairav (one of the guards or protector gods) – which will be seen outside to assure the security and protection of both the temple and people. The main shrine room doorway separates the devotee from the deity so the divine has its own separate space, and the threshold is only crossed by the priest to perform the rituals in the mornings and in the evenings.

"The main flame or light inside the temple represents the one true light, and one can admire the main statue with the light of the flame reflecting on it and back on to the devotee. External light is seen as darkness, *maya,* or illusion, which is ever-changing, but inner light is seen as absolute and balanced."

They had a *parikrama* (walking around) around the main temple, and Dani said that it always had to be clockwise, representing the journey from earthly to divine. They rang one of the big brass bells hanging from the ceiling and then sat down for a few minutes on the mat. They also saw some drums and musical instruments, which were customary for a temple.

Dani said, "They are to play during the morning and evening prayers as well as during ceremonies and festivals.

They greeted the priest, and he offered them some sweets, flower petals and a colourful string as an auspicious protection or an amulet to repel bad luck. They thanked him by bowing in respect and said "goodbye" while stepping out of the temple. Dani told Roland that people normally offered fruit, sweets and other eatables to temples so that the priests and monks had enough to eat and didn't need to worry about hunger or other-worldly matters but instead could concentrate their energies on much higher aspects of spiritual well-being for themselves and all humanity.

"Some old temples have special *dharmshala*, or a big open hall, where people stay overnight, sleeping on a mat with a little sheet to cover them as beds or *charpoys* are not allowed in some of the temples as no one should be higher than the divine statue. But by four or five o'clock in the morning the mats have to be rolled up and put away so that the village children can come to practise yoga and Sanskrit mantras, and even in some parts or villages of India, particularly the south such as Kerala and Tamilnadu, a very old marshal art called *Kalaripayattu* (with or without weapons) is taught and practised in the temple in front of great masters and in the presence of God, because it is seen as a divine force given directly for physical and spiritual advancement. Mainly nowadays though, in most traditional temples, it's limited to yoga and breathing exercises as well as to morning Sanskrit mantra practice and singing, but in the Sikh religion, marshal arts (called Sanatan) are still practised in the same way as they have been done for generations.

"I have heard that due to their profound knowledge and practise, some of the martial arts masters don't even need to touch their opponent to attack, but can do so purely through vibrations and invisible force. Because of their body language, facial expressions, eye contact and vibrations, and because their whole physical, mental and spiritual appearance or presence is so powerful, the opponent will not even be able to come close to making contact with the master but will drop away as though they've had an electric shock. But that is only achieved because these masters do it for spiritual advancement, not to destroy, or compete or show off. They are egoless. Their goal is simply to harness the force of the physical body and the temple, which God has made his residence, and they strongly believe in this. Their sole purpose is to help, share and achieve a higher level during their journey towards peace or *Moksha*." Pointing at the priest, Dani explained that the priest had gone through some extreme tests, commitments and practices in his childhood including walking on red burning coals before he was confirmed a priest.

"Nowadays some priests have made their temples a commercial business, so the general public don't feel as comfortable or peaceful there and the real benefit of their visit is being eroded by the desire and greed of people who have no knowledge of the history of temples and their meanings. But temples in the mountains tend not to be affected by this trend and I hope people will again understand the real importance of these ancient places that exist for the well-being of humanity, instead of just somewhere to make money from donations."

"Why did we have to ring the bell?" asked Roland, "and why did he put the red dot on our foreheads? I notice that some of the ladies have a red dot on their forehead too."

Dani replied, "The bell is there to prepare our minds for entry into this sacred place and for our relaxation. There are three steps in a temple – relaxation, concentration and meditation. First we are required to wash our hands and ears and feet to assist our physical body in fully relaxing, as most of our nerve endings are in our hands and feet. Very often people will come to the temple in freshly washed clothes. Relaxation, in turn, is seen as three levels: physical, mental and spiritual. That's why they have fragrance in the temple, so you are not disturbed by any bad smells in the environment. So one can feel comfortable, inspired, uplifted and positive.

"The paste applied on the forehead consists of different herbs, the main one being sandalwood. The herbs are mixed with red colouring from rocks and applied on the forehead, but traditionally they used to apply it on the forehead and in some cases all over the body, including the arms and chest. Many *sadhus* or wandering monks still do this or use ash, and they hardly wear any clothes – these are mainly *sadhus* who live in the jungles. But it is very rare that people do the full paste ceremony nowadays. In the old days it was to protect their body from the heat, dust and the harsh weather conditions, both hot and cold."

"Like the Aborigines in Australia and the Bushmen in Africa still do?" Roland asked.

Dani went on. "Yes, also, the fragrance makes you feel good, and a layer of that paste keeps the mind calm. If you only have that simple small tika, or dot, in the temple, it can remind you that you're doing something extra special and spiritual for yourself, which is purely between you and the almighty, to narrow the bridge between you. So this is part of that process of relaxation.

"After the sounds of the bells, the mantras and the chanting or singing, and the sounds of drums, the weight of worldly worries should recede to enable the mind to focus on a more positive level. Finally, you ring the bell for the final time and close your eyes while observing the light and sound. As that last sound echoes, the mind automatically creates an image of that sound, and if one is focusing a hundred per cent that image of light and sound will disappear and no more concentration will be needed. The mind will become empty and the person will be completely calm and peaceful. This is called meditation. This is the benefit of a visit to these temples and the importance of these rituals, nothing else. That's why in India people visit temples whenever they can and pray on their own. And when you open your eyes, you find a kind face offering you flowers or sweets or other things donated by people to the temple. So in one way a temple takes it, and in another way it gives it back. And it is all done without any pay or salary. It is all about keeping the mind and inner self peaceful. It is only us who can hear and fulfil the prayer. "In Sanskrit the mind is likened to a devil or a naughty monkey that jumps from one interesting thing to another. To calm him down is almost impossible unless you give him a repetitive task, the same thing over and over again. There is a story in the scriptures that once there was a genie, and when his master had found him, the genie imposed a condition that he had to be kept busy otherwise he would harm the master and would have to be set free. One day, the master was busy chanting his *mala*, or beads with mantras, and the genie kept disturbing him for more and more tasks. In the end the master asked him to climb a tree to the top, which was fifty feet or so, and then to climb back down and to repeat the process again and again. The genie happily accepted the task and went off. After the master had finished his chanting and meditation he looked for the genie, and to his amazement he found him asleep under the tree. Then the master realised that, yes, the mind is like a monkey, jumping here and there, but now it's calm after the repetition of the task. So, likewise, he understood that the mind can be tamed through repetition of the mantras and the beads, just like the genie."

Roland loved the story. "So it means that the purpose of meditation is to calm the mind from activity and agitation?"

"Yes, that's the goal," Dani replied. "It sounds easy in the story, but with the mind in real life, desires and thoughts drive everyone mad. Even the luckiest, wealthiest person doubts himself too, due to the mind, and constantly desires others things."

"That's really interesting," Roland said. "But what about the red dot, Dani? Many ladies have them on their forehead."

"That red dot is called a bindi and is a symbol of marriage for ladies," Dani explained. "Once a lady gets married she will use a bindi, the modern version of which is a ready-made sticker quickly fixed with glue. Previously, it used to be similar to the paste of herbs and colours to keep the mind calm. It tells other men to keep their hands off, because normally if one is attracted to a woman, the way to get attention is to make eye contact. Eyes are the windows to connect first. But before that contact is made, you would notice this big red dot between her eyebrows and instantly understand that she is a married or taken lady and respect that. If a woman is wearing no bindi but her clothes look very subdued and conservative, it will usually mean she is a widow. That's why it was considered important, but these days the practice is getting less and less common.

"Traditionally, married women also used to apply that colourful paste on to the parting of their hair all the way from the forehead to the centre of the head, so the paste would keep the mind calm and diffuse the heat. That's why it was known as the symbol of a husband's long life. Because they used to say that any woman who wore this paste regularly was calm, and consequently her husband would live a long life."

"Well that may well be true," Roland replied. "It would be interesting to do some research on that paste to see whether it really does have this calming and cooling effect. In the West, people use the wedding ring as the symbol of marriage. Some very traditional men in Britain don't use the ring, which I have never understood, but most of the modern ladies and gents do. Do they use wedding rings in India?"

"It is not customary for Indian men to wear wedding rings or any other symbol to identify them as married. People who are wealthy will often wear rings or other jewellery but not for the purpose of marriage. It is considered irrelevant as due to arranged marriages you always expect them to be married after a certain age."

By this time their walk had taken them up to the main road and they passed a few shops. Dani went to a store and greeted the people sitting on a wooden bench outside the shop. Some of them spoke good English and talked about the English cricket players with Roland. By then, Dani had bought some snacks and a few more things to take home for the evening.

They waved goodbye to the men and walked down the road, which had taken them across a bridge over a little stream and there was a primary school situated on the left. This had been Dani's first school. The students were sitting in rows on thin mattresses on the ground and were writing on wooden boards.

"That's the way children learn how to write," Dani explained, "They still learn to write using handmade bamboo pens and an ink pot."

Dani added that in his day if you made a mistake you would be caned on the hand. Roland asked if he had ever been caned?

"Unfortunately, yes, for the difficult word tests. One hit on the palm for each mistake!" said Dani, laughing.

They followed the route back home through the fields and were welcomed again by the barking of Tigger.

"That is so impressive," Dani said, "how a dog can smell you from far away. How do they do that? If it is an animal, stranger or a family member, they know the smell."

"Well, dogs are very intelligent and have extraordinary senses. It is amazing," replied Roland.

Dani's sister *Satya didi* and *Amma ji* were waiting and asked them why they had taken a long time to get back, and their excuse was that they had been to the temple.

"You must eat on time," *Satya didi* moaned. "If you eat too late then you will not be hungry for the evening meal."

Lunch was waiting for them and *Satya didi* made sure that they had water to wash their hands and plenty of food. After the meal they had a rest and Roland caught up with his diary and book. After a while he went outside to join Dani who was helping his brother dig some holes in the garden for some plants and a new avocado tree.

"This could be the only avocado tree in North India. The seed came from England in a little plastic bag which I had planted in a flowerpot in London, and when it sprouted I thought I must try it at home. I always like to bring different plants to experiment with the courtyard garden. The little garden was created in our father's memory after his death in 2004." In it were useful plants like rosemary, basil, mint, lemon balm, aloe vera, chillies, garlic, onion, turmeric and ginger as well as some green vegetables and roses, marigolds and some other flowers.

When the house was originally built by Dani's *Dada* (paternal grandfather), they'd had a kitchen garden there, but that had changed during his father's time as they turned it into a protected place for the cattle, due to the threat of wild animals. But now the cattle were moved outside the courtyard to the right side of the house, and the cowshed area was protected by a wire fence. They were kept inside the cowsheds at night as the threat of jaguars and leopards was high.

Roland helped them water some of the plants and after a while went to collect some gardening tools. They moved some of the chairs inside as it got a bit colder in the late afternoon as the sun started to go down.

After the gardening they all had tea in the kitchen and discussed the following day's rafting plans as well as the subsequent trekking plans, as Dani's younger brother, Roop, was organising and leading the trekking trip. Roland was keen on experiencing some trekking in the high Himalayas in Kinnaur before the snow arrived and winter was upon them. A list was drawn up for their trekking supplies and soon after he went to bed.

***

The next morning they had an early start at sunrise as the sun got warmer. Roop and Dani went to the field to bring in some of the fresh vegetables. They brought a full basket of cauliflower and cabbage and some mustard and spinach leaves. Roop was a very keen and knowledgeable farmer, as well as his other skills, as he had looked after the farm since his older brothers left home to study in Shimla, when he was hardly 15 years old.

After packing and breakfast, they got ready for rafting. They walked down to the wooden bridge by the river and then a Jeep took them to a place called Chaba. This was the place where the British had built a hydroelectric power station to produce the electricity for the capital of the Raj, which was then Shimla. Roland could not believe that despite not having any roads they had managed to import their huge machines and turbines all the way from Europe all those years ago.

Dani and Roland had a quick tour of the power plant and Roland was proud to learn that this project was realised by a British man named Colonel Basil Betty in 1909. It produced 1.75 megawatts of electricity, and all the machinery was original and had operated continuously for the past century making it now a heritage site as well. The station was built on the banks of the Satluj River, but the water it used was from a small river which was further up in the hills called Nauti Khad – *khad* meaning 'stream'.

Five heavy iron pipes channelled the water from a large reservoir on the top of the hill and from there it flowed down a very steep hill to create the heavy force required to operate the European-built turbines. Roland imagined the British officers arriving here surveying the foothills of the Himalayas in order to find a suitable location for their electric power project.

"As this hill is hidden away, how did they find this location? Amazing work! And with marginal investment they created their own power source to supply electricity to their summer capital – Shimla – not long after electricity was discovered in England. How wonderful is that?"

Dani said, "That's why India admires the work the British did in India."

Roland was struck by how often the officer, Mr Gunpat, giving the tour referred to and acknowledged the British workmanship, pointing out the building as well as the old electric wiring and the machinery. When he learned that Roland was English, he offered them a visit to the workshop and explained that if they have any serious problems with any of the parts they still send them to London for replacement even now. He also pointed out that most of the buildings and infrastructure built by the British in India, such as the railways, were still going strong after all these years, and were considered as heritage sites in India.

The officer asked if they wanted to have tea, but they declined politely as their raft was ready and they had to find their way through the bushes and rocks down the steep cliff.

They got down to the sandy bank and Roop handed them their life jackets and paddles, and their Nepali guide, called Naure Bahadur, briefed them about the safety rules on water. They had four other tourists from Israel as well as a second group on a different raft led by Ramesh Sharma. They all got onto the rafts and the guide started with some practice paddling. He took them up river first and then they turned round and started under a rope bridge down the hill, leaving the power station behind.

As they went through the first rapids the adrenaline started to build. Roland realised that the water was quite cold but very refreshing. Soon, the quiet and peaceful river valley started echoing with their happy screams. They could see bats and owls on trees on the high cliffs as they passed by. Someone noticed a deer running uphill into the bushes.

Now they were near the place where they'd met the other rafting group the day before and they carried on down past the other wooden bridge in Thali village.

Soon after, the guide instructed them to be ready with forward paddling, as they were about to go through their last big rapid. Most of them were now soaking wet. A short while later, they got to a more open space and landed the raft on a sandy beech. They all got out and helped to lift the raft onto a Jeep which was waiting there with their bags and belongings.

Dani and Roland rushed off to find the natural hot springs as they were soaked through. As they got closer, they saw lots of people bathing in the small hot water pools created in the sand. One of the men looked like he was doing a few exercises and stretches in the pool. Dani recognised the man, and greeted him and asked him how he was. The elderly man indicated with his hand gestures that he was fine, and smiled.

As Dani and Roland got closer, he answered in a poetic manner, *"Ho Rahe hai Jivan Mele,"* which means "life meetings are happening". He went on: *"Naye naye chehre mil rahe hai, naye naye mahanubhavo se meeting ho rahi hai…,"* – "I am meeting new faces every day, meeting new, new, great souls every day. Look at this wonderful world, isn't it like heaven? Isn't it like heaven? Look at these birds, they are flying free here and there, and look at these trees, the clouds, the sky and this beautiful river flowing day and night, giving water to the thirsty, who need it. Not only here but down in the plains, irrigating the land of thousands. The cold holy river is flowing from the Himalayas, and hot springs are sprouting from Mother Earth. This is a most beautiful thing. Oh, this life is just wonderful. Meeting beautiful new people every day, doing our duties and karma, as much as is offered and donated to us by almighty nature. Oh this is simply heaven. Aren't we in heaven? This is heaven. You are in heaven here now! Nothing is better than this," – "*Hari vayapt sarvatr Smana* ('Vishu' or the preserving force or energy 'lives equally everywhere'). People make a story about the afterlife, but if they can't feel and live this real heaven now, they have lost the afterlife too."

The man's arms were flying in the air and his facial expressions were mirroring his words, pointing at and describing the surroundings. Dani could not believe what he was hearing and how it was possible for this man to experience such a level of happiness and joy.

Dani said, "You are absolutely right, and I am so grateful and fortunate to have seen you and hear your precious and priceless words."

He asked Dani how long he was staying, and how his family was, and also paid condolences on his father's death and said how he he'd known him very well. The man then put both his palms together and bowed his head. Dani did the same and wished him farewell. Dani explained to Roland that he was a simple man from the village, had children studying in school and did some farming as well as selling milk in the mornings and evenings and helping part-time in a local restaurant. Dani had noticed him before playing the flute on the river banks, and it was his routine to play the flute every morning and evening on the way to the market and on the way back home after selling his milk. He was very humble and kind too. Dani came to the conclusion that this man's level of thinking and being was incredible; he understood the joy of nature and life around him so much, which others could grasp much less.

"They call him Hari Baba. Hari Ram is his proper name, but locals have given him the nickname of Hari Baba, or 'blessed sage'. It is not that he lives the life of a *sadhu* or a monk. No, he lives and does everything that a normal farmer and family man does. But he is humble, kind and ready to help, without any ego, pride or demands. I have heard about him and his extraordinary selfless actions."

After their dip and a bite to eat at the nearby guesthouse, they drove to the Shiva cave which was situated a few kilometres from the hot springs. They bought a few bottles of water and some sweets from the only local store in this little village called Saroar before their hike.

After descending about 300 steps, they arrived at the cave entrance where they rang some bells, and there was a pool of water inside the cave where people were washing their feet and hands before entering.

Inner part of the cave
and 109 Shiva Linghams

Main entry to the Shiva Cave

c–Natural Shiva cave with 109 Shiva Lingams
(stalagmites), now submerged by the dam lake.

"Caves have great importance in India as they are seen as the natural homes for gods, and any spiritual practice and meditation within these places has a more profound effect," Dani explained.

Electricity had been connected to the cave and as they walked to the centre of the cave they saw many lingams (stalagmites) all around the floor. Some big ones were decorated with flowers, garlands and leaves. Dani explained that these were called Shiva lingams, highly regarded as symbols of the Lord Shiva in Indian traditions. By worshipping the lingams one would please Lord Shiva.

Some of the lingams were three to five feet high and others may have been much higher previously. People were ringing the bell, lighting incense sticks and candles and offering fruit and donations at the foot of the central lingam.

Dani said it was a common practice in India to worship caves and mountains, trees and rivers, the Sun, the Earth and the other planets. He explained that Shiva was the first yogi to arrive in the high Himalayas, with his seven disciples who were called the *Sapt Rishis* or 'Seven Sages'.

"They are supposed to be the first people to have roamed the Himalayas before anyone else, and one of them, Jamadagni Rishi, had spent time at the hot springs in Tattapani before Nagas, Dasyus or Khash or any of the other races in the Himalayas. These *Rishis* all had received the knowledge of life directly from Shiva. Shiva is depicted as an omniscient yogi who lives an ascetic life on the frozen world referred to as Mount Kailash in the Himalayas and he is also known as the Adiyogi, a practitioner from the origin. One of the primary forms of god or the Hindu Trinity of the primary aspects of divine. He is the god of transformation: he transforms old to new; he destroys everything so it can be reborn. Shiva is also known for wearing snakes and skins and living in the wilderness without any possessions. His pleasure does not come from the material world, but from a stable inner world. He is known for saving earth by consuming negatives, dreadful and bad things or any kind of poison from the universe so that it can be a safe place for all beings to live."

As they came out, Dani told them that the cave had to be removed due to the rising water level from the dam, and it was going to be transported up to the top of the hill piece by piece. The company involved in the dam was paying for rebuilding the cave in a temple and the whole project. He hoped that they would not just build a cement structure and make the lingams stand without a natural design or setup.

"It won't be possible to create what is natural here in this cave," Roland said. "All the water which has dripped down in the cave over centuries and has created these wonderful structures should be fully preserved and the government should employ someone knowledgeable to do the job or simply the cave could be preserved under water, before being spoiled for commercial use."

After a hard climb through these continuous steps, soon they realised that it was not that easy, but they took it as a very good exercise for Roland's trek. It was late afternoon, when they arrived home and they saw Roop getting ready and packing all the trekking equipment. Roland was excited having watched numerous documentaries on the area and on the exploits of Sir Edmund Hillary, Chris Bonington and the like, but at the same time a bit anxious, as it was almost getting to be the wrong time of the year for trekking as winter was about to arrive. A little change in weather could bring about heavy snow which could stay for the next six months and make the mountains impenetrable.

Dani would not be going with them on this journey as Roop was the expert trekker in the family now, but he made a phone call to check that the horses arranged for the trek were ready in the base village and all the arrangements were confirmed. All the bags and rucksacks and tents were placed near the door in the courtyard for their early morning start.

***

The next morning, after a quick breakfast, Roop, Roland and Chaman, the driver, loaded up the Jeep and set off at around seven o'clock, and Dani wished them the best of luck for their adventure, with some warnings and instructions. They followed the Satluj River on the right-hand side just after Suni and the road changed to a much smaller road at the edge of river. They were all chatting away and they had Hindi music on. The scenery was dramatic as the road zigzagged its way up the mountains with hard corners and curves regularly having to be negotiated. They would often have to stop or reverse to give way to big trucks as well.

Soon they reached the main road to Rampur, and it was a little wider than the previous roads so Roland was able to sit back and relax. A few big trucks passed by and Roop informed him that they were loaded with green peas and potatoes as they were the only crops that could grow in the highlands, and they were making their descent before snow blocked the roads in the upper highlands in Spiti.

A few more hours of journeying saw them pass old villages, mud houses painted with natural earth colours, some very beautiful old wooden houses, winding gorges cut into the mountains by millennia-old rivers, isolated houses by the river banks and a myriad of faces going about their daily business: sweeping their front steps, brushing their teeth by the roadside with twigs from local plants, while others were cutting through narrow hillside paths to catch the bus to work.

They stopped at the town of Rampur (previously called Bashahr) for lunch. Roop explained that this had been the winter capital of the Rampur Bashahr, one of the old powerful dynasties of the Himalayan kingdom. This city had been an important stop on the trade route with Tibet in the old days, where horses, swords, dry fruit, wool and arts and crafts would be exchanged, a main fort or defence town for the whole Satluj Valley. So the king had a very powerful seat in relation to Tibetans and the Gurkhas, or anyone else who wished to enter the hidden kingdoms deeper in the Himalayas. So it was a powerful area and the dynasty had built other strongholds and palaces in Saharan, Rampur and Sangla in the Himalayas for added security.

The Rampur Bashahr dynasty could be traced back to Mahabharata times from Dwarika near the Taj Mahal. Written records show fifteen rana and rajas from the day when their ancestors arrived from the Deccan plains as Rajputs and first took over the kingdom seven or eight centuries before, and the present descendant, Raja Virbhadra Singh and family had an active role in the political responsibility of the state.

They passed the Padam Palace, set strikingly against the beautiful mountain backdrop and carved exquisitely from wood.

They stopped to buy some fruit and vegetables from a small shop as the shopkeeper was sorting his produce, taking out and throwing the waste to a cow which was patiently waiting nearby. Roland was impressed with the whole display: beans, cabbage, cauliflower, apples, bananas, grapes and many different fruit and vegetables.

A friend of the shopkeeper came in, joked with the shopkeeper and ran his eyes over the apples. Then he chose a damaged apple, cut the rotten bit off and threw it towards the cow and ate the rest. Roland kept watching as they chose green beans, potatoes, apples and bananas for themselves.

Roop noticed Roland's amused expression and commented: "Tourists find it strange to see cows or animals on the roads and in the towns, but they are left loose by owners so that they can collect food from these stores, so no food ever goes to waste. Now they have even banned plastic bags in this state in case they accidently eat them."

Roland explained: "In England if there is a little mark or sign of damage on fruit or veg, people will not buy it, and if the expiry date has passed, people will not touch it at all. Because many are not used to eating food from the garden or from farms, they think that it's supposed to be spotless and the sell-by date is final. In big supermarkets and in the corporate world, staff can't just pick or bite a damaged product, it has to be accounted for. Consequently, hundreds and thousands of tons of food waste is produced constantly despite the fact that these things are imported from thousands of miles away at huge environmental cost. It's really terrible that in the UK every week a family waste food worth twelve to sixty pounds, such a shame."

Roop found this difficult to comprehend as he'd not heard about food waste or food bins. In his village leftover or waste food went to cattle.

Soon after, they drove off and the road was now getting higher and the river was disappearing into the distance. The road was wider, but it was still close to the cliff edges, so Chaman's skills as a driver were being put to the test. They passed a little village where some of the shops were perched on the edge of the cliffs as if they could fall off in a strong wind.

Soon, after a while, there was breathtaking scenery, and they drove through apple orchards and villages as the road zigzagged up the hill, and the view to the Satluj Valley and to the high Himalayas became more and more real. Apple orchards and children playing cricket and local ladies carrying bundles of grass and wood were a common sight as they continued to climb.

Soon they arrived in Sarahan, where they were going to spend the night. Roop pointed at the snow-topped mountain opposite, which was called Shrikhand Mahadev, 5,227 metres above sea level. Finally Roland had caught his first glimpse of the real snow-capped high Himalayas. Soon they approached the authentic-looking beautifully carved wooden temple with its well-carved doors to the courtyard.

Chaman and the *chokidar* from the Temple Guesthouse helped them to unload their bags. The *chokidar* pointed them to their rooms, and rest of the equipment they left in the Jeep.

The guestrooms were situated on the lower courtyard and could be entered through two huge wooden doors which were embedded with silver and brass ornamentation. The most fascinating building there was the wooden temple built in the Himalayan pagoda style. After checking in, Roop had planned a little walk up the hill to admire the view as well as to visit a rare bird park. They were breeding very precious birds there, in particular the local *monal*, a colourful Himalayan bird with purple, green and blue feathers, which is the state bird of Himachal Pradesh. After the birds, they drifted down through the pine trees towards the little market and the guesthouse. Through the trees they could see the beautiful temple and the stunning mountain view behind, as well as the royal palace of the same Rampur dynasty. Again, it was a beautiful wooden building, well protected by gates and walls. Roop moaned that they had to have special permission to visit and it was rare for ordinary people to get in.

They passed a large area that was like a playground or stadium on their left and then walked down by the royal palace through the market back to the Temple Guesthouse. The little market was very colourful, with people selling various types of sweets, coconuts and things for visitors to take into the temple.

Back at the guesthouse they dropped a few things in their rooms and decided to visit the temple. After taking off their shoes and washing their hands and feet they climbed the steps up to the main shrine.

There was one more courtyard and a wooden-built gatehouse where they had to wear colourful caps as it was considered respectful to do so. As they entered, they could see the two beautiful wooden towers. Roop explained that the temple was built for a very famous goddess called Bhima Kali, who rode a lion and had protected the Himalayan kingdoms many times in the past, so she was highly respected and worshipped in the Himalayas.

An elderly gentleman also explained that the wider temple area had been renovated a few years ago, but the main temple had been built in the twelfth century and the shrine itself was much older. It was all built using local wood, stone and mud, and the local name for this style of architecture was *dhaji* (timber) and *cutkuni* (cut corners). One of the two towers was bowed due to an earthquake, but had been left untouched in the hope that it would realign itself in time. Roland also noticed that the doors of the towers were very small and had few windows. Every gate and door was built from extremely thick wood so no one could possibly break in. From the doors hung vast handmade iron chains which could shut the doors from the top floor just by pulling them up in an extreme emergency. The old man explained that in the old days when different communities existed in these regions, there was an ever-present fear of looting and robbery from bandits, so people used to keep their valuables in these towers as they were well protected. Hence in many parts of the Himalayas, wherever there was a well-established community and ruler, one can find a fort, temple or palace with a high tower, for the local people and their wealth. These were also safe places for their most worshipped deities and idols in the event of attack.

Both towers were built on much higher platforms and after climbing the wooden ladders, they could peer out of the small windows and appreciate the view. They also noticed some ancient gold and silver palanquins through the windows, and Roland remembered from his chats with Dani that these must be the palanquins that they carried to village fairs and festivals.

Back on the main temple floor there was a beautiful display of precious statues and idols, all well-decorated and preserved. The main evening worship was about to commence so candles and incense were being lit and bells and chanting were underway. It was very gentle and the chanting and singing was very soft and sweet and the vibrations echoed throughout the temple and towers. The ceremony seemed very unique to Roland and more serious and intimate than many other temples.

One by one the priest attended everyone and he offered them sweets and fruit as is the custom. They also received a coloured tika on their foreheads.

Roop explained that the local priests and authorities had maintained that temple's ceremony for generations, and it was very profound and peaceful. It wasn't like some more commercial temples where the ceremony was rushed and the priest was loud and more concerned with gathering donations.

They also visited a small museum within the temple compound, which was interesting.

After, they went to find a place for dinner. They were really keen to try some highland food, which was noodles and *momos*, not unlike Chinese food. They found a little restaurant to enjoy their evening meal and by the time they re-emerged all they could see were the stars in the sky and it was peaceful and pleasant.

Roland talked about the book he was reading – *Breaking Dawn* by Stephenie Meyer – and said that it was getting very interesting, and it was about love and life and he was enjoying it.

After exchanging a few words about next day off they went to their rooms.

***

The next day they awoke to the soft sound of the bells in the temple ringing in the early morning light. Roland stayed in bed and enjoyed his book for an hour or so and then they met at the restaurant for breakfast at around eight o'clock.

After breakfast they checked out and resumed their journey in the Jeep. They followed the road as it cut through rocks and steep cliffs on either side of the mountain.

Huge herds of sheep, goats and horses often passed the car. Roop explained, "These are *gaddis* (shepherds). They migrate every summer up to the highlands, and every winter back down to the lower land."

"To move with these hundreds of sheep and goats must be a nightmare on these narrow roads," Roland remarked. He remembered Dani explaining how countless footpaths had been taken away from these shepherds, making it almost impossible for them.

"It takes them much longer these days due to the cars and traffic as well," Roop added, "and very often they lose a lot of their herd on these cliffs because they panic."

The Jeep came to a standstill and Roland took the opportunity to use his camera. Roop advised him not to get out of the car as the shepherds had very aggressive dogs so it was better to avoid them, and after ten minutes or so had passed, the herd was gone.

After that, they passed a huge hydropower station which generated a good deal of electricity for the area. Unfortunately, since the dam had been built it had not been as productive as when the river used to flow freely. Other hydro projects in the Satluj Valley had been similarly affected and landslides were on the rise.

As they drove nearer the river, they could see one of the typical metal bridges in the area, the Wangtu Bridge. This had been built by the army and previously had often been washed away by the river before the dam was built. A higher bridge had been built further up the gorge. Roland could feel the wilderness of the high Himalayas now. The river was fast and clear and the mountains were very steep, wild and rocky.

Roland was shocked to see a half-sunken Jeep in the river, which must have dropped from the main road higher up. Though Chaman's driving skills were excellent, it was hard not to watch his every move as they climbed higher and higher.

Finally, they were on top of the mountain and the road levelled out as they approached the village of *Katgavan* before the Kafnu area.

"Thank goodness," exclaimed Roland. "Why on earth do these people want to live here? It's impossible to get here!" he laughed.

A few children and villagers gathered around them as the Jeep came to a stop. They were all wearing woollen hats and thick woollen jackets. There was much shaking of hands taking place before the group were welcomed and led off to the house of Roop's friend Laxmi Negi. Laxmi, who was about sixty or so, was the owner of the horses they were to use the following day and would be escorting them on their trek.

Laxmi took them to his house, where they were warmly greeted by his wife. Laxmi had been organising horses and trekking with Roop and Dani for the past ten or twelve years.

They discussed the trek over tea and Laxmi's wife was relieved to hear them confirm that they were not proposing to do the full trek which would have taken them over the 4,900 metre-high Bhaba Pass to the Pin Valley and the snow deserts of the Himalayas to Spiti, close to the Tibetan border. With snow threatening to arrive any day, this would have been highly dangerous.

Roop asked about "Helicopter", and she smiled and said, "Oh, you remember him? Yes, he is very well and still working for us."

Roland was surprised at the thought that they were talking about a rescue helicopter operated in the area, and when he enquired they all laughed out loud at the idea.

"No Roland, there is a horseman called 'Helicopter' because he is really like a helicopter. He is very fast and never stops moving. If he comes with us he does everything – cleaning dishes, helping with the camp, you name it, he will take over everything before you even realise it needs to be done. You don't have to tell him anything."

This time, however, he was not in the village so they were going to be joined by Laxmi himself.

They thanked Laxmi and his wife and then left the house for a brief excursion around the surrounding area. The first stop was in two villages called Yangpa 1 and 2. The first village involved a very steep hill climb which was hard work. They saw many people dressed in the same woollen jackets and hats they'd seen earlier travelling up and down the steps past them. Some of them were collecting fruits for spreading them on mats to dry, or collecting and carrying firewood, or grass for the cows. Everyone they passed had a smile and greeted them. Most of the houses were built of wood and a few were large and very well built with carvings and slate roofs.

Outside one such big house, a young man invited them for tea. They entered and were taken to a room with sofas and some family albums were produced which showed the traditional attire at weddings and other special occasions. The man said that everything they wear was made from local wool and they hardly use any materials from outside the area. Their tweed was their pride and the patterns on their shawls and jackets and hats were very unique, warm and artistic.

After questioning Roland about himself and his life and what he did and whether he was married or not, the young man explained that these villages were the only Himalayan people who were both Buddhist and Hindu, as they were devotees of both Lord Shiva, because of the Kailash Mountain 6,050 metres high in that area, which represents the home of Shiva, and also of Lord Vishnu, as Buddha is considered to be the incarnation of Vishnu.

He carried on that the two villages were also divided on the basis of caste. The one near the temple was the higher-caste village and the other was the lower-caste village.

Roland told him that was a shame, but they were lucky to live in such a peaceful valley and that it was very beautiful. He also found out that their main crop in the past had been wool, but now it was apples, apricots, peaches, almonds and pine nuts. They thanked the man for the tea and then shook hands to say goodbye.

After that, they toured the second village and saw more wooden houses together with a few more modern cement houses, which Roland thought must be freezing in the winter. Roop said that the older houses were much better and the wooden houses with little windows were much warmer than the modern houses with big windows, which often had no additional heating except maybe small electric wire heaters or just a kitchen fire.

There were lots of school children around and they passed some of them on the way. They all had school uniforms on and were carrying their bags on their backs and rushing uphill. They seemed casually physically fit, and they all greeted him, saying "*Namaste*". What struck Roland was that most of the older people that he had seen earlier had been wearing woollen jackets, woollen trousers, woollen hats and other thick warm clothes, but these children now were wearing very thin, modern, machine-made materials, cotton or fabric of some sort. He wondered why they weren't wearing the warm woollen clothes which were used by their elders. He asked Roop about it, and Roop said that the uniforms were probably chosen by a head office somewhere in a warm state by government officials who have never been to these places, so they had the same uniform for those who lived in hot places as for those who were living here in the cold mountains. Roland was incredulous and couldn't understand why they had forsaken the natural, warm and beautiful woollen local dress for the sake of unsuitable modern materials. If they wore the local attire it would be much more sustainable and it would help support the community and the local skills.

By now they were halfway down, near to the Bhaba River next to Kafnu village, and a few village ladies, beautifully dressed in their local outfit with hats on, were walking uphill with another lady tourist. They had stopped to catch their breath as they were climbing up. They all smiled and greeted each other, and Roland found out that the beautiful tourist was from England too, and they chatted away together. Her name was Anna, but to Roland's disappointment, she was on her way down after completing her trekking, and she was going with the local ladies to have tea in the village before leaving the next morning. Roland would have liked her company for the trekking, but alas not!

Soon, further down, there was a bridge to cross to the other side of the Bhaba River, and they walked by the riverside and up to the centre of Kafnu and on towards the nearby dam. It was a beautiful spot and the adjoining man-made lake was open and beautifully surrounded by the high mountains.

The evening meal was taken with Laxmi and his wife. Roop called them uncle and aunty as it was the custom not to call elders by their first names, and Roland also found out that they had sent their children to Chandigarh for further studies, which was some distance away. Roop explained that uncle and aunty worked very hard and lived a simple life themselves in order to provide the best education for their children. Education was very important to everyone, not only for their own benefit but for the benefit of their home village.

They planned the next day and then went to bed after some hot tea.

***

They were woken by the horses from the courtyard early the next morning. Aunty greeted them and set out some omelettes and chapattis for breakfast. After a final check of their lists, they started loading the horses. They were taking four horses to carry luggage and a spare horse to ride in emergencies.

They set off via a checkpoint in order to obtain a special permit required because it was on the border with Tibet and China and they kept records of people crossing this area. It was also for the safety of trekkers, so they know how many people cross from this side and how many arrive safely on the other side or turned back or went missing or were lost. In the old days, border officials used to hassle guides and tourists for under-the-table baksheesh before allowing them to cross, but now it was much more civilised: a simple entry in the book with a permit from authorities and a brief introduction to the area by an official to tourists and you were on your way.

Laxmi told Roop that some of the villagers were planning to introduce a new charge for camping on their land, and it would be charged on a per tent basis, so that they could make some extra money from the tourists. Roop thought that it would put tourists off and the villagers could lose horse business as well. He asked Roland what he thought.

"If they created a nice camping ground with public toilets, water facilities and cooking facilities, then everyone would be happy to pay. But if they just impose a charge to set up a tent, that would definitely make the trip more expensive and then people might choose to go to other places instead," said Roland. "Alternatively, they could build some nice lodges or huts along the trek with facilities and people would be happy to pay for those too."

As they left all the houses behind, all they could hear and see was the sound of the fast-flowing river and the whispering trees and the colourful prayer flags fluttering in the wind over the Bhaba Valley.

After an hour of walking up by the stream they had a serious uphill climb through walnut trees, and on top was a flat plateau with a huge fir tree. On the right-hand side of the plateau were a few old wooden houses, and Laxmi said that that used to be the summer village, but in time people found it difficult and it was not very safe due to heavy snowfalls. So they moved out and down the mountain. Also, the younger generation could not be bothered to plough the terraced fields, and he remembered the time when potatoes, peas and other crops were grown here by the elders, including by his parents. He doubted if the modern generation with their iPhones and computers would ever return back to this isolated spot in the Himalayas. It was all growing wild and trees were reclaiming the land. All the wooden buildings built by their ancestors were being left to fall into ruin.

Roland was saddened to hear this. "Why don't they lease them to someone who could renovate them and convert them into huts for trekkers?" he suggested. "Trekkers could stay here a night or two and that could bring in some revenue for local families."

"The tourism department, or the forestry department, could renovate them and it would be a very good spot for tourists to stay here and have adventure activities around the area or even for use as storage or first aid," agreed Roop.

"It has to be done by the youngsters who are educated and know what they are doing," Laxmi said. "But local people need to be taught about these options so they can give access. This forest was donated to the Kinnaur district by the Raja of Rampur Bashahr. It used to belong to his kingdom, so his influence as king, benefactor and important minister of the state would be significant and could ensure the future of these precious wooden buildings."

The sun was shining and they chose a spot to have their picnic in a lush green meadow with trees around them and a thick pine forest on the other side of the stream. While they were sitting, they noticed a large number of goats and sheep coming towards them, together with horses loaded with shepherds' belongings. The bleating of lambs and goat kids echoed around the whole valley. They quickly grabbed their picnic and stood watching the animals crossing the stream over a thick broken tree which had been carefully cut to make a small bridge. It took some time for them to cross and approach the little group. Laxmi had a brief exchange with one of the shepherds who said that they'd had trouble with a bear, but luckily he hadn't taken any sheep, and he assured Roland that they don't come near humans. The shepherds were also in a hurry as they wanted to be out of the mountains before the snow arrived and they knew that the snow would be falling any time soon.

After their picnic, they packed everything up and crossed the stream using the tree bridge. They met a group of Dutch tourists coming from the other side of the valley who were pleased to see them as it was their sixth day trekking and they told of some snow on the passes. They were pleased when Roland told them that his group were not going over the pass and were coming back after the second camp.

After waving goodbye to them, Roland caught up with Roop and the horses, the bells around the horse's necks helping to lead the way through the thick woods. After a little while they emerged from the woods to a breathtaking spot from where they could see the vast range of the high Himalayas, and their first camp area was visible now.

When they all made it to the top, they caught their breath.

Chaman said jokingly, "You have brought me up here to die, Roop. I am not used to it anymore. It is really bad because I drive everywhere and so this walking is killing me. I am not doing this again!" Though he joked, it was clear he was pleased that he could see this spectacular view, because he thought he might never get a chance to see it again.

"It's just the first day," Roop joked back. "See how you feel on the way down!"

Roland was mesmerised by the stunning views all around. They were surrounded by a circular wall of high mountains with a huge green valley and beautiful trees and a river flowing through it. He asked the others about the piles of stones and the prayer flags on the gigantic boulder nearby. Roop told him that this was one of the oldest ways of marking footpaths. Also, people were very scared of storms and bad weather in the old days, so to appease the gods and ask their permission to enter this sacred land they used to offer piles of stones and hang prayer flags and pray for good weather and safety to Shiva, the god of Mount Kailash and all the Himalayan people.

Laxmi was unloading the horses, and they rushed so they could pitch the tents up before it began to rain. First, the make-shift kitchen tent went up. Then Roop went to fetch some fresh water from a little stream next to the camp, and Laxmi lit the stove and soon its comforting sound was buzzing in the tent. They put a big pot of water on to heat while they prepared the ingredients for cooking. The kitchen tent was windproof and the heat from the stove was making it much cosier. Laxmi asked Chaman and Roland if they wanted to join him to collect wood for the fire. They followed him into the woods nearby to collect broken branches to create a pile of wood. Laxmi added some oil and paper to the pile and then with a single match there were flames flying in the air.

Soon after, Roop came out with a tray containing tea cups and biscuits and Bombay mix. They all gathered around the fire to enjoy their tea. Roop pointed out that it had only taken them five hours and twenty-five minutes to reach the first camp. Roland was overjoyed to finally be there and said he couldn't believe how wild, natural and beautiful the whole valley was and how lucky they were to have it all to themselves as everyone else had left.

They finished their tea and Roland sat quietly with his book. Roop went to check that the tents were properly erected and assured Roland not to worry about the camp and that his tent was in a safe place, away from rock falls, the river and flooding risks, so there was no cause for any concern.

Roland, unpacked some of his things and sleeping bag and went back to reading his book, leaning out of the tent for light.

Laxmi fed the horses some grain and then left them nearby. He covered the horse equipment under a big plastic sheet and brought all the woollen blankets to the kitchen tent for him to use for the night. There were a number of cows gathering near a big rock away from the camp and they were all jostling each other for a drier spot under the sheltered rocks.

In the make-shift kitchen, Roop and Chaman were preparing soup and other food for the evening meal.

When the soup was ready they called Roland and he came to the kitchen tent with a torch on his head and his waterproof jacket on. They had all taken their shoes off outside the tent, so Roland did the same, while keeping his warm socks on. They had set up a few folding camp chairs and a metal box as a table in the middle. With a few candles, it was a perfect setting for dinner. They enjoyed their soup while talking about the day's events.

They all took turns telling a few stories and after dinner they played cards until the fire was nearly out. Laxmi was tucked under his warm woollen blankets. He didn't use a sleeping bag and never had done.

Roop went out to check the horses and noticed a few clouds in the sky, though he could clearly see the skyline and the mountains. He stoked the fire, saying that wild animals don't come near the camp if they smell any smoke.

It was an incredible spot for camping, Roland thought. They filled a few bottles with boiled water and then after brushing their teeth went to bed wishing each other goodnight.

***

The next morning as the cows and horses started moving, flakes of wet snow were landing on the tents. By the time the younger men woke up, the fire was doing well and Laxmi had collected some more wood as well as heating some water for washing and for tea. He teased them, saying, "Come on, wake up, there's lots of snow on the mountains."

Laxmi served tea to Roland in the tent, and within an hour or so they were all ready for their porridge which Roop had prepared for breakfast. Discussing the weather conditions over breakfast, they concluded that they wouldn't move to the second camp as the weather was deteriorating. They would just hike further up the valley to Kara, around 3,560 metres above sea level, and then return to the same camp that evening. They packed boiled eggs, fruit, sandwiches and a Thermos of boiled water for tea, together with their trekking gear.

Chaman decided to stay behind in the camp and the rest of them set off. It was a beautiful bright day despite the clouds. They walked by the river, all the time getting higher and higher into the mountains. Most of the pine and other fir trees had disappeared further down and only birch trees were still growing at this height. Roop pointed at the silver birch trees and took some bark out from a fallen branch with his Swiss knife so that he could show the different layers, and he explained that this was one of the first materials used for making paper in ancient times, and many Sanskrit texts were written on this.

"Yes, it must have been very precious when there was no paper and people used to just write on leaves and canvas," said Roland, "but now machines produce so much paper it's lost its value and people just use it like water. And with recent innovations like computers and electronic books people don't need to use paper much anymore which has devalued it further."

By now they were near a stream which they could hear but not see as it was hidden about 20 metres or more underground below the rocks. They noticed that the whole area of the mountains further up from them were very bare with no trees at all now. By this time they had walked for around two hours and a break was needed, so they sat on some huge boulders that were the size of a double decker bus and had some tea and some snacks.

"The valley further up is called the Kara Valley," Roop explained, "and it's a beautiful place for camping. But the river is much stronger and isn't easy to cross except in the early mornings."

"After Bhaba Valley there is the Pin Valley and Spiti Valley, and there is no vegetation at all. It's like a desert, cold and windy," Laxmi said. "But there are communities living up there, and if they need any wood, they travel down to this valley to cut trees overnight and by the early morning they've loaded their donkeys and yaks and rushed over the high pass to the other side so they can't be detected. They're not allowed to cut the trees, but forest guards can't really stop them as this is too far up for the guards to patrol and there's no chance of catching them when it's cold at night. Although the forest department has built a post in Kara, the people in Spiti are really tough and for them the high altitude or cold is nothing and they can climb these hills like a marathon runner on flat ground. As they have no trees and wood higher up where they live, for them every root and piece of wood they collect is extremely precious."

Roland commented that it was important to save the forests from being destroyed, otherwise flooding, land erosion and global warming could really harm the Himalayas and threaten the lives of the wider community in the mountains.

Roop noticed some clouds over the high peaks and realised that it was now snowing on the mountains.

"Not a good sign," Roland said. "I'm afraid we'll have to abort our plan to go to Kara and keep a watch to see whether it's heavy snow or just light flakes in the distance."

They decided to do a circular route back to camp that would take them over the river and up a steep hill on the other side of the river. After half an hour's steep climb through huge rocks they got to the top of the hill which was full of more huge boulders and rocks, as well as heather and highland basil and flowers. From there they could see all the way up the valley to the main Bhaba Pass, which was around 4,900 metres above sea level.

"Most of the mountains are over 5,000 metres around that valley. The base camp for that pass is at Pushtirang which is about 4,200 metres above sea level."

After lunch, Laxmi suggested they'd better hurry as it was more than two hours of trekking back to camp. Within half an hour the clouds had taken over the valley and it was turning into a "still zone": the wind had disappeared and black clouds and thunder were warning them, telling them of imminent heavy snowfall. Light flakes of snow began falling and within minutes all they could see was a white landscape and it was snowing heavily. The tops of the mountains were no longer visible and everywhere was getting whiter and whiter. Despite the obvious risks to their safety, Roland couldn't help but marvel at the sheer beauty of the dramatic scene unravelling before his eyes. It was what he had always dreamt of seeing in the high Himalayas.

They carried on their steady descent back to the camp. It was hard work and their legs were now aching but there was no time to stop. A while later they could see the camp in the distance and the cows gathering back to the safety of their shelter too. Laxmi told them that these were all village cows that are brought up the mountains for the summer, as there is plenty of water and grass for them up there, but in winter they come down to the village, or if any cow is about to have a calf then they will take her down early. Otherwise they are roaming free in the hills for months. They must be the healthiest cows on earth, thought Roland.

Roop joked that Chaman might be worried about them after seeing the snowfall, and wondering whether he was trapped alone in the middle of nowhere, or worse still, that he may have abandoned the camp and gone home.

"He'll be missing his car," Roland said. "Poor Chaman, I'm sure he'll be glad to see us."

It was true. Chaman had begun walking in their direction from the camp and was relieved to see them finally in the distance. They waved at him and he started walking back to the tent.

Roop asked Laxmi, "What do you think of this weather, do you think it may really snow heavily tonight at camp? If it has started snowing on higher land it may come down to our camp."

"Yes it could," Laxmi said, "and if we were to have heavy snowfall at camp tonight it could be quite difficult to pack up and leave in the morning. But we will see …"

They'd had a tiring day trekking, and it was time to warm up in the tent and to have something to eat and drink.

Chaman said he'd had a good sleep while they were out and he'd enjoyed his rest, but he'd been getting bored and then worried when he saw the snow. He'd started preparing things for dinner and had some tea ready for them in the tent. But they noticed that the temperature was falling and it was getting much colder.

Laxmi tied up the horses as he was concerned they might want to run away from the cold weather.

They ate their dinner shortly and all the while the snow was picking up a pace and the mountains around them were getting covered in a white sheet. Daylight was disappearing so they hurriedly packed up the kitchen equipment. They filled the Thermos with boiled water while Roop and Laxmi walked a little distance from the camp to inspect the conditions. It was absolutely silent and everywhere was white further up. They assured that the snow was likely to be about 3 foot deep at their level by morning due to the volume and speed with which it was snowing.

Packing the tents and walking the horses down the mountain would be very difficult if they were buried under snow, so the decision was made to go back down the valley that night. Winter had finally arrived and they were the last trekkers in the mountains to witness this magical sight.

It was already nearly 8 o'clock, so they quickly packed all the tents and bags. Soon they'd loaded the horses and covered them with blue plastic sheets so the load didn't get wet and heavier. The horses seemed happier to be walking away from the snow as they began their descent slowly by torchlight. By the time they got over to the other side of the mountain, behind them most of the valley was pure white. Laxmi told them that all the wild animals, such as snow leopards and mountain bears, would be descending too down to the woods near to the villages, seeking shelter from the extreme cold. Roland replied that this might not be the best time to be telling him this, to which Laxmi laughed and said that many shepherds spend nights walking alone in these woods, sleeping under trees and rocks, alone and isolated, as they had thick layers of woollen clothes and blankets. He assured them that with all the up-to-date equipment they didn't need to worry.

They carried on through the forest down to the river again and wondered if they should camp there for the night. The trees provided very good shelter and there was a big enough area to put up their two tents. They were tired as well and it had been a very long day so far. The weather was better here and so Laxmi unloaded the horses and they pitched the tents, much to Roland's relief. They thought it would be a good idea to make a fire, but the wood was so wet and damp that they struggled to light it. Laxmi got the stove oil out saying that they could use that up as tomorrow they would be back in the village. They managed to light the fire and by then it was nearly midnight, quiet and still.

Laxmi was pleased that they'd taken the decision to come down, and Roland suddenly remembered about a brandy bottle he had brought with him in his rucksack. They toasted their exciting adventure and their last night in the wilderness, and after one last check of the horses, and shaking the snow away from the tents, they were fast asleep.

***

The next morning, as soon as light broke, the sound of water flowing down the river woke them up, and Laxmi was already breaking wood for a fire and warming the water in a big pot. Roland got up and was surprised that the weather was so much better. It was clear and the view had improved, but further up, the highland was all covered in snow.

After a quick wash and a much welcomed cup of tea, they started their trek, which was uphill for half an hour and then another hour all the way downhill. It was cold and the path was wet and slippery, and the horses struggled on the steep zigzagging paths. They had to hold them firmly and steer them to stay on the path.

Roland enjoyed the fact that he was experiencing more challenging conditions than expected and told Roop that although they might explain it to their friends at home, they might not be able to understand it in same way.

They past a few villagers who were going upwards towards the woods, and they weren't wearing special boots or rain jackets. They looked very resilient to the harsh weather. Roop told Roland that they were going up to collect their cows and they would bring some wood with them on the way back, and now they knew they were quite close to the village.

Roland realised why the early summer was much easier for the trek, but he liked that he had experienced these conditions and seen how people live in the region too. It was much more interesting to be there when all the tourists had disappeared, after the real highland winter had arrived.

"I'm really looking forward to seeing the village again, and I'm excited about the Lavi fair too," Roland said.

By now they were by the first bridge they had crossed over the river and the horses had regained their confidence on the normal footpath to the village. Laxmi let the horses walk ahead, saying that they knew where to go now, and the men followed behind. The weather was cloudy but perfect for the morning walk.

They continued around the lake and arrived back in the village. After sorting out their unloaded luggage, they bid farewells to Laxmi and agreed to meet him in the evening for a meal as they wanted to have a hot shower and a rest at the hotel. Roland was pleased to have a hot shower, and then after an hour or so they met for lunch at the restaurant.

In the evening they all met to have dinner at the one restaurant in the village, called Lake View. The owner of the restaurant was a friendly old man, but he was complaining about not being able to find good staff in the villages.

***

The next day they woke up to the sights and sounds of large crowds and traffic outside in the main square. Everyone was dressed in beautiful traditional clothes, and they were nearly all wearing the same woollen hats that Roland had seen everywhere in the village before, including Laxmi, who had a smart new hat. Laxmi had rarely taken his hat off throughout the trek. They found out that it was the day of the fair and that everyone was going. Again Roland noticed the younger men wearing peaked caps, jeans and modern, thinner clothes. He wondered if these were providing them with the same warmth as the more traditional clothes worn by the majority of the people.

d–Friendly Kinnauri ladies dressed in handmade woollen clothes, posing proudly with the British tourist.

Roland recalled Laxmi mentioning that the famous Lavi mela festival was happening in Rampur the following day and that his wife had taken a horse down to the festival in the hope of selling it, and he wondered whether she had managed to sell it. He couldn't stop thinking about the fact that Laxmi only possessed one woollen jacket, one woolly hat and a simple pair of shoes for trekking, but he was satisfied and warm, which defined the toughness of these local people. In developing countries most young people aspire to dress like they have seen on television or in magazines, by films stars and other celebrities, whereas here each mountain area had its own unique and colourful style.

Roop had told him that Kinnaur and Spiti were areas of Himachal Pradesh where life was extremely hard in winter, and snow and avalanches could routinely cut them off from the outside world for many months at a time. Similarly, the lower part of Kinnaur and other Himachal areas got lots of flooding from the melting snow, and lakes were created by landslides and rain in the monsoons too. So life was very difficult year after year and they needed to wear clothing that suited their environment and had stood the test of time over the centuries.

Roland thought about these people who must have arrived in these mountains with their sheep and goats millennia ago, and their forefathers had developed the ways they now practised to live and dress and survive in this extreme climate, making their own woollen dresses, blankets, shawls, hats and scarves to keep warm. Their natural handmade clothing was both ecological and practical and could be repaired with materials from the village again and again. But instead, they'll throw away the modern clothing after a little use, and then buy more, sending money out to big companies instead of supporting their own communities to keep the skills alive.

Roland wondered how long it would take for city attitudes towards cheap and disposable clothing to infiltrate these villages as it would create a lot more problems to their lifestyle than they could imagine. It would increase their dependence on non-local products, and village skills and lifestyles would be destroyed. A person dressed in thin modern clothes in this climate could easily get ill, whereas a person dressed in traditional clothes would be less likely to fall ill, require hospital care or even modern medicine.

He blamed the media and celebrities for promoting the wrong messages. A simple boy from a village is encouraged to think that he should dress like a Hollywood or a Bollywood star. It may make him feel good, but it can lead him away from reality, because he is not a film star, he is a village boy who has just bought the clothes with all of his hard-earned money. In return he may not be as warm or comfortable as he would have been in his handmade traditional woollen clothes. This boy needs to survive in these harsh conditions but he may act like a star in his poor mud hut. He doesn't realise that the celebrity whom he admires may have countless staff and servants to work for him and live in a centrally heated home with all the modern conveniences.

Local people don't understand these days how they make much more money than previous generations but it all disappears – where does it go? They don't realise that it goes on the products they buy from the outside world. This means village money and village life is slowly disappearing; it becomes a race by companies to make money. They should consider, before buying anything, whether it is helping them and their community.

These were the thoughts going on in Roland's head before Roop knocked on the door. Roop told him that they were leaving for the fair in Rampur shortly and was Roland ready to go?

The morning was cold and the villagers had made a big bonfire outside to keep warm. Laxmi arrived and he was dressed so smartly that they didn't recognise him at first. He had a brand new hat with some feathers on top and a woollen overcoat on top of his woollen jacket.

The atmosphere was very festive and uplifting and everyone looked happy. Many Jeeps were being filled with people and they were all chatting away and waving and smiling as they drove off.

Roland was told: "If you hold the hand of a girl and ask her to marry you at that fair, she will be your wife forever, that's the tradition!"

"Oh, really?" Roland laughed. "We'd better get a move on then!"

They climbed into the Jeep to make their way to Rampur where the fair was being held. Soon they came out of the Bhaba Valley, and Roland remembered the zigzagging road and the dangerous winding corners which they had to follow back. After driving through some snow they got to the main road at Wangtu and they could see the crush of buses and Jeeps going to and from the festival. Many of the cars were overflowing with people or drums and some had people sitting on their roofs.

There were lots of fast-moving cars. It was a chaotic scene and Chaman complained that that's why they have some accidents in these parts, especially during weddings and festivals, where cars drop off the cliffs as drinking was a big part of life in these mountains and sometime drivers were a bit too casual about the roads.

As a result of the traffic jam they had to park away from Rampur near the college campus. Roop, Laxmi and Roland got out and Chaman decided to wait until the traffic cleared so that he could transfer his car to the hotel at the other end of the town, where it would be safe to leave it.

Laxmi had been to the fair almost every year of his life and he was very pleased that he could now take Roland to it. As they got to the fairground, Roland noticed many interesting stalls, all looking very colourful with various types of crafts, lots of wool produce, blankets, shawls, hats, jackets and *paatis* (long rolls of woollen materials to make jackets), and people dressed in traditional dress to present their folk dances and cultural programmes.

Roland wanted to buy a woollen jacket, overcoat and hat for himself like the local people were wearing. He then also bought scarves and shawls for presents to take back home to England.

He was also intrigued to see many shepherds were selling dried goat meat, which they dried (and sometime smoked) over the summer to see them through the harsh winters with protein. This had been done for centuries.

Roland asked Roop about the dry meat and also wanted to know how goat sacrifices fitted in with religious festivals. Roop had told Roland that they had some shaman ceremonies and animals were often offered to these deities or *deos,* as they called them.

"Yes, there are plenty of shamans in the Himalayas, and almost every family in the Himalayas will have some connection with shamans through their family or through the village community." explained Roop. "These are quite secretive practices, and the Himalayan shamans work as mediums for people to converse with deities and spirits. A good proportion of community leaders have connections with it but responsible people are well connected to it, and they may not disclose it publicly."

"The age-old Himalayan communities have their own ways of celebrating, and when they get together during these events or gatherings, or on the arrival of a deity in a village or home, a goat or sheep or ram will be offered, and there is a specific way to do it. This is still a very old and powerful tradition. I don't know if you know, but there is a village called Malana in the Kullu Valley further up in the western Himalayas in the Beas Valley, considered to be the oldest democratic local government in the world, and it is all controlled and ruled by permission of the local deity, or *deo,* through the shamans. They have their own courts and decision-making process with a committee locally called PUNCH or five responsible persons. Animal sacrifice is one of oldest native traditions of the Himalayas, so they could have a feast on fresh meat.

"According to these traditions, one may offer an animal, typically a goat or sheep, if prayers have been answered, or to please the arrival of the *deo* in the village or at the festival. Very often the cost is shared by the family or the community. Whatever is offered has to be healthy and well-nourished. The way it is done is that the whole community will gather around in a circle and the animal will be placed within the circle. They will wash his feet and horns and then offer flowers and water, flower petals or even some grains such as rice or mustard seeds with some red or orange powder on his spine from his forehead to his tail. In some traditions there will be a main priest or shaman who may be in a trance at the same time, and punch with some community leaders will perform the rituals and direct the decisions. Once the flowers, grains, colours and water are offered, the whole circle of people will start to pray for their sacrifice to be accepted without any disrespect or hassle to the animal. Then they wait for the permission from the animal as he surrenders, as well as acceptance of the offer from the *deo.* If all are united in their decision and prayers it may take a few seconds, or if there are some doubts or issues in the community, or if the animal is not well fed and healthy, it may take hours. If the animal doesn't surrender, then the sacrifice cannot be done. The surrender takes place when the animal shakes its body and contracts and relaxes its muscles, causing uncontrollable quivering, and every hair stands up on its body. This reaction can happen due to many things; it also happens in orgasms or when the mind and body is fully relaxed and balanced or blissful. When an animal is in the middle of it, at this moment a special skilled man, called a *fatbai,* or chopper, will swing his sword or a specially made sickle to chop off the head, while a second person might grab the back legs of the animal, or the head chopper himself will grab one back hoof, so that the animal can't move. It's believed that this moment is very important as the animal's mind is motionless, balanced and in a blissful state. That's the moment when the animal has surrendered his life, and that's the time to accept his surrendered body. Then the whole meat eating community will feast on the fresh meat. This is a very serious ceremony involving constant prayer and supplication that the sacrifice should go smoothly and not take too long. There are also rules – which part of the animal should be offered to whom, like the drummers, *fatbai* and so on. The problem these days is that those people who were skilled in these things are now slowly disappearing and non-meat eaters and governments are against it, and due to that the sacrifice has become badly managed, and the ways are being twisted in panic.

"I had a chat with some local traditional drummers who were complaining that even long-established families, known to do traditional things like playing the drums, music pipes, ancient oral hymns and singing, are now losing interest in these skills. It is very sad, because although the traditions are still carried on, the skills are being lost. I hope that they record and write down all these rituals and skills, so they are not lost forever."

Roland was quite surprised and said, "So it's like in the African bush where the Bushman would track and run behind the animal for many hours, and sometimes even for days. The whole idea used to be to make the animal so tired that it said 'no more' and surrendered its body. That's the moment the Bushman will kill the animal and then pray for it and thank it for giving its body to nourish the Bushman's family."

"Roland, that's interesting, because I have heard that in the highlands in Spiti in this state, quite close to the Tibetan border, they use the same technique and chase the yak all over the highlands before killing the animal," added Roop.

Roland continued, "That is incredible to have these matching traditions between these two distant continents, fascinating! I wonder if anything like that ever existed in England? Nowadays, huge slaughterhouses mechanically kill and chop up thousands of animals. Some of them are even large animals like horses or bulls, and God knows how they control them. It can't be a simple process and seems less respectful to the animal.

"Here, the public will witness the event, where as in big slaughter houses the public can't really see what is being killed and how. It's very different to the old ways of the Himalayas, Roop," said Roland.

"Yes, Roland. The traditional system, or ritual, acknowledges the animal's sacrifice and it seems that these ideas in the Himalayas and in the African bush may have come from similar sources."

"Is that because if the animal does not give up, or fights for its defence, it releases different chemicals into its body than when it is relaxed or surrendered and is instantly killed? It would be very interesting to know why these old techniques developed and from where?" Roland also stressed that India talked about non-violence and vegetarianism.

Roop added, "For survival we have to eat something, and even plants were seen as living things too. But the whole idea of non-violence is that we should do the least harm to any beings so we can all survive in harmony together. With the dry meat at the Lavi festival, the shepherd will have saved and dried the best bits of meat during the summer to sell at this festival," Roop explained.

Roland was fascinated by the eye-opening stories, scenes and market stalls.

Among the other attractions were the traditional palanquins of deities, or *deos*. They represented the different clans and races of the old times, like Nagas, Devi and other sages and gurus. They were well-decorated with gold and silver masks, and were covered with beautiful materials and a golden crown, or *chatra*. There were lots of traditional drums made of brass and other metals, using the skins of cows and goats. It felt like the whole mountain valley was echoing with the joyful sounds of singing and dancing together with other local instruments such as long brass pipes and curly shaped horns. When they started playing, it seemed that the whole Himalayan valley was dancing and everyone was in a joyous mood.

By now, Roland was dressed in his new hat and woollen coat and looked very much a part of the highland Himalayan community. Even if it was just for a short time, he felt very much a part of it.

By this time, Chaman had found them at the fair. "You both look like Kinnauris now. I couldn't recognise you at first, seems that the fair has already affected you," he laughed.

An old man approached Roland to speak to him and to find out where he was from and how he was enjoying the festival. He told Roland about the fair and its history.

"Its purpose was mainly to say farewell to the summer and to prepare for the winter season, as it always used to be very harsh and cold. It was an opportunity for people to meet and greet each other as many would not see each other again for a few months. Not only that, but people needed a last chance to stock up on food, meat, wool, nuts, dry fruit and handmade crafts as well as livestock like horses, sheep, goats and utensils, and this was the time to provide for their survival for the winter ahead.

"People were very tough and hard-working in the old days. They only travelled on foot or on horses up and down the mountains. But nowadays it's changing and it's much easier as they have roads and cars, and every village has shops. So its not urgent to stock up like they used to but the fair has been going on for over 600 years and still goes on."

Meanwhile, Laxmi had received news of the sale of his horse and was really pleased with the price. He offered to buy everyone a few drinks, so they took refuge at a hotel called the Bushahr Regency and celebrated over a drink. Soon after, Laxmi had to leave and they thanked him for his great contribution to their trip and bid him farewell.

The whole valley was echoing with loudspeakers and crowds singing and dancing in front of the stage, when they decided to call it a day.

***

The next morning they made the long drive back to Dani's village. *Amma ji* and *Satya* were happy to see them back safely, as they'd been anxious until they were back home. Roop busied himself unpacking all the equipment and hanging the tents on the washing lines to dry, while the others put away the other equipment for him.

"You must be really tired and cold," *Amma ji* said. "You should go to the hot springs and warm yourself." Roop and

Roland gave *Amma ji* the shawl they had bought for her and showed off their new hats and jackets.

After lunch, they took Roop's Royal Enfield motorbike for a few spare rides around the area after which they drove to Tattapani to the hot springs as he had missed it so much. It was a strange coincidence that Roland's grandfather had worked with the Royal Enfields in the UK, and his family were still members of its club.

They had a hot bath in the pools so that their aching muscles could fully recover from their trek. It was Roland's last night at the farm and he wanted to spend it with the family in the old kitchen by the fire as he had missed it a lot in the mountains. They talked about the Lavi mela as they shared the sweets and dry fruits he had brought after the meal.

A little later Roland went to bed, feeling revived and exhilarated.

CHAPTER ELEVEN

Sustainable and harmonious living within the community, and the Wonders of the World

Roland had such a good sleep that night that he hardly noticed the dog or anything else. *Satya didi* served tea, and soon after that he got up and helped with the packing and to put the tent away as Roop was joining Roland to Shimla too. Then they had their breakfast and Roland thoroughly enjoyed it, because he knew that after this his next meals were going to be in hotels.

They heard the car arriving and were all set to go. Roland thanked the family for his stay and they all wished him well for his long journey and flight home. They assured him that he was welcome to come back and stay with the family again anytime, and he promised to come back soon.

The whole family came out to see them off and waved goodbye as the boys got into the car and drove off. Roland was very touched by their hospitality and quite sad and heavy-hearted to leave the family behind.

They were soon going through the winding roads into the hills, passing a few stations on the way, like Basantpur, where they bought a few bottles of water in a local restaurant, and then on to higher roads through alpine woods as the view of the Satluj Valley became less visible, and after a little while they took a sharp left at Devidhar and left the whole valley behind.

After that, the road became much more winding and they had some quite serious steep drops downhill to navigate. They drove through Naldehra golf course and Mashobra, and then after driving through a very thick forest they arrived in Shimla.

A room had been booked in the Woodville Palace Hotel for Roland, and he gave a good tip to Chaman before saying goodbye to him as he had already driven Roland a few times on his trip. The location of the hotel was perfect for those who wanted to get away from the heat and the plains of India, but Roland would have preferred to be closer to the town as he wanted to do some shopping. The old Palace provided a lot of ambience and more than two hundreds years of the old ways of operating things. He felt safe to be back again after his trip and wanted to see the town, the mall road and colonial Shimla. Roop rang Mr Raaja Bhasin, the famous historian of Shimla, and a friend of Dani, to confirm their meeting in order to introduce Roland to Shimla and the history of the Raj. After a brief conversation, Raaja invited them to meet him in the town at the Ashiana Restaurant.

They walked from the hotel to the town centre, along the famous mall road, passing the chief minister's house on the way, as well as some wonderfully painted old buildings opposite. These made Roland feel at home. They were beautifully maintained old colonial wooden houses. Soon after that they passed the famous Hotel Oberoi Clarkes on their left and as the road curved to the right, the best thing was the view of Shimla from that point. Roop said that most of the markets were this side of the main hill due to the sunshine from the east as Shimla was cold in winter. He pointed out different monuments and buildings from the British Raj, like the main town hall and the post office, as well as the library and the old Sikh temple. They walked further up by the Hotel Willow Bank and Roop pointed out an old stream. He said that when the British arrived in Shimla the stream had been clean and drinkable, and he had heard that there used to be a wooden bridge and locals used to come here for drinking water, but now most of it was lost under the new buildings and hotels.

"It's been more than two hundred years since these foothills were taken over, and everyone from around the world wanted to come here at the time. As the weather's so good and it's such a beautiful location, it soon became a fashionable summer place for the rich and famous," said Roop. "The British had also managed to connect a railway to Shimla and it was a very good base and trade centre for them to explore the highlands up to Tibet."

They walked and roamed around the mall, enjoying the shops selling all sorts of souvenirs and other touristy things. As well as many international stores there were local shops too. Roland also had a quick look through an old bookstore selling historical maps and books. They climbed the road to the right by Jhansi Park and within a few minutes were on top of the ridge near the beautiful Golden Statue of Mahatma Gandhi. Roland really liked this part of Shimla as it was clean and free from cars.

"Have you noticed the signs notifying you of fines if you smoke or spit on the mall road or in any public place here?" Roop asked.

"Yes, Dani pointed them out," Roland said. "It's very impressive."

After a while they noticed that they were getting a lot of attention from people, and they realised that it was because they were dressed very differently from everyone else. They were dressed in the mountain hats and woollen jackets that they had bought at the craft fair. Roop pointed out that everyone else was in modern clothes and they must have thought that they were from a different planet.

"They must think we are a bit crazy, but who cares, we are much warmer than they are, and it is a traditional dress for people from the highlands," Roop said.

They walked to the mall and met with Raaja Bhasin, who was waiting for them. Roop introduced Roland to Raaja, and as he had a few other things to do in Shimla, he left them to talk about the British History of the Raj and find out more about Shimla.

Raaja took him for a short walk to the mall to point out a few interesting buildings. Roland soon realised that Raaja spoke excellent English. Raaja asked if he had enjoyed his trekking and Roland was delighted to share his trekking experience and told him about it and about the Lavi fair, saying how very different it was, even though it was just a little distance away from Shimla itself. They had a good conversation about the trekking and about Roland's time in the mountains.

Raaja pointed out at a well-built circular shaped restaurant and explained, "You will be surprised to know that this place used to be a bandstand. The British could not live without their music concerts, theatre, wine and tennis, and that explains the circular shape of this place. Over the years it has changed hands and at one point it was even converted into a children's crèche. But they soon realised that it was best as a place for entertainment and now that's what they do. They opened a restaurant upstairs and a bar underground."

"But what happened to the bandstand?" Roland asked.

"Present Simla (as Raaja called it) had become the summer capital of the state of Himachal Pradesh and the population had multiplied from the days of the Raj and so they needed a much higher bandstand to accommodate larger crowds. That's why the present government have built a new bandstand much further up, higher from the Mahatma Gandhi statue," Raaja pointed out.

"There's also a beautiful theatre called the Gaiety Theatre, as well as a club, which is quite exclusive. They have a members-only policy, but once in a while some of my friends have drinks or dinner there. The club is quite strict, but one can take friends as long as they follow the dress code and behave well," Raaja continued, with a smile.

As they walked, Raaja mentioned the different names of the buildings of the Raj and threaded them with dates and familiar names from British history to Roland in way that it soon became a colourful and memorable story of the past.

Raaja's knowledge of British history and the history of Shimla was incredible. He explained about Shimla, its history and formation, and he knew almost every story about how certain members of the British Empire had come to Shimla, as well as their family histories, and then how they had adapted Shimla to become a comfortable British hub. He told how they had built Shimla from the first house in 1822 by Lord Kennedy, which was now the house of the government state assembly, to how within sixty to seventy years they had made it a summer capital of the Raj by building the Viceroy Lodge in 1888. He said that at that time one-fifth of humanity was ruled from this place.

"I bought the book you wrote about the Lodge. It was very impressive," said Roland.

"Yes, it was very well built and they did really well without any trains or motor cars. Local labour and horses and donkeys transported most of the stones, carried from a long way away."

"Dani spoke of you very highly," Roland said, "and he believes that due to your publication and work Shimla has achieved a lot with regards to heritage and historical value, otherwise much of the historical charm and legacy would have been lost. Dani also thought that your work will continue to shed light on Shimla so many more will come to visit this summer capital of the British Raj in future. He told me that you have received many titles: historian, lecturer and author. Some call you 'King of the Hills' or 'Raja of the Hills'. Many famous BBC stars like Michael Palin and Sanjeev Bhaskar have documented your work and you have made documentaries for the BBC."

Raaja was very humble and laughed this away. "I just love Shimla and I like scribbling. Often, magazines seem to like it. I'm working on some government tourism heritage projects and I'm able to produce a few books as well. I live in Shimla most of the year and like it very much."

Roland was surprised to find out that Raaja had never been to England and yet he knew much more than him about British history. Raaja had just finished working on a book for his old school, Bishop Cotton, which was established in 1858, and that had already been sent for print.

As they walked back to the meeting place, Roland asked, "After all the years of the British Empire being in India and in Shimla, how is the relationship of Indians towards the British now?"

"To try and answer your question," Raaja said, "I think that most Indians of today's generation are quite indifferent to the British–Indian connection. In more ways than one, we've moved on, and few, if any, know or care whether they built the railways or whatever. As far as the older generation goes, the attitude is still mixed. We appreciate some of what the British did, but also condemn them for other things – the avoidable famines, the arrogant repressions, and so on."

"That's really interesting, because whomever I've met in India so far have all been very friendly as soon as they discovered I was British or knew about cricket!" replied Roland.

"To be honest, Roland, now it does not matter and things are changing fast here," Raaja said.

By now Roop had arrived. Raaja concluded sagely: "After all, we are all visitors and no one can hold the fort for that long."

After a brief chat, Raaja had to rush off, and he wished them well, saying to Roop that it was really nice to meet Roland and they should meet again for a drink."

Roland thanked him and said that he really appreciated that Raaja had taken time to meet him and they waved each other goodbye after a good handshake.

Roland wanted to buy a few more presents for Christmas, so they strolled through the Lakkar bazaar, a crafts market, for a few things. After that they walked back to the Himachal Tourist Information Office, where Roland bought a few more Himachal maps. Roop told Roland about a Tibetan market further along and asked if Roland wanted to see it. To Roland's amusement, there was not much there as they mainly sold lots of modern jeans imported from China. Roland had been expecting things made from natural materials from Tibetan villages instead. They had a look but Roland decided to leave it and go back to the main mall.

Roop pointed out a bookshop called Minerva for Roland to buy a few cards. "Do you know what Minerva means?" Roop asked Roland.

"Yes," said Roland. "Minerva is a Roman goddess of knowledge."

"Really?" Roop said with a smile. "Oh, so you also have gods for different things in Europe. That's really good to know, and we call her Sarswati in India – the goddess of knowledge. That's why books are highly regarded, and we don't touch any books with our feet as knowledge is sacred, and if you touch with shoes or feet, that is disrespectful."

"Oh, well, yes we had, but it's a pity not many people know about them now," said Roland.

They entered the shop and bought a few postcards as well as a few more books. After that, they decided to go for dinner at a restaurant belonging to Roop's friend, Niraj, called New Milap, which was just along from the Gaiety Theatre further down the steps. It was a traditional vegetarian restaurant, and they wanted to try authentic food for the evening, so this was the perfect place in town because they still followed age-old recipes. Here, they also met another friend called Gajender Sason, who worked in a bank as well as with Western tourists. He came up to greet them and asked after Dani.

Roop told them that he had spoken to Dani and that he had to go to Delhi to meet some of the members of his Spanish group, and he was going to meet Roland at the New Delhi train station. He had booked a room at the Grand Godwin Hotel for him. Roland had to drive to Kalka next morning to catch the train. So this was going to be their last night in Shimla and they should make the most of it.

They had their meal and, after having a meeting with Niraj, another friend of Roop's, Dhiraj, arrived. Roland found the names easy to remember as they were quite similar. Dhiraj joined them and they decided to explore the town's nightlife.

They wandered around the mall after a few drinks and met a few other locals who wanted to have a chat with Roland and have their photo taken with him.

At around ten o'clock, they decided to drop Roland at the Woodville Palace and then head home, as Roop was staying with his friend Dhiraj. Roland invited them to the hotel bar, and they enjoyed their final drink in a very grand bar in the centuries-old hotel.

Roop made sure that Roland was clear about his travel arrangements for the next day for his journey to the train station in Kalka, and then Roland presented Roop with a thank-you gift. Roop was deeply touched and said that it had been a great experience for him too and hoped for another adventure in the future. They wished each other well and said their goodbyes.

Roland went to his grand bedroom, and, after a nice shower, enjoyed the luxury of a royal palace for the night.

***

The next morning he had breakfast and after that he had a look around the hotel and its grounds and found out a little more about the history, as well as about the other facilities they provided.

He had a conversation with the accountant, Mr Sharma, who told Roland that the hotel was quite popular for Bollywood films and many movies were filmed there. He also pointed out some of the portraits of the family who owned the Palace – the family of the Maharaja of Jubal – and that some parts of the Palace were still occupied by members of the family occasionally.

At around eleven thirty in the morning, his car arrived to pick him up to take him to Kalka station, which was a three-hour drive from Shimla.

During the journey, the driver stopped for a late lunch at a hotel in Parwanoo called Timber Trail. The hotel owner was quite an elderly man who came out and had a chat with Roland and told him that they had an amazing spa called Moksha at the top of the hill, and he had imported a cable car from Europe so that people could travel to the top of the hill to enjoy it. Roland liked the place and its wonderful setting in the beautiful foothills.

Soon after lunch, they left and met a policeman who took a lift with them, and then Roland was dropped at the small colonial station in Kalka. It was not too busy, but there were still a few people rushing in and out with their luggage and red uniformed coolies on the look-out for people with heavy luggage.

He made his way through the entrance and, after a little wait, the Shatabdi Express train was ready to board, so he searched for his name on the list and went to find his seat. The cost was about six or seven pounds for the four-hour journey to New Delhi in an air-conditioned coach, and included a bottle of water, tea and dinner. It was a comfortable and enjoyable journey for Roland, and it reminded him of all the things he had seen on his journey from Delhi to Shimla with Dani.

The train was quite empty at first, but after stopping at Chandigarh, it filled with a lot of people. They may have been people finishing after work, as they were all busy on phones and laptops. What Roland found interesting was that they were all served tea and snacks and meals too. Not a bad way to finish work and then get some rest on the way home as well as being served dinner!

Roland was soon lost in the beauty of the scenery, but none of the other passengers seemed to be bothered about it, so he took a few more photographs as it was getting dark outside.

They passed a few more stations and finally he arrived at New Delhi Station. As soon as train stopped he got his rucksack out and went off to find the exit. By then a few people were chasing him to help him get a taxi or carry his bags, but to their disappointment Roland found Dani and he took one of his bags.

"You were on time. How was your journey?" asked Dani. The touts tried their best, but Dani told them off, telling them that they were "fine, thank you very much." They walked to the busy main junction and jumped into one of the three-wheeler rickshaws which were waiting around.

After a short drive they got to the Grand Godwin Hotel and Roland was relieved to be back in a hotel again after his long day. It was quite late, but they decided to go out for a drink and Dani wanted something to eat, as well as to try a new hotel and restaurant in the main bazaar in Pahar Ganj. Roland put his luggage in his hotel room and then they both jumped back into the rickshaw again. It was a short ride of ten minutes through the busy streets of New Delhi, and after another interesting zigzagging journey through all sorts of traffic, travellers – Western and Indian – and of course beggars and people selling all sort of things in the street, finally they found the Hari Piorko Hotel and restaurant that Dani wanted to check out. He had heard that it was good. As they went up to the rooftop restaurant, they realised why it was popular with tourists and students. There were natural huts made of reeds and bamboo on the rooftop, and the whole atmosphere was very village-like and full of Western tourists. They ordered a drink and some snacks, and Dani also ordered some food, as he hadn't had dinner. While the order was coming, Dani went to check some of the rooms and was pleased that the rates were good and the rooms were clean and well-maintained.

Dani said that he was looking for a cheaper hotel near the train station and this one could be suitable for some of his student guests staying in New Delhi. But for mid-range guests the other hotel was fine.

Their food arrived and Roland tried a garlic nan bread and had a drink as well as a cup of chai. They both enjoyed it and Dani said that it was delicious. Dani asked how his journey to Delhi had been and if he had met anyone on the train.

"It was a good journey but the road from Shimla was a bit windy," Roland said, "but we took our time and had a few breaks. We had a policeman travelling with us for part of the journey, but the driver didn't like him, and he told me afterwards that they don't pay any money and they just use the car for free. If you try to ask for money, they get irritated and check your documents for any faults as an excuse to fine you. So you have to just ignore them."

"Yes some officers are corrupt, but some of them have few resources and they try to depend on the public and it is a very difficult balance," said Dani, "and yes, these habits of corrupt officers are taking time to change and they give a bad name to the whole police department and it's disappointing."

The conversation then moved on to trekking and the challenge that Roland and the others had gone through in the snow.

"It couldn't have been better, and I had an amazing time," said Roland. "It wasn't easy, as we had some snow fall and some real mountaineering experience."

Dani laughed. "Oh, so you had a snowy experience? It's alright if the wind is blowing from behind and the snow is not thrown in your face."

"Yes, that's right. Luckily there were lots of trees and we were quite well protected by them," Roland said. "It was cold, and we were trekking through the snow, but the good thing was that the families in the village were very hospitable. Laxmi's family was very helpful and we had a great time with him. He took us to the Lavi fair too, which was the best way to experience the culture and the way they have been trading for centuries."

"I'm really pleased that you got the chance to see all these things and the ceremonies, Roland," said Dani.

"Did you see any traditional drums playing in the festival as well?" he asked.

"Yes, I did, and its sound was echoing all around the valley: drums, horns, long brass pipes too. It really was beautiful. And how was your trip to Delhi, Dani?" asked Roland.

"I had a most interesting journey," replied Dani. "I came by bus, which was fine, but not comfortable like the train. I met two very unlucky boys on the bus. They were travelling all the way from Kaza and Manali, before the weather closed in and they were stuck there for the whole winter. One of the boys was very ill due to a combination of altitude sickness, hash weather conditions in Spiti (3550m) and malnutrition, so he had to leave his job after just a few days work and he didn't have much money. The other boy came with him to make sure he got home safely as he was not well enough to travel on his own. They had journeyed for four days using local buses and third-class trains, and they wanted to get to Delhi so that they could catch a train to Patna in Bihar in Eastern India. I was shocked on hearing their story and they were very poor. I bought a few things for their journey – biscuits and fruit and bottles of water. You would not believe it, they had nothing. Whatever money they had they were holding on tight to. I felt really sad for them, and they said that their contractor had told him that if he wasn't fit to work he had to go home. That's it, so they had to rush home before the roads got blocked for six months due to snow. They were pleased that they were leaving the freezing weather behind. I feel so angry with the government for allowing contractors to take these boys to these remote places where the conditions are really very rough and then abandon them with no rights."

"What kind of work do they do?" Roland asked.

"They work on the roads, digging and working manually with tarmac, concrete and cement. They have no proper equipment, and after six months or so they look black like tarmac themselves, due to the smoke, the low temperatures, the stinging cold wind and the dust and dryness in summer. I have seen these people working during my trips to the desert parts of the Himalayas in summer. They are sometimes stuck in the middle of nowhere. One has to drive around eight or nine hours or for days to get to these roads, and there you find these boys who are brought from the lovely hot weather from Bihar, and they look like they have been blackmailed or kidnapped. I'm sure that the introduction of modern machines will save their lives, but if the attitude of the government and the contractors is not changed, then nothing will change and that is a crime. They should be paid double or triple what they get now, and they should be provided with special equipment and medical help to work in these remote wildernesses where many labourers die unaccounted for under huge landslides year after year. They also told me that some boys are trapped there for years working for families or guest houses and they can't leave easily, if they try to run, they are blamed for robbery and brought back, explained Dani.

"These poor boys travelled with me and it made me think how millions of youths continue to be trapped in the grip of poverty in this country due to a lack of accountability and care. Some people in authority don't do their job properly and that creates a lot of suffering for the vulnerable people below them.

"As we are travelling, the buses routinely stop at certain food stalls, where the driver gets good treatment. I am not sure if those are official places designated by the government for the bus to stop or if they are unofficial arrangements between the drivers and owners, but some of these roadside stalls just don't know how to serve food or deal with customers. They treat everyone like beggars and then they charge you much more afterwards because they think that once you are there you have no choice, and they probably won't see you again, while the drivers and conductors get a superior meal inside in a private room. So the passengers are being cheated. These are the places where private cars and luxury buses don't stop. So the regulators and food hygiene officials may not have seen how bad their standard of cleanliness is. I did not buy anything there except some sealed juice. These poor passengers already have enough problems and others are trying to squeeze the life from them. They don't care what's going on with you."

"Well it sounds just like marketing companies or shops in Britain, who just want to sell to you or sign you up for deals, and they don't care if you are struggling to pay your bills or not," Roland said. "Phone companies try to squeeze you, too, so that they can achieve their targets and the company can make more profit. It's woeful, Dani, that people only think of themselves, and sometimes people ring you at home to sell insurance and take marketing surveys so that they can sell you more or hassle you. They ring you when you're in the middle of something, saying they will only take a few seconds, and after a few minutes you realise they're wasting your time.

"That's the problem with the modern world: a shop may look wonderful, but it's all designed to trap the buyer. Everything these days seems to be there to trap people. The more you look around, the more your time is wasted. It's a commercial world where you get nothing for free, but they extract anything they can from you through flyers, emails, newsletters and other lures: they bombard you with information, but the ultimate goal is to take, not to give and we forget that!" added Roland.

"That's the sad thing about the world, Roland," Dani said with frustration. "The difference in England is that at least there is a respected system. People are generally polite and respectful, and customer service and accountability is good. If you see these roadside food stalls in India though, they treat you like dirt while they themselves don't trust anyone. Maybe they are cheated too."

"But it is the responsibility of the authorities to regulate them and make sure that they have a system and that they're accountable and supervised," added Roland.

Dani countinued, "I had a few busy days in the village and spent my time in and out of revenue offices trying to apply for some land demarcation, as we needed to check a few fields. Roland, you would not believe how corrupt and useless some of these officers are. They just don't want to help. If you go to these admin offices they just ignore you, and they won't ask if there's anything they can do for you.

They see you as another obstacle disturbing their leisure time.

"They make excuse after excuse – they need approval from a magistrate or a certificate from a village president or office or clerk or someone. You can bet on it, they will try to object. Even an educated man ends up feeling desperate to end his suffering in these places."

"What about the villagers who can't read or write?" Roland asked.

"Well those people are happy to pay under the table, and they spend lots of money doing so, and some of these corrupt officers are used to this system. If you are honest and you don't want to pay under the table or you have no connections, they make you suffer. Sometimes I wonder whether this stems from those ancient ideas of survival and victory from the Indian scriptures: *saam, daam, dand* and *bhed*. The desire for success, whether individual or family-oriented, is embedded in the culture and it is really funny to think that people may still be employing these old techniques in India referred to *char bhed* or 'four secrets'

"Sam, daam, dand and bhed," Roland asked. "What are those?"

Dani explained, "*Saam* means manipulating others through the use of charm, conversation, talk, and emotions, such as putting on an act.

"*Daam* means using money or bribes to get what you want. This can include gifts, offers, parties, meals, alcohol, games or even women, depending on what the recipient's weaknesses, interests or habits are. This method seems to be on the increase around the world.

"*Dand* means manipulation by force, whether verbal, physical or mental, through demonstrations of power, praising their own side, name-dropping to make connections to famous people, lifestyle, clothes, luxuries, or direct mental or physical threat, or war.

"*Bhed* means manipulation by division and the word also means secret, whether covert or created ('divide and conquer'). This was the technique used by the British during the Raj. Creating trouble or conflict between friends – even in their own families, and singling out the enemy so he becomes weaker and insecure – is a way to win because an insecure enemy won't make good decisions."

Dani continued, "These are the ancient ways of moving forward to win and survive. But people forget that these methods originated only for the benefit and protection of *dharma* and the well-being of societies as a whole, to achieve a prosperous and peaceful life for all. Krishna initially applied them in the *Mahabharata* to avoid war, but the ruling and unrighteous side, which was stronger and continued to wage war, forced Krishna to utilise these 'four secrets' to win and to save the *dharma*. But today, those methods are being misused for selfish and individual purposes, so victory is being forced at any cost, or being achieved at the expense of society as a whole. Under-the-table bribery through old-boy networks – fairness is being ignored and its effect will be serious in years to come."

Dani laughed, saying, "The desire to win must be in the genes, and bribery is the quickest way to win, so all the unrighteous people are at it! What a shame to manipulate something for the wrong purpose. Where is the fairness and *dharma* in that?

"Krishna uses all four secrets to avoid a war. He talks to the Kauravas (the hundred princes, the sons of the blind King Dhritarashtra). He is willing to accept just five villages for the Pandavas (the five princes and sons of dead king Pandu). That is all he asks for. He narrates to the Kauravas tales of the powers of the Pandavas but when all this fails, he decides to divide the Kauravas with the last technique, *bhed*, and as a result their friend Karna is affected badly, and can no longer fight with conviction anymore.

"The lasting lesson from this is that victory and pleasure can only come from a terrible struggle, whereas inner peace comes from the path of righteousness. Being on the right side of the *dharma* will always help one to achieve inner peace, which is more important than a victory for the ego or for pleasure. But people have forgotten that, or they don't know about it."

"The best thing would be to film them or record these corrupt officials in action," said Roland.

"Yes that's true," said Dani. Nowadays, due to phones having cameras, many of these officers are being dismissed from their jobs as people produce live recordings of them taking bribes. So I hope it will get better. I hate the bureaucracy so much. India must move on and update their corrupt and lengthy system. We may leave India or its old natural customs behind, but we can't wash our hands from the responsibilities of climate change and looking after nature and other beings."

"Dani, now I know why your mother said you were very busy and that you were fed up with the bureaucracy."

"Yes, exactly. Anyway, enough of corruption. How was your meeting with Raaja, Roland?"

"Really very interesting. He knew a lot about British history, and he was very English in his manner and in his speech," joked Roland.

"Yes, he is old-school, Roland. I am always amazed with his articles and his knowledge of Britain, despite the fact that he has never been there."

Roland said, "I asked Raaja what people thought of Britain today, because India still has many old British schools and institutions, even after all these years. Raaja also mentioned some avoidable famines which I didn't know about."

"Well, Roland, many people have forgotten the famines, but he is a historian and knows much more about the famines of Bengal and Bihar which claimed millions of lives due to huge rises in tax and changes in crops. British officers were not there to help the natives, only to make money, and they demanded increases in taxation. No gravestones or memorials were ever erected for the millions who died as a result of being forced to grow cotton and opium so that the East India Company could sell it to China and other countries to make a very lucrative profit. Who cared about the millions of farmers dying of hunger in India? Those officers were put in India to use all the resources at their disposal and to make money out of it to fund their lavish lifestyle. In some cases it was just pure arrogance and greed. Whoever stood in their way was removed; freedom fighters or fair and responsible people who tried to protect their communities were punished. These famines and, subsequently, partition claimed millions of lives in India due to their arrogance and their attitude of believing themselves to be superior to the native population, who they considered were uneducated fools and inferior to their pets. They were desperate to import their own way of life from Britain into these native lands."

"I see," replied Roland. "I didn't realise. Shimla could almost be a town in Europe. The old churches and buildings are still standing and are well managed, but on the other hand, you see the contrast of the villages around Shimla living sustainable and traditional lifestyles, unlike those in Britain."

Roland mentioned about the beautiful yellow church in the mall at Shimla, which was in a wonderful position, and he wondered how the church had managed to acquire the land in such a good position. "Was that through the generosity of local people, or was the land bought or just occupied for nothing, as it seems that, in contrast, the local temples were built on small corners or on steep slopes. And there are many more such wonderful buildings built by the British all over the place."

"Well that's true, Roland. I'm not sure how they acquired those spots, but they built the first house in 1822, and that beautiful church was built in 1857. They did build incredible architectural monuments till around 1900, but after the first mutiny things changed a bit. All those buildings and monuments have become just landmarks now, and things have changed in all the years since Independence. The most interesting thing is that maybe old churches, cemeteries or some of the social legacy is fading. But the old system of morals, structure and overall bureaucracy is still alive in the government system. Some of those things have moved forward in England itself, but India still drags those things on.

"In terms of the relationship between India and Britain, it was very interesting for me when I had to organise a tour for a retired group of people, whose interest was an army one. Roger Massie, the son of a 9 Gorkha Rifles officer Lieutenant Colonel TA Massie, had planned a trip to recreate the footsteps of his late father, who had served in India during the British Raj before Independence. I was the civilian companion tasked to organise and coordinate the itinerary for this group. Murray Campbell, a family friend from

England, had put me in touch with his friend Roger Massie to plan this trip for him and his wife, Claire, with several other British friends who had a similar connection, and most of them were old friends from Oxford. They were hungry for knowledge and an exploration of British history in India. As soon as we got in touch with the colonel commandant of the regiment there, Major General Kishan Singh VSM, we received an astonishing response, welcoming and offering to host Mr and Mrs Massie to India in order to maintain the British pre-partition connection, as they treasure the glorious history of their regiment and the memories of all its officers. Mr and Mrs Massie were given access to explore their family connection in Dehradun, and special events were hosted for Mr and Mrs Massie in Pune to acknowledge his father's work as part of that regiment and his later years in the Wellington Club in Coonoor in South India.

"Roger said that things were preserved to a high standard and both countries still valued their shared history, army connections, training, ties and exchanges. The army had very strict rules that access was purely for Mr and Mrs Massie, and it was limited for anyone else, which was very interesting, and special care was taken to entertain and protect them. Major Samir Lama was deployed to receive the couple and it was overwhelming for me to witness officers greeting and saluting us. I had to send them all the lists and the detailed itinerary for Mr and Mrs Massie's tour in advance, and they had to verify all the hotels. They were in constant touch with me on the phone for any issues. Later, Mr and Mrs Massie had a private invitation for a few days to Pune, where they were entertained and hosted by the army. Roger and his group really liked Shimla, with its glorious and peaceful history. Roger Massie subsequently wrote in an article that, *The mountain boy proved the ideal guide to the hill country around Shimla, the former summer seat of government of the British Raj whose twilight – so much better than bombs and blackouts – I was lucky enough to witness, even if only as a toddler.'* (Article: The Bonds of the Regiment – A visit to 9 GR in the Kukri – the Journal of the Brigade of Gorkhas).

"So this is what I find interesting, Roland. In some cases, India and Britain share the past and still remain constant partners like with the army and the railway system. Because Britain and India have spent more than four hundred years together, learning from each other, they share some cultural and moral values, which have been embedded in their respective lifestyles. But there are various different aspects to colonialism. One is the hierarchy and the other is the friendship and sharing between the officers and the workers who worked side by side giving their lives or saving each others' lives. That trust and faith lives a long time, whereas the arrogant and superior side of colonialism has faded and will disappear soon."

"It's natural that the good done by the British will live on and other things done for purely personal or selfish reasons will be forgotten," said Roland.

"But that's history, Roland, and here we are in a new modern world with new ties and new goals, and India is moving fast, but still, as you know, the old schools, army, railway and banking systems left by the British remain visible today. India is a strange place in that sense. On the one side they practise ancient rituals and ceremonies, and on the other, some of the English schools will still punish their pupils if they speak their native Indian language. Also, all children are now studying English, IT and engineering and India is sending missions to space to compete with the world. It is so difficult to say in which direction India is heading," said Dani as he started to get up.

31 Old wooden pagoda Sarahan Temple and snowy Shri
Khand Mountain peak above the clouds (5227m).

32 The guide, Roop Singh standing by a
rocky glacier and river Bhaba.

33 Camping in the Bhaba Valley at Kara
(356m), below the high mountains.

34 Himachali Shepherds dressed in homemade woollen clothing,
cooking on an open fire and drying meat on the rocks.

35 Mountain drummers performing at night as their echo resounds in the mountains.

36 Fascinating sculptures made from concrete and discarded broken glass bangles in Nek Chand's Rock Garden, Chandigarh, North India.

37 The life of a cycle rickshaw driver in New Delhi using his energy to cycle many miles a day leaving no carbon footprint, unlike other motor car drivers polluting the atmosphere.

38 Waiters serving food and drinks on the Shatabadi Express train, New Delhi to Kalka.

39 Roland Bourne, Puran Bhardwaj, Hellen Faus, Isabelle Lahoz, Prem Adriano Merola and Yuko at the Taj Mahal.

40 Carved Brah statue (Boar – 3rd incarnation of Vishnu) at the Amravati Cave, Madhya Pradesh. 5th century and inset statue of Brah Avatar at the farmhouse.

"That's true, Dani," said Roland. "It will be interesting to see which direction it takes in the next twenty years or so. But it will be a shame if India loses its traditional ways and lifestyle in the process."

They left the restaurant, and after a little walk through flying dust and pieces of paper, boxes dumped by shopkeepers outside their stores, cows finding the best bits in these piles to eat in the main bazaar, in the dark, with just some dim street lights and confused late-night walkers and back packers, they managed to find a cycle rickshaw in the chaotic busy street to take them to their hotel, driven by a skinny man who moved his whole body as he stood on the peddles to push it forward. Roland felt sorry for him, but it was the quickest way to go short distances.

There was less traffic now in front of the New Delhi train station, but paper and rubbish was strewn everywhere and a few beggars were still chasing passers-by, while others were huddled in groups in corners to divide and share the money they'd earned or food they'd found.

Dani asked the rickshaw man where he was from and what his name was. He replied, between catching his breath, that his name was Govinda and he was from Bihar state. They found out that he used to come to Delhi every year for many months to make money, and all his family was in Bihar, which was like the distance between Rome to London, Dani explained to Roland. They also found out that he lived on his rickshaw and all he had was a bag and a bundle of sheets, hanging down from a fence near a temple sheltered by a tree, and he used to park near there. That was his residence, and he never spent any of his earnings to rent a room.

"That's his life, Roland," said Dani. "Imagine this, he is contented earning money by peddling people around, and the earnings are going to his village to support his family and community."

Roland thought that it was incredible to think that a few rupees paid to him were going such a long way, and lives were being transformed in a different part of the world.

"A man running around any city in the world, whether in London, Paris, New York or Delhi, can be supporting another community around the globe," said Roland.

"That's the beauty of the world today," Dani said. "The world is connected in a very complex way."

"Govinda is also using and burning his own energy and keeping fit," continued Roland. "His contribution to the world and to nature is much more sustainable than those people who are driving and rushing about in smart and expensive cars. In that sense, this man is contributing much more than those huge industries producing cars that are causing harmful pollution as a few hundred thousand cars pass by every little town around the world now, and which not only may bring every living thing to an end, but humans may lose the natural capacity and resilience to survive."

Dani also found out that his rickshaw was on lease and that whenever he went back home to Bihar, he returned it to its owner, and he said many rickshaw people didn't own their rickshaws either.

As he took his money, he thanked them, saying, *"Mehrbani Sab time kat raye hai, jo malic or bhgya ne buksha hui."* ("We are all passing the time, with whatever is destined to us by the real owner and fate.") Govinda seemed a satisfied man, happy with his work. He made sure they didn't forget anything. They paid him well and wished him well too. Roland shook his hand and said goodbye, and with a respectful smile he drove off.

They entered the hotel as the *chokidar* opened the door for them. Dani said goodnight to Roland, saying that he would see him early in the morning at reception with his bag at 5.45 a.m. Roland was happy to have a rest after his long journey from Shimla. He had an early start the next day to catch a train to the Taj Mahal in Agra. Roland wished him a good night, and they went to their separate rooms.

***

The next morning, Dani woke up thanks to his Nokia speaking alarm, "It is time to get up. The time is five thirty-five." He punched the mobile with his thumb, and then he jumped out of bed, ran to the bathroom and, after a quick shower, dried himself and got ready.

He made a phone call to reception to check the taxi and told them that they were leaving in a couple of minutes. Grabbing his things, he opened the door and shut it behind him, taking the stairs.

Everyone was already in reception waiting for him; the friends he had collected at night as well: Hellen Faus, her friend Isabel (Seby) Lahoz from Spain, Dani's Italian friend, Prem Adriano Merola and his girl friend Yuko from Japan.

He wished them all good morning and they all jumped into the waiting taxi. They soon faced the main entrance of the New Delhi Station. It was a shock for Hellen and Seby as it was their first morning in India and they couldn't believe the chaos on the roads. The driver had one or two close encounters with rickshaws, buses and other cars, but they all rushed off after thanking him, and Dani handed the taxi driver a fifty-rupee note as a tip for the early morning drop-off.

They followed Dani through the morning rush in the station, although a few touts were chasing the ladies, but they soon realised that they had no luggage and someone was leading them so they had no chance. They found the train and their names, and made themselves comfortable. Adriano and Yuko sat on two seats further away. They had arrived quite late last night and they wanted to have some rest on the train. Adriano was in his forties, a flight steward by profession and a saxophone player and traveller by hobby. He had met Dani for the first time in Goa in a resort called Dreamcatcher in 2001. After that, Adriano had been on a group trekking trip to the Himalayas led by Dani, and he was a frequent traveller to India and knew Dani well now.

They were all very comfortable in their seats by now. After a long whistle at six fifteen, the train left the station. Everyone was quiet and still half asleep, so they took some time to energise, but for Hellen and Seby this station was a wake-up alarm and the scenes outside were very exciting. Lots of people were rushing about and going in and out of the station or waiting for their trains. It was quite something for them to see. Some children and beggars were being chased out by policemen, and lots of people were just lying down or sitting down on the floor with a pile of their belongings providing a backrest or a headrest while they waited for trains. Hellen noticed that they were sitting and waiting very peacefully; there was no panic or strain on their faces. They were just watching the passers-by as if they were made of wax.

Hellen got her guidebook out and started to look through it, but soon the waiters with colourful turbans and long jackets came round with serving trays piled with tea bags, sugar, biscuits, coffee and powdered milk, while the second waiter followed him with red Thermoses, and they handed things out one by one to everyone.

Dani wasn't bothered about having tea or coffee; he preferred to have a nap. Hellen pointed out to Roland that Dani was tired.

"Yes," Roland said, "he's had a few long journeys, a night-time airport pickup and very little rest."

They asked Roland about his trip and the itinerary he'd had. He told them that it was his first time in India and about what he'd done, and that he was fascinated by the country and really enjoying his experience.

It was getting brighter outside and they could see the small houses as they passed them by. Roland told them about the shock he'd had with all the rubbish and litter along the railway tracks the first time he had taken a train. Hellen said that she had heard about children who spent most of their time going through rubbish alongside the trains and in the landfills. She had heard about the railway children as well and about the child labour and beggars in India, and she was interested to see and understand how they scavenged and survived around the big crowds and stations.

A waiter cleared all the trays and then the ticket collector came. Dani opened his eyes and handed over the tickets, while pointing out the other members of the group. Next, breakfast was served, and Dani was looking forward to it now that he'd had a snooze and was feeling refreshed. He joined in the conversation between Roland and Hellen. She was full of fun and couldn't wait to see the Taj Mahal.

After putting his tickets back in his bag, Dani said, "I'll tell you a funny story. Once I had a friend who was travelling on the train from Delhi, and she had great difficulty finding the platform and the coach. Eventually she found the correct train and her seat number and the train departed, and she had wonderful service – water, juice, tea, breakfast, newspaper and so on. She thought it was the best train ever as she had hardly paid a pound or two for the nine-hour journey. After four or five hours, the ticket collector came and asked for the ticket. She handed it over but the ticket collector said, 'Oh madam you are causing offence.' She said, 'Oh, I beg your pardon, what's the matter?' 'This is first class, madam, and this ticket is general class.' She said, 'No, no, look, I could not find the coach number on the ticket, but it says F for first class and thirty-four is the seat number.' He burst out laughing. 'No, this is your age and gender, madam.'"

They all burst out laughing.

"Oh, that's fantastic," said Hellen, "but what happened to the lady?"

"Well, the ticket collector wanted to fine her a few hundred rupees, almost ten euros or so, but she refused to pay and said, 'I will go to my own seat at the next stop.' As more than half the journey was done and she was not going to pay, he could not believe it, but he said, 'Please change at the next stop, madam, and don't worry, it's okay.' She was really pleased that she'd had at least a few good hours in first class and now the train was going higher in the hills, so air conditioning wasn't needed either!"

By now they were all enjoying their breakfast and the train staff were collecting the empty trays. After they finished breakfast some began reading newspapers while Hellen and Seby kept watching out of the window as they passed through different stations; they thought it was like watching a movie. Most intriguing and disturbing for Hellen were the young children, running with tea kettles, glasses, or selling bottles of water or fruits and candies.

Dani said that it wasn't far now. It was eight o'clock and within fifteen minutes they would soon be there. Some of the passengers were gathering their things and waiters had passed comment forms around to sign for whoever took them willingly. There were many Western tourists as well as some officials and local people going to work. Soon the train stopped and they got out quickly as they didn't have any heavy luggage.

As soon as they came to the main exit gate, they were faced by a huge wall of people; it looked like they were about to burst into arrivals like a flood, but luckily they were being pushed back by the policemen.

Dani explained that it was a crowd of taxi drivers, touts and local guides who were trying to find or grab tourists to earn some money. They were trying to think what to do when suddenly a police officer with stars on his shoulders jumped among the crowd and commanded them to empty the space. Within a few seconds the wall of people had scattered and thinned; the police officer grabbed a man by the collar and a few voices were raised.

Dani gathered everyone together as they were being followed by people offering their services to them. As they came out of the crowd, Dani noticed a man with a name board, who was their driver waiting for them. They got into their car and were relieved to leave the packed station behind as they drove through the busy traffic.

Hellen asked Dani about the many young children selling things in the railway stations, and she had also noticed lots of them by the side of the tracks. They didn't look healthy and some of them had no shoes or clothes. Hellen asked if they went to school or not, and how did they live?

"Yes it is awful seeing these children and beggars passing stations and no one to notice them or to stop and think why that child isn't going to school or to provide some support for them," said Dani. "Some families will be spending fortunes on their own children, but on the other side of the road a child may be begging for a coin to buy a loaf of bread and his plea will go unnoticed. Sadly, they really are unnoticed children. Those children are so unfortunate. From birth they are in a race for survival. The fittest will survive, but even they have to fight for a suitable roadside spot to sell their products, to collect things from the dump, or fight for a suitable shelter or a space under a tree to place their mat for the night. Who knows what happens at night to these children in places where the nights are ruled by powerful criminals or hooligans in the underground world. The problem is that most people are in a race for survival here, wherever they live. Many who manage to earn a little want to move and send their children to school, but they are still struggling for their basic needs. Who has time to stop or notice?

"Although there are many social problems in some parts of India, poverty is the biggest curse and the root of many problems. People think that their child is more precious than the child who is born in the streets or roadsides or in the households of the poor and the lower class. That means that the nation is lacking serious foundations for the welfare of its people. Until authorities and people start thinking that children are just children and that they should all be provided with proper education, basic food care and an opportunity to do well in life, a nation cannot be healthy, because they are the future of a nation. Even many animals look after their own better than us humans."

Hellen asked, "What about the government? Why don't they send them to school or take them away to hostels and other safe places?"

"The problem is that they are children who are used to moving from station to station, and they have also developed skills in how to go unnoticed," replied Dani. "Very often they are victims of the shopkeepers or even of the authorities. Sometimes, a policemen or ticket collector is not paying enough attention or they are not bothered if an underage child is being abused of his rights. Due to a lack of cooperation, many children are unrecorded. Nobody knows where they come from, their date of birth or any ID or address. All the social workers and authorities are trying to remove or settle those who are on their lists, but the rest are still in hiding or unnoticed, living like shadows.

"In India, primary education is free for all, and the government schools provide free books, uniforms and midday meals. However, the biggest problem in India is that the bureaucracy and paperwork is so shambolic that no one will just say, 'First let's improve the life of this child, and then once he is studying in a school and he is settled, we will figure out his details.' No, they have to have legal certificates and documents and those things take much longer even for well-established citizens in the country, and the chance of producing those certificates for a street child is impossible.

"Another problem in India is that there is a lack of practical and technical education. If parents are careless or the children find education very difficult, they may just drop out of school at a very young age, and that can be due to disability or disease also." Dani pointed out other interesting things on their way, saying, "There are no institutions that can give these children a technical or practical education. This could include handicrafts or any other skilful trades.

That is really lacking. Education should be much more than theory and books. They are lacking in hands-on experience-based education.

"We need education about practical skills related to the local environment. How to work practically with cattle, goats, sheep and chickens, or how to grow crops – rice, wheat and vegetables. Whatever jobs exist in the children's surroundings, they should be taught practically, because that is what they need first to revive local skills.

"There could be visits to farms and workshops so they can gain work experience in real life during their school years. If they are studying about a flour mill they should visit a flour mill in real life to really understand the work behind this. That would be a real education. If the topic is a guest house or hotel, they should visit a five-star hotel to see how it works, how to be a better waiter and how to do these jobs. The same applies for any work one wants to choose after school too. That will perpetuate skills and sustainable ways of living. If someone wants to study music, he should have the experience of playing traditional drums and songs within villages and visits to real concerts should be free and encouraged. The government needs to encourage science museums to have exhibitions and workshops on the topics of science and technology. If we have organised exhibitions, these could be mobile and could travel from village to village and school to school. People's minds could be opened up through these exhibitions and workshops.

"Very often topics are just memorised, with no practical thinking at all. If you ask a child about the topic of a cow, the student will sing it out as a song. But if you show them the cow and talk about it, then ask them about the cow, that would make much more sense to a child's mind and he will start thinking and creating things from there.

"They should also have training scholarships, post-school, run by the government, or NGOs to give scholarships to those students who can qualify and pass tests for further technical training.

"Financial support should be there so the needy can benefit from it. Our leaders need to know about our children and students. How many are qualified, employed, unemployed, and how many are finishing school in the next year? This should be their job, so that society and government start thinking about how we are going to create jobs for each of them and how to make them skilful and eligible for jobs and how to create places for them according to their qualifications. It should be for leaders to decide how each child is going to get a few hours' work in day-to-day life so they can earn a living. So they don't roam around hopelessly. Internships with small local businesses could help. It may be just selling tea or helping a farmer to do weeding in his fields for a few hours a week. Otherwise, if there are no options, then one person will have long hours of work and a regular job and someone else will have nothing. How can that make a society safe and crime free, without any social security?

"Many educational institutions are privatised without any conditions or regulations. So they charge fees that are much more than one normal salaried person can afford in his whole lifetime. And very often, student recruitment and places are not regulated. Personal links and connections are prioritised. Government schools and institutions are cheaper, but there are still fees to pay and competition for places is high. In recent times there has been an increase of around thirty per cent in rates for transport, and landlords in towns have their own rules and regulations, so often rates for rent are high too and health and safety is an issue. There is so much under-the-table corruption that a normal, sensible, hard-working man is struggling and he can't do anything as everything is controlled by this network of people who show red tape to others but have no rules of any kind for themselves. Some of the leaders and top government officers never use private transport as they have free government transport for whole families and relations to carry them around. How will they know what goes on for ordinary struggling people? The day these authority employees and officers start paying for government services, that's the day when the normal man will be respected. Otherwise the number of poor people is going to rise, and it's no wonder they are left to their own devices, which is a big shame for India."

"In the big cities, like Delhi, Calcutta and Mumbai, where the population of these homeless children is so huge, it must be a nightmare for the authorities," Roland said. "I was shocked to see the homeless children at the New Delhi Station on my first day too and found out lots of stories about them from Dani and learned that thousands of them travel on Indian trains from place to place and survive on the railways."

"Nowadays there are a few good new charities formed especially for railway and street children, and many of the older children are working hard to help remove younger children to permanent accommodation and schooling. The lucky ones are taking advantage, but many unfortunate ones still live underground in the world of the unknown," said Dani.

"The challenge for India is huge, as a greater proportion of the Indian population is young and many are struggling to survive. Another big challenge for the government is the farmers, who are suffering due to drought and competition from mass producers, and they have taken huge loans to keep up farming in their villages. But due to the changes and the increase in farming expenses, they are no longer able to keep up on their loans and the debt has forced them to sell their land, and they have sometimes killed themselves out of despair. It usually happens to the younger families, who have no resources to fall back on and no wide-ranging set of skills, and as a result they become unemployed and useless. These are some of the current problems India is facing and very often these people end up working for big contractors and brokers, where they soon fall into bad habits like drinking, drugs and finally end up on the streets."

Prem Adriano added, "The biggest difference is that the West has moved beyond the state of living for survival, and they have got all the basic comforts and facilities as well as a social security system, including medical help, education, law and order as a back-up, and they provide support in the event of unemployment, funds to guarantee a basic level of existence."

"Yes, Adriano, that's the thing," replied Dani.

Adriano carried on. "So now what people in the West are exploring, or craving for, are other and higher standards. They want better air, ever more beautiful environments and gardens, which are good for all, but on top of that are some extreme desires for countless luxuries plus an economic dominance over the world ... mama mia, too much, I say! Spending billions of euros or pounds on the improvement of a stadium or a shopping centre, or huge funds for fireworks for opening or closing ceremonies, or just to celebrate a festival like New Year, for example. That's the problem with the world. They can't share or have their big budget compromised by even a little. If thousands are dying in Africa without water or food due to drought, not one government in the world will make any changes to these kinds of events, to say, 'Okay, this year no fireworks for New Year or an opening ceremony. Let's send the whole amount to a needy country in Africa.' Every year thousands die without water in the deserts. Let's build a water reserve or transform a village in Africa by building a fence to help them grow and save their crops. Or let's change our yearly budgets or plans a little, so that we can remove poverty in those countries where thousands of children or people are dying due to lack of food. Thank goodness there are a few kind people in the world who have started charities to think beyond their borders and are making a change to the world today. I get upset when I think about this. It is really bad."

"There are thousands of rich people in India too," Dani replied, "but the attitude of surviving and gathering has not changed and people are still gathering more and more. This applies equally to politicians who are hungry for power or greedy individuals or corporations who have donated zero to the community, while their own shopping is done in the top boutiques of London, Paris, Singapore or LA. This contributes to the cause of these children who are suffering here in the streets. These people who spend money around the world on expensive brands, they need to think deeper and see their neighbourhood, they need to start buying things from local craftsmen, local shoemakers and local tailors, so their local brands can be popular and the money go to these skilful workers who are losing their livelihoods and ending up on the streets.

"But we can't cure this problem overnight, and it will take time," Dani said, "but you must not forget to enjoy the day, after all, this is the wonder of the world. This is India and very often tourists end up in tears on their first day after seeing the beggars and children in the streets."

"Because in the developed world you don't see them, they are all moved into shelters, away from public view. But here they all gather wherever they see lots of people or tourists, because India has no social security or unemployment support," Roland added.

Dani continued, "It is part of India, but the amazing thing is that if we talk to them you realise that they do enjoy life too, and they have impressive selling skills, and some of them even speak a few languages, and as they grow up, they become expert salesmen. Some of their minds are much sharper than average due to necessity. The *Slumdog Millionaire* film describes it very well."

By now the driver had stopped the car and told them they had to walk from there, as this was the point where they picked a local guide. They hadn't opened the windows, but their car was already surrounded by an excited crowd. They got out and were faced with offers to buy things as well as for guide services. Young boys were selling replicas of marble Taj Mahals, elephants, camels, flutes, peacock feather fans and beautiful wooden and marble chess sets.

Dani came up with a charming young man and introduced him to the group saying that he would be their guide for the Taj Mahal and his name was Rahim. He was about thirty years of age and was local to Agra. As soon as Rahim joined them, other potential guides slowly disappeared.

Rahim led them through a tall raised portcullis-type metal gate, explaining that traffic was prevented from going beyond this point and they had to take electric four-wheelers or camel carts to the entrance.

So two of the electric carts were organised and off they went. By now the sun was quite warm and they could see the high red stone or granite walls of the gate and huge queues of excited tourists beyond. They had to walk a bit to get to the ticket counter where they purchased their tickets and they deposited some of their bags in a cloakroom. The tickets were much cheaper for Indians than for Europeans, and they had to pay extra for their cameras too. They stood in the queue and after a while got through security and in they went.

At first they couldn't see any signs of the Taj, just a big open space inside the gate with a few trees and beautifully constructed walls, paths and arched gates. They could see the crowd turning left and they followed their guide. Rahim pointed out some of the noticeboards and explained about the dates, as well as pointing out some of the gates to the workshops and exits. Soon they could see the marble building in the distance. There were thousands of people taking photos and capturing their first image of the Taj Mahal.

Rahim led them to one side, to the right, where they stood in a huge Mughal garden with water fountains, beautiful flowers and many old trees and lawns walled by hedges and plants, and there they could see the symmetrical formation of the garden and of the Taj Mahal itself; it was half and half – a mirror image. Everyone was amazed by the vastness and beauty of the Taj Mahal.

Rahim explained the extraordinariness of this Seventh Wonder of the World: "The Taj Mahal is no ordinary architectural monument, but is about mortal love and the divine. The transformation from one life to another, from the earthly, external world to the eternal world.

"What went on around four hundred years ago was incredible. More than twenty thousand craftsmen, labourers, stone carvers, mahouts plus thousands of animals, camels and elephants, worked for around twelve years to create something which became the dome of love, *Jannat* (heaven), and a resting place for the Mughal emperor's beloved wife and childhood chosen one, the queen, Mumtaz Mahal."

They noticed that the whole compound was well protected by garden walls and the external buildings were built of red stone, but the central heavenly dome was built of pure white marble, the spiritual colour of peace and absolute purity. The guide explained that the stone was transported in blocks on round wooden logs, pushed and pulled by almighty elephants from Rajasthan more than 400 kilometres away.

"This project was no ordinary project. It was the desire or call of the great emperor, Shah Jahan, who was heartbroken and in mourning for his beloved, that every effort be made to realise the dream of his wife and create a heavenly dome where she could rest for all eternity. The scale of the project was something that had never been attempted by any lover or emperor in the world before, or indeed since.

"This was also a peak period for the Mughal emperors, and this emperor was the most powerful of their emperors. He had a great tolerance for other faiths and an equally high understanding of music, love, and entertainment. He came from brave and fierce Mughals. Their powerful armies would ride to the Indian plains and whatever was in their way and whoever stood against them was crushed or chased away."

Rahim was excellent. He recreated scenes from history with hand gestures and his style of English, which made it much more interesting.

"One of the first Mughal emperors, or sultans, King Humayun, the son of Babur, placed the foundation of his Mughal kingdom in Delhi."

Dani replied, "One can still see the wonderfully built Humayun tomb in Delhi today."

Rahim added, "Yes, the first great emperor was Humayun's son, Akbar, who ruled and centralised power in India in the 1500s. He became king at the age of thirteen or fourteen. He was born in 1542 and became the emperor in 1556. He ruled India until his death in 1605 and was known for his openness and tolerance, love of knowledge, warfare and music, as can be seen in the newly produced Bollywood film *Jodha Akbar*.

"He created a library which housed a collection of over 24,000 books in various languages from Persian, Sanskrit, Hindustani, Arabic, Latin and Urdu. They were collected from scholars of all faiths and diverse regions. Monks, fakirs and *sadhus* were welcome in his kingdom and he was open to acquiring knowledge and wisdom from all kinds of people, and that knowledge was all recorded for later use and study. He amassed great knowledge, especially from the Sufis and Sants in his lifetime. In spiritual practices, he sought to achieve a higher level of being. He married a Hindu princess and had a Hindu temple especially built for her to worship the god Vishnu in. He had a genuine desire to understand the meaning of life and how to be a people-loving emperor.

"Akbar had great respect and tolerance for Indian faiths and customs, in sharp contrast to Babar, his grandfather, or previous rulers, who thought that only their faith was legitimate, and they were happy to kill those who defended their own faith and customs and refused to be converted to Babar's. The bloodshed, suffering, and looting had reached such a scale during that period that Indian priests and the public felt a terrible threat to their existence and their culture. They emptied the temples and buried and hid lots of their precious statues and treasures. It was the time when

Indian maharajas started to reorganise themselves against these powerful and dreadful armies. Out of this bloodshed and suffering a wise teacher known as Guru Nanak Dev was born, the founder of the spiritual army now called Sikhism. He was born in Lahore, in modern-day Pakistan, and had worked for the rajas of Afghan descendants. His wisdom and teachings brought people together and his Sikh army was the only one that could make Babar's intolerant regime rethink its attitude to humanity, equality, tolerance, and how to be a great emperor and achieve respect in the public's eye. Guru Nanak Dev created social and spiritual platforms to achieve equality for all. He merged two faiths to remove castes and other superstitions which were causing so much suffering and conflict among men."

Dani added, "It was very interesting that the son, King Akbar, later paid great respect to Indian traditions and the science of yoga and *Vedic* Sanskrit knowledge. In some of the Hindu hymns, Akbar's name is still sung. That was the greatness of this emperor, and his glory and reputation grew not only in India but throughout his ancestral land of Persia. No one wanted to fight against him, and therefore his goal became to seek beyond the material and the earthly world to the higher heavenly level, which could provide the answer and absolute inner peace."

Rahim went on to explain that his knowledge and wisdom was embedded in his teachings to his own generation, and special mosques were commissioned with precious stones and grand domes to create a link between people and the divine.

"After his death, Akbar was succeeded by his son, Jahangir, and then after Jahangir it was a young prince called Khurram, later known as Shah Jahan, who was dear to his father and had grown to be passionate about war and power. He became emperor after eliminating his elder siblings from his path. It was a time when the Mughal dynasty was at its peak and they had huge power. Art and craftsmanship flourished. Trade with the East and West was expanding, and India had a thriving trade in precious stones, spices and so on.

"Shah Jahan married early to his first wife, but his real love was his second wife, Mumtaz Mahal, who had been his childhood sweetheart. During this time there were a few uprisings as he had forgotten the tolerance of his grandfather and father and he had started destroying temples and forcing sharia law on his public. Although his education and knowledge came from all faiths and Akbar's library, he had grown to have faith only in the Kuran and he had forgotten all the wisdom collected by his grandfather, Akbar.

"It was at this time when his dearest queen lost her life giving birth to his fourteenth child, and that was the time when the emperor did not listen to any music, and the king was so heartbroken that his hair went grey and he ceased to listen to music and lost interest in life. He went into a long period of mourning. He decided to create a monument or tomb which could provide an eternal resting place for her. He gathered the best craftsmen and architectural experts in his land to study all the old monuments built by his ancestors, and the eventual creation was a combination of the past and the future to display his love for his dearest wife.

"Thousands of people and animals worked day and night like slaves on the site full-time for around fourteen years to satisfy their king. It was an achievement of gigantic proportions for that age. He had to divert some of the deliveries of rations and food to that region, and consequently many villages near and far suffered due to famine. Shah

Jahan spent most of his wealth on the monument in the end and a disagreement within the family erupted as a result.

"The Taj Mahal was eventually completed in 1648 and it had cost the treasury dearly."

Roland pointed towards the minarets, which seemed to be gently bowing sideways. The guide pointed out and explained that if they were to collapse they wouldn't ruin the main tomb. By now the group were moving forward closer and closer to the Taj. Rahim pointed out the well-known benches at the front and suggested that they may want to take photos there later on. They could feel how vast and imposing the building was. The white marble was shining like milk and the sun was making it brighter and more beautiful. Some of them took their shoes off and some preferred to use white slip-on covers which were provided for them to cover their shoes in order to protect the marble steps and floors.

Security was high and filming wasn't permitted, only photos. Standing beside it felt like an illusion, something other-worldly.

They visited the main centre where a replica of the king and queen's tomb was laid, protected by carved marble *jali* (marble lattice screens). Below that, the real tomb lay, wherein the precious queen and mother of fourteen children could be found.

Roland thought how moving it was that a lover would do something extraordinary like this for his beloved. How precious and lucky she was!

The group moved outside and Rahim took them around and pointed out the various incredible artistic designs skilfully carved into the hard white marble and inlaid with multicoloured precious stones and jewels. The minarets above the main tomb were so high that Roland couldn't imagine how on earth people in those days had built them. He was amazed to consider that they had no machines of any kind at that time – no trolleys, lifts or cranes – and yet they managed to give a smooth finish with such accuracy and beauty. The guide pointed out the special words and verses carved into the marble from the Kuran, which defined not just the material value of the monument, but the significance of the bridge between the earthly and the spiritual.

The guide also pointed out the Yamuna river behind the Taj and the land on the other side of the river with some foundations on it. This was an attempt by Shah Jahan to build another identical black Taj Mahal, but he had stopped after the foundation, when he ran out of resources. In addition, by then, Shah Jahan had been captured by his own son but in a gesture of compassion he was put into prison at the Red Fort of Agra close by so he could still admire his masterpiece and pray to the love of his life.

After admiring the Taj and the surrounding building and monuments where royals had enjoyed their leisure time in days gone by, they walked to the left where there was an old mosque and the guide pointed out that Muslim people of Agra still prayed in that age-old mosque every Friday and that's why the Taj Mahal is closed to visitors at that time. Finally, they made their way to the famous bench to have photographs taken, made more famous in recent memory by the late Princess Diana.

Roland found it interesting to see the well-maintained garden. It was divided into four squares and there was a raised platform in the centre as well as fountains on both sides of the footpaths.

Rahim was very good with his dates and numbers and could recount how many kilos of marble was used, how high and how wide various sections were, and other such detailed facts.

A museum by the right-hand side of the main gate was their final stop before they headed to the exit. Inside, Roland found it interesting to see a collection of images and historical details of the Mughal emperors and the way they lived and dressed, including various objects and antiques on display from those times. Equally fascinating was a plate for testing food which used to change colours if poison was added.

There was also a photographic exhibition showing all the historical architecture or art ever built or discovered in India. Soon everyone was lost in the photos illustrating the origins of Indian art.

"Early humans created wall paintings more than 30,000 years ago in Bhimbetka," said Dani, "and there are signs that in the heart of India, in the state of Madhya Pradesh, humans created wall paintings of animals and people in caves to show the dangers they faced, as well as some illustrations of their way of life."

The most interesting and famous photograph they saw was of a carved ritual scene of a Hindu god, called Varah, a boar-headed incarnation of Vishnu. It was from the Udayagiri Caves in Madhya Pradesh and dated back to the fourth and fifth centuries. It included hundreds of figures of gods, horses and a ten-headed serpent protecting Vishnu, the preserver god, and a big statue of Varah who was lifting a lady with his nose.

"This lady represents the earth," Dani said, "and the whole scene is supposed to be taking place under the sea and the serpent provides a step for Varah to rest his foot on, as Varah rescues the earth out of the water."

Hellen also pointed out the Meenakshi temple in Madurai, South India. She knew about the temple and had really wanted to see it while she was in India, but sadly didn't have enough time. She said that it was one of the most fascinating temples in India, and its highest tower was one hundred and seventy feet high, and it had around 33,000 statues and sculptures built inside the temple.

"Meenakshi means 'fish eyed goddess'," Dani explained, "and she was the wife of the famous God Shiva. Its history goes back more than 2,000 years to the Pandyan Dynasty, and the city of Madurai goes back more than 2,500 years. The first mention of Madurai was by Greek and Tamil writers in the fourth century, and it was famous for its spice trade."

Roland also noticed some images of stone circles from the Mauryan period from Bairat in Rajasthan and from Mahachaitya in Amaravali, from the third century BC, similar to Stonehenge in England. He wondered if there was a common belief, or practice behind these sites and he kept thinking that it must have been fascinating for Britain when these new discoveries came back from India, showing parallels in distant parts of the world, including colourful spices and the discovery of erotic statues and art, showing an intimate and amusing knowledge of the *Kama Sutra caves* hidden deep inside *India*.

As they came out, Rahim took them through a different gate to the left-hand side and soon they ended up in some workshops, where there were young boys working hard at carving white marble, and inlaying it with precious stones, or carving elephants and other Indian gods and chess sets out of the stone.

Back outside, many street children noticed them and recognised them from earlier that morning. They kept saying, "You promised in the morning …" and they were pushing things to buy. Some of them bought marble replicas of elephants and the Taj Mahal, and the children tried to sell drums, wooden snakes and chess sets to them too. They would quote a high price first and then keep reducing it, and Roland wondered how much the items really cost.

Once the children had left them, and they had said farewell to Rahim, they drove back off through the busy streets of Agra to the Taj View Hotel where the doors were opened by well-dressed staff and all the street noise disappeared behind them.

They headed to the dining room for some lunch, where they found the time to really reflect in silence on the idea of the wondrous monument.

They were all really impressed and couldn't believe the way they must have carried rocks and marble, and created the whole monument without any machines.

Dani said, "In a way, the Taj Mahal is a monument of perfection, where an artist has created a symmetrical mirror image of perfection and balance. The Taj Mahal is not just a historical building, but a mystical ornament, or *tabeej*, of India, which provides a wonder of the material world to the spiritual world and ultimately leads one to great feelings and to a balanced mind. White marble is a symbol of purity and peace, and when you add love, it makes it much more precious. It's almost like a beautiful piece of classical music, which ultimately leaves one with profound joy."

Dani was amazed at the idea, and he went on, stressing how powerful one idea can be, one single idea, a thought from a single mind, how could it be this powerful to create something like this. He went on, saying that one idea or thought can create or destroy so much.

"Just imagine, just imagine that thought and that very idea came into his mind to build the Taj Mahal! My goodness me, and it applies to the creation of a bridge, house, engine, computer, phone, book or a space rocket, or anything we use. Without that one little idea, these things would not be here. This was incredible self-realisation, and if an idea comes from a balanced mind, that could benefit the whole universe or humankind."

Dani said that during his yoga studies they had learned a story about how different parts of the mind work. He explained, "The mind is divided into four parts: conscious, subconscious, intellect and ego, or self-assertive principle. If you are walking and you suddenly see two eyes glowing in the dark, that picture is taken and scanned by the senses immediately. First, it's taken by the visual sense, and then it's sent to the conscious mind, and that sends it to the subconscious mind, or the memory store, to find more detail about it, what that is, almost like the google search today. If there is any information about that picture in the memory, it brings the information back to the conscious mind. That information will be analysed by the intellect – this could be a lion and it could be harmful. In that moment, the ego, or self-assertive principle, will say, 'Oh no, this is dangerous', and at that point the conscious mind will give the command to send more blood to the muscles, so that it can take action or simply run. Remember, this all happens in seconds within our mind. It's amazing how advanced the system is!"

That's where the topic of discussion turned to whether India's age-old practices of yoga and meditation may have had an influence on the many artists, craftsmen and even on the king himself to create such a perfect monument as the Taj Mahal, and it may be due to the collected knowledge descended from Akbar the Great through the accumulated books and wisdom of India.

Dani explained, "Yes, exactly. Yoga, or *Yog* in Sanskrit, actually means union, and it starts with the union of five balanced and healthy elements (air, fire, water, earth and space or emptiness) within an individual cell, and the cell then forms tissue and then tissues unite to form organs and the organs unite to form a system, and many systems form the body itself. So yoga first applies to that physical union. Once the body is working harmoniously, then yoga deals with the union or coordination of the body and mind. Once one has achieved that balance as well, then yoga takes a person to higher levels of spiritual union or inner balance.

"I'm really impressed that old breathing exercises make scientific sense because they are correct in physiological and anatomical ways. I wonder how those ancient practitioners were able to discover these things? In ancient Sanskrit wisdom, the breath is known as the king of the mind and the mind is known as the king of the senses. Only the breath has the ability to control and balance our mind. If we observe a little baby, he moves his abdomen up and down as he breathes naturally."

Roland put himself forward, saying, "Yes. Recent biological knowledge has shown us that whenever a body needs more oxygen, it is not the lungs which receive the first command from the brain. We have oxygenated blood coming from our heart through a thick pipe called the aorta, and there we have some cells which are like supervisors called chemoreceptors. They supervise the oxygen level in the blood coming out through the aorta. If they think there is not enough oxygen in the blood and they need more, they will send a signal to the brain and the brain will then send the signal to the diaphragm to contract, telling it that we need more air or that we are short of oxygen. Then the diaphragm will contract to provide more space, and air automatically comes into the lungs. If the diaphragm is dull, or not moving much, then the lower portion of the lungs may not get enough air or stimulation. And a dull diaphragm does not lead to healthy belly organs, and ultimately most illnesses start from the stomach. Another interesting thing is that if we hold our abdominal region tight, one cannot laugh at all. To laugh or to be happy, we need our navel region or abdominal region to be fully active, and a deep abdominal breath or a full contraction or stretch of the diaphragm helps one to achieve that easily. Breathing is a crucial part of our life. It connects and keeps alive every cell in our body. Through this, we form a direct link with plants too. The air we exhale is taken in by other plants and the air they breathe out is inhaled by us, so breathing is a very uniting factor within nature."

"To do yoga practice you don't need any machines or any equipment," Dani said. "All you need is a mat and that's it. Through a few sets of exercise, one can transform one's life and achieve real balance."

Hellen asked whether everyone in India knew about yoga.

"Not everyone," Dani said, "but most people who are interested in health and spiritual well-being do it. They may not have any scientific understanding of it, but they have a long trust and belief in yoga, and they do it almost like a ritual or prayer. It is embedded in the culture from thousands of years ago and it is a way of life. In the early morning you wake up, wash your face and then go for a walk to fetch water as well as doing the sun salutation over simple exercises as the sun rises. It is part of life. The problem is that yoga is much older than any organised or newly formed religions. It is now associated with Hindus, as they represent the native or oldest race of India. But it is practised by lots of people, regardless of their religion, who are seeking well-being and mental or spiritual peace. Sadly, some narrow-minded religious groups now see it as a threat. Some religious leaders would appear to prefer their followers to carry on their problems and keep coming and following them in big numbers, so they can control them more easily. Hence they see yoga as being dangerous to their religion.

"Yoga is simply an age-old technique which provides well-being. Any tool which can help humanity to achieve a healthy body and mind and well-being belongs to all.

"Before these religions existed, lots of people used to practise exercises in the form of dance. Many Hindus practised Sufi dance, and even today in Himalayan villages, when they have folk or cultural dramas performed in open-air theatres called *Kariyala,* they still open with a Sufi spiritual dance called *Chandrawali.* People did not see the Islamic aspect behind it but rather the benefits that dance provides. These included spiritual uplifting and increased concentration, together with devotion and respect. Hand mudras match even in Nutraj dancing Shiva statue and Sufi dance, right hand upwards blessing or raising and left hand pointing downwards. Today there may be different names for these ceremonies – *Kariyala* in North India and *Chaam* in Tibetan Buddhism – but they relate to pre-religious practices that inspired people to spirituality and well-being. Yoga is a similar practice, or technique, which helps to achieve both physical and spiritual well-being.

"There are many famous people in the world, who have made yoga their routine practice. Yoga is a life-transforming tool and all can benefit from it. Of course yoga cannot fix everything and one should not pretend or misuse it in that sense. It can provide good exercise, inner balance and an overall understanding of body, mind and self.

"A deeper concept that also runs through yoga is called *dharma or* righteousness. Again, this is an ancient attitude designed to promote positive action in our day-to-day life to gain contentment and inner peace. My mother used to tell me when I was a child: *"Beta, dusre ke hisse main kabhi hissa nahi dharna chahiye,'* 'Son, never desire a part of someone else's share'. In this one statement or action, I see duty and *dharma*, or righteousness and pleasure, within this one performance. This applies equally to the sharing of food or the sharing of one's country. Eating something alone may bring momentary satisfaction, but it will not bring *shanty* (peace) or *anand* (bliss) in the long term if you have taken what should have been shared.

"The joy of *dharma* is greater in the long term. A brother may like to eat chocolate alone and may hate that he has to leave half for his sister after school, but in the long term, sharing will give him a feeling of peace, patience, compassion and respect, not just from his sister but also from himself. And the bigger a thing is, the greater it can produce either peace or suffering. So when you consider this deeper concept embedded in yoga, the more significant it becomes.

"The main purpose of yoga is human sustainability on earth, healthy body and balanced mind, so that they can adapt to survive with nature. One who has that balanced mind and wisdom, will plant that tree with scientific or practical tool to sustain the life of, not only human, but of every living thing, so they can all live in harmony to sustain life on this planet. Today's science has achieved a lot. One can fix broken bones or replace joints and teeth. Science has evolved over the years to help humanity and nature to survive."

432

"Yes, that's true," Roland said. "Science has done wonders and it can do complex surgery which humans couldn't imagine a few years ago. Its advances in exploring the earth, sea and its weather, as well as the rest of the universe, have opened new dimensions, showing that Earth is a small planet moving around the Sun, while some of the planets are thousands of times bigger than our Earth."

"Science has done so much, but the world is still a very fragile place, due to the greed and monopoly of some nations," added Adriano.

Dani announced that in some ways we are becoming too sophisticated in our habits. For example, in nature, a tree drops its leaves in autumn which provides fertiliser to the ground below as they rot during winter, so that the soil can then provide goodness back to the tree. But in the modern world, we want to keep the grass green and tidy all year round. So we collect the leaves and then produce complex fertilisers to do a job which had been naturally happening for thousands of years. We have substituted a natural system for a complex and expensive system and added the expense of huge machinery. Similarly, we can't do simple walks or runs or exercises anymore. No, we need huge indoor gyms to exercise, with loud music and machines, but if we just used the simple methods of exercise, such as gardening, walking, running, swimming and yoga, we wouldn't need all that."

"Yes," Hellen agreed, "moderation and the right balance between machines and the natural way of doing things is needed. It is like if you boil an electric kettle for one cup, but fill it up every time, it's a waste."

They had been enjoying their lunch and were now ready to explore more as it was getting cooler outside. It was nearly three o'clock and they asked for the bill. They decided to visit the next destination – the Agra Fort. They were dropped off by their driver near the busy square by the main entrance to the Red Fort in Agra after lunch.

The guide's name was Mohammad Uslam, but Dani referred to him as *chachu*, which means "uncle" in Hindi or Urdu. He was a tall, thin man, wearing a white traditional kurta pyjama and plastic sandals, which he dragged along as he walked. He put on a very unusual accent to impress the group, and Roland and Dani couldn't stop imitating some of his expressions and giggling. But Mohammad was very experienced and his knowledge of the fort and its overall history was impressive.

"The main fort is around a thousand years old," he explained. "It was first built in brick by the Rajputs over the next 500 or so years. It changed hands several times due to dynastic battles until eventually, having been captured by the Mughal Akbar in the Second Battle of Panipat in 1556, it was torn down and a process of rebuilding began. At first, it was intended by Akbar to rebuild it as a military base, but by the time it was completed by Shah Jahan, Akbar's grandson, it's use had been changed to that of a private palace, resplendent in red stone and white marble, of which Shah Jahan was very fond."

As they toured around they were told about the huge hall which was used for public audiences, with its huge marble pillars set out so that the emperor could be seen from every corner of the hall. A separate hall for private audiences was even more impressive as it was built with very fine marble inlaid with precious stones. The guide explained that this was the place where the famous Peacock Throne had been, a throne so opulent and precious it had been more costly than the Taj Mahal itself. It contained the famous Koh-i-Noor diamond, now found in the British Crown Jewels at the

Tower of London. Because the throne was later plundered by the Persians, it was suspected that after the Persian king's execution the throne simply disappeared from all records, taken apart and its gold and jewels were distributed.

The guide was so knowledgeable that he recreated fascinating scenes from the past, describing where the emperor and empress lived and how every wall and chamber was built, how sound or cold air travelled from one room to another. It was built with extraordinary architectural skill.

Looking over to the other side, they could see the high raised walls, around 20 metres high, and a deep-water moat, as well as areas of woodland where wild animals like lions and tigers would roam. The high walls ensured it was a highly secure fort and nothing unknown could enter from any direction. The guide explained that underneath lay many secret tunnels and passageways, as well as private ghats for royals to bathe in the river.

They also saw cannons for protection, and behind them lay the river Yamuna as well as the beautiful Taj Mahal to the right. They could see where Shah Jahan had been imprisoned in the Agra Fort by his son Aurangzeb until his death in 1666.

After the extensive tour, they were all exhausted, so, after taking some photos of the guide and paying him a good tip for his wonderful narration, they said their goodbyes. Mohammad looked tired too as he must have been around sixty-five or more and he must have had many tours since the morning.

Soon they departed on cycle rickshaws to find the local market in search of gifts. They explored lots of showrooms for marble objects, pashmina shawls and carpets and were amazed at how expensive some of the showrooms were.

Dani and Roland went to a small local market to have a drink in a little garden cafe and then afterwards they went and bought a few things and browsed around some bookshops. Roland bought a few books about old Indian monuments and sites such as the Ajanta Caves, and Dani bought a book called *A Brief History of Time* by Stephen Hawking, whom he greatly admired.

Roland also found a small internet cafe to check emails quickly. After that, they headed back to the hotel where they were reunited with the rest of the group, laden with shopping bags.

Dani laughed. "Oh, so the salesmen finally won you over?!"

Hellen smiled in agreement. "Oh, it was so difficult. Every showroom and store wanted to sell us something." She showed her marble white Ganesha and wooden elephant and some books she had bought as well. She was amazed to find a book called *Sita*, because her mother was called Sita, and Dani told her that Sita was the wife of Lord Rama, the Prince of Ayodhya from the Ramayana era.

After that they had tea and a few snacks by the pool, after which they packed and departed the hotel for the train station. Their train was the 8.30 p.m. NDLS Shatabdi train, one of the fastest trains to New Delhi from Agra, which only took two hours.

The sun had almost gone down now as they waited on the platform, and the rush of people getting home after work had simmered down, but many children were still running around on the platform, mostly around the wealthy-looking tourists. Some of the children were really young, hardly five or six years old. They were with their older siblings who would train them how to act and how to put their hands out with a sad face. Dani felt so sorry for them and started to speak with them. Soon they gathered around him and he was amused that the girls, who were about eight or nine years old, were very grown-up and were asking him to convince his tourist friends to give them some money. He asked them what they would do with the money, and why didn't they study and go to school, and he told them that it wasn't a good thing to be dragging their little brothers and sisters barefoot around the platforms. He gave them fruit and they wanted his bottle of water too, which he also gave them. Soon they realised that he was kind and they started telling him the truth: that some of their parents or guardians were living nearby and they were sent to beg by them. One of the girls pointed out a lady in the distance who was keeping an eye on them and said that they had to give everything to her. Dani found out that she travelled from place to place and slept with her mother on mats and sheets in the open at night. They spent some time chatting together and Hellen gave them some sweets. Some groups of beggar boys collected plastic bottles in big bags or bullied each other as they chased each other here and there. They seemed happy and normal, despite their circumstances and the way they lived and roamed around the roads, traffic and railway line.

Dani asked a policeman about the children, and he said, "Oh, they are sent by their parents to beg. There are so many of them in the tourist areas that we have no idea what to do with them."

The reality was that they had nowhere else to go where they would be provided with accommodation, food or schooling in a safe and a protected environment.

Adriano remarked that that's why he had a policy against giving anything to beggars, because it incentivised them to exploit their children.

Hellen protested that they had to be provided with some sort of support. "If everyone neglects them, God knows they could sleep hungry or thirsty for many days or even die somewhere unnoticed. Everyone chases them out and they resort to crime because they have to survive. The best thing would be for the government to open a few children's centres and take them away from the parents that force them to beg. Otherwise, plenty of innocent lives are being ruined in the streets."

Soon the train arrived and they found their coach and got in. As soon as they settled in their seats they were provided with tea and coffee, which they enjoyed, and a quietness descended among them as the dark streets passed outside their windows. It wasn't long before they arrived at the New Delhi Station. They walked out of the station and found a few cycle rickshaws to take them to the hotel.

Finally, in their hotel, it was time for everyone to have a drink to celebrate the last evening, so they went to the rooftop for a quick drink and to plan their next trip. Dani was staying in India to develop his charity further to support children in the village by opening a sport academy and an art academy, as well as to encourage local craft centres and give power to local woman and craftsmen to revive some of their practical and sustainable skills. Roland was thrilled with his two-week trip, and he wanted to come back to do a motorbike expedition to the higher Himalayas to cover the remote villages in the Kinnaur, Spiti and Ladakh region. He had made his mind up to buy a Royal Enfield on his return to England. It was quite emotional and sad for Roland to leave, but he was already excited about his next trip to India and thrilled that he had safely completed his holiday.

It was time for their goodbyes. Several of them, including Roland, had very early flights to catch the next morning and a taxi was arranged to drop them at the airport.

Roland thanked and said goodbye to Dani with a certain sadness as their travels together were coming to an end. They wished each other well in their onward journeys and promised to look forward to their next expedition together.

As Roland was already packed, he set his alarm, and he was soon asleep.

***

The next morning, as soon as his alarm went off, he got ready and had a cup of tea. Soon he had a call from reception telling him that his driver was there, and within a few moments he was downstairs. Hotel staff put his things in the car and he was driven off to the airport, leaving the colourful streets behind.

Roland found his flight check-in desk and stood in the queue to wait. However, there was more excitement for Roland. After a little while, he saw a familiar face in the queue just a few passengers ahead of him. Straight away she said, "Hi!" and smiled, waving.

At first Roland couldn't remember where he'd seen her before. Then she asked him, "So how was your trek? I hope you had fun." That's when Roland realised it was the girl he'd seen at the remote village on the day he arrived for trekking.

"Hi, I'm Roland," he said.

"I'm Anna, really nice to see you again."

"And you, Anna. We had hoped, when we saw you in the village, that you had been heading the same way as us, but it turned out you had already finished your trek. But I thought of you in the mountains later. You were so lucky with your trekking timings. We had two great days, but the third day was cold and we had a heavy snowfall which made us turn back earlier. But never mind, what a surprise that we meet again here," said Roland.

"Are you going to London?" she asked.

"Yes!" he replied.

"That's really strange," Anna said with a twinkle in her eye. She waited with him to check in, and after getting rid of their heavy bags, they walked through security and entered the lounge.

"You must be brave to travel around all on your own," Roland said.

"Oh no, this is my second time. I'd been teaching in India during my gap year for three months with a friend. Now, after finishing university, I wanted to come back and see some places, especially the Himalayas. But my friend couldn't join me at the last minute so I decided to travel by myself. So here I am."

"That's what happened to me too," Roland said.

They found a cafe and ordered two coffees, and Roland couldn't believe his luck, that after their brief encounter in the Himalayas, they were having a coffee together. They talked about their time in India and he found out that she had been to Kalpa, a very beautiful village right inside the Himalayas, and also saw the Kinnaur Kailash mountain. It was only three or four hours' drive from Kafnu, the trekking base, and after that she had been to the Lavi festival too. Roland couldn't believe that they had both been at the fair and then taken the same journey back.

She had also visited the holy river Ganges at Rishikesh and Varanasi and the Golden Temple in Amritsar, as well as some of the old temples and historical monuments in South

India. Anna had a particular interest in the archaeological history of the Mauryan Empire of ancient India.

"The whole concept of life and living in India is both fascinating and practical, truly a world within, and it seems that there is so much to experience and learn in this colourful country."

"We have acceptable reasons to come back again," he smiled and agreed with an excitement.

As the announcement to board was heard, and they moved towards their gate, a huge crowd of passengers rushed to the desk as if it was the end of the world. Roland and Anna smiled at each other in amusement, and as soon as the rush ended, they and a few other passengers moved forward, their hearts full of emotion as they left behind the country they knew they would miss so much and will visit again soon.

The End

APPENDIX I

Quotes on climate change and the sustainable living:

Bill Gates:

"Climate change is a terrible problem, and it absolutely needs to be solved. It deserves to be a huge priority."

Mahatma Gandhi:

"Earth provides enough to satisfy every man's needs, but not every man's greed."

David Attenborough:

"It's coming home to roost over the next 50 years or so. It's not just climate change; it's sheer space, places to grow food for this enormous horde. Either we limit our population growth or the natural world will do it for us, and the natural world is doing it for us right now."

Ban Ki-moon:

"Climate change is destroying our path to sustainability. Ours is a world of looming challenges and increasingly limited resources. Sustainable development offers the best chance to adjust our course."

President Obama:

Our efforts "will help us begin to meet our responsibilities to leave our children and grandchildren a cleaner planet."

Prince Charles:

"Remember that our children and grandchildren will ask, not what our generation said, but what it did. So let us give an answer of which we can be proud."

Governor of Virginia:

"We need to communicate and explain to people who do not understand climate change and keep communicating."

Additional Information on the Intergovernmental Panel on Climate Change (IPCC) Summit at Copenhagen, Denmark, December 2009.

December 15, 2009.

India Minister Ramesh has also pointed out that India is committed to act in a manner that would ensure that global temperatures meet the two degrees threshold by 2050.

December 17, 2009.

Persistently deep divisions threatened to scupper a climate change deal in Copenhagen. "I know my proposal today will disappoint those Africans who, from the point of justice, have asked for full compensation of the damage done to our development prospects," said Ethiopian Prime Minister Zenawi on behalf of African nations present in Copenhagen. Addressing the plenary, Zenawi endorsed UN proposals for fast-start aid of $10 billion per year between 2010 and 2012.

Points from the article in *Times of India*. December 19, 2009, China triumph: No legally binding deal for now.

COPENHAGEN: President Barack Obama said the United States, China and several other countries reached an unprecedented breakthrough" The agreement, which also includes the developing nations of India, South Africa and Brazil, requires each country to list the actions they will take to cut global warming pollution. In announcing the five-nation deal, Obama said "We have come a long way, but we have much further to go," he said the nations of the world will have to take more aggressive steps to combat global warming. The first step, he said, is to build trust between developed and developing countries...

APPENDIX II

Glossary

abhyas – practice.

acha – good.

achkanor sherwani – cocktail jacket with close collars.

adrack – ginger.

ajgar – snake, refers to a big snake.

alaturka – name of a ground-level toilet.

ammaji – "amma" means mother and "ji" is more polite and respectful.

anand – blissfulness.

anta – end.

astra – weapons that can be used away from body, like arrows or missiles.

astu – means "is" in Sanskrit, or refers to the ashes of departed one.

Atithi Devo Bhava – guest is equivalent to God. A very old Sanskrit phrase.

avatar – incarnation or form.

ayu – age.

Ayurveda – the knowledge of a long life.

Baba – holy man or father.

baldu – a clay pot, but this name refers to a particular clay pot used for death ceremonies.

balti – bucket.

baturu – a puffed and swollen thick circular bread.

beaul – name of a green tree that produces plenty of leaves for cows, and bark and sticks for farmers.

berr – round berries, almost like olives, but with a very thin skin and a round stone.

Bhagavad Gita – Holy Book of Hindus. The words of Krishna to Arjuna in the middle of the battlefield to protect righteousness and fairness.

bhaiya – brother.

bhanartie – white skin or bark-free sticks used for kindling.

bhegre – small black figs.

Bhima Kali – name of the Goddess Kali, mainly famous in the Himalayas.

Brah or Varaha – boar, but refers to the third incarnation of Vishnu.

Brahmin – priest caste or highest caste and scholars.

burphi – fudge-like sweets made from milk.

caru or kaddoo – a hot water drink made by boiling herbs and spices to cure cold and flu.

Cham – Buddhist name for a spiritual dance performed in the Himalayas by monks in the monasteries to remove evil energies.

chachaji – uncle, and "ji" is more polite and respectful.

chachu – uncle on the father's side.

chai – tea, but it is boiled with tea leaves, sugar, milk and a few spices like cloves, ginger and cardamom.

Chandrawali – A Sufi dance performed for the opening ceremony of an open-air theatre in the Himalayan villages by a male performer dressed as a female.

chapatti – hand-made round wheat bread.

Charpoy – Bed made from strings and used to sit on in the sun or to sleep.

chatra – wheel.

chowkidar – a guard.

Churu – name of highland cows in the Highlands of the Himalayas.

chutany – a thick liquid made from sour and spicy leaves and fruits.

cutkuni – the building style where logs are used to point the corners.

Daan – charity or offerings or donations done to liberate physical or mental suffering.

dada – grandfather.

dadi – grandmother.

dadiji – "dadi" means granny.

dai – midwife, sister, or in some dialects it refers to brothers as well.

Dakus – bandits.

dal – lintel.

dalals – brokers.

dalchini – cinnamon.

Darshan – an opportunity to see or have a personal meeting with a holy person or a deity.

Deo – deity or god. The same word is used in Sanskrit and Latin.

Deobade – deity, god or divine, and bade means great.

Devi – goddess, or can refer to a girl too.

Devtas – deities or heavenly gods.

dhaji – wooden planks, but refers to the old architecture or pagoda-style houses, with walls built with stone, mud and wooden planks.

dhanyabad – thank you.

dhar – mountain range or a hill.

dhargiri – "dhar" means hill and "giri" means fell.

dharma – righteousness or duty.

Dharmshala – a shelter or inn built to provide shelter for the needy, inspired by charity and righteousness.

dhekli – a hit and run game using a tower of flat circular stones or slates broken by hitting a ball.

dhoti – a sheet of cloth worn around your hips.

dubra – a circular bowl.

dudhjalebi – milk and jalebi.

dudhpina – milk drink.

elaichi – cardamom.

fatbai – a man who chops an animal's head off.

gachak – dry hard sweet made in winter from sugarcane juice and peanuts.

gaddis – shepherds or nomads.

garbhagriha – main centre part of the temple.

ghee – purified or boiled butter.

ghiya – gourd.

Gita – name of a holy book, refers to a female name now.

gulabjamun – round sweets made from milk and oat flour and dipped in sugar syrup.

gulli-danda – name of an Indian game more than 3,000 years old. "Gulli", or "gilli", is a little pointed stick about five inches long, and "danda" is a stick.

guna – quality.

gurr – brown sweet made from sugar canes.

Guru – "Gu" means darkness and "Ru" means the remover in Sanskrit, but "Guru" means a master in his field, therefore a great teacher.

haka – call.

halo – flax.

Harijan – "Hari" means Vishnu and "jan" means people– God's own people.

imli – tamarind, a sour fruit used to make chutney.

jail – prison.

jakha – a clay dish to keep or store freshly home-made butter or a treasure.

Jalebi – round hollow sweets made from oat flour, deep fried in oil and then dipped in sugar syrup.

Jannat – Islamic term for heaven.

jhinjara – name of grass or straw used to thatch the roof.

Jodha Akbar – name of a Bollywood film.

jyoti – flame or light.

Kachcham or Kurma – a tortoise, but refers to the second incarnation of Vishnu.

kala – black.

kalaripayattu – a south Indian martial art and is the basis of other martial arts in the world.

kalgi – a shoot, but refers to the highest tip on top of a crown or tree.

Kali – means "the black one", or the name of a Hindu goddess.

kalipati – black wool length.

Kama sutra – "Kama" means pleasure and "sutra" means formula or tie.

kamarband – a piece of material rolled around the waist and used with a black tie or with Indian closed collar coats.

kanugo – revenue officer who is responsible for documents, demarcation and measurements.

Kariyala – open-air theatre act that entertains the public with a story as well as with dramas and comedy plays in the Himalayas.

khad – stream.

khaliyaan – a circular platform used to harvest crops.

khatru – means holes, but refers to a very old mancala game played with rubble or marbles using six or twelve holes.

kherkath – solidified juice of a wood called "kher" and widely known as "kotechu".

Kheru – name of a curry made from frying lassi or yogurt.

Khichuri – a pilau or biryani rice, but only cooked with lentils or with rice.

khoji – investigator.

kiltas – bamboo basket, which is carried only on the back.

kools – name of water channels connecting from source to irrigate fields.

kshatriya – warrior second caste.

kui – a squeaky and sharp sound.

Kurta – a man's shirt. Mainly refers to the old Indian shirt which comes down to the knees.

lassi – a liquid left after making butter from yogurt.

loung – a clove.

lungi – also known as a sarong. A sheet of cloth worn around the waist.

mahouts – a man who looks after elephants.

mala – a necklace made from beads or flowers, could be a garland as well.

Mamleshwar – a name of Shiva and refers to a shrine of Shiva.

Mancala – name of an African game. "Man" means mind and "Cala" means black.

Manusmriti – a book of memories of kind Manu.

Matsya – a fish, but refers to the first incarnation of Vishnu.

maya – illusion.

moksha – nirvana, or entry into a heavenly plane, or union with the absolute.

momo – name of a Tibetan snack or dish, almost like Italian tortellini. These are stuffed and steamed.

monal – name of a Himalayan bird, a very colourful pheasant.

mudra – a form, or shape or hand gesture. Refers to old coins too.

mulethi – liquorice.

Mungal – means auspicious, Tuesday and Mars.

munji – name of a grass known as a reed.

Nag – snake or cobra.

namaste – applies to all greetings such as hello and good morning, evening or afternoon.

Narayan – refers to Vishnu, who can descend to earth as a human.

Narsingh – fourth incarnation of Vishnu as a half lion and half human, "nar" means human and "singh" means lion or king.

nimboo – lemon.

aorta – a major artery, which takes oxygenated blood from heart.

Omkar – absolute supreme or emptiness or omnipresent energy, which is within everything, beyond cosmos and nature, that who made that first movement ever and who drives everything with its force.

Patti – long lengths of woollen material, especially made to make woollen coats.

padu – fall.

pakora – a snack deep fried with vegetables and covered with gram flour.

panchayat – local village council.

paneer – a cottage cheese or soft cheese.

pani – water.

panijhadna – "pani" means water and "jhadna" means to shake off or wipe off. This is the name of an old ritual of making bubbles on a heated metal sheet by sprinkling water on it.

panijharna – to rinse with water or shake off water.

parantha – a stuffed chapati or bread with vegetables and fried with oil.

parat – a circular bowl with low sides.

parikrama – a holy path around a shrine or temple is called a parikrama.

Parshuram – sixth incarnation of Vishnu, and also refers to a stoneage man with a long beard.

patda – a rectangular wooden stool, about six inches high, or a square or rectangular mat.

patwari – revenue officer who is responsible for all the land documents and measurements.

pazama – men's trousers made in the old Indian style.

Per Braham – supreme almighty – which cannot be known by any means.

pilia – "pila" means yellow and this refers to an illness called jaundice.

prakriti – nature.

pravalior Pharkaval – "pravali" refers to the slope of a roof as well as to pharkaval, which is a way to create wind to grade crops and husk or hay.

prem – Hindi word for love.

pudina – mint.

puja – worship.

Rajas – the active quality.

Ramayana – name of an epic poem, or the era when the Lord Rama was born to the Ayodhya dynasty.

rath – chariot.

Rishis – sages.

roti – refers to any bread, but mainly used for corn bread or a circular yellow bread.

Sadhu – sanyasi, or a man who has left every material procession behind seeking enlightenment.

Sakrant – mame of the first day of the month in Hindu calendar.

sanatanadharma – eternal order.

Sanatana – eternal.

sanjivini – name of a Himalayan life-giving herb used to save Lakshmana in the *Ramayana*.

sanyasis – people who has renounced all worldly materials and pleasures.

Saptarishis – seven scholars, or seven sages in the high Himalayas.

Sarsokasaag – "sarso" means mustard and "saag" refers to a dish of green leaves.

sattva – true quality.

Satyadidi – "satya" means truth and "didi" means sister, used as name here.

shal – scarfor shawl.

shanti – peace.

sharbat – a cold water drink made from aniseed, rose petals, saffron and sugar, as well as other herbs.

shastra – weapons that are used by hand, like swords.

shlokas – mantras or verses.

Shudra – worker or farmers, fourth caste.

shup – three-sided basket. One side is flat, which sits on ground, mainly used to grade grain and husks.

Sita – name of Prince Rama's wife from *Ramayana* times.

sua – natural water fountain.

such – satya or truth.

sukh – pleasure or comfort.

tabeej – an amulet.

tamas – or tamo refers to laziness or anger or low quality.

tamba – copper.

tambia – "tamba"means copper; this is large copper pot with a narrow top used to heat water.

tanga – a rikshaw pulled by a man.

tangawala – a rikshaw driver.

tarpai – a table the size of a plate, which is about a foot high to put your food plate on.

tawa – a thick circular metal sheet to cook chapatti or bread on.

Teljhadna – to shake or rinse oil treatment used for illness.

thali – plate.

The *Mahabharata* – Indian story of ancient maharajas and royals, when Krishna was born.

theka – means contract, or refers to a local alcoholic liquor store.

tika – a coloured dot or mark on the forehead.

tokari – a circular bamboo basket.

tulsi – Himalayan basil.

uple – cow dung cakes made to light fires.

Vaishya – traders, third caste.

Vaman or Baman – fifth incarnation of Vishnu, and refers to a dwarf-like human.

varnas – refers to types, colours, classes and castes.

vastu – Indian old architecture.

vastushastra – the knowledge of the old Indian architecture.

ved – knowledge.

veda – knowledge, or that knowledge that removes vedna, or suffering.

vedanta – knowledge of bringing an end to suffering and seeking.

Vedic – ancient knowledge from the time of Vedas.

vedicvastuvidya – the ancient knowledge of building houses, which helps to remove all obstacles.

vedna – pain or suffering.

yog – means union, and applies here to the physical, mental or spiritual exercises or techniques to purify and liberate ourselves from any sufferings.

yogi – master of yoga and one who has practised and mastered yoga.

PHOTO CREDITS

Captions for all photos with authors name, image or page numbers – The Himalayan Bond

Images 1 to 10 (on pages 100 to 104)
Images 11 to 20 (on pages 205 to 209)
Images 21 to 30 (on pages 290 to 294)
Images 31 to 40 (on pages 398 to 402)
Image a (on page 79), Image b (on page 215),
Image c (on page 336), Image d (on page 364).

Alison Fairbank – 8, 10, 11, 13, 16b, 18, 20, 27, 30, 33, 34, 35 and the front Cover image.
Elexandra Mohoney – 2.
Puran Bhardwaj – 1, 3, 4, 5, 7, 9, 12, 28, 37, 38, 39, 40, A Palanquin of Deity photo b on page 215 and Kinnauri ladies with British tourist photo d on page 364.
Eleanor Marriott – 15, 16a, 17, 19, 25 and bucket bath photo a on page 79.
Baily Galwin-Scott – 36.
Brendan James – 24.
Kirk Newton – 31, 32.
Alex and Mark Berthon – 14, 21, 22, 26, 29.
Prabhoo Janabalan – 6, 23.
Prem Raina – Shiva cave photo c on page 336.
Ingrid Timmerman – Author profile image on the last page.
Zoe Kay – Map for the book on page xiv.

ABOUT THE AUTHOR

Puran Bhardwaj was born in a small village called Thali in the foothills of Shimla, North India and he began his career as a school teacher in the Himalayas after his business degree. For the past fifteen years he has set up trekking expeditions and community projects in the area as a founder of Expedition Leaders and the Asra Charity. The issues in his book are very important for both man and the environment as they threaten his family home, village and the farming. His insight of both cultures east and west has enabled him to speak at many European schools, clubs and organisations.